“Too long has this world been with[illegible]ddess!” Malystryx cried. The great r[illegible]n her haunches, her neck st[illegible] long has there been no [illegible]tting the course of Ansal[illegible] am all!”

D0957534

“Malystryx!” Gelli[illegible]immered white around him, as ice cry[illegible] from between his jagged teeth and instantly melt[illegible] in the hot air.

“The new Dark Queen!” Beryl and Onysablet cried practically in unison. Acid spilled from the Black’s jowls, hissing and popping and melting coins and bits of jewelry on the altar.

By Jean Rabe

DRAGONS OF A NEW AGE
THE DAWNING OF A NEW AGE
THE DAY OF THE TEMPEST
THE EVE OF THE MAELSTROM

BRIDGE OF TIME SERIES
THE SILVER STAIR

THE DHAMON SAGA
DOWNFALL
BETRAYAL
REDEMPTION

The Eve of the Maelstrom

Jean Rabe

THE EVE OF THE MAELSTROM

© 1998 TSR, Inc.
©2002 Wizards of the Coast, Inc.

All characters in this book are fictitious. Any resemblance to actual persons, living or dead, is purely coincidental.

This book is protected under the copyright laws of the United States of America. Any reproduction or unauthorized use of the material or artwork contained herein is prohibited without the express written permission of Wizards of the Coast, Inc.

Distributed in the United States by Holtzbrinck Publishing. Distributed in Canada by Fenn Ltd.

Distributed to the hobby, toy, and comic trade in the United States and Canada by regional distributors.

Distributed worldwide by Wizards of the Coast, Inc. and regional distributors.

DRAGONLANCE and the Wizards of the Coast logo are registered trademarks owned by Wizards of the Coast, Inc., a subsidiary of Hasbro, Inc.

All Wizards of the Coast characters, character names, and the distinctive likenesses thereof are trademarks owned by Wizards of the Coast, Inc.

Made in the U.S.A.

The sale of this book without its cover has not been authorized by the publisher. If you purchased this book without a cover, you should be aware that neither the author nor the publisher has received payment for this "stripped book."

Cover art by Matt Stawicki

Cartography by Diesel

First Printing: February 1998

Library of Congress Catalog Card Number: 2001097181

9 8 7 6 5 4 3 2 1

US ISBN: 0-7869-2860-3
UK ISBN: 0-7869-2861-1
620-88270-001-EN

U.S., CANADA,
ASIA, PACIFIC, & LATIN AMERICA
Wizards of the Coast, Inc.
P.O. Box 707
Renton, WA 98057-0707
+1-800-324-6496

EUROPEAN HEADQUARTERS
Wizards of the Coast, Belgium
P.B. 2031
2600 Berchem
Belgium
+32-70-23-32-77

Visit our web site at **www.wizards.com/dragonlance**

For Mary and Jerry

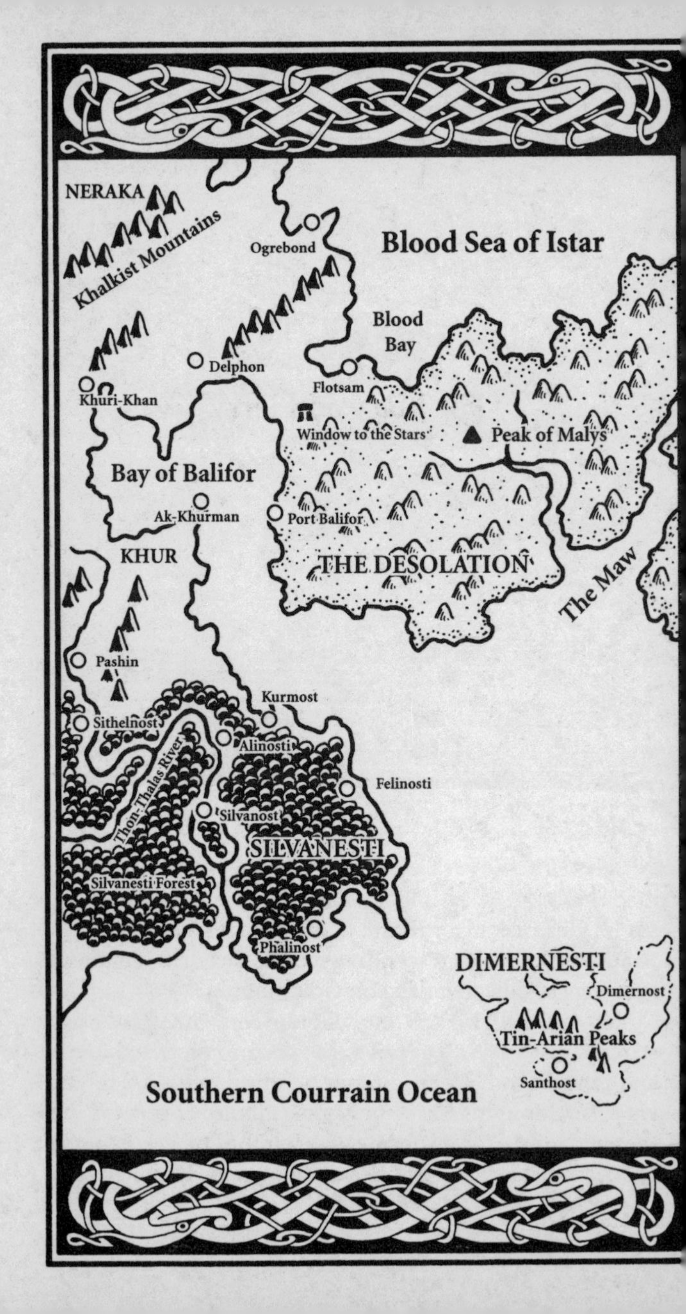
NERAKA
Khalkist Mountains
Ogrebond
Blood Sea of Istar
Blood
Bay
Delphon
Khuri-Khan
Flotsam
Window to the Stars
Peak of Malys
Bay of Balifor
Ak-Khurman
Port Balifor
KHUR
THE DESOLATION
The Maw
Pashin
Kurmost
Sithelnost
Alinosti
Thon-Thalas River
Felinosti
Silvanost
SILVANESTI
Silvanesti Forest
Phalinost
DIMERNESTI
Dimernost
Tin-Arian Peaks
Santhost
Southern Courrain Ocean

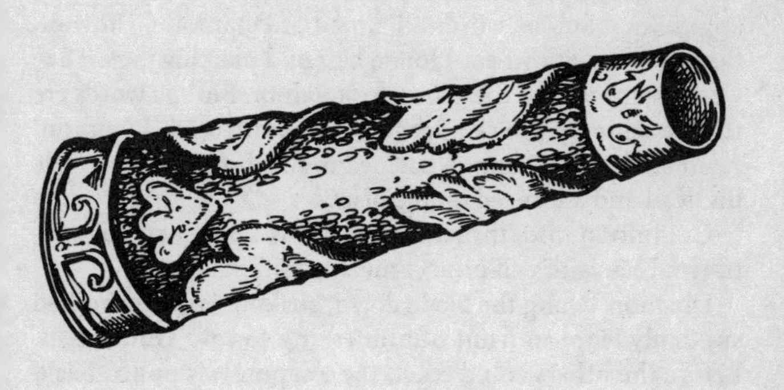

Prologue

Kindred Spirits

The glaive Dhamon Grimwulf clutched was simple in design yet starkly beautiful, an axelike blade affixed to a long, polished wooden haft. The edge, curved gently like a smile, gleamed silver in the light that spilled through the window. The weapon was drawn back, steadied. Dhamon's eyes were steady, too, fixed on Goldmoon's.

"My faith will protect me," Goldmoon whispered as she stepped back, trying to put some distance between herself and the weapon. A few moments would buy time to convince Dhamon this was wrong. Goldmoon's fingers touched the medallion about her neck, a symbol of her departed goddess Mishakal, and of her undying faith in the goddess.

"Dhamon, you can fight this. Fight the dragon. . . ."

There were other voices in the chamber beside hers—that of the dwarf, Jasper, her favored student of many years, and those of Feril, Blister, and Rig. Shouted words, pleading, angry, incredulous words all aimed at Dhamon Grimwulf, the tall man with wheat-blonde hair and piercing eyes. They were meant to stop the glaive, to stop him. But the words ere thrust aside by the red dragon who controlled Dhamon. Against his will, Dhamon listened to the dragon voice inside his head and advanced on the healer.

Goldmoon, too, thrust all the words aside, and concentrated. "My faith will protect me. My faith . . . no!"

Dhamon swung the blade down, striking Jasper, who had suddenly leapt in front of him trying to save Goldmoon. Before the others could react, the weapon was pulled back, this time gleaming red with the dwarf's blood.

"Jasper," Goldmoon whispered.

The blade poised for the most fleeting of moments. It was suspended for a heartbeat, no more, before continuing on a lethal path toward the famed healer and Hero of the Lance.

"My faith will protect me," Goldmoon repeated in a slightly stronger voice. Then she felt the coolness of the metal as it touched her; surprisingly she felt no pain. The gleam of the blade filled her vision. Then she saw nothing. Dhamon and the voices of her friends were gone, as her life was gone.

She slipped from Krynn.

A welcoming blackness swallowed Goldmoon, tactile like velvet and somehow comforting. This was death, she knew, and she was not afraid of death. She had never been afraid of it. Death had claimed her husband and one of her daughters years before, had claimed cherished friends—Tanis, Tasslehoff, Flint. Jasper too? In death, she expected to greet them all again.

The darkness, like a gentle vise, held her briefly, then

receded. As the darkness changed to a charcoal gray, it lessened its grip, but it did not release her. Then the space around her lightened further, until her surroundings became almost white, the shade of pale smoke. No floor to stand on, no walls, only a limitless mist. She hovered in its soft embrace, seemingly alone. But she knew he must be here with her.

"*Riverwind.*" She spoke the word, though her lips didn't move. She spoke the word with her mind and heard it clearly, as she also heard the response.

"*Beloved.*" He appeared before her as if by magic, young and strong, looking as he had on the day she'd first glimpsed him. His skin was tan, his eyes dark and full, his arms muscular and now wrapped around her. His long black hair fluttered in an intangible breeze.

"Riverwind . . . husband, I've missed you so." Goldmoon clung tightly to him and inhaled his scent. Memories flooded her mind: his courtship of her under the disapproving gaze of her father; the exhilarating danger they had experienced together during the War of the Lance; the time they had spent apart; and, above all, his death far from her side. Even after Riverwind had been killed helping the kender against Malystryx the Red, she had sensed that he was with her, part of her.

"I've missed you, too," Riverwind answered. "I've not been complete without you."

"To be together again," she said wistfully. "Complete. Forever."

"Forever." He stared at her. She looked as she had decades ago, full of hope and life, skin shining, silver-gold hair festooned with the feathers and beads of the Que-shu tribe. "Forever, yes. But forever must wait. Goldmoon, you can't stay here. You must go back."

"Go back? To what? Krynn? The Citadel of Light? I don't understand."

"It isn't your time to die. You have to go back. Feril . . . the Kagonesti . . . she can heal you."

"Not my time to die?"

"No. Not yet." He shook his head. "At least not for a while, love. Forever will have to wait a while longer."

"I think not, husband."

"Goldmoon . . ."

"I'm more than eighty years old. I've walked more than enough years on Krynn. Few people are fortunate to live as long. And I've had enough of living."

He ran a finger across her cheek, his spirit form as vibrant and warm as it had been in life. "But Krynn hasn't had enough of you, beloved. Not just yet, anyway."

"And who or what force decides this? I am dead, Riverwind. Am I not?"

"Dead? Yes. Still . . . it's not easy to explain," he began. "There is still time, if you hurry. Feril can—" He tried to say more, but she cut him off.

"I will admit I hadn't expected to die this way. I didn't think Dhamon would kill me, *could* bring himself to kill me. I thought he was strong enough to resist the beast that possesses him."

"Malystryx."

Goldmoon nodded. "She controls him through a scale on his leg. I was so certain he could overcome that. I thought he was the one, the man who could lead the fight against the overlords. I myself *chose* him, Riverwind, chose him months upon months ago as he kneeled outside the Last Heroes' Tomb. I looked into his heart. I erred. . . ."

"Things don't always turn out the way we expect," Riverwind replied.

"No."

"The others need your help."

"They can continue the cause without me. Palin, Rig, Blister, Feril . . ."

"They need you." Riverwind's voice was firm. "There are things you've yet to accomplish. The dragons . . ."

"How do you know this? Are the gods not truly gone? Do they speak to you? Are they . . ."

"You weren't supposed to die this day. That's all I know. And that's all you are permitted to know right now. Another was so fated."

"Another was to die? Not me?"

Riverwind drew his lips into a thin line. With a gesture of his hand the mists parted. They were hovering above the chamber in the Citadel of Light—ghostlike, for no one saw them there. The floor below was covered with blood—Goldmoon's, Jasper's, Rig's. The dwarf was seriously wounded, barely clinging to life, but he was clinging to Goldmoon's body, sobbing, his eyes wide with disbelief.

"I will miss them all," she whispered, her fingers reaching out toward the dwarf.

"There is still time. Return to them, beloved. Let the Kagonesti aid you. Then help Jasper. Hurry."

"Let Feril help Jasper."

Riverwind and Goldmoon could faintly discern words swirling in the air—grieving words over Goldmoon and Jasper, venomous words about Dhamon, words of shock that something like this could have happened, words demanding revenge.

"It wasn't Dhamon's fault," Goldmoon said. "They have to understand that. They'll eventually realize that."

"One of them was to die," Riverwind repeated. "Not you. Not yet. Dhamon wasn't meant to kill you."

"It wasn't Dhamon's fault. The dragon . . . the scale on his leg . . . who was supposed to die instead of me?"

Riverwind shook his head.

"Who?" she insisted.

"I can't tell you. All I can tell you is that you must go back." Riverwind's voice was firm, tinged with sadness. "We'll be together again, I promise. It will be soon enough. And you know I'll always be with you."

"In the very air I breathe."

"Yes."

"No. That isn't enough." Goldmoon tilted her head upward, drifted toward the ceiling, through the domed roof. Riverwind followed her, his arguments lost amid the heated words still audible from the chamber below. Again they were surrounded by the pale mist. "I'm not going back, husband. Only forward—to wherever spirits are destined to go. To see Tanis, Tasslehoff, dear Flint—wherever they are. My daughter Brightdawn. My mother. Perhaps finally to reconcile with my father. It is long past my time to join them all. And to join you."

"That may be what I wish, too," he offered. "But it is not what was meant to be. There are powerful dragons to consider."

"Ansalon always has dragons." She placed a finger to his lips, then drew him close. "Precious Riverwind, Krynn does not need this old woman any longer. Nor do I need Krynn. I need you. We are together again—finally and forever. Complete. One old woman will make no difference against the dragon overlords."

"Goldmoon, one person can always make a difference."

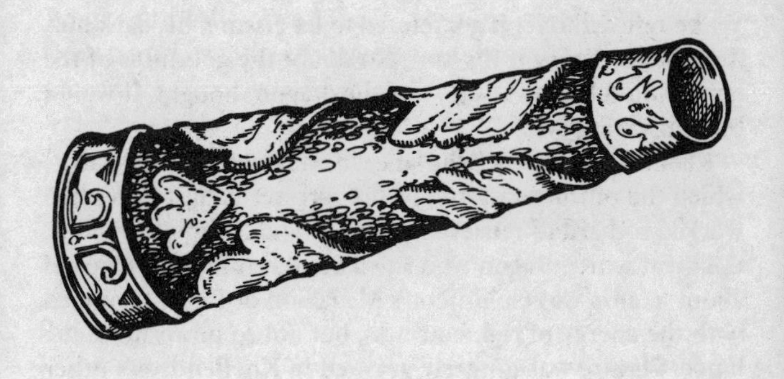

Chapter 1

After the Storm

Pain raced up the dragon overlord's claw and into his massive blue body.

"This damnable lance," he hissed in a zephyrlike voice. He threw back his great, horned head, opened his maw, and spewed a bolt of lightning into the belly of a thick cloud high above. The sky thundered its response, and what had begun as a steady rain deepened into a driving storm. The night was intermittently brightened by the lightning that danced down to his indigo-scaled back, a sensation he normally found pleasing. The wind keened fiercely, and the rain hammered obligingly against his thick hide. But no element of the storm was enough to assuage his suffering.

The powerful lance burned the dragon, was continuing to burn him with every beat of his enormous wings, with each mile that he crossed. He had been carrying it for the past several hours, ever since he claimed it from the heroes he slew. Yet he refused to let it go, refused to let Fissure, his dark huldrefolk ally, carry it for him. No doubt the goodness of the lance would harm Fissure, too, the dragon thought. It would burn anything evil.

Khellendros clutched the lance in one claw—Huma's lance, which the pitiful associates of the sorcerer Palin Majere had worked so hard to retrieve from the frigid realm of Gellidus, the great white dragon who ruled Southern Ergoth. Hooked about a talon was Goldmoon's Medallion of Faith, also filled with the energy of righteousness, but not so powerful as the lance. Fissure was gingerly grasped in Khellendros's other claw. A second medallion, a seeming twin of the first, was about the huldre's neck. Three artifacts from the Age of Dreams. Three the dragon had acquired. There was one more at his lair, a ring of crystal keys. Four should be enough, he remembered Fissure saying.

"The lance is filled with god-magic! That's why it burns you so!" the gray-skinned huldre offered, shouting above the gale. "It was crafted to slay dragons, after all!" The tiny man, drenched, hairless, and looking as if he were freshly-sculpted from smooth clay, craned his bald head around so he could look into Khellendros's flashing eyes. "That lance is the most powerful of these three artifacts—and certainly more powerful than the keys the Knights of Takhisis gained for you."

The most powerful and the most painful, Khellendros thought. The dragon growled and tried futilely to thrust the pain to the back of his mind. The lance could do more than simply cause him discomfort. It would scar him certainly. But it could not kill him—probably not even if it plunged into his flesh. He was, after all, a supreme overlord, one of a handful of Krynn's most awesome dragons, and he would use this hurtful, hateful lance—and the other three artifacts—to open a portal to The Gray.

The spirit of Kitiara, his long-ago partner in the Dark Queen's army, wandered somewhere in that dusky dimension. And he would snare her spirit, as he had snared this lance, and by that act return Kitiara to Krynn. Four artifacts ought to be enough.

But first he had to craft a new body for her spirit.

He *had* one, a fine blue spawn—muscular, elegant, perfect. It had been birthed in part from one of his rare tears. But Palin and his conspirators had unknowingly killed the blue spawn, along with dozens of others, when they destroyed his favorite lair in the desert of the Northern Wastes. That he had slaughtered Palin and his companions less than an hour ago was some small consolation. He should have seen to that task earlier, not so much out of revenge—a human motivation that was beneath him—but as a tribute to Kitiara, who in life had been vexed by Palin's father and uncle, Caramon and Raistlin Majere. The Majeres had plagued her life, and now they haunted her in death.

For a time, Palin and his fellows had proved useful to Khellendros. On the advice of one of the dragon's planted spies, an old sycophant who had managed to pass himself off as a scholar, the wizard's party had unwittingly gathered these artifacts for him.

On a stretch of ground on the island of Schallsea, not far from the Citadel of Light, they had placed the artifacts. The fake scholar had advised shattering them, claiming that the energy released would increase the level of magic in the world. They had had no idea that it was all a ruse, that Khellendros had been alerted and intended to steal their precious artifacts.

Their usefulness was at an end. Palin and the others had realized too late that the blue dragon overlord had cornered them. As Khellendros slew them, Fissure killed the sycophant to tidy up loose ends.

However, Khellendros hadn't known that holding this damnable lance would be so agonizing. Still, any amount of pain was worth bearing if it meant Kitiara could be welcomed back to Krynn. She had to return, had to be made whole. Khellendros had made a pledge to her—out of loyalty and respect—long ago when she was his partner. He had promised that he would keep her safe. Then one day, when she strayed from his side, she was slain. A grieving Khellendros searched and searched for her spirit, eventually finding it in The Gray. He would keep his pledge by rescuing her from that faraway dimension. There was no one to stop him—Palin and his friends were now dead. And, best of all, Malystryx the Red and the other overlords were oblivious to his ultimate goal.

He and Kitiara would be reunited. Soon. But first Khellendros had to endure this hellish pain all the way back to his lair.

* * * * *

"Khellendros thinks we're dead," Rig said. The dark-skinned mariner glanced up, peering in the direction in which the great blue overlord had disappeared. He ran a hand through his close-cropped hair and breathed a sigh of relief.

"I certainly *hope* he thinks that. Otherwise he'll come back and try again. And I wouldn't want him to try again 'cause I don't think there'd be any *trying* about it." The strained, high-pitched voice belonged to Blister, a middle-aged kender who was ambling toward the mariner. "Nope. No trying to it at all in my opinion." Her gnarled hands were busy—one tugging at Jasper's sleeve, the other fiddling with her frazzled blonde braid. "Y'see, if he did come back and try again . . . well . . . I just have this feeling that he'd be pretty darn successful. I'm kind of surprised to be living and breathing. He's certainly a very *big* dragon. I never saw one so big. Did you see his teeth? Big teeth, too." She paused, her face contorting into a puzzled expression. "So what happened? How'd we escape?"

"Palin," Rig supplied the answer.

"Oh. What did you do?" Blister turned her attention on Palin Majere.

The sorcerer brushed a long strand of graying hair out of his eyes. "A spell," he said softly. He hadn't the energy to speak louder. His shoulders stooped, he leaned against Rig, and sucked a deep breath of damp air into his lungs. The climactic enchantment had taken the last of his resources. He was the most powerful sorcerer on Krynn and one of the few survivors of the Battle of the Rift in the Abyss. But at the moment he felt far from mighty. He was weak, vulnerable, his spirit as ravaged as his mud-stained tunic and torn leggings.

"An amazing spell," Blister said. "Very effective. Wouldn't you say so, Jasper?"

The dwarf clutched his side, nodding in agreement. A wheeze escaped his thick lips. Though the wound Dhamon had inflicted on Jasper was mending—thanks to Feril's ministrations—the dwarf would never be the same. His lung had been punctured. Though in earlier times he might have used his own clerical magic to heal himself, such power was now beyond his reach. His faith had died with Goldmoon, and with it had died his healing abilities. He offered Blister a slight smile.

"Amazing. Yes, Jasper thinks so, too. A very impressive spell," she clucked. "You made us all invisible?"

"Not exactly," Palin returned.

"You spirited us away to some other place?"

"Not precisely."

"Then what?"

"For a few brief minutes, I disguised us, made us blend into the landscape. Then I created a magical illusion of us a short distance from where we were hiding. Khellendros slew the illusion. And, fortunately, he appeared to be in a hurry and left without examining his handiwork. Had he lingered a moment longer, his keen senses would have ferreted us out."

"Wow. So how did you create this illusion?" the kender persisted in asking.

"It's not important," Jasper cut in. He glanced back at Groller, his deaf half-ogre friend. Fiona Quinti, the young Solamnic knight who recently joined their number, was using rudimentary sign language to translate what was being said, so Groller could understand. The dwarf turned to face Blister and pawed at a clump of mud stuck to his red-brown hair. "It's not important at all. What is important Blister, is that . . ."

"Couldn't Palin use some of his magic to find Dhamon? I want to go after Dhamon, find out why he went all crazy, hurt Jasper, and killed Goldmoon. We could . . ."

The mariner set a hand on the kender's head, leveling his gaze at Palin. "We could kill him is what we could do. It was indirectly because of Dhamon that Shaon died. Now Goldmoon—there was nothing indirect about that. He almost killed Jasper, too. And he sank my ship."

"*Flint's Anvil*," Jasper whispered. The dwarf had purchased the carrack many months ago, and his beloved vessel had taken them from Schallsea far north to Palanthas, then back again. It had been their means of transportation and their home.

"We *should* kill him before he causes any more harm," Rig finished. The mariner motioned for the rest to gather around—Feril, the Kagonesti; Groller and his wolf, Fury; Fiona; Gilthanas, the lanky elven sorcerer whom they had rescued from a Knights of Takhisis stronghold; and Ulin, Palin's son.

Swirling high above them were two dragons, a gold and a silver—Sunrise and Silvara—who had carried Ulin and Gilthanas to Schallsea and who had been instrumental in distracting Khellendros in order for Palin to cast his spell. The dragons and their riders had just returned from the Dragon

Isles, where they had informed the good dragons there of what was transpiring across the face of Ansalon.

"Rig . . ." Feril cleared her throat to get the mariner's attention. A breeze whipped her wild tangle of auburn hair about her face. "We need to find Dhamon. Help him fight the scale's influence. We must have faith. . . ."

"Faith?" Jasper looked up at her, fixed his eyes on the oak-leaf tattoo on her tanned cheek. His ruddy face was uncharacteristically grim. "*He killed Goldmoon.* We haven't even had time to grieve for her, or to bury her properly. She preached faith—breathed faith. And forgiveness. But right now I have no faith and little forgiveness. Right now I'm siding with Rig."

Feril closed her eyes and let out a long breath. "I'm angry, too, Jasper. Maybe I won't ever be able to forgive him. But I have to know what happened and why."

"It's pretty obvious what happened," Rig cut in. "He told us he once *was* a Knight of Takhisis. I'm betting he still is. Fooled us, like the scholar fooled us into collecting the damned artifacts. No ship. No Goldmoon. No Huma's lance."

"No medallions. Goldmoon's medallion, and the second medallion I . . ." Jasper forced back a sob. "The one I took from her after she was dead. Both gone and in the hands of the dragon."

"The only artifact we have left is the scepter," the mariner said. He held it out. It was fashioned of wood and looked more like a mace, though it was bedecked with jewels.

"The Fist of E'li," Feril whispered softly. "The Fist of Paladine."

"What good'll one lousy artifact do?" Blister asked as she looked up at the sorcerer. "We can't increase the level of magic in the world with just one artifact."

"The scholar tricked us into gathering artifacts for the dragon," Palin said. "The dragon must want the ancient magic for an important reason. Maybe we should concentrate on finding other ancient artifacts. At the very least, we can keep them out of the dragon's clutches. And at the most. . . somehow we might be able to use their energy to block Takhisis's return to this world."

"Father, Gellidus—Frost—claimed Takhisis's return was imminent," Ulin said. The younger Majere looked as Palin had, two decades earlier. He gestured to the silver and gold dragons circling above. "Sunrise and Silvara confirm what the white overlord boasted. Takhisis is coming back."

"So where are we gonna get enough ancient magic to stop Takhisis?" Blister's eyes widened.

"Dalamar's ring," Palin said. "That's located in the Tower of Wayreth. The Master of the Tower said he would give it to me, but only when we knew how to use it and when we were safe from Khellendros."

Ulin sniffed. "Safe! That will take a long time! Can you persuade the Master how important is our need for the ring?"

Palin considered a moment, then nodded to his son. "Yes. Yes, I think I can."

"With the Fist of E'li," Blister said, pointing at the weapon in Rig's hand, "That makes two artifacts."

"I know of a third—the Crown of Tides," Palin finished. "It rests in the realm of the Dimernesti, the sea elves, a long way from here."

"Then we better get going," the kender said.

"Wait a minute." Rig scowled and shook his head. "I want nothing more than to take a stand against the dragons—even the Dark Queen herself if it comes to that. But there's a little matter of justice that needs to be taken care of, too. I mean Dhamon."

"Rig, please," Feril appealed.

"We can't let him wander around free—not with that weird glaive. No telling who or what else he'll destroy." The mariner's eyes narrowed darkly.

"Rig!" The Kagonesti glared at him.

"Enough." Palin eased himself away from Rig's side. "Arguing won't do us any good. Neither will revenge. But, yes, we also need to find Dhamon."

The mariner grinned smugly.

"We especially need to find him because we need his weapon," the sorcerer said.

"His *weapon*?" Rig scowled.

"That glaive cuts metal like cloth. It must be some kind of artifact, perhaps as powerful as Huma's lance," Palin returned. "Even more powerful," he added softly.

"So how are we gonna do both at the same time? Collect artifacts and find Dhamon?" Blister asked.

"I'll need your help, Blister," the sorcerer told the kender. "You and I will form one team and head to the Tower of Wayreth. My wife Usha is waiting for me there. We'll use the resources in the tower to trace Dhamon."

"And in the meantime, we'll go after the crown," Feril said excitedly.

"Great. How do we get off this island without a ship? Swim?" The mariner tucked the scepter into his belt and glanced to the west. It was too dark to see the Schallsea shore.

"We'll help there," Gilthanas offered. He pointed to the dragons. "We'll take you to the edge of Onysablet's realm. From there . . ."

"Let me guess. We're on our own," Rig grumbled.

Gilthanas nodded. The elf did not need to explain that the dragons would not prefer to venture into an overlord's realm, at least one they were unfamiliar with.

At the edge of the gathering Fiona Quinti squared her shoulders. Though Groller towered over her, she looked tall and formidable, if haggard, in the silver plate of her Solamnic knighthood. Her mailed hands painted pictures in the air, as she did her best to explain to Groller what was about to transpire.

The half-ogre's heavy brow knotted in thought. He looked up at the dragons, nodded, and swallowed hard.

* * * * *

It was the hazy hour before dawn, when the sky lightened just a little and the world seemed at its quietest. Usha stared out a window in the Tower of Wayreth. She drew her robe tight around her thin form, shivering from worry, not cold.

Blister was sleeping. Palin, too, had fallen asleep shortly after arriving a few hours ago. She hoped he would rest long enough to regain his energy.

She was exhausted, too, but couldn't sleep. Her mind was too preoccupied with the Fist of E'li that Palin had told her about. She had traveled to the Qualinesti forest with Palin, Jasper, and Feril in search of the Fist. But she hadn't accompanied them on the most dangerous part of the mission. When they had been caught by a band of distrustful, freedom-fighting elves, Usha had volunteered to stay with the elves as a hostage, insurance that her husband and the others were there for only one thing—the scepter—and proof that they were not spies for the green dragon overlord.

Something happened during her time with the elves. Something about the scepter. Something she was trying desperately to remember. Something, perhaps, that might help against the dragons.

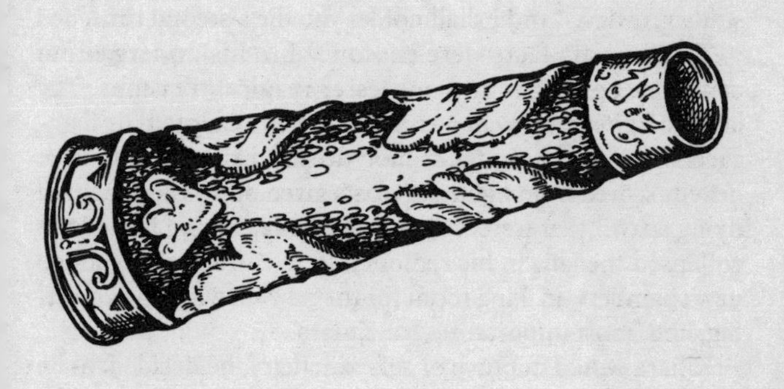

Chapter 2

A Gathering of Evil

The Storm Over Krynn sprawled just outside the mouth of his lair, basking in the late afternoon sun and idly studying his claw. Huma's lance had left a crimson welt deep across his thick skin. The wound throbbed, though the blessed heat somewhat eased the pain. It had been a few weeks since the battle over the artifacts, time enough for the wound to heal—if it would ever heal. He had carried the hateful lance hundreds upon hundreds of miles to the Northern Wastes. Perhaps it had marked him eternally.

Khellendros knew he could live with the pain—a small price to pay in his quest to resurrect Kitiara's spirit, and an unremitting memento of his easy triumph over the great

Palin Majere. He smiled inwardly. It would be sweet to tell Kitiara of his victory, though even more sweet had she been there to share it with him.

"It will not be much longer. We shall be partners again," he softly growled. "And I shall not let you die a second time."

The four artifacts were ensconced in his underground cave—along with numerous lesser magical treasures. The latter had been excavated recently as he resculpted his damaged lair. The walls in the section deepest below ground were heavily scored from lightning blasts given off by the dozens of dying spawn that were trapped when Majere and his fellows collapsed the lair. In his remodeling, the dragon had added new chambers, making room for the new spawn he was creating, and, most importantly, for Kitiara.

Kitiara would approve of this sanctuary, he decided, as he thrust his wounded claw in the sand and stared across the seemingly endless white expanse, broken only by the occasional cactus he had allowed to grow. She will approve, and together we shall . . .

A shadow fell across the sand, momentarily blocking the sun. Khellendros set his thoughts of Kitiara aside and glanced up to acknowledge the approach of Gale, his lieutenant. The smaller dragon glided to a landing several dozen yards from the overlord, sniffed the air to hone in on the Storm's precise position, then slowly advanced.

"You desire my aid," Gale hissed. The smaller blue brought his head to the ground in a show of respect.

Khellendros stared into his lieutenant's eyes, sightless from a battle with Dhamon Grimwulf, and waited several beats to answer. "Follow me, Gale. We shall discuss things inside."

The shadows of the overlord's lair swallowed the massive dragons. The great chamber, barely large enough to hold the pair, was dimly lit along one wall by the light that spilled down the tunnel from the surface.

"Fissure!" Khellendros's voice reverberated against the

walls and caused the lair to vibrate. Sand filtered down through cracks in the ceiling, dusting the four artifacts laid out in the center of the chamber and covering the huldrefolk who had been gazing intently at the ancient magical items. The faerie took a few steps back.

"These treasures are not yours to trifle with," the great dragon growled.

"I didn't so much as touch them, O Portal Master," the huldre answered. His form shimmered, and the sand disappeared from his features. "But I have been looking at them. Very closely. We should use them, Khellendros. Now. We shouldn't wait and risk the chance that Malys might discover your great prizes and take them for herself. Gale is finally here, and he can watch over your realm while you and I are in The Gray. We should take them out on the sand this very night. Together we can . . ."

Khellendros's rumble silenced the huldrefolk. "There remain a few things to attend to, faerie, before we dare open the portal."

"Hmm, yes. Selecting a spawn for Kitiara." The diminutive gray man scratched his smooth head. "Gale can do that, while you and I are visiting The Gray. You showed him how to train spawn. He can pick one out. There are more than a dozen to choose from."

"*I* shall be certain a perfect spawn is ready *before* we leave for The Gray. *I* shall select the vessel."

"Fine. And how long until you make this selection?" the huldre dared to insist.

"Gale will be training the few spawn below. He must also find more human females to serve as spawn. When the time is right, I shall select the most appropriate of them."

The smaller blue dragon edged closer to the faerie, nostrils quivering to take in Fissure's scent. He cocked his head and sniffed again, listening with ears that were increasingly an acute substitute for lost eyes. From farther in the cave came a skittering sound, at first no louder than the huldre's beating heart, a definite clacking against the stone floor. Within moments the noise was loud enough to interrupt Khellendros and the huldre.

Two great scorpions, as black as night, scuttled forward out of the shadows. Their unblinking yellow eyes gleamed malevolently, and their pincers snapped open and shut.

"You wisssh sssomething," they said in unison, their strange voices hissing like shifting sand. From their clawlike feet to the tip of their curved venomous tails, they stood a little taller than a man. Their hard, segmented bodies were long and thick, glistening like wet stone in the meager light.

"You will guard my lair while I am away," Khellendros instructed the pair. "And you will make sure none of the spawn touch these." He gestured at the lance, medallions, and crystal keys. "Do you understand?"

"Yesss Masssster," they replied. They skittered past the dragons, toward their post at the entrance to the lair.

"Away?" Fissure asked. "You're going somewhere? Where?"

Khellendros narrowed his eyes. "Where I go is none of your concern, faerie." The overlord turned toward Gale. "Malys desires my presence, and I would not like to give her cause to suspect my plans by refusing her. I shall be gone for some time. How long, I am not certain. But in that time . . ."

"I will train your spawn," the lesser dragon finished.

Khellendros pivoted and glided up through the tunnel that lead to the desert above. Gale followed at a prudent distance.

"There are barbarian villages to the east," Khellendros advised when they were back on the sand. "I raided them and captured their strongest warriors. It was from them that I fashioned the spawn in my lair. Take care, for the villages' remaining warriors might come seeking their stolen brethren."

"It will be my pleasure to slay any who come uninvited. They will pose no threat."

"Take care that you do not underestimate them," the Storm said. "Malystryx, who calls me, has no fear of humans. Neither, it seems, do the other overlords. But I know better."

"As do I." The lesser blue closed his blind eyes. "One did this to me. One I once called partner and friend. I never underestimate humans."

He sniffed the wind and turned toward the east. "The faerie," Gale added. "While I am training the spawn, can he be trusted with your treasure? The artifacts?"

"No," the Storm answered. "I do not underestimate him either. He can be more formidable than a human. But he is far, far less a threat in this instance. Besides, I took steps to protect the artifacts."

The blue overlord took to the sky, the draft from his wings sending a shower of sand across Gale and toward the immobile scorpions who stood guard at the lair.

Deep inside, Fissure shuffled toward the artifacts. "Khellendros, The Storm Over Krynn. Khellendros, the Portal Master. Khellendros, the Procrastinator, he should call himself. He wants to wait to open the portal to The Gray. Wait . . . wait . . . wait," the huldre muttered. "Time to a dragon is . . . well, the mighty Khellendros will discover how waiting has cost him. I have been absent from The Gray for far too many years. And I have no desire to wait any longer. I thought I'd need his help to open the portal, was certain I did. But Huma's lance . . . There is so much power contained within it. Maybe I don't need The Procrastinator's help after all."

He held his small hands a foot above the medallions, sensing the magic that pulsed in them. It was a pleasing sensation. "No. Maybe I will not need Khellendros any longer, now that I have these within my grasp." He passed his fingers over the keys, sensed the cool smoothness of the crystal, the tingle of the enchantment. His fingers lingered a few inches above the smallest key, one crafted to open any lock, and he closed his eyes to bask in the arcane aura.

"No. I certainly will not wait. I must try to go home. I will destroy these myself and open a portal to The Gray with the released energy. If I cannot do it myself, perhaps Gellidus the White or the big green can be duped into helping me. The Storm Over Krynn will be angry, but he will not be able to follow me; he has no more artifacts to destroy, nothing to empower his plans. I will be safe, safe at home. And he will be stranded. Stranded so very far from his poor, lost Kitiara afloat in The Gray."

The gray man giggled and stretched his fingers toward Huma's lance, felt the intense vibrations of energy the weapon loosed into the air. "I saw how the lance burned Khellendros," he whispered. "It will not burn me. I am not so evil as the overlord. No, not evil. Not at all. I just want to return home. Pity that the humans who once wielded this magnificent weapon could not feel this power." He edged his hands closer to the lance handle. "Pity. Such a . . . argh!" The surge of power scalded him as if he'd thrust his hands in boiling oil. Waves of energy crashed into his tiny form, jarring him, sending him reeling and writhing to the cavern floor.

Through a haze, the dark huldrefolk shuddered uncontrollably and glanced at his seared skin. "Khellendros . . . cast a spell on the items . . . warded them. He did not trust me." He gasped for breath, then mercifully lost consciousness.

Overhead, Khellendros banked toward the southeast, toward Malystryx's realm. The first rays of the setting sun painted his desert a pale red. "No," Khellendros murmured softly. "The faerie is far less of a threat."

* * * * *

The ground was cracked like a dry riverbed: flat, desolate, and warm beneath the claws of the five dragons gathered in a circle atop it.

Gellidus, the white dragon overlord, did his best to veil his discomfort at his hot surroundings and stared straight ahead at the distant mountain, the Peak of Malys, ringed by glowing volcanoes. Called Frost by men, ruler of ice-covered Southern Ergoth, he presented a stark contrast to Malystryx. Frost's scales were small and glistening, white as snow,. His crest looked like a halo of inverted icicles, and his tail was short and thick compared to the other dragons.

The red overlord was easily twice Frost's size, with shield-shaped scales the hue of freshly drawn blood. Massive twin horns curled into the air, and twin streams of smoke spiraled from her cavernous nostrils. She glanced briefly at Frost. Then her dark eyes drifted skyward, following Khellendros. To her right was a lean red dragon, who, curled like a cat, looked slightly smaller than the white overlord.

Khellendros landed nearly a mile away from the circle and took in the other two dragons with his stare as he approached. Beryllinthranox, the Green Peril, sat opposite Malys. She was the color of the forest she ruled—the lands once held by the proud Qualinesti. Beryl's narrowed eyes were intent. Perhaps she was trying to gauge the others' reactions to Khellendros. Her serpentine tail, extended straight behind her, undulated slowly. Beryl gave the blue overlord a perfunctory nod, then turned to the Black.

Between Beryl and Gellidus sprawled Onysablet. Acid dripped from the black dragon's equine-shaped leathery jowls, forming a bubbling pond between her claws. Unblinking eyes that gleamed like twin pools of oil, so dark that irises could not be distinguished from pupils, were fixed on Malys. Her thick, glossy horns swept forward from her narrow head.

Beryl was regaling the Black with tales of her domination over the elves, but Sable showed bare interest. Malys held most of her attention.

Khellendros took a position between Beryl and the smaller Red, Malys's lieutenant, Ferno, sitting back on his great haunches. Malys was the only dragon larger than he, and he was careful, for propriety's sake, to keep his head lower than hers. Too, he kept his wounded claw flat against the earth, not wanting the other dragons to question him about his injury. He nodded to Malys. He was the Red's acknowledged consort, openly favored by her. But the Red's continued glances toward Frost hinted that Malys was sharing her ambitious affections.

Malystryx returned Khellendros's nod. "We can begin now," she said, her voice resonant and booming across the arid land. The noise touched the Peak of Malys and echoed hauntingly. "We are the most powerful of dragons, and none dare stand up to us."

"We crush our opposition," Beryl hissed. "We dominate the land—and those who live upon it."

"None challenge us," Sable said. She drew a talon through the pool of acid in front of her, as the liquid trailing from it sizzled and popped over the barren ground. "None dare, because none can."

"Those few who try," Frost added, "meet death quickly."

Khellendros remained silent, listening to the overlords' boasts, and watched Gellidus squirm almost imperceptibly in the heat.

"Yet our power is nothing," Malys interrupted. She craned her neck toward the sky so that she towered above the others, who listened to her remark with wide eyes. "Our power is nothing compared to what it will be when Takhisis returns."

"Yes, Takhisis is coming!" Frost cried.

"But when?" That was Sable.

"Before the year ends," Malys answered. She brought her head lower, making sure that Khellendros kept his lower still.

"And how do you know this?" Beryl's voice was laced with venom. "What great knowledge do you have of the gods?"

Malys's immense jowls edged upward in the approximation of a smile. Ferno uncurled himself and stood, his eyes boring into the green dragon who dared ask such a question.

"Malys knows," Frost offered. "Malys told us how to gain

power, before the Dragon Purge. Malys directed us to grab territory. Because of her we are overlords. If any among us would know of Takhisis's return, it would have to be Malystryx."

The Green cocked her head to the side. "I am an overlord because of my own ambition and power. What power, Malystryx, do you have that I do not? What power allows you to know of Takhisis's return?"

Malys regarded the Green for several silent moments. "Perhaps rebirth would be a better term," the Red purred.

Khellendros remained quiet, noticing that Frost and Ferno had moved closer to the great Red and that Sable was carefully watching Beryl.

"Rebirth?" the Green hissed.

Flames flickered about Malys's nostrils. "It is a new Takhisis who will appear on Krynn, Beryllinthranox. That Takhisis will be me."

"Blasphemy!" Beryl shouted.

"There is no blasphemy when there are no gods," the Red sharply returned.

The Green arched her back. "And without the gods, we bow to no one, serve no one. We are our own masters—Krynn's masters. Only gods are worthy of our deference. And you, Malystryx, are not a god."

"Your gods left this world. Even Takhisis vanished." The air grew warmer as Malys continued, and the flames about her nostrils rose higher. "As you say, Beryl, we are the masters now. We are the most powerful beings on Krynn—and I am first among us."

"You are mighty, I will grant you that. Alone, none of us could stand up to you. But you are not a god."

"I am *not yet* a god."

"Not ever."

"No, Beryl?"

Sable moved closer to Frost. The two had broken the circle,

formed a line with Malys and her lieutenant, all facing Beryl, who was looking at Khellendros out of the corner of her narrowing eye.

Beryl wants to know where I stand, the Storm mused. *The Green recognizes my strength and is looking for support. Malys is also waiting. She has been devoting her time to forming alliances, with the White and the Black. She is more clever and calculating than I thought. Paired with others, she cannot be challenged.*

Khellendros cast a sidelong glance at Beryl, then moved to join the line, taking up a position next to Ferno and dwarfing the smaller red dragon.

"I will ascend to godhood before the year is out," Malys hissed at the Green. "I will ascend with the heavens—and my allies—as my witnesses. Where do you stand?"

Beryl dug her claws into the baked ground, glanced for a moment at the myriad cracks she had added to the land, then tilted her head to meet the Red's stare. "I stand with you," she said finally.

"Then you may live," Malys said.

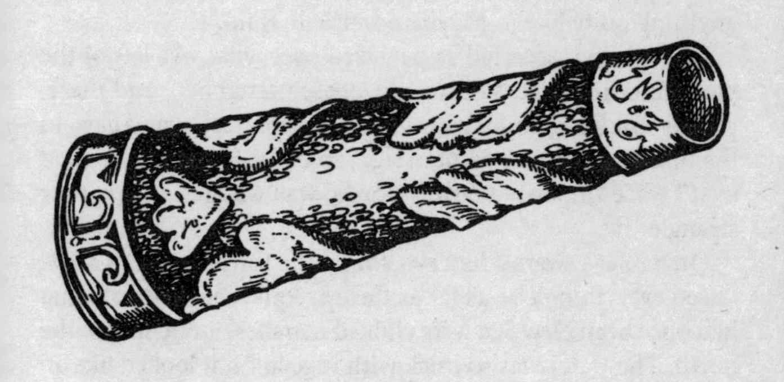

Chapter 3

A Dark Domain

"Decent people used to live here." Rig sat heavily on a rotting willow log and swatted at the mosquitos swarming around his face. His dark skin glistened with sweat.

"How would you know?" Jasper asked.

"Years ago Shaon and I stopped here for a few days." He smiled wistfully at the memory and swept his hand to indicate the small clearing they'd selected for a campsite. "This was once a town, here on the banks of the River Toranth. S'funny. I don't remember the name of the place, but the people were friendly enough, real hard-working folk. Supplies were cheap. The food was warm—and good." He took in a deep breath, let it out slowly. "Shaon and I spent an evening on the docks, which would have been somewhere over by that cypress. There was this old man; I think he passed for their barge master. Talked all night with him and watched the sun come up. He shared his flagon of Stone Rose Ale. Never tasted anything quite like it. Maybe never will again."

The mariner scowled as he gazed over what was left of the place. Bits and pieces of wood were scattered here and there, poking out from under round, leafy buttonbushes and gaps in the thick sawgrass. A painted sign, so badly faded that "boiled oyst" were the only legible words, was wedged into a pale strangler fig.

Onysablet's swamp had swallowed the town, as it had swallowed everything else as far as the eye could see. Parts of what had once been New Sea were choked marshes, stretching to the north. The water was so thick with vegetation it looked like an olive plain. In many places it was difficult to tell where the land ended and the water began.

Several days ago Silvara and Sunrise had deposited the travelers on the shore of the New Swamp, after flying across the navigable part of New Sea. Though the ride was unsettling, the mariner wished the dragons could have taken them farther. But the Silver and Gold had no desire to encroach on Sable's realm. So Silvara and Sunrise left to take Gilthanas and Ulin to the Tower of Wayreth. Rig hoped the two sorcerers could pool their wits with Palin to discover Dhamon's whereabouts.

"I'm hungry." Jasper sat next to the mariner and gently deposited a leather sack between his legs. It contained the Fist of E'li, of which Jasper had volunteered to be the caretaker. The dwarf was still favoring his side, his breath was raspy, and he was also hungry. He patted his stomach, offered Rig a weak smile, then batted away a thumb-sized black bug that was inching too close for comfort. The dwarf pointed a stubby finger toward what he could see of the sun between breaks in the tree trunks. "It's getting on toward dinner time."

"Your belly'll be filled soon enough," Rig said. "Feril

shouldn't be gone too much longer. And I hope she brings back something other than a fat lizard this time. I hate lizard meat."

The dwarf chuckled, patting his stomach again. "Groller and Fury went with her. Maybe the wolf will spook out a boar. Groller likes roast pig. So do I."

"You shouldn't be so particular, Rig Mer-Krel and Master Fireforge," Fiona called over. "You should be appreciative of any fresh meat." The Knight of Solamnia was busy picking through the more intact remnants of the town. She brushed back the leaves of a massive bladderwort, lifted up a decaying chair back and shook her head. Retrieving a moldy doll, she held it up, looked into its absent eyes, then carefully replaced it on the ground.

Fiona's face and arms were gleaming with sweat, her red curls plastered against her high forehead, the rest of it piled in ringlets atop her head and held in place with an ivory comb borrowed from Usha. She'd taken off her metal arm and leg plates yesterday as well as her helmet, and was toting them around in a canvas sack. Though they were cumbersome and heavy, she refused to leave them behind. Neither would she completely surrender to the heat and take off her silver breastplate with its Knight of the Crown etching. "Even lizard is more nourishing than the usual rations," she observed. "We have to preserve our strength."

"The rations are a little more tasty as far as I'm concerned," Rig muttered half under his breath. "Though not by much. Lizard. Yuck." He kept his eyes on the Solamnic as she continued rummaging, moving farther away from them. "By the way, it's just Rig, remember?"

"And Jasper," added the dwarf. "Nobody calls me Master Fireforge. I don't think anybody even called my Uncle Flint that."

Fiona glanced over her shoulder, smiled, and resumed her search.

"Keep poking around all you want, but you're not going to

find anything worthwhile," Rig called to her. "When the black dragon moved in, most of the sensible people picked up what they could—their children, valuables, mementos—and moved out."

"I'm just browsing while we wait for dinner. Something to do. I just can't sit around."

"You like her, don't you?" Jasper winked at Rig, keeping his voice low. "You've been watching her like a hawk since Schallsea."

The mariner grunted in reply.

"Hmmm, there's something here," Fiona said. "Something solid under this mud."

"She's got spunk." The dwarf nudged Rig. "She's lovely for a human, polite, brave too, according to Ulin. He said she didn't run when Frost attacked them in Southern Ergoth. Stood her ground and was ready to fight, even though it looked like certain death. She can handle that sword she totes, and . . ."

"And she's a knight," Rig said in a voice the dwarf had to strain to hear. "Dhamon was a knight, *is* a knight, of Takhisis. I've had my fill of knights. All their talk of honor. Just a shallow word."

"I'm betting there's nothing shallow about her."

"Look at this!" Fiona's arms were buried halfway to her elbows in muck. She tugged at a small wooden chest. The ground grudgingly released it with a loud slurp. She grinned and held it up for them to see. A cloud of mosquitos immediately formed around her.

Fiona batted the insects away and carried the chest toward Rig and Jasper. Banded in thin iron, a tiny lock dangling from its front, the chest was thickly rusted and covered with slime.

Jasper wriggled his nose, but Rig was instantly interested. Fiona placed it on the ground in front of them, knelt, and drew her sword. "I'm going to need a bath after this," she said. Muck dripped from her arms and fingers onto the pommel of her sword. She thrust the tip at the small lock, which quickly gave way.

Rig reached for the chest, but she stayed his hand with a wry smile. "Ladies first. "Besides, I went to all the trouble of digging it up. I'm hoping there's a book or papers inside, something that might tell me more about the inhabitants of this place. Maybe some information about the dragon." She eased the lid open and frowned. Brackish water had seeped in, filling it to the brim and ruining the velvet lining. She drained it out and let out a deep sigh, holding up a long strand of large pearls. She scowled and dropped the necklace back in the chest, where a matching bracelet and earrings rested.

"Careful! That's valuable!" Rig said.

Fiona shrugged. "Riches never much interested me, Rig Mer-Krel. Any coins I earned, I gave to the Order."

"Then I'll hang onto those," the mariner advised, as he snatched up the pearls. "We're probably gonna need money—more than we've got—before this is all done. Clothes. We're wearing all we have, and they won't last forever either."

"Food," the dwarf offered.

"Renting a ship to get to Dimernesti—provided we can figure out where Dimernesti is," Rig continued.

"And that's provided we can make it through this swamp," Jasper added as he looked up at the giant trees draped with moss and vines. "Provided the black dragon doesn't find us and . . ."

"I wonder if there's more treasure," the mariner speculated aloud as he pushed himself off the log and tucked the pearls in his pants pocket. "No way to tell unless we look. I might as well do a little digging myself. Dinner's not here yet." He took off his shirt and arranged it on the lowest branch of a palm-leaved sweetbay tree. Leaning his sword against the trunk, he started scooping through the muck near where Fiona had discovered the chest. "Join us, Jasper?"

The dwarf shook his head. He stared into the sack, fixated by the Fist of E'li. "Wonder how much longer Feril will be?"

* * * * *

The Kagonesti breathed deep, inhaling the intoxicating scents of the swamp as she strolled farther away from where she'd left Rig, Jasper, and Fiona. She moved barefoot—agile as a cat—through the dense foliage, never tripping among the thick roots or making the branches rustle, pausing only to smell a large orchid or watch a lazy insect. Her short leather tunic, fashioned from a garment Ulin had surrendered to her, didn't hinder her movements.

The half-ogre, who followed a few yards behind, picked up all the scents as well, though he did not appreciate them as much. Nor was he fond of the branches that tried to snag his long brown hair and claw at his broad face.

Deprived of his hearing, Groller knew his other senses were far more acute. Rotting vegetation, wet earth, the cloying fragrance of the dark red blooms of the water hickories, the sweet scent of the tiny white flowers that hung from the veils of lianas; he noticed them all. There was a dead animal nearby, the acrid odor of its decaying flesh unmistakable.

He could not smell the snakes that were wrapped like ribbons around the low branches of practically every tree, nor could he smell the small broad-tailed lizards and shrews that scampered about the soddened ground. Their scents were overpowered by the loam. But he could smell Fury, his loyal wolf companion. The red-haired wolf was trailing behind him, ears standing straight up and head twisting from side to side, panting from the heat. The wolf was listening, as Feril was listening, as the half-ogre could not.

Groller wondered what this place *sounded* like. He tried to imagine the sounds of the birds and insects. He remembered them from years ago, but the memory was elusive. Perhaps later he would ask Feril to describe the forest sounds.

Feril was so caught up in this place, Groller thought. And she was "talking" to many of the snakes and lizards she passed—all of them too small for dinner. The half-ogre suspected she was immersing herself in the swamp as a way to forget what had happened to Goldmoon at the hands of Dhamon Grimwulf. She was sad, Groller knew, confused and out of her element except in places like this—the wilderness. She was more relaxed here, seemingly content. How much longer would she stay one of the companions? he wondered. How long would it be before she decided to leave their fractious company in favor of an appealing forest?

When he had hunted with her two days ago, they had not roamed so far from the others or dallied as long, and she had not chatted with nearly so many animals. Then they had gone straight to the business of getting meat—snaring the fat lizard that didn't put up much of a fight. Yesterday, they had walked deeper into the swamp, and the elf had paused often before deciding on a large lizard the size of a cayman and stalking it for dinner.

Today was the worst yet. Feril was lingering longer here and there, walking farther away from the others, becoming ever more distracted, talking to birds and frogs. She was happier in one respect, the half-ogre knew. But her behavior worried him.

Time to focus on food, he decided. If Feril was too preoccupied, he would let the task fall entirely on his broad shoulders and let her escape into daydreams for a while. The half-ogre had been collecting handfuls of the fist-sized purple fruit that grew in profusion on the giant silk bay trees. The fruits were sweet and juicy, richly fragrant, and he intended to gather enough for tonight and for breakfast tomorrow. They were safe to eat—he had watched the tiny monkeys pick at the fruit. Groller popped a piece into his mouth and let the juice dribble down his throat and over his lips. The fruit would have to do if he could not find meat. He dropped his gaze to the ground, looking for tracks, hoofed ones preferably. They'd spotted a deer earlier, but it was too far away and had moved away too swiftly. Deer would be delicious—if he could kill one before the Kagonesti decided to befriend it. She wouldn't kill anything she first conversed with.

Ahead, Feril stopped. Groller glanced up and saw that she was studying a massive boa constrictor. She stood on her tiptoes, nose to nose with the snake, the exact length of which was hidden by the branches of the water hickory in which it was curled. The snake was dark green, the color of the leaves, and its back was spotted with brown diamonds.

"Furl? Furl be careful. Znake's very big." The wolf moved to Groller's side, brushing against his leg, and growled up at the snake. The half-ogre reached for the belaying pin at his waist, his fruit-sticky fingers tugging it free from his belt. "Znake be dinner." He moved a few steps forward and raised the weapon, saw Feril's lips moving, the snake flicking its tongue at her. He relaxed a little, pursed his lips. "You're dalking do the znake," he said. "Thad means znake iz nod dinner. Good. I dod like znake meat."

She nodded and motioned him away with her hand.

The snake was talking back, he guessed. He watched for several moments, saw Feril smile, close her eyes, the snake's tongue flicking out to touch her nose, then he replaced the weapon. "Furl wod led us kill the znake fur dinner," he told Fury. "Furl made 'nother friend. 'Kay. I really wand deer." He moved away, continuing to look for hoofprints.

"Great snake," Feril hissed softly, "you must be old to be so large. Ancient, most wise."

"Not so old," it replied in hisses that the Kagonesti mentally translated into words. "No older than the swamp. But much wiser than the swamp."

Feril reached a hand up and ran her fingertips over the snake's head. Its scales were smooth, and her fingers tarried, enjoying the luxurious sensation. The snake flicked its tongue and stared into her sparkling eyes.

"This wasn't always a swamp," the elf hissed. "My friends said this was an immense plain. People lived in villages around here."

"I was born with the swamp." The snake dropped its head lower. "I belong to the swamp. I know of no place else. I know of no people, save you."

The Kagonesti held her hands open in front of her face, beckoning with her fingers, and the snake moved down to rest its head on her palms. Its head was heavy and wide, and she ran her thumbs along its jawline. "I belong to a land that's covered with ice," Feril told the massive snake. "So cold. A land changed by the white dragon. The land is beautiful in its own way, but not so beautiful as this place."

"A dragon rules this swamp," the snake hissed. "The swamp serves her. The swamp is . . . beautiful."

"And you? Do you serve her?"

"She made the swamp. She made me. I am hers, as the swamp is hers."

The Kagonesti closed her eyes again, focused on the feel of the snake in her hands, centered her thoughts until the supple scales filled her senses. "I want to see how she made this swamp," she said, finally opening her eyes and returning the snake's gaze. "Would you show me, great one? Show me what you can?"

The constrictor flicked its tongue and dropped more of its body, a thick ribbon of scaly flesh, down to the lowest limb. More than twenty feet long, the elf guessed. She began humming an old elvish tune, the notes soft and quick like the babbling of a brook. As the melody became more intricate, Feril let her senses flow down her arms into her fingers, let her senses edge into the snake's form and flow over its body like the multitude of supple scales that covered it. In an instant she was looking at herself through the eyes of the snake, staring at the tattoos on her tanned face—the curling oak leaf that symbolized fall, the red lightning bolt across her forehead that represented the speed of the wolves with which she had once run. Then the snake's gaze shifted, and she was looking beyond her form, staring at the thick broad leaves of a massive gum tree.

The green filled her vision. The color was overwhelming, hypnotizing. It held all her attention and then melted like butter to reveal a sheet of blackness. The blackness came into focus, breathed, became scaly like the snake.

"The dragon," she heard herself whisper.

"Onysablet," the snake answered. "The dragon calls herself Onysablet, the Darkness."

"The Darkness," Feril repeated.

The blackness shrank, but only barely, so she could just make out the dragon's features rimmed by the gentle green of what was once the plains. The scents were not so strong and rich, the area not so pleasantly humid. It reminded her of the land in which she had been raised. "Home," she whispered.

"This swamp could be your home," the snake said.

The dream image of the black dragon closed its eyes, and the pale green of the plains around the overlord darkened. Feril sensed the dragon becoming one with the land, mastering it, coaxing it, nurturing it like a parent seeing to the development of a child. Trees grew about Sable's form, raced like running water to cover settlements and farmland. The changes chased away the humans who foolishly thought they could hold onto their homes. The plains' beasts began to claim the land. They no longer feared the people who had once hunted them, people who were now hunted by the dragon and her minions.

The willows that had once dotted the plains survived. Now they took on gigantic proportions, their roots spreading and their size swallowing up the birches and elms that formerly grew in small copses, the tops forming a dense canopy that became the feeding ground of black birds and passerines. The tips of the willows' umbrellalike branches kissed the water that pooled on the ground. Feril's gaze followed the water, which led her to sloughs, basins, and limestone outcroppings.

Saplings sprouted everywhere and became tall trees in the span of a few years. Giants, stretching more than a hundred feet to the sky, should have been ancient trees, but they were only a decade old. And the ground, even the high spots once covered by thick prairie grass, was quickly covered in ferns, greenbriars, and palmettos.

In the Kagonesti's vision the earth continued to dampen. Thick pools of water became foul fens, the river slowed and became clogged with vines and weeds. Alligators lined its banks. The bay of New Sea, once crystal blue and inviting, took on a gray-green sheen. Then the sheen darkened and grew thick with moss. Plants rose from the bottom of the bay and poked through the surface carpet.

There was no longer any sign of much of the eastern half of the New Sea. There was only this expansive marsh, this extraordinary swamp—warm, primordial, and inviting to the Kagonesti. She allowed her senses to slip further from her body, to become drunk on this place and the vision of its existence. Just for a little while, she told herself.

Clouds of insects gathered and danced across dark, malodorous bogs. From the waters' edges crawled snakes, small at first. But as they slithered farther from the bog, they grew. Egrets, limpkin, and herons skimmed the surface, larger and more beautiful than Feril had expected. Cricket frogs and mud turtles assembled at the edge, feeding on the insects and growing. The magic of the dragon, which was the magic of the land, enhanced them, nourished them, embraced them. Embraced Feril. The swamp enfolded her as a mother's arms would comfort a small child.

"The swamp could be my home," she heard herself whisper. "The beautiful swamp . . . the swamp." The words were harder to form. "For just a little while." Breathing was harder. Her chest was tight, her senses reeling. She didn't mind; she was merging with this place.

"Furl!" The word intruded into her perfect world. "Furl!"

Groller clawed frantically at the snake, which had slid down the tree and wrapped itself around the Kagonesti. The half-ogre cursed himself for being deaf and unable to hear what was going on, for not being more alert, for not paying closer attention, for thinking the elf was all right. He had strayed, following deer tracks. Fury, snapping at his heels, drew him back to Feril's predicament.

The elf was not fighting the snake. Instead she lay on the ground, limp in the serpent's tightening grasp. Its tail was wrapped around her throat, and Groller's large hands pulled at a coil, so thick he could barely get his fingers all the way around it. But the snake was one giant muscle, stronger than the frantic half-ogre and determined to crush the elf.

Fury growled and barked, repeatedly sinking its teeth into the snake's flesh. But the serpent was so large that the wolf could not seriously wound it.

Groller tugged the belaying pin free and began thrashing at the snake, moving along the length of it toward Feril, closer to the head of the creature, where Fury continued the attack. The snake's head rose and bared a row of bony teeth. Groller raised the pin and brought it down hard between the serpent's eyes. Again and again the half-ogre struck, oblivious to the snake's hissing, the wolf's growling, unable to hear the constrictor's skull crack.

The half-ogre's arm rose and fell, bashing at the creature long after it was dead. Exhausted, Groller dropped the belaying pin and fell to his knees. He began to unwrap Feril, as he prayed.

"Furl be all ride. Please." His words were nasal and slurred.

"Furl be 'live."

Her eyes fluttered open. Groller effortlessly picked her up and bore her away from the dead snake. "Furl be all ride," Groller kept repeating. "Furl be all ride."

She focused on Groller's face, upon his knitted brow. Shaking her head to clear her senses, she returned her mind to a world from which Goldmoon and Shaon were absent, a world that had corrupted Dhamon Grimwulf. She dropped her chin to her chest and pointed toward the ground.

"I'm all right, Groller," she said, knowing he wouldn't hear her.

He released her, holding her arms until he was certain she could stand. The wolf brushed against her leg with his wet nose, and somehow gave her strength. Feril looked up again and met Groller's worried gaze, then brought her thumb into her chest, her fingers splayed wide. She waggled them and smiled. It was the gesture for fine. But she didn't feel fine. Her chest burned, her ribs were sore, and the contentment that she had found in this place was gone.

Groller pointed to the bulging sack resting near the dead snake. "Got dinner," he said. "Meat. Fruit. Znake. No mer hunting today. No mer talking to znakes."

She nodded and let him lead her back to Rig and the others.

* * * * *

Jasper was disappointed in the food at first, but he found the fruit to his liking and the massive constrictor more palatable than lizard. He devoured enough to fill his stomach, then settled back against a trunk and looked toward the setting sun. He listened to Feril talk about the swamp, of how she had watched it come into being.

The air was filled with Rig's questions, Groller's hand signals pantomiming his fight with the snake, and Feril's replies about her experiences. Fiona worked on preserving the snakeskin. It could be made into excellent belts.

Reaching inside the leather sack, the dwarf let all the competing sounds recede into the background. His fingers brushed aside the big ivory belt buckle Rig had found in the muck and closed instead on the scepter's handle. He pulled it out into the fading light and admired the jewels dotting the macelike ball. It made his fingers tingle.

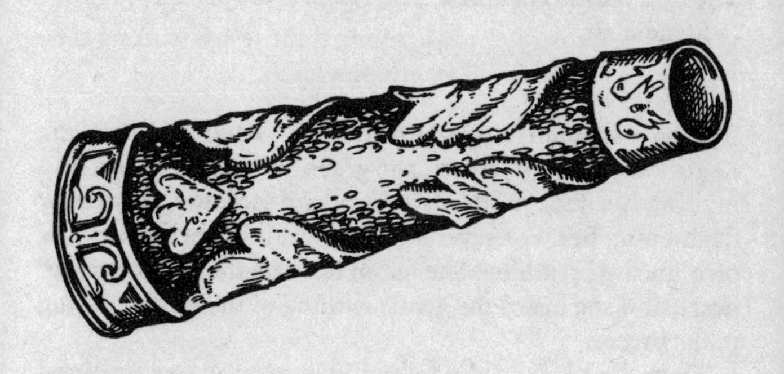

Chapter 4

Stolen Thoughts

"The Fist of E'li," Usha whispered. She paced up and down the hall, passing by the closed door to the sorcerers' study. She let out a deep breath and finally stopped before a painting, one of a willow birch she'd finished nearly two decades ago. Palin sat beneath the tree, with a very young Ulin between his knees. Usha's fingers traced the raised paint swirls on the trunk and dropped down to linger on Palin's face, then rose to touch the weeping leaves that shaded him.

There were trees like this on the island of the Irda, and more like this in the Qualinesti forest—though those willow birches were much larger. She had seen them when she stayed with the elves, when Palin, Feril, and Jasper went after the

Fist. Were Feril and Jasper in a similar place now, an overgrown forest corrupted by a dragon?

She closed her eyes and tried, one more time, to remember. The Qualinesti. The forest. The Fist of E'li.

Remember.

* * * * *

Usha watched Palin leave, the forest swallowing him, the Kagonesti, and the dwarf, the green filling her vision and making her feel suddenly empty and isolated, somehow frightening her. For several moments all she heard was her own uneasy breathing. She felt in her ears the beating of her heart, and she heard the gentle rustling of the leaves turning in the breeze.

Then the birds in the tall willows around her resumed singing. The chittering of chipmunks, chucks, and ground squirrels reached her, and she sagged against the thick trunk of a shaggybark and took in the myriad sounds of the tropical forest, trying to relax. Had the circumstances been different, or had her husband been with her, she might have enjoyed her surroundings or at the very least appreciated and accepted them. As it was, she couldn't help but feel uncomfortable, a leery intruder in the elven woods. She couldn't help but inwardly jump at every snap of a branch.

Usha inhaled deeply, summoning her resolve, and scolded herself for being nervous. She offered a silent prayer to the departed gods that her husband would be successful and would safely return to her, and she also prayed that he would find the ancient scepter, that she would be safe, too, that the elves would realize she and Palin were whom they claimed to be.

Usha wasn't nearly so confident as she had sounded when she volunteered to be left behind. She wasn't certain that Palin could find what he was looking for during the brief time frame of a few weeks allowed by the elves. Nor was she entirely certain that the scepter even existed. It might, after all, be nothing more than the figment of a senile scholar's mind.

But there was something she was certain of: she wasn't alone. The elves who stopped her and Palin, and who didn't believe they were really the Majeres, were still nearby.

Though the elves had left the clearing when Palin left, she felt their eyes still boring into her, felt the prickly sensation of being watched. Usha imagined the elven archers, their arrows trained on her. She tried to appear composed and aloof, determined not to give them the satisfaction of knowing that they had successfully unnerved her. She stilled the trembling of her fingers, gazing straight ahead, and didn't flinch when suddenly words came from behind her.

"Usha." Her name sounded like a brief puff of wind. It was the female elf's voice, the leader of the elven band. "Usha Majere, you call yourself." The tone was sarcastic and sounded like a curse. "The real Usha Majere would not trespass in our woods." The elf silently stepped into the clearing, brushing by Usha's side, the bushes moving slightly in front of the pair, hinting at the presence of elven archers.

"Who are you?" Usha quietly demanded.

"Your host."

"What's your name?"

"Names confer a small sense of power, *Usha Majere.* I'll give you no power over me. Create a name for me, if you think you need one. Humans seem to require labels for everything and everyone."

Usha sighed. "Then I'll simply not refer to you. I'll consider you my host, as you wish, nothing more. There'll be no closeness, no hint of friendship. That, I suppose, is also a measure of power."

The elf smiled. "You are brave, *Usha Majere,* whoever you truly are. I will grant you that. You stand up to me. You stayed behind while your dear *husband* heads toward his doom. But you are also foolish, human, for there is a good chance he will never return, and then I will be forced to decide what to do with you. You cannot stay with us. So just what will I do with you? Leave you for the dragon, perhaps?"

"Palin will succeed, and he will return." Usha continued to stare straight ahead. "He is who he claims to be, as I am who I claim to be. Palin Majere will find the scepter."

"The Fist of E'li," the elf answered. "If he is not Palin Majere, and if he does manage to succeed, we will take the Fist from him."

So that's why you let him go, Usha thought to herself, so he could get the Fist for you. "He is Palin," she repeated aloud. "And he *will* succeed."

There, straight ahead near a tall, broad-leafed fern, Usha picked out part of a face, a gently curving pointed ear. The elves weren't so invisible after all, she thought smugly. Then she pursed her lips. The elf archer had met her gaze. Perhaps he'd wanted to be seen, serving as an implied threat.

"He will succeed?" The female elf parroted. "Hardly." The elf took several steps beyond Usha, pivoted to face her, green eyes boring into Usha's golden ones. "Dozens of my men have learned the folly of approaching the old tower where the scepter rests. How will three—a dwarf, a Kagonesti and a human—win where dozens of others have failed?"

"Palin is—"

"What? Different? Powerful? If he is truly Palin, he's the most powerful sorcerer on Krynn, they say. But Palin Majere would have more than a ragtag handful with him, I think, and he would not be exploring these woods. So who is he really? And who are you?" The elf's eyes remained unblinking, mesmerizing, taunting. Usha could not look away.

"He *is* Palin! He *is* the most powerful sorcerer on Krynn, just as the tales say."

"So your *Palin* is magical? This entire forest is magical. And I'm not without my own magic, *Usha Majere*. Indeed, you will discover that. My magic will tell me who you really are and what your friends really want in this forest. Your mind will reveal the truth."

Usha felt a sensation, a persistent pulling that registered on her mind. She shook her head, trying to throw off the feeling. Instead, the tugging grew stronger and her limbs began to tingle, her head to throb. Still, her eyes remained open and fixed on the elf's, as if a thread of energy ran between them.

The elf chuckled softly. "Tell me, *Usha Majere.* If you are who you claim, tell me about the Abyss where Palin battled Chaos. You would know the true story. The real Usha was there."

Usha tilted her head, felt the tugging grow even stronger. "We were in the Abyss, Palin and I. There were dragons there. Chaos." The tingling in her limbs became an uncomfortable soreness and she saw in a vision the cavern in the Abyss, relived the heat, and smelled the death. "The war . . ."

"Only a part of the war, human. The Abyss was only a part of it. Across Ansalon elves fought and died in the war. So did kender, dwarves, and more. Dragons died, evil dragons to be certain, but the good ones, too. More of the good ones, they say. More good than evil had joined the battle. But none of the dragons or knights who fought in the Abyss survived." The elf paused. "Even Raistlin Majere has not been seen since the Abyss," she finally said. "None survived the battle in the Abyss, they say, save Usha and Palin Majere."

"There was so much death in the Abyss because of Chaos. He was huge, a giant who batted away dragons and trampled armies."

"The so-called Father of All and of Nothing?" The elf's voice was softer, now with a trace of compassion. "But why didn't you perish in the Abyss, Usha?"

"I don't know why we were spared, why I lived. I had expected to die. I don't know how we escaped. All the death. The dragons. I don't know . . ."

"The Chaos War upset the balance of power throughout Ansalon. The dragon overlords who control our world now would not have become so powerful, I think, if the good dragons who fought in the Abyss had lived—at least some of them had lived—to challenge them. The Dragon Purge might not have happened. The Green Peril would not be so all-encompassing. There were bronzes in this forest, brass dragons, too. They fought in the war, and died. And without them protecting the forest, there was nothing to stop Beryl."

The elf's voice was louder now. It rang in the clearing, harsh and bitter. "I am uncertain why the Green Peril settled in this land, changed the forest, enslaved my people, butchered us as though we were cattle. Men slaughtered in front of their families, children kidnapped and disposed of. I don't know why Beryl started massacring elves, using what little magic flowed in my people's veins to create enchanted items. And I don't care why—not anymore. But I do care that she is still here and that each day my people and I have to wonder if we'll live to see another sunrise."

"Palin has helped your people," Usha countered. "He helped save all of the Qualinesti. If it hadn't been for him, many, many more elves would have been sacrificed to Beryl. He risked his life in the Abyss, risked it for all of Krynn. He is risking it now. Surely you must have some faith. Surely you've learned enough from my memories to realize . . ."

The elf moved so close that Usha could smell the sweetness of her breath, like fresh rain clinging to spring leaves. "I do believe he is Palin, as I now believe you are his wife, Usha. Tales reveal much about your husband. But I know little of you. You are an unknown. Who *are* you? How did you come to be with Palin Majere? And why did *you* survive the Abyss?" The elf's eyes seemed to grow larger, coaxing, imploring, extracting more of Usha's memories.

With a bat of the elf's eyes, Usha's past came alive. The vision of the Abyss faded, the Qualinesti forest melted away, and different trees sprang up—pines and great, spindly willow-birches, pin oaks and summerwoods. Sand spread out below Usha's and the elf's feet, and ice-blue water ebbed away from them.

"Home," Usha whispered. In the distance, through the rows of willow-birches, she spotted the simple dwellings of the Irda. "No!" She fought to push the image aside. The Irda of the island, though now extinct, had long worked to cloak their presence from the rest of Krynn. "This is a secret place," she spat at the elf. "You've no right to intrude."

"This is our forest you've intruded upon, and that gives me the right to probe you," came the reply. "Concentrate, Usha. Show me more."

As if she were a detached observer, Usha helplessly watched her memories unfold. The Irda, in their unmasked, perfect, beautiful forms moved about their homes, performing the simple daily chores.

"So you are a child of the Irda," the elf observed as Usha's gaze drifted toward one Irda in particular, the tall man who had raised her, the Protector. "Quite beautiful by human terms, plain by theirs. An unfortunate, modest child."

"No," Usha said, a hint of sadness to her voice. "I am no child of the Irda."

"Then how did you come to live among them?"

Usha sadly shook her head. "I don't know, not really. Raistlin . . ."

The elf's eyebrows rose. "Go on."

"Raistlin told me I was born there. My parents certainly died there. He didn't say how they happened to find themselves on the isle, if they came from a ship, or . . . It doesn't matter. Raistlin said the Irda took me in."

"Where were your parents from?"

Usha drew her lips into a thin line. "The Irda told me nothing. But they did take good care of me."

"Quite so," the elf observed. "There is something of them

about you. Perhaps living with them, on their secret island, for so many years—"

"There is nothing special about me."

"Not that you realize, perhaps. Nothing that the Irda or Raistlin told you. But I sense otherwise, Usha Majere. Your eyes, your hair, your seeming youth. There is something unique about you indeed. But . . . continue."

Usha desperately fought the urge to reveal more of her past, but it was a futile battle. In the space of a few heartbeats, she and the elf witnessed a young Usha walking among the Irda, learning from them, growing older, but always different from her adopted people.

"Then they turned you away," the elf noted flatly. The Irda called the Protector led a lithe young woman with golden eyes to a boat along the shore, pushing her off, bidding her a farewell. Then the boat was gliding across the water, Usha in it, clutching a bag she'd been given, holding on earnestly to the memories of her Irda upbringing.

Within a day the Palanthas shore came into view. Usha, still clutching her bag, climbed up on the docks, drinking in the sights and sounds of the human city. Those first wondrous impressions came rushing at her anew like a strong wind, overwhelming her. Through a haze, Usha noticed that the elf was also affected by the powerful vision. Her expression showed curiosity and excitement.

Then weeks melted in moments, and young Usha's path crossed with Palin's. Usha relived the moment, her heart beating with exhilaration, a flush rising to her face. She was flooded with emotions and hopes, private feelings she did not want to share with the elf. She recalled all the little half-truths she had first told Palin and the others she met. She remembered Tasslehoff Burrfoot and how he believed she was Raistlin's daughter because of her golden eyes. She had not corrected him, but had let the kender believe what he wanted.

At the time she'd wanted her new friends to believe whatever they desired—so long as they would accept her and help chase away her loneliness.

More time melted away, and she found herself, Raistlin, and Palin standing in a burnt clearing and wishing she had told the younger Majere that she wasn't related to his uncle. She could have admitted her emotions then, could have learned if he felt anything similar toward her. She feared she would never see Palin again, that he would die and so many things would remain unsaid between them.

Someone was sending Palin to the Abyss where the war against Chaos raged. The younger Majere was quickly swept up in a spell, transported to another dimension. Her eyes met Palin's for what might be a last time. Then suddenly she was traveling with Raistlin.

The world ran like watercolors around her and the elf. Rocky spires and cavern walls appeared, turning brown, orange, and slate gray. The air was instantly dry, though some part of Usha's mind knew that she was still in the Qualinesti forest, with trees all around her and the air damp and sweet. But her memory felt the heat and smelled the sulphur of the Abyss. The elf too experienced everything. Her eyes drank it all in, as her mind continued to draw the images from Usha.

Shadows fell across them, heralds of the dragons overhead. Usha and the elf raced them along the ground. Many dragons were with riders—Knights of Solamnia and Knights of Takhisis. Far ahead Usha thought she recognized the form of Steel Brightblade, Palin's cousin.

The air was filled with the sounds of battle, and men's screams echoed off the walls. There was blood and death everywhere, wounded dragons and men who were crumpled and discarded like dolls. And there was Chaos, giant and impressive beyond human words.

The elf was captivated by the incredible scene. Tears spilled from Usha's eyes as she recognized Tas, so full of life and moving up behind the Father of All and of Nothing. She saw the halves of the Graygem in her hands and remembered that somehow she'd been entrusted with them.

"Draw a drop of Chaos's blood and put it in the gem," she recalled Dougan Redhammer saying. Their first attempt to do that had failed. But Tas inched into position for a second try.

Palin opened an ancient book. It was a powerful tome, Raistlin had told his nephew, the enchantments inside penned by one of Krynn's greatest war-wizards.

Usha hadn't understood it all then. She'd been thrust into this world from her protected home, where war was only a word and dragons were creatures unseen.

But she trusted Dougan's words about the force in the broken halves of the Graygem, and she had placed all her faith in Palin Majere, for whom she felt more than friendship. She found herself praying.

She watched as words tumbled from Palin's lips and saw from the corner of her eye Tas's dagger glowing with the eldritch light Palin had called forth to blind Chaos.

The young sorcerer's spell ended and a dragon fell from the sky, slain by Chaos. Its tail struck Palin and pressed him to the floor of the Abyss, sending him beyond the brink of consciousness.

But Usha was still alert, and she rejoiced to watch Tas's dagger pierce the god-boot of Chaos. It cut through the thickness to the god-skin below. The dagger sliced at the form taken by the Father of All and of Nothing.

The dagger drew blood, and she was there, halves of the Graygem extended. One crimson drop, that was all they needed. One crimson drop fell into the shattered gem. One drop. Her hands closed the broken halves.

She and Palin lived. How? The feeling of the Graygem in her hands disappeared, and the forest of the Green Peril again sprang up around her and the elf.

"My apologies for making you relive that remarkable

experience," the elf said simply. "It held questions you cannot answer."

Usha felt the spell lessen and then withdraw altogether. She blinked her eyes, dry from being open so long, and fixed them on the elf's. She looked away and caught more than a dozen faces staring at her through the ferns and bushes. Had the elven archers also experienced her life story that began on the isle of the Irda and climaxed in the battle in the Abyss? Had they been privy to her innermost thoughts?

"The Abyss," Usha whispered. "There was so much death."

"There is still so much death," the elf said sadly. "Beryl, whom we call the Green Peril, has slain so many of our kinsmen. Our numbers are less than half what they were a few years ago. It will take us centuries to recover, to become as strong as we once were. Perhaps we will never be the same nation again."

"But if Palin gains the scepter—"

"If," the elf cut in. "This item Palin seeks, this scepter . . . the Fist of E'li." The elf paused, stared at Usha. "Your thoughts revealed that you are uncertain about it. You don't even know if the power of the scepter is real."

Usha's eyes narrowed. Was the elf, even now, still reading her thoughts? "It doesn't matter what I think. It's more important what Palin believes."

"Oh, the scepter is real enough. It is indeed called the Fist of E'li, an ancient thing once wielded by Silvanos himself. Ornate, it is said, bejeweled and pulsing with strength. Perhaps if we had the Fist, we could do something against the dragon's minions. But so far, the draconians have kept us from that treasure."

"If Palin gains it, you can't take it away from him!" Usha raised her voice for the first time against her hosts. "We need . . ."

"I'll not take it—*if* he finds it. I'll be glad enough if the Fist is kept from the occupants of the tower. Who knows what terrors the draconians could inflict upon us with it. But I'll extract a promise from you." The elf's eyes practically glowed. Usha felt weak, her tired mind unable to defend itself as the elven woman continued her mental magic. "If the scepter is not consumed by whatever your husband has planned, you will do everything in your power, Usha Majere, to keep it safe and eventually to return it to us. You will risk your life for this scepter—the Fist of E'li—if need be. You will risk your very spirit, for the scepter is far more precious to Krynn than you are. Do you understand?"

"Risk my life," Usha whispered. "Keep it safe. I promise." She paused, then asked, "Silvanos—what did he use this scepter for?"

"I will tell you, Usha Majere. I will tell you everything." The elf smiled, words tumbling from her lips.

Usha fought to remember them. They were locked away. They were . . .

"You were telling me about your voyage to this forest," the elf said.

Usha's fingers passed across her temples, rubbing away a small headache. "Yes," she said haltingly. "A ship brought all of us here."

"What did you call it, this ship?"

"*Flint's Anvil.* Jasper named it, bought it with a gem his Uncle Flint gave him."

"Uncle Flint?"

"Flint Fireforge. One of the Heroes of the Lance."

"The legendary dwarf." The elf cocked her head. "Is something wrong, Usha?"

"I seem to have forgotten something. Maybe about the scepter. Maybe something I was going to say. Maybe . . ."

"It must not have been important."

"I suppose not."

* * * * *

"Usha!" Blister's hand was tugging on her skirt, rousing her from her reverie. "You better come inside. The Shadow Sorcerer's found Dhamon—with my help, of course."

Usha's golden eyes smiled down at the kender. "All right," she said softly. "I'd like to see."

A large crystal bowl filled with rose-colored water sat in the center of a round mahogany table. A dozen thick candles spaced evenly on sconces set into the walls reflected the stern visages of the sorcerers who peered into the water's gleaming surface.

Palin sat next to the Shadow Sorcerer, an enigmatic figure cloaked in gray. Though the Majeres had worked with the sorcerer for years, they actually knew little about him—or her. The folds of the sorcerer's robes were too voluminous to provide a clue, and his voice was soft and indistinct. Indeed, it might belong to either a man or a woman. They knew only that the Shadow Sorcerer had walked out of the Desolation, possessing magical abilities none could mimic and willing to assist the Last Conclave in its campaign against Beryl.

Across from the sorcerer sat the Master of the Tower, who, Palin had confided to Usha, was not a man at all, or a woman. He was the embodiment of High Sorcery, birthed when the tower in Palanthas fell decades ago. The Master and Wayreth were one.

And there was Ulin. Usha observed her son. He had recently joined the young gold dragon, Sunrise, attempting to learn more about magic. The dragon was elsewhere in the tower, in the guise of a boy, roaming and exploring, no doubt. The creature had an unending curiosity. Ulin had not returned home to see his wife and children in months, had not even communicated with them, and it looked as if he had no plans for a visit in the immediate future. He was changing before her eyes, becoming more obsessed with magic than ever his father was. He reminded her of Raistlin.

Gilthanas stood away from the table, his thin elven arms draped across the shoulders of a comely Kagonesti—who in truth was no elf at all. She was Silvara, his silver dragon partner whom he'd met decades ago and whom he'd finally come to admit he loved. In her guise as a Kagonesti, she presented a striking figure, though as far as Usha was concerned it was a false mask.

Half the people in the room were cloaked in mysteries and half-truths, Usha had to admit she was a bit of a mystery herself, as the elven woman in the Qualinesti forest had pointed out. Where *had* she come from? And where were she and Palin ultimately headed?

"Usha! Quit daydreaming!" Blister tugged her closer to the bowl.

She peered over the crystal lip and saw a hazy image, that at first seemed merely like ripples on the surface. But as she stared, she saw that the ripples were curls. Dhamon's hair. His face came into focus, pained and determined.

"They needed my help, because I knew him the longest," the kender babbled. "Well, the longest of anybody they knew about. I even met him before Goldmoon did and, well . . . The Shadow Sorcerer asked me all sorts of questions about Dhamon. Down to the scars on his arms I'd seen. His eyes, the way he talked, walked, everything. They really did need my help to find him."

The water shimmered green, and leaves came into view, framing Dhamon's sweat-slicked face. Water dripped from the leaves, fell to ground covered with moss. His feet moved swiftly over rotting twigs and puddles.

"He's in the swamp," Palin explained. "Ahead of Rig and the others, and moving quickly. They're practically following his trail, though they don't know it."

"Where is he going?" Usha asked as she pulled back from the table.

The Shadow Sorcerer passed a pale hand across the surface and the water turned clear. "Toward an old ogre ruin. Farther and farther away from us."

"Toward Malystryx," Blister suggested.
"She owns him," the Shadow Sorcerer said.
How would the Shadow Sorcerer know that? Usha wondered.

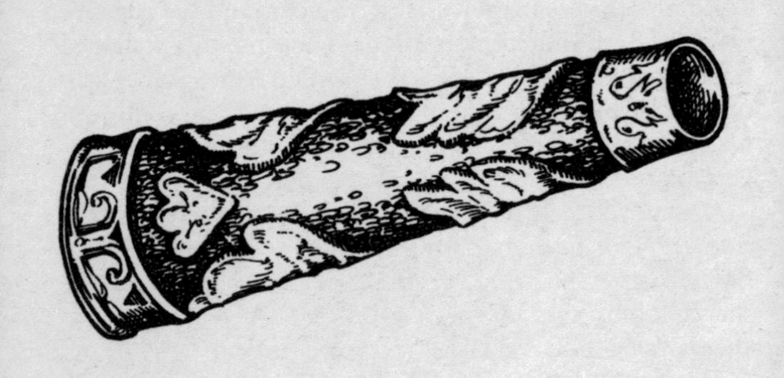

Chapter 5

Black Thoughts

"No!" The scream cut across the darkening fen. "I'll go no farther, damn you!" Dhamon Grimwulf dropped the glaive and fell to his knees, cupped his throbbing palms and hugged them to his chest. He rocked back and forth, tucking his chin down and gritting his teeth. His hands, though visibly unmarred, stung horribly from contact with the mysterious weapon, sending jolts of fire up his arms and into his body. His chest burned, and his head pounded. "No farther!"

Tears rolled down his cheeks, from the pain, the memory of killing Goldmoon, of killing Jasper, from the memory of striking Blister, Rig, and Feril. Beloved Feril, now forever lost to him. "You've cost me my friends, my life!"

His hands dropped to his thigh, where his leggings were cut. The red scale, shining through, glimmered in the light of the setting sun. Goldmoon had examined the scale, trying to free him from it and from the dragon who controlled him. Dhamon's fingers trembled as they ran around the edges of the scale, flush with his skin. His nails dug in near a scalloped corner and pulled hard. He was rewarded with another stab of pain. He bit his lip to keep from crying out and continued his efforts. Blood ran down his leg, over his scrabbling fingers, yet the agonizing scale would not budge.

"Damn you, Malys!" He gasped and rolled onto his side, into a stagnant puddle. "You've made me into a murderer, dragon! Made me a thing of evil! That's why the glaive burns me so! It burns those who are evil!" He sobbed and stared at the glaive lying several inches away.

Dhamon had dropped it the instant he felt the red dragon's presence withdraw, only a few heartbeats ago, here in the fading light of the sun. An early evening was fast overtaking the swamp.

Had he finally—successfully—pushed the dragon from his mind? Or had she merely backed away to tend to other matters? In the end, the reason for her absence was unimportant. What was important was that he was finally free. Free after running days upon days through this seemingly endless swamp and existing on pieces of fruit and foul water. Free after killing Goldmoon, Krynn's famed healer, the woman who had met him outside the Last Heroes' Tomb and coaxed him to take up the cause against the dragons—the woman who once told him she'd looked into his heart and found it pure and honorable.

He was free after sinking the *Anvil.* Free after losing Feril.

Free? I can't go back to Schallsea, Dhamon thought. I can't go back to face Rig and Feril. I'm a murderer, worse than a murderer. A betrayer, a turncoat, a slayer of an old woman and a dwarf whom I called a friend. He closed his eyes and listened for a moment to the insects all around him, listened to his still-pounding heart. He felt the pain in his hands lessen. Perhaps I should go back, he mused. Rig would certainly kill me, and that would not be so bad a thing, would it? Certainly it's preferable to being a dragon's puppet.

"I deserve no better than death," he whispered. "Death for killing Goldmoon." A branch snapped, and he opened his eyes but made no move to rise. He saw nothing except his glaive, inches away, and the growing shadows of twilight.

The glaive, given to him by a bronze dragon who had saved his life, was a most remarkable weapon. Meant to be carried by someone of sterling character, the weapon had begun to burn him the moment the dragon entered his mind, the moment he damned himself. Dried blood marred the blade's silver finish—Goldmoon's and Jasper's. He wouldn't wash it off, though the wetness of this place might tend to that task for him. The blood was a reminder of his heinous deeds.

So weak, he thought. I was so weak in spirit that I let the dragon take me over and force me to slay her enemies. Dhamon had managed to stave off the dragon—at least he thought he had—until he was in the Citadel of Light with Goldmoon. Perhaps I was too weak all along, he thought, and she merely waited for the right time to claim me.

And perhaps the dragon was able to claim me because my heart is tainted, still mired in the ways of the Knights of Takhisis. Maybe I have been only fooling myself, letting the darkness within me rest while I kept company with Feril and Palin and pretended to be on the side of good. And perhaps that darkness welcomed the opportunity to surrender to the red dragon and draw righteous blood. Who is more righteous than Goldmoon?

"Damn me!"

Branches rustled nearby. And from somewhere in the depths of the swamp a bird cried shrilly.

What to do now? Dhamon wondered. Lie here until some

swamp creature decides to make a meal of me? Find my way back to the Knights of Takhisis? They'd slay me: a rogue knight carries a death sentence. But do I deserve better than death?

What did he have left but death? Could he possibly have a prayer of redemption?

"Feril . . ."

The insects quieted, and the air became unnervingly still. Dhamon pushed himself to his knees and peered through the shadows. Something was out there. Closest to the ground, the swamp floor blended with the muted greens of the low-hanging branches. The black trunks fused to create a near impenetrable wall. Scant light filtered down from the stars and the moon that peeked through a gap in the overhead canopy.

Little light, but just enough to see some of the shadows separate and come closer. There were three figures.

"Spawn," Dhamon whispered.

They were black, roughly shaped like men. Wings scalloped like a bat's sprouted from their shoulders. They flapped their wings, almost silently, just enough to lift themselves above the soddened ground. Closer. Their snouts were lizardlike and crammed with teeth, and the teeth and their eyes were the only parts of them that were not black. Both gleamed dull yellow.

As they neared, he could smell them. They carried the scents of the swamp, though stronger, the fetid odors of decaying vegetation and stagnant water.

"Maaan," the largest creature said. He drew out the word and ended it with a hiss. "We have found a man for our noble mistress."

"The man will be a spawn. Like us," another hissed. "The man will be blessed by Onysablet, The Living Darkness."

They spread out, began to encircle him.

Dhamon laughed then, catching the creatures off guard. That he would find himself finally liberated from the red overlord only to stumble into the clutches of death was darkly comic. He could never be truly free, he realized. He could never be redeemed. Death, then, was the only solution—the one he deserved, and a more apt fate than becoming a spawn. He laughed louder.

"Is the man mad?" the largest asked. "No sanity in his fleshy husk?"

"No," Dhamon answered, drawing a breath and reaching for his glaive. "Not mad. But damned." The haft of the glaive was warm in his hands, slightly uncomfortable but no longer painful. It did not burn him as it had when the dragon was manipulating him.

"Perhaps there is hope for me." Dhamon whispered. "If I live through this." He swung the weapon in a wide arc, forcing the three spawn back. "I'll not become one of you!" he yelled.

"Then you will die," the largest hissed as it leapt into the air above the sweep of the weapon.

Dhamon slashed at the closest spawn, the magical blade effortlessly parting the creature's skin and plunging deep into its chest. The beast howled and fell back, released a stinging spray of black blood. Acid, Dhamon realized. Instinctively, he shut his eyes as the spawn's burning blood showered the immediate vicinity. His face and hands were scalded, and he nearly dropped the weapon. His eyes stung.

"You will die most painfully!" came a sibilant voice from above him.

Dhamon tried to open his eyes, but the acid felt like hot daggers. Blindly, he drew back the weapon for another attack, aiming for where he thought the spawn was. But as he swung the weapon, the spawn bit into his shoulder, its claws digging deep. It was all he could do to keep on his feet and withstand the searing pain.

Another spawn darted forward and wrenched the glaive free. A scream pierced the swamp, guttural and earsplitting. "Fire!" the would-be thief howled.

Dhamon heard the soft thud as the spawn dropped the glaive. "The weapon burns evil!" Dhamon shouted, as he struggled with the large spawn hovering above him. Still blinded by the acid, he flailed his hands, finding the spawn's muscular arms and trying to grab hold. The creature's scaly hide was too thick to be harmed, too smooth for Dhamon to seize, but he hammered it with his fists.

The spawn tightened its hold on Dhamon's shoulders and flapped its wings, trying to lift him above the swamp floor. It shook him violently as flecks of acid dripped from its jowls onto Dhamon's upturned face.

"I will smash you!" it cursed. "The fall will crush your frail human bones, and your blood will seep into my mistress's swamp. You killed my brother and wounded my comrade. The Living Darkness can do without the likes of you."

"No! Do not kill him!" the one below Dhamon shouted. "Onysablet, The Living Darkness, would covet him. He is strong and determined. The dragon will greatly reward us for catching such a prize!"

"Let him come to her broken, then."

The spawn flew lower and tossed Dhamon into a stagnant puddle. His fall was cushioned by the soft, wet ground. He fought to catch his breath, batting his eyes to clear them of the acid. His vision was blurred, but he could dimly see. The shapes were indistinct and gray—tree trunks, curtains of vines hanging down. There! A glint of silver. The glaive. And near it a spawn, a manlike black shape moving clumsily.

Dhamon gritted his teeth and dove for the weapon. The glaive did not burn, now. He lay there for several heartbeats, clutching the weapon, listening, waiting.

The soft flap of wings above him signaled that the one in the sky was coming closer. Dhamon rolled onto his back and swung the glaive upward in an arc.

The blade parted spawn flesh, nearly dividing the creature in two from sternum to waist. Dhamon rolled quickly aside, taking the glaive with him and narrowly avoiding the eruption of acid from the fatally wounded spawn.

"I will never be a spawn!" Dhamon spat at the advancing survivor. "I will never serve your black overlord! I will never serve another dragon again!" The glaive, wet from the blood and fetid water, nearly slipped from his hands as he hoisted it toward the remaining creature.

"Then you will die!"

The creature's charge forced Dhamon back several feet, the spawn's weight bearing him to the ground. Drops of acidic moisture fell from the creature's lips and struck his chin.

"You will die for killing my brothers,"the creature snarled. "For refusing to serve Onysablet."

I will die for killing Goldmoon, and for killing Jasper, Dhamon said to himself.

You will not die, said another voice, this one coming from the back of Dhamon's mind. *You must defeat the spawn.* The red dragon had returned, Dhamon realized. "No!" he screamed. "I will resist you!" He tried to push Malys out of his mind.

Fight the spawn! Use the strength I give you!

"No!" Against Dhamon's will, he felt his arms rise and his hands move against the spawn's chest. His limbs, powered by the dragon's magic, forced the spawn away. The muscles in his legs bunched, forcing him to stand.

His legs pushed forward. He bent and picked up the discarded glaive. The searing pain returned as his fingers enfolded the haft. A grin formed on his lips, one fostered by Malys. Dhamon's body advanced on the remaining spawn.

"I am safe, man. You cannot fly. But you are not safe. You will die, man! Die by the claws of Onysablet. The Living Darkness comes!" The creature flapped its leathery wings and rose, angling its body between the thick branches of a strangler fig tree. From a place in the back of his mind, Dhamon watched the spawn fly higher as the swamp grew darker. Then he heard the crack of trunks breaking and trees being uprooted.

The inky darkness carried with it an overpowering stench of decay. It reminded the former knight of the smells that had assailed him more than a decade ago as he walked among the fallen on a battlefield in Neraka.

Though the red dragon manipulated him, she could not stop his involuntary actions. Shivers raced down Dhamon's back, and he found himself retching from the nauseating odor.

"The Living Darkness will slay you!" came the cry of the spawn from high above him. "Or she will make you serve her until the flesh withers with age from your body! Until you die!"

Dhamon felt a jerk, and now he stared at a wall of blackness. He gasped as the blackness breathed and blinked to reveal a pair of drab, massive yellow orbs. The blackness returned his gaze.

Sable, Dhamon thought. The black dragon overlord. Despite the unnatural strength his link with Malys provided him, Dhamon knew he hadn't a prayer of standing against the Black. And he knew Malys realized this also.

The blackness drew closer, her breath so foul Dhamon's stomach roiled. So huge was the Black that Dhamon's eyes could not absorb her entire form. *I'll not serve you*, were the words his lips tried to form, but they were doomed words. *I'll not be a spawn. Kill me, dragon!*

"You will not kill him, Onysablet," emerged from his mouth. The words were rich and drawn out, inhuman sounding. Malys was speaking through him. "He is my puppet. He brings to me his ancient weapon. The scale, Onysablet. Look at the scale on his leg. It marks him as mine."

"Malystryx," the Black returned after several moments of silence. She dropped her gaze to Dhamon's leg and then lowered her head in deference to the red dragon overlord. "I grant him safe passage through my land."

No! Dhamon's mind screamed. *Slay me! I deserve my fate!*

"He will bother no more of your creations, Onysablet." Malys continued. "I will see to it."

The Red turned her thoughts inward, admonishing her puppet.

You will continue through Onysablet's realm, she instructed him. *You will travel southeast until you near the border of mountainous Blöde. There are ruins at the edge of the swamp, an old ogre village called Brukt. A band of Knights of Takhisis is on their way there—my knights. I will not let them kill you, as your mind has told me is the custom with rogue knights. You will travel with them to my peak, where you will surrender the glaive and what, if anything, remains of your spirit.*

* * * * *

Brukt consisted of a makeshift village surrounding a crumbling tower of chert and limestone propped up by two massive cypress trees. The tower was pointed and jagged at the fanglike top, and flower-covered vines grew up its sides.

Cobbled around it was a collection of huts made of bamboo and thatch and several lean-tos draped with lizard hide. There were a few sturdier buildings made of stones and planks, and one large structure with doors made from a wagon bottom. Some of the buildings carried weathered wording that suggested the planks had once been crates: Morning Dew Mead, Shrentak Leathers read some. A few others were in a language Dhamon couldn't fathom.

A kender, a dwarf, and a small group of humans who were gathered at the base of the tower halted their conversation and stared as he approached. They were a scraggly lot, barefoot and in worn clothes. One motioned with his hand toward a lean-to, and a female dwarf stepped out of it to quickly join the others. Her fingers drifted to the handle of the axe stuffed in her belt.

"Friend?" she called in a rough voice.

"Friend?" the dwarf repeated. The kender joined her, whispering something into her ear.

Dhamon tried to answer, to tell them he was far from a friend, but instead was an unwilling agent of the red dragon. They should flee or kill him. But Malys held his tongue.

"He is with us." The voice came from one of the stone and plank buildings. A woman pulled back a hide covering the doorway and stepped out. Despite the heat of the swamp, she wore armor—black, with the emblem of a skull in the center of the breastplate. A death lily grew from the top of the skull, encircled by a thorny vine. The red flame on the lily indicated she served Malystryx. A black cloak draped down to her ankles, held in place by an expensive clasp. Military decorations covering a shoulder of the cloak glinted in the morning sunlight. "Welcome to Brukt, Dhamon Grimwulf."

"So he's definitely not a friend," the female dwarf muttered glumly.

"Commander Jalan Telith-Moor," Dhamon heard himself say.

She nodded only slightly and walked toward him. A half-dozen knights followed her out of the doorway. "We arrived here very late last night," she said in an imperious voice. "Here, in this desolate place, there seem to be a pair of spies sympathetic to Solamnia. We will root them out before we leave." She pursed her lips in thought and studied Dhamon's face. "Or perhaps . . ." She gestured, and two knights flanked him, indicating he should follow them inside the building.

"You must be very important," one of the knights whispered, "to merit Commander Jalan's presence. She broke off recruiting ogres near Thoradin just to come here to meet with you."

Dhamon went inside the building and placed the glaive against the wall. He allowed the knights to strip off his tattered, acid-burned clothes. "Do not touch the weapon," Malys warned them in his voice.

They indicated a carved wooden bowl filled with fresh water. The dragon let him drink his fill; then he washed, letting his hands linger in the water to ease the pain from the weapon. As he dressed in the padding and armor the knights provided, he listened to their whispers about the scale on his leg. The armor did not fit him well, as it had been made for a slightly larger man.

He hated both the armor and the knighthood. He tried again to push the dragon from his mind, but Malys easily controlled him.

"He's ready, Commander Jalan," one of the knights called.

She entered and inspected him up and down. Her cold eyes lingered on his face. She was young for her rank, Dhamon guessed, probably in her late twenties, though with a few age lines. No, tiny scars, he decided, as he stared more closely. Her expression was hard, her mouth thin and unused to smiling. Her blonde hair, much lighter than his, caught the sunlight. Dhamon had heard of her: She was among the top-ranking officials of the knighthood.

"We questioned some of the villagers—refugees, when we arrived last night," she began. "We were concerned they had . . . done something . . . with you. As it turns out, they'd never heard of you. But during our interrogation, one of them revealed the presence of Solamnic spies. You were once close to the Solamnic knights, weren't you . . . Dhamon Grimwulf?"

I was close to *one*, Dhamon thought, an old knight named Geoff who saved me though I had tried to kill him. The Solamnic had successfully turned him from the Knights of Takhisis. Or so Dhamon had once thought.

"Perhaps you could root out the Solamnics for us. They're in the building at the end of the street. Save us a little trouble." Jalan moved closer to Dhamon, whispering in his ear. "Malystryx has told me of you and your impressive weapon. She thinks killing a few Solamnic spies should make you more . . . malleable, more useful to her. You'll not be so defiant, always trying to resist her and run away. We'll make your corruption complete and allow her to fully concentrate on more important matters. That's why I saved this trifling business for you. Go, and kill them."

From the secret place in his mind, Dhamon stealed himself against the pain as he wrapped his fingers around the hateful weapon once again. He brushed by the commander and strode out into the makeshift village, gazing with dragon-heightened senses at the door to the building at the far end of the road.

Dhamon's black armor gleamed in the sun. The tabard draped over the top of the mail was pressed. Not a wrinkle was visible, not a loose thread. The white of the lily was bright, the miniature red dragon scale looked like a flame on a glistening petal. The dragon forced him toward the building.

"Hey, why aren't you back inside there with the rest of the knights?"

Dhamon looked down at a tow-headed kender, the one whom he'd seen earlier whispering to the female dwarf.

"Did the other knights kick you out or something? If they did, you shouldn't be wearing that nasty black armor. Silver would look much better on you. Or none at all—armor, that is." The kender wrinkled his little nose in disgust. "Did you do something wrong? Is that why you're out here all alone? You can tell me all about it. I'm a terrific listener, and I've nothing to do today except listen to people."

Dhamon ignored the persistent kender.

"Hey, that's a nice-looking weapon. Mind if I look at it?"

Malys forced Dhamon to speak. "No, you cannot look at my glaive."

"How about your helmet? Let me see it! Bet it would fit me better!"

Dhamon frowned. Malystryx had no patience with the small man. She was considering having Dhamon kill him.

"Where are you going all grumpy anyway?"

Dhamon looked down at him balefully.

"There's nothing in that old place. I should know. I've been inside. There're many more interesting things around Brukt. I could show you."

The dragon allowed Dhamon to stop. He let out a slow breath.

"I was just trying to be friendly."

"I do not deserve any friends." Dhamon was surprised the dragon had let that comment escape his lips. "My friends have a tendency to die."

The kender backed up a step. "Gee, I don't really and truly want to be friends with you," he said with a hint of huffiness in his voice. Then he raised his voice, practically to a shout. "Most of the people around here have got plenty of their own friends already."

"What?"

"Well, you're a *Knight of Takhisis*," the kender said more loudly, as he wrinkled his little nose again. "People don't really care for *Knights of Takhisis*, do they?"

"Stand back," Dhamon advised, as he felt the dragon shift the glaive to one hand. He was right outside the door now, and he reached out for the handle. "You've already done enough, trying to warn those inside of my approach."

"Is that what you think I was doing?" the kender said, sounding genuinely surprised. He fidgeted with something at the small of his back. "You really thought I was trying to warn someone?"

The dragon muttered a soft curse in Dhamon's voice. The

door was locked.. Dhamon saw through cracks in the wood that it was reinforced by bars. The dragon flexed the muscles in Dhamon's arm, and he yanked. The door fell off its hinges, and with minimal effort Dhamon tossed it aside.

"Well, I guess you'd be right if you thought that I was trying to warn someone!" the kender continued. He pulled a small, curved blade from a sheath at his waist and jabbed it into the back of Dhamon's leg. "Company!" the kender announced.

The pain in his leg competed with the burning in his hands. The dragon forced Dhamon to ignore both. He quickly noted the occupants—eight armed men—then whirled on the kender. Dhamon fought to get another warning out. "Get out of here!" he cursed through clenched teeth. "The dragon'll make me kill you!"

"I don't see a dragon!" the kender shouted. "I only see a lousy Knight of Takhisis!" The kender, not budging, slashed at him again with the knife.

Dhamon balled his fist and brought it down on the kender's head, hard enough at the very least to knock him out, possibly to kill him. The kender crumpled, and the dragon inside Dhamon seemed satisfied.

"The Dark Knight bastard killed little Tousletop!" cried one of the men inside, wielding a spear. "Get him!"

The eight surged forward. Four were armed with crude spears, four with swords. Of the latter, two looked *different.* Dhamon's mind registered their appearance. They were dressed like the others, he realized It was their eyes that were unusual: strangely unafraid and fixed on him.

He sensed the dragon lock onto his thoughts, felt her raise his lips in the approximation of a smile.

"You're badly outnumbered, Takhisis bastard. Surrender!" the tallest of the two men barked, as he tried to get the others to stay their weapons.

Chivalrous, Dhamon thought from the secret place in the

back of his mind. *Don't make me kill them! Let them kill me! Let me drop this cursed weapon!* It was a prayer to the departed gods. He met the man's stare.

"Surrender to you?" Dhamon heard himself ask. The dragon brought the glaive up. At the same time, Dhamon kicked out, landing a solid blow against one of the Solamnics. The man fell, his spear clattering away, and Dhamon swung the glaive at another man holding a spear. The blade smashed the spear and knocked away another being thrust at him. Dhamon sensed that Malys was enjoying the situation.

"Gods!" one of the villagers cried. "The blade cuts metal like butter!"

"As it will cut you," the dragon spat in Dhamon's voice. Reflexes honed in countless fights made him duck, avoiding a thrown spear. He swiveled to the right, avoiding another sword thrust. *Let me drop this glaive!*

One of the warriors charged forward, darting beneath the glaive and stabbing with his broadsword. Dhamon brought the glaive down, slicing through the offending weapon. The Solamnic sympathizer leapt back. Dhamon's opponents were no match for him—he and the dragon knew that. Despite their superior numbers, they could not hope to bring him down.

"Run from me!" Dhamon cried, wresting a small measure of control from Malys. "Run before I kill you!" He watched with some satisfaction as four of the men turned and raced for the back of the building. The others did likewise when he took a few menacing steps toward them.

With his dragon-enhanced eyesight, he watched the men claw at a few loose boards, create an opening at the back. They began squeezing through it. One warrior who still held his sword protected their retreat. Dhamon studied the man's eyes—they spoke defiantly, telling him the man was ready to die to keep the others safe.

"Run!" Dhamon barked at him. He glanced from the

Solamnic to his own fingers, knuckle-white and on fire. *Let me drop the glaive!* He put all his efforts behind that thought. *Drop the . . .*

The warrior crouched and moved forward, drawing his sword back and swinging it at Dhamon. In one fluid motion, Dhamon brought the glaive down, slicing through sinew and bone and cutting off the man's sword arm. The man grabbed his stump, refusing to scream, dropped to his knees. Dhamon backed away several steps to avoid the spray of blood.

Outside, from behind him, Dhamon heard murmurs, the voices of curious townsfolk gathering. He picked out General Jalan's stern words.

"Foul Knight of Darkness!" the wounded warrior shouted. "Finish me!"

"You heard him," Commander Jalan said. She was standing only a few feet behind. "Finish him."

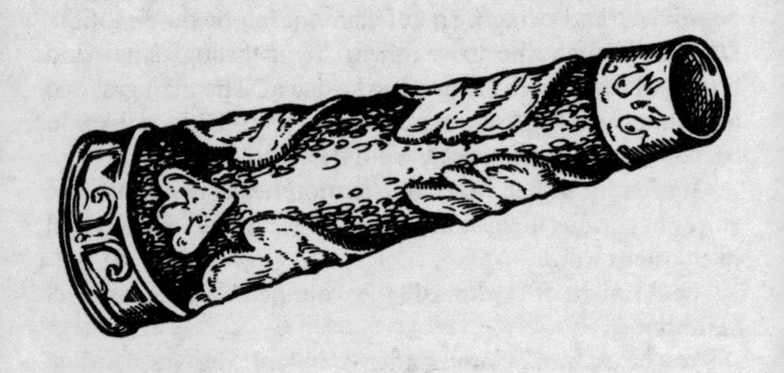

Chapter 6

Dismal Futures

"You want to kill him, don't you?"

Rig shrugged his shoulders. "Fiona, sometimes that's all I think about. Part of me holds him responsible for Shaon's death. The dragon who killed her . . . well, the dragon and Dhamon used to be a team. And Goldmoon. How can I not want revenge?"

The young Solamnic knight peered into Rig's dark eyes. "What does the other part of you want?"

The pair kept their voices down as they sat on the willow log and watched over their sleeping companions. The mariner had refused the dwarf's offer to take a turn at watch—he wanted Jasper to get as much rest as possible. And after

Groller's tale of Feril and the snake, Rig didn't trust the Kagonesti alone. She might wander off and make a home for herself in the swamp. Or she might mistake a hungry alligator for a friendly one, what with the smile and all. Groller and his wolf would take the watch just before dawn, a few hours away. That left Fiona, who had decided to keep the mariner company.

"The other part?" Rig softly chuckled. "The other part just wants to wring Dhamon's neck—after he tells us why he attacked us and killed Goldmoon. Maybe Palin was right, the scale was responsible. But Palin could be wrong, too. Sorcerers aren't always right. You know, I halfway liked Dhamon once. Sometimes I even admired him. And I guess . . . *maybe* . . . a small part of me wants him to turn out innocent."

The Master had contacted them shortly after sunset, magically appearing like a ghost in the center of their camp, announcing that Dhamon Grimwulf and his glaive had been located. Dhamon was on his way to an ogre ruin called Brukt. Gilthanas and Silvara had struck out after him, but considering all the ground the pair had to cover, Rig and the others could get there before the silver dragon without much of a detour to their original course.

Just beyond Brukt stretched the mountains of Blöde, and the ogre ruin was near the Pashin Gap. After dealing with Dhamon—one way or another—they could pass through the mountains to Khur, rent a ship somewhere along the coast, and set sail for Dimernesti. The Master said he was working on finding the exact location of the underwater realm of the elves. "Just so you've it found by the time we get to Khur," Rig had told him. "I don't want this trip through the swamp to be for nothing."

"We'll have a long time of it tomorrow," Fiona said. "And the next day. And the next." She brushed at mud on her breastplate. "We'll have to cover more ground than we've been doing, if there's a chance of catching him. Do you think Master Fireforge is up to it?"

"Jasper's tough. He'll make it. But you . . . you ought to consider leaving that armor behind," Rig advised. He pointed to the canvas sack that carried the rest of her suit of plate. "It's heavy, and lugging that around for a couple added hours a day will only wear you out faster. We can't afford to be slowed for a few hunks of shiny metal."

"I've managed so far. A few more hours a day won't matter."

"If you say so."

"Besides, the armor is part of who I am. The most important part."

Rig started to say something else, but a muted noise to the south cut him off. It sounded a bit like the snort of a big horse, and whatever made it was coming closer. He put a finger to his lips, unsheathed his sword, and motioned for Fiona to stay put. He disappeared into the foliage without noticing that she had followed him.

The canopy was so dense they could barely see more than a few feet before them, yet the noise became more distinct with every yard they covered. The mariner moved slowly, testing the ground ahead with his feet.

They were only a hundred or so yards distant from the camp when they spotted a clearing ahead. Krynn's single pale moon shone down on a small moss-covered pond, ringed by a half-dozen grotesqueries.

"Spawn," Rig whispered to Fiona. "Black ones."

The young Solamnic stared with wide eyes. She'd heard of them when she listened to Rig's and Feril's accounts of battling the spawn they had inadvertently stumbled upon in Khellendros's lair months ago in the Northern Wastes. But their descriptions didn't do the creatures justice. Krynn's moon revealed them in all their freakish horror.

Half of the creatures were vaguely man-shaped with sweeping batlike wings, the tips of which grazed the top of the leather ferns. Their snouts were equine but covered in tiny black scales. The scales were larger elsewhere on their bodies, sparkling darkly in the moonlight. Their eyes were dull yellow, as were their fangs, their talons long, curled, and sharp. A thin ridge of scales started at the back of their heads and ended at the bases of thin, snakelike tails.

The light was too dim to see if the others matched these three. Their noises had no pattern to hint at a language. They seemed reminscent of pigs snorting.

As the others came into the moonlight, Rig and Riona could see that these three differed from their companions. One had wings, but they were short, scalloped and uneven, extending from the creature's shoulder blades to just above its waist. Its head was more manlike than equine, and long horns grew upward from the base of its jaw. Its arms were short, ending in misshapen claws where its elbows should be, and its tail was forked and thick.

The remaining two were the largest, easily eight feet tall. Their skin looked leathery, with no trace of scales or wings, though there were malformed nubs on their shoulder blades. They were a dull black, with nothing shiny about them. Their heads were overly large for their bodies, long snouts filled with crooked teeth of vastly uneven lengths that prevented their mouths from shutting entirely. A ribbon of drool ran from the one with the longest snout and disappeared into the ferns with a sizzle. Acid, Rig decided. Their arms were longer than suited their bodies. They reminded the mariner of baboons he'd seen in his youth on the Misty Isle.

"Yesss, drink," the lead spawn hissed. "Drink, but hurry. We have important work this night."

The two apelike spawn moved into the shallow water, and Rig's eyes widened. Their arms didn't end in claws at all. Their arms looked like snakes tipped with fanged heads that eagerly lapped at the stagnant water.

Rig's fingers closed about the pommel of his sword. The beasts looked evil, had to be evil, like the blue spawn he had fought. They should be attacked and slain, he knew, to prevent them from inflicting horrors on anyone. They should . . . He released his grip and motioned to Fiona to retrace her steps.

From a safer distance, they watched the three spawn and the three grotesques drink their fill and then move toward the west.

"We might have been able to take them by surprise," she whispered when she was certain the creatures were far enough away. "Horrid creatures."

"Maybe we could have," Rig quietly answered. Maybe we should have, he said to himself. He spoke aloud. "But there's three other people back there in the clearing. I'm responsible for them. And we've other priorities: Dhamon, his glaive, the Dimernesti crown. I couldn't risk jeopardizing our mission." Inwardly he added, Rig Mer-Krel, you've changed. And I'm not sure it's for the better.

* * * * *

It was late the following afternoon when the hair on Fury's back rose. The wolf's ears lay flat, his lips curled. He pawed nervously at the ground.

Groller was the first to notice his animal companion's unease. He motioned to Rig, pointed at the wolf. The half-ogre cupped his hand and scooped at the air, bringing it to his nose and inhaling deeply.

"The wolf smells something," Rig said.

"I smell something, too," Feril whispered. "Something smells *wrong*."

"I never thought anything about this place smelled right," Jasper said.

Fiona drew her blade and moved to Rig's side. He'd been leading the small band in the direction toward where the Master said they'd find the ogre ruin. The ruin should be at least another day away.

"I'm going to scout ahead," Rig said, his voice low.

"You're welcome to join me if you leave that sack of armor behind."

She dropped it on the driest spot of ground she could find.

"I'll go too," Feril offered.

Rig scowled. "Next time," he said.

Groller looked at Rig, brought both hands to his mouth, fingertips touching and covering his lips, then dropped them to his sides, as if he were discarding something.

The mariner nodded. Don't worry, he signed by shaking his head and rotating his hands in front of his forehead. I'll be very quiet. Rig drew his cutlass, motioned for Fiona to follow, and quickly disappeared.

"Think it's Dhamon?" Jasper asked so quietly that Feril had to bend over to hear him.

"We're not close enough to the ruin," she answered.

"Yeah, but . . ."

"Okay, let's *all* find out." She took the trail Rig and Fiona had left.

Jasper started after her, but Groller's hand fell heavily on his shoulder. The half-ogre whirled his fingers, indicating himself and the dwarf, then pointing to the ground.

"Yeah, Rig wants us to stay here," Jasper whispered. The dwarf nodded his head in understanding. Then he held his hands in front of his chest, as if he were holding the reins of a horse, pantomiming. "Who put Rig in charge anyway?" the dwarf said. "I want to go see."

Groller shrugged, picked up Fiona's sack, and followed the dwarf. The wolf growled softly, padding after them.

Rig, Fiona, and Feril were ahead, crouched behind a thick patch of spike rushes. Beyond them, wending their way through a stand of moss-draped dahoons, were four lizard creatures leading a sorry-looking group of elves.

"Scaly men," Feril whispered. "Spawn? No. Something different."

The four creatures were green and covered with thick,

raised scales. They were stoop shouldered and had thick chests covered with lighter green leathery plates. Their heads looked like alligators, perched upon short necks. Three of them carried spears festooned with orange and yellow feathers, and they chatted among themselves in a lost tongue. The fourth held a long vine attached to the band of prisoners.

"The elves are Silvanesti," Fiona whispered. "I count a dozen." Feril nodded.

The fair-haired elves were tied together with ropelike vine. Thorny vines that cut into their skin were wrapped about their wrists and ankles. They were gaunt, and the few clothes they wore were tattered and filthy.

Without a word, Jasper reached into his sack and pulled out the Fist of E'li. The scepter felt good in his hand. Rig caught his eye, and he, too, rose from behind the rushes, brandishing his sword. They dashed toward the creatures. Fury streaked past them, a red blur.

Fiona was quick on their heels. Groller dropped the canvas sack, reached for his belaying pin, and barreled through the rushes. Behind them, still hidden in the spike rushes, Feril had closed her eyes. Her fingers played across the rush blades as a musician might stroke harp strings. She let her mind drift to the swamp and began singing.

The wolf barreled into the first lizard creature, knocking it down into the saw grass.

Rig struck the one directly behind, dropping beneath the jab of the thing's spear and thrusting forward with his cutlass. The weapon bit into the creature's thigh, spilling black blood. The lizard thing made no sound, didn't flinch, and Rig manuevered a step to find a better opening.

Fiona effortlessly parried a jab by a third lizard creature and slashed at its plated abdomen. The creature was swift, despite its size, and easily dodged her blow.

Rig narrowly sidestepped a well-aimed jab. His sword knocked aside the next stab, while the fingers of his free hand reached into his waistband and retrieved three daggers. He hurled these at Fiona's target. "Yes!" he shouted. The first two daggers lodged in the creature's chest. The third missed its intended mark.

"Thanks, but I can fight my own battles!" the young Solamnic called.

"Just trying to help!" Rig returned as he feinted to the right, then drove his blade into his foe's side. The creature hissed, slimy spittle flying at the mariner's face. The butt of the lizard man's spear slammed into Rig's stomach. The mariner fell back, dazed, and drew three more daggers.

Fiona's lizard creature struggled to stay on its feet, as black blood poured from its wounds. "Surrender!" she shouted, hoping it could understand her language.

The creature shook its head, but she began to wear it down, shifting from side to side, making repeated jabs and thrusts.

Meanwhile, Groller wrestled with the lizard creature that had been leading the captive elves. The half-ogre was wielding his belaying pin while trying to avoid his enemy's long, curved dagger. Jasper was busy, too, the Fist in his right hand, distracting the creature with his shouting and whirling.

The creature was no match for the two of them. The half-ogre hammered the belaying pin into the side of the creature's head. Jasper grinned at the crunch of bone.

The lizard creature sank to its knees, then pitched forward as Jasper and Groller jumped out of the way.

In the rushes, more than a dozen yards away, Feril's fingers continued to play on the blades of tall grass. "Let this one live, Fury," she whispered. Her senses raced past the spike rushes and floated above the saw grass toward the wolf.

Fury's jaws were black with the thing's blood; he'd been nipping at the lizard man's stomach, biting through its tough skin plates, keeping the thing on its back. Again and again, the wolf darted beneath its claws, snapping.

"Let this one live." Feril's song became louder, her senses

touching the tips of the tall saw grass. The blades near the wolf and lizard creature began writhing, randomly at first, and then with a purpose. They twisted about the creature's legs and arms, throat, pinning it to the soddened ground. Yet, the blades did not touch the wolf.

"Fury!" she called as she distanced her senses.

The wolf looked up, muzzle dripping, then loped toward Rig's lizard man. The mariner had a dagger between his teeth and two more in his left hand. In his right he held his sword. Taking a few steps back, he tossed the left-hand two daggers at the creature in front of him. Only one found its mark, though, sinking into the lizard man's stomach. "Losing my touch," the mariner cursed, as he took the dagger from between his teeth.

Fury leapt at the creature. His jaws clamped tight on the lizard man's wrist, preventing him from throwing the spear. Rig took advantage of the opening and swung his sword at the creature. Spattered with black blood, the mariner retreated to watch the thing flop onto its back, twitching horribly. Fury vaulted onto the creature's chest and tore at its throat.

Rig whirled to see Fiona slashing at the remaining lizard man. She dropped below a feeble spear thrust, her long sword slicing into the creature's waist. The creature emitted the first howl of pain any of them had surrendered. Fiona tugged her sword free, then thrust it up and forward, finishing the thing quickly.

"See? I didn't need any help," the knight said, as she tugged her sword free and rubbed it in the grass to wipe off the blood.

Rig touched Fiona on the shoulder, pointing at Feril and Groller. The Kagonesti and half-ogre were working quickly to untie the vines that held the prisoners together. The mariner and knight headed toward them.

"We cannot find the words to thank you," an emaciated

elven woman said. She gazed into Rig's eyes. "We had no hope left."

Rig and Fiona carefully set about the task of removing the thorny vines that had hobbledthe prisoners. Jasper replaced the Fist in his sack, padded over to study the elves' wounds, and shook his head.

"The thorns, this place," he said sadly. "These people need tending. Most of their wounds are infected. This will take me quite some time, if I can do anything at all."

"I will help," Feril offered. "No matter how much time it takes."

"Time isn't something we have a lot of," the mariner cut in. "We've got to hurry to find Brukt. And Dhamon."

"These people need rest and tending," the dwarf persisted. "I'm not going to abandon them in this condition."

The Kagonesti's eyes bore into the mariner's. "None of us will leave them like this."

"We know where Brukt is," the thin woman offered. "We could guide you there. We owe you our lives."

"Then lead us after we've healed you," Feril said.

"How long is this going to take?" Rig softly asked the Kagonesti. He pointed toward the east. "We've got a few hours of light left and—"

Fury's barking cut him off. The wolf was chasing the sole surviving lizard creature, the one Feril had trapped with the help of the grass. Her concentration interrupted, the plants had released their scaly prisoner.

"We need that one alive!" Feril called to Rig, whose legs were churning over the damp ground toward the fleeing creature. "We need some questions answered."

The mariner closed the distance and slammed the creature hard in the back. The lizard man fell face forward, and Rig was on top of him in a heartbeat, rolling him over and straddling his chest. A blade flashed in the air.

"Alive!" Feril hollered.

"Then you'd better hurry with your questions!" Rig called back. "This thing might not be alive much longer."

The mariner held the dagger at the lizard man's throat, staring into its black eyes. "The lady wants some information," he spat. "You'd better hope you speak her language."

"I . . . understand your words . . . some." The lizard man's voice was raspy.

"What are you anyway?" Rig demanded while he waited for the Kagonesti.

The lizard creature's scaly eye ridges furrowed in puzzlement.

"You're not spawn. What are you?"

"Bakali," it said after a moment.

"Never heard of ba-kah-lee," Rig mumbled. "What's a ba-kah-lee?"

"I bakali," the creature returned.

"That's not what I—"

"What was supposed to happen to these elves?" Feril interrupted.

The mariner pressed the blade harder against the bakali's throat , creating a line of black blood under its edge. "Loose your forked tongue, ba-kah-lee," Rig said, stumbling a bit over the unfamiliar word. "Answer her."

"Spawn," the creature returned. "Mistress Onysablet wants elves made spawn."

"That only works on humans," the mariner said. "We know. So come up with another answer."

"Spawn," the creature insisted. "Abominations. Humans make perfect spawn. Elves, ogres make spawn-abominations. Ugly. Corrupt."

"The creatures by the pond," Fiona breathed.

"Mistress Onysablet wants abominations. She likes things corrupt."

"Are there more elves being held somewhere?" Feril edged closer. "Humans? Ogres?"

"Not know," the creature answered. "Not care."

"Then where do you take them?" Rig asked .

"Deep swamp. Mistress Onysablet find us there, take prisoners. We hunt more. Return deep swamp. Our lives a circle for the dragon."

It was Jasper's turn. "How deep into the swamp?"

The creature tried to shrug. "Don't know. Until Mistress Onysablet comes."

"Let's get out of here," the dwarf suggested. "If the dragon shows up . . ."

"Yeah," Rig said. "If the dragon shows up, we're dead."

"Or abominations," the emaciated elven woman added, nodding toward Feril and Groller.

With a single slash, Rig cut the creature's throat. The mariner stood, glancing down at the black blood coating much of his clothes.

"You didn't have to kill him," Jasper whispered, as Feril gathered the elves and started ministering to them. "He cooperated."

"If the dragon shows up, let her find only corpses. The dead don't talk, my friend. Now see if you can help Feril, so we can get going."

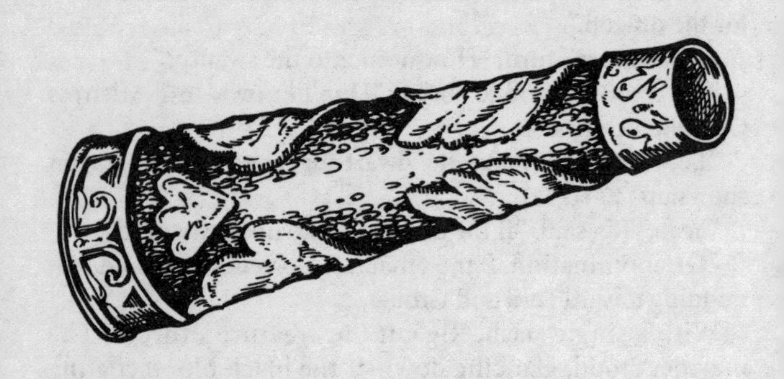

Chapter 7

Lofty Plans

The dead lay all around them, butchered by sword, trampled by dragon claw, slain by strokes of Khellendros's lightning breath. They were all unrecognizable: faceless husks among shattered pieces of armor.

Their deaths spoke volumes—of the bravery of the fallen. But to the great blue dragon the carnage was one more fine trophy. The acrid smell that rose from the bloodied ground was sweet.

The invasions of Tarsis, Kharolis, and the Plains of Ash to the south were grand. The conquests mounted, each more cherished than the one before. There were numerous victories in Hinterlund and Gaardlund, and Solamnia had been invaded. All for Kitiara, the human woman with a dragon's heart.

As he lay on Malys's plateau, The Storm Over Krynn could envision Kitiara plainly. The massive red overlord sat nearby, her eyes fixed on a volcano in front of her, as she repeated softly, "Dhamon, you must never drop the glaive." Preoccupied with something, she had left Khellendros to his own thoughts.

Kitiara stood before Khellendros in his mind, wearing the blue armor that complemented his indigo scales. More dear than a daughter, he thought. More treasured. Soon she will be rescued and reborn. Soon they would be together, and there would be no more squandered time with Malystryx the Red.

Malys had adopted Khellendros as a companion of sorts, treating him not quite like a servant, as she had begun to treat the other overlords, and more like a lesser partner. But The Storm Over Krynn knew others occasionally shared Malystryx's dark affections. He was certain the white, Gellidus, had played consort to her. But he kept silent on this matter and on many others, listening with mild curiosity as the Red directed a human pawn, Dhamon—he'd heard Gale mention that name—to follow the orders of someone named Commander Jalan and not to discard a glaive.

The blue overlord had given little thought to Malys's schemes, or to her relationship to the other overlords and the Knights of Takhisis. His own alliance with the Red was one of convenience to keep himself above her suspicions. It was not against dragon nature to feign cooperation as he was doing.

However, in ages past Khellendros had defied dragon nature. He had been true to only one other dragon, a calculating blue named Nadir.

Nadir died during the Third Dragon War, but not before she had laid a clutch of eggs. Several of the eggs survived the

Cataclysm, growing into Khellendros's proud brood in the wastes of western Khur. Malystryx's plateau was in Goodlund, and he was not so terribly far from Khur now.

One daughter distinguished herself in her zest for battle, joined Khellendros in service to the Dark Queen. Khellendros's daughter, called Zephyr by men, was ambitious, but her father thought she lacked the military mindset needed to survive. So The Storm manipulated the pairing of partners in the Blue Dragonarmy and caused his daughter to be partnered with a young human woman rising in the ranks. Kitiara uth Matar. It went against custom, as dragons were usually paired with humans of the opposite gender, but then Khellendros had been reputed to go against tradition.

Khellendros's choice of Kitiara was wise. Zephyr learned much from the human. She ascended to become first lieutenant to Skie and his partner, who was a cunning she-warrior named Kartilann of Khur. Together, the foursome could not be bested, leading strike after victorious strike above the battlefields.

Until a long time ago, during the battle on Schallsea.

Schallsea Island, Khellendros mused, was the place of ultimate sadness and destined revenge, where he had recently bested Palin Majere and stolen the precious artifacts. Where dreams died and dreams began.

"Do not discard the glaive," The Storm Over Krynn heard Malys repeat. He ignored her presence; her words were not meant for him anyway. Instead he focused on his memories of the island.

It was decades past. Khellendros and Kartilann led a sweep of the island. There was no reason to fear the inferior enemy, no reason to suspect disaster. But a sniper's arrow slew Kartilann, and shortly thereafter Zephyr, too, was killed. In the midst of Khellendros's sadness, another breach of tradition occurred. In the Dark Queen's Dragonarmies whenever a partner was killed, dragon or human, the surviving partner was ordinarily dishonored. And to be dishonored in the eyes of Takhisis was something Khellendros could not, *would not*, abide. He shrewdly made a pact with Kitiara, quickly re-teaming with her—in part to honor Zephyr, in part to save face before the Dark Queen.

Their partnership, born from dragon and human death, from two dissolutions, was a stroke of creative genius. So perfectly suited to each other were Khellendros and Kitiara that at first they appeared omnipotent. Together they carried the Blue Dragonarmy to one conquest after another—Tarsis, Kharolis, the Plains of Ash, and more.

Blue Lady, Kitiara was called. Highlord.

The humans called Khellendros Skie. An inadequate name, one lacking any hint of power, and one he had grown to despise—except when it rolled off Kitiara's tongue.

The Blue Lady stood before him now in his dream vision, her form perfectly imagined in the steamy air that rose off the baked earth of Malystryx's peak. Like a mirage, the vision beckoned soothingly to his spirit. Soon he would bring Kitiara back to Krynn and keep his promise to her. Soon he would not need to acquiesce so completely to the red overlord's commands. He would have Kitiara, more dear than a daughter. . . .

"Khellendros?" The word sounded like an earth tremor.

He let the image of Kitiara fade and stared into the smouldering eyes of the Red. "Yes, Malystryx. Your plan has merit. Uniting the dragons under a new Takhisis will forge a new epoch." A part of him had been listening.

"The Age of Dragons," Malys purred. "No more will this be called the Age of Mortals."

Khellendros nodded. "This ascension of yours . . ."

"Will require exceptional magic," she finished. "A grand artifact is even now making its way to us, carried by a lowly human pawn. He will be escorted by other humans to afford more protection to the item. Commander Jalan leads the Knights of Takhisis. My knights."

"And will other magic be necessary?"

"Onysablet, Gellidus, even Beryllinthranox will search and provide their greatest magical treasures. As must you. Gather the magic for me: ancient artifacts filled with raw, arcane power."

"Of course."

"I will need the energies stored in all these things to aid in my transformation." Her eyes glimmered darkly, and flames lapped the corners of her vast mouth. "We will unleash the magic when enough artifacts are gathered and when the time is right. We will unleash it in Khur."

The place where Nadir had laid her clutch, Khellendros reflected, where he and Kitiara once fought side by side.

"I will be reborn."

The blue overlord nodded.

"Near the Window to the Stars."

Khellendros knew the location. In ancient times, it had served as a portal to the Gray, where in ages past he might have perhaps more easily found Kitiara. It was a human place.

"When I am Takhisis, I will completely dominate the humans. I will crush them. There will be no more pockets of resistance. None will dare to defy us. And none will be able to hide. Not even the greatest of creatures who still—"

"Like the shadow dragon who so troubles you?"

A rumble started deep in Malystryx's belly. "The rogue defies me. He continues to slay lesser dragons and to draw strength from their carcasses."

"As we all did during the Dragon Purge. You set the example for us. You showed us the way."

"But I called an end to the purge."

"And he did not obey."

"I will find him," Malystryx said, her tone as matter-of-fact as possible. "Now or when I become the new Takhisis, I will find him and purge him. His energies will be mine."

"And the good dragons?"

"They will join me. The silvers and bronzes, the coppers and brasses—even the golds. They will join me."

"Most will die, I think, Malys."

"Not all of them." The Red breathed deep and exhaled slowly, watched the twin curls of smoke drift up from her nostrils. "Life will be more precious to some than death, even life under my rule. I have been busy planning and I have identified those who can be swayed. You see, I have been busy. And you, Khellendros? What has been occupying you in the Northern Wastes?"

"I have been controlling the land. I have built my army."

"Gathering followers?" she asked dryly. "You have only one who shows any real promise."

"Gale."

"A *blind* dragon?" The Red's tone was laced with scorn.

"He is capable."

"Capable of ruling the Northern Wastes?"

Khellendros's golden eyes narrowed slightly.

"Is he capable of controlling Palanthas and of shepherding the Knights of Takhisis or guiding legions of brutes? Is he capable of creating all the necessary spawn? Of dominating all the insignificant tribes of barbarians that litter your great white desert and pester your blue dragon servants?"

"Do you intend to replace me with him, give him my territory?"

A hint of a smile played upon the red overlord's mouth. "Of course," she said silkily. "As Ferno will eventually replace me as overlord of this land."

She rose to sit on her haunches and towered above him, her head as high as the tops of the volcanoes that ringed her plateau. "But I will need no designated territory, for all of Ansalon will be mine. And as Dark Queen, I will need a king." She dropped her gaze to meet his. "Rule by my side. Only your intellect and ambitions are great enough to complement mine."

Khellendros raised his head slightly, keeping it judiciously well below her gaze. "I am honored, my Queen. And I accept. I will relinquish my land to Gale when the time is right."

"The time will be soon. Ferno comes to me now. I will tell him of our agreement. He will inherit my domain. Then you and I will possess Krynn."

* * * * *

The shadow dragon glided on the updrafts birthed by the mountains of Blöde. The morning sun shone bright upon his back. His snout was long and thick, filled with faceted teeth that resembled sharp bits of smoky quartz. His eyes were fog-gray with black pupils. Twin fog-gray horns swept up and back from his head. Smaller horns, looking like jagged onyx, ran from the bridge of his nose to the top of his head, edging his jowls. The undersides of his wings were the darkest parts, dark as midnight, black as a corrupt spirit.

Onysablet, too, was black. Yet the shadow dragon was, strictly speaking, not a black dragon. His scales were shadowy, but somehow translucent, the color in them shifting with light and darkness. He usually hunted at twilight, when the world's shadows were the thickest. It was his favorite time, although sometimes he hunted very late at night, when he blended in with the ebony sky, invisible to all but the most discerning. That he found himself hunting this sunny morning disturbed him a little. He was out of his element, but his quarry was about. And that necessitated this unaccustomed foray.

He dropped lower and craned his long inky neck so he could better inspect the ground and peer into the jagged outcroppings and foothills. An ogre village was nestled between two peaks. Smoke twisted up from ruined huts, scenting the air with scorched wood and charred bodies. Ogre bodies. The dragon had no love of ogres, but he did not hate them either. He had killed enough of them in his life. But he also tolerated them at times, as he tolerated a great many things in this land. However, this day at least the sloppy despoilers who did not consume or bury the dead after their deeds were done bothered him.

The Knights of Takhisis, the despoilers, his quarry, were not terribly far away, he sensed, less than a day's march, just beyond the mountains. He banked to the southwest, noting more bodies as he went. Scores of crows feasted, fleeing as his shadow moved over them. The miles slipped by beneath his wings. The hours passed. And then something else caught his attention.

Below him, a mile or so away, was a red dragon. Flying northeast, the red was large, perhaps two hundred feet from nose to tail, its horns curving up as its talons curved down.

The shadow dragon banked higher and watched the red for a few moments, gauging its age, guessing its strength. Red dragons, the shadow dragon knew, were among the most formidable.

The shadow dragon studied the land below him, looking for mountains that might cast just enough shadows to conceal him so he would not have to fight the red. Looking . . . there. He folded his wings into his sides and dropped toward a nearby summit.

As he dove, he watched the red dragon continue on its course. He saw the dragon slow and glance his way, and he wondered if the dragon would ignore him, since he was certain it had spotted him.

Ferno was headed toward Goodlund, summoned by Malystryx. The red dragon lieutenant knew not to tarry in Blöde, but he also knew that to bring his queen this trophy would raise him in her esteem. She hated the shadow dragon, and though there were rumored to be a few of these creatures on Ansalon, only one would be so bold as to fly during daylight hours. It must be the rogue that so vexed his mistress. Malystryx would reward him greatly.

Ferno beat his wings faster and banked to the east, opening his jaws wide. He coaxed the heat as it mounted in his stomach, as though stoking a furnace. The closer he flew to the shadow dragon, the more he anticipated the red overlord's gratitude.

From his inadequate hiding place, the shadow dragon glanced one last time at the approaching enemy. Too late to find better shadows. Not now, not that the red had made its decision. The shadow dragon angled to face the red, beating his wings slowly as he rose, focused his strength, concentrated his energies.

Flames burst from Ferno's mouth, a crackling ball of fire that raced to engulf the shadow dragon. Translucent black scales sizzled and popped, the heat and flames threatening to overwhelm the shadow dragon.

The shadow dragon beat his wings harder, faster, taking him above the flames and the furnace-hot air. The red dragon stretched out his claws and drove them deep into the blackness of the shadow dragon's chest, sending a shower of scales into the air.

The shadow dragon howled, inhaled deeply, and let loose with his own breath weapon, a cloud of darkness that expanded to envelop the red. Dark as ink, the cloud folded in upon itself, coating the red and sapping its strength.

"How dare you!" Ferno hissed. The red dragon flailed, flapping to keep aloft, and struck out again with its claws. "Malystryx will reward me well for slaying you!"

But the shadow dragon had slipped above its grasp, hovering now over the red and the blackness. His adversary was temporarily blinded. He listened to the red's taunts, watching and waiting. Then he breathed a second cloud of darkness, even as the first was dissipating, and then dove into the blackness that surrounded the red, his own talons outstretched. His eyes pierced the darkness as easily as others saw in light. His talons sliced at the red's wings, ripping through them and filling the air with hot dragon blood.

"For this affront you will die painfully!" Ferno bellowed. Although virutally sightless, the red dragon was hardly powerless. He twisted his head back over his shoulder, and his furnace breath rushed out to set the air on fire.

Translucent black scales melted under the intense heat, and wave after wave of hot pain pulsed through the shadow dragon's body. Another blast of fire surrounded him. The shadow dragon only dug his claws deeper into the red's back, bringing his suffering head down closer to the red's neck. Smoky quartz teeth sunk in, parting red scales and discovering the flesh beneath. The shadow dragon clamped his teeth down, dug his claws into the red's sides, then released his prey, pushing off his back and flying away to escape the heat and pain.

The red cursed and flapped his wings madly. At last he broke free from the cloud of blackness that had continued to sap his strength. "Malystryx!" he cried. "Hear me, Malystryx!" Still blind, he fought to focus his other senses.

The shadow dragon glided above him, silent, scentless, regaining his strength and absorbing the strength lost by the red. He followed the red, noting that its wounds were not fatal.

"Curse you, blackness!" the red bellowed. "Where are you? Fight me!"

Above, still silent, the shadow dragon opened his maw, summoned the last of his energy, and released yet another cloud of blackness.

"Malystryx!" Once more Ferno felt engulfed by blackness. It was like a cool, wet blanket. It smothered his flames, sapping his energy and his willpower. "Malystryx!"

"Your overlord is too far away to save you." The shadow dragon spoke at last, his voice raspy. He was weak, burned horribly, and no doubt permanently scarred. He considered fleeing while the red was still dazed. In the shadows he might heal. The red would let him go now, he was certain.

"I need no one to save me!" the red retorted. Ferno had listened closely to the shadow dragon's words and could pinpoint where his opponent was. The red inhaled deeply, twisted his head, and breathed another blast of fire.

The shadow dragon had dove just as the red's jaws opened. He twisted onto the red's back even as the crackling flames passed over his head. Scalded, he fought to master the moment and keep his hold on the red. His claws dug in, as his jaws found the red's neck again. Hot blood flowed over his quartz teeth and rained down on the mountains below.

Ferno's last fire breath had sapped his waning strength. Now he could barely keep himself aloft, especially with the weight of the shadow dragon riding him. "Malystryx." The word sounded like steam escaping, so little strength was behind it. "Malystryx, help me." It sounded like a prayer.

Black claws dug deeper, smoky teeth tore at flesh. And the shadow dragon felt a rush of energy as he began to absorb the red's life essence.

* * * * *

Malystryx watched the sky, studying Khellendros's retreating form. The blue dragon, dismissed so she could tend to other matters, was returning to the Northern Wastes. He would inform Gale, his lieutenant, of the red overlord's plan.

At the back of Malystryx's mind, she heard a muted voice of some significance. "Ferno," she said. She closed her blood red lids, slipped her senses to the back of her mind, and wrapped her thoughts around the whisperer. She willed herself to find her red lieutenant.

* * * * *

Dhamon Grimwulf stepped toward the defenseless Solamnic spy, raised the glaive to finish him, then felt the pressure of the red overlord lessen. She retreated just a bit further, and he was able to stay his hand.

Behind him, in the large makeshift building, Commander Jalan moved closer. "The Solamnic . . ." she began. "Finish him—or if you are incapable—I will be obliged to do it for you."

* * * * *

"Malystryx!" Ferno called in desperation.

The shadow dragon would not relent.

His strength lost, his wings unable to support his weight, Ferno plummeted down, the shadow dragon riding him while continuing the wild assault that was purging the red's energy.

Ferno felt the warmth of his own blood on his neck and back. His claws flailed uselessly. He felt his wings tossed by the wind. Then, blessedly, he felt the shadow dragon's claws pull away and the vicious jaws unclench. Ferno felt the dragon shove off his back and was glad to be free of the weight.

With a shock, he realized how close he must be to the ground. Still he saw only blackness. But he sensed the earth, now close below him, and he made one last strenuous effort to work his wings.

Too late. Ferno sensed Malystryx's mind caress his. Then he felt a spear of rock thrust into his belly, impaling him on a mountaintop. Then he felt nothing.

The shadow dragon hovered on the updrafts for several heartbeats, looking at the streams of red that poured from the dead dragon. Then he descended to absorb the last of the red's power.

* * * * *

"Ferno!" Malystryx's cry echoed off the volcanoes that ringed her peak. The thunderous word rocked the plateau. As if in reply, the cones glowed red and sent gouts of sulfurous smoke into the air. Streams of lava ran down the volcanoes' sides. Ribbons of red and orange, they glittered brightly in the morning sun.

"Ferno!" The great red overlord was enraged. Shared plans were lost. Schemes half-hatched between the two were now dashed and broken.

But more than the loss of her lieutenant, she was angered at the disrespect shown by her by the shadow dragon. The Dragon Purge had ended by her command. No more were dragons to draw power from the luckless spirits of those they defeated. Never again!

Ferno could be replaced—would be replaced—within the next few weeks. But the shadow dragon . . .

A rumble started deep inside her, growing until the noise filled her plateau. Fire streamed from her mouth, touching the bases of the volcanoes, and her anger deepened.

* * * * *

Stronger from the red's absorbed energies, the shadow dragon resumed his course. As the minutes passed, the mountains seemed to shrink, and in the distance he spied the verdant greenery of Onysablet's swamp. And there, practically between the mountains and the foothills, where the steamy mists of the jungle lay thick, a jagged fang jutted defiantly into the sky. It was ringed by lean-tos and crude huts—ant hills crawling with life.

The despoilers milled about, unsuspecting. Dressed in black plate mail despite the heat, the Knights of Takhisis gathered outside a large building. The clang of metal, evidence of an ongoing fight, cut through the air. Men and women stood behind the knights, curious about what was transpiring inside the building, wanting to catch a glimpse of the combatants. A dwarf and a kender, kneeled and peered through the armored men's legs.

Too close. Their fault. Could not be helped.

The dragon drew his wings to his sides and dove, creating a shadow on the ground that grew as he neared.

"You heard me, Grimwulf! Finish him!" came an imperious

voice from inside the building. The shadow dragon's senses picked up that lone voice with a commanding air. No others spoke when this voice sounded. "Finish him!"

The shadow dragon opened his mouth, releasing a cloud of blackness on the black dressed knights below. The cloud descended on them, smothered them, as it smothered the innocent bystanders, robbing them of sight and energy.

Screams filled the air, shouts of shock, terror, disbelief. The shadow dragon watched as knights and commoners alike scurried blindly away from the cold blanket of suffocating air he created. They crashed into each other and ran into their crude homes. A few stumbled headlong into Onysablet's swamp. Foolish ants.

The dragon dropped closer, picking out his armor-clad targets. His claws sought out the knights one by one.

Inside the building, Commander Jalan heard the first screams and wheeled around to glimpse the impenetrable blackness as it fell beyond the doorway. She drew back, pulled her sword, and called to her closest men.

Behind her, Dhamon Grimwulf felt the weight of the burning glaive in his hands. The ever-present red dragon in his mind faded, and he stared at the man before him. "Run!" he cried. The Solamnic spy cradeled his stump, acting dazed. "Run!"

The spy paused for only a moment more. Then, meeting Dhamon's wide-eyed stare, he staggered toward the back of the building. Boards had been hastily peeled back to create an exit. Sunlight streamed through the opening. He took a last look over his shoulder at Dhamon, then stepped through.

Dhamon breathed a sigh of relief. Behind him Commander Jalan cursed. Dhamon searched his mind for the dragon and found no trace. He took a tentative step toward the back of the building.

Still there was no countercommand from the dragon. A trick? Dhamon wondered. One more trick of the dragon's to let him think he was free? Salvation was beyond him, he realized, now that he had drawn Solamnic blood. He was eternally damned. But where was the dragon presence? He took another awkward step. Was this one more game the dragon would end by pulling his puppet strings?

Dhamon considered dropping the glaive and running. Maybe the dragon intended Commander Jalan to take it now. The screams outside made him grit his teeth, and then he saw the Commander square her shoulders and step into that ominous blackness.

Dhamon Grimwulf shouldered the weapon and quietly slipped to the back, ducking through the opening and stepping into the light.

Foothills stretched to the east, and nearby he saw a pass through the mountains. Not the pass, he decided; it would be too easy for someone to follow him. He glanced about for signs of the villagers or Solamnic sympathizers. There was blood on the ground, a trail. Dhamon ignored it, darting instead toward the foothills. Clambering up moss-covered rocks, he took a last glance at the village, seeing the cloud of darkness. He glimpsed what looked like a long black tail flicking out of it and heard the horrible screams and the clang of metal. The Knights of Takhisis were battling something inside the darkness. The cloud looked too small to cover Onysablet. Perhaps it draped one of her minions.

He struggled up the rough terrain of the Blöde foothills and made his way toward the mountains. The dragon voice was gone.

* * * * *

The shadow dragon had had its fill. It had slain all but one Knight of Takhisis. Only Commander Jalan remained. The dragon knew only that she was an important leader, given the decorations on her armor. She must also have rare courage to confront him.

The commander walked forward, blinded by the cloud, stumbling over the few bodies the dragon had not yet swallowed. She waved her sword before her, slowly, searching for her unseen foe.

The shadow dragon studied her determined face for but a moment. Then it flapped its wings to soar above the cloud of blackness. The cloud would dissipate within a few heartbeats, though the woman would remain blind for longer than that. He would leave her be, the lone survivor, to tell her red dragon mistress of the triumphant assault. Survivors were necessary; otherwise there would be no accounts of his great deeds.

The dragon banked away from the village, coasting over the foothills of Blöde, heading toward the mountains. He watched for shadows, eventually finding one to his liking that was halfway up a peak. Gliding toward it, he discovered the narrow mouth of a cave, whose interior shadows were thick and pleasing. His dark form shimmered, shrinking just enough to let him pass beyond the opening and into the welcome embrace of the shadows beyond. Time to rest, he decided, to savor his successes and make his plans. He closed his dark eyes.

Hours later, he opened them. Within the cave resounded the footfalls of an intruder.

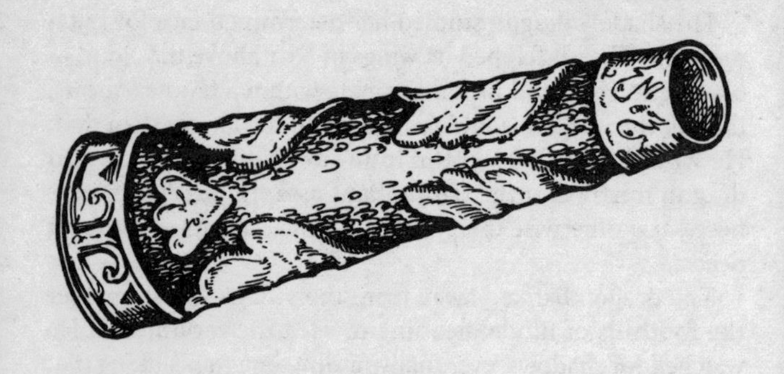

Chapter 8

A Matter of Timing

"Where you heading, Ulin?" Blister stood in the hallway, feet spread wide, blocking Ulin's path. The curving passage high in the Tower of Wayreth was narrow, and though Blister was small, there was no easy way to get around her.

Ulin shifted the leather pack on his back and gestured with his head, indicating she should move to the side.

She didn't. "Where you going?" she persisted.

"Away."

"Away where? Home to your wife?"

"Just away, Blister. I don't know where yet." The mage ran his free hand through his chestnut hair and stared down at the determined kender. "Away from *here*," he added evenly.

"Need some company? I could tag along. It's getting boring around here."

"Not this time."

"Palin and Usha know you're going?"

He let out a long sigh and nodded. "Yes. Of course. I told them. I'm a grown man, Blister. I can do what I want, go where I want."

"But the dragons and everything. Rig and Feril and . . ."

"I'm leaving *with* a dragon. Sunrise." The younger Majere had met the dragon when he journeyed with Gilthanas to the icy land of Southern Ergoth. Sunrise taught him how to draw on a dragon's essence to enhance spells. The first time Ulin tried the technique, more than a month ago, was during the battle with Khellendros on Schallsea Island. He hadn't yet mastered the ability, and he longed to do so. He always hungered for more where magic was concerned. "So you're leaving with a *good* dragon, a gold one. Lucky you. But I'm worried about the evil ones."

"So am I. And so is Sunrise."

"So you should be helping us—and your father."

Ulin drew his lips into a thin line, closing his eyes for a moment. "I don't have time for this conversation, Blister. Sunrise is waiting outside, and time is slipping away. There's nothing more I can do *here* to help."

"Then maybe you and Sunrise should be flying after Gilthanas. Silvara took him to . . ."

"Brukt. I know. Where Dhamon and the glaive are. But I'm not going there. I'm going to where I can learn more about magic and study with Sunrise."

"You could do that here. Or at home with your wife."

"You're right. I could." A hint of color crept into his face. He glowered at the kender. Then he softened his expression, gave a hint of a smile. "I could study right here, except I don't want to. We're going to where there are other good dragons. And while I work with Sunrise, we'll learn from them. If we can more firmly unite the good dragons, they will present a great challenge to the overlords and offer my father their assistance when the showdown comes. So, you see, I *will* be helping my father."

"Sure, your father. Of course, he does pretty well on his own. But your wife and . . ."

Ulin kept his temper in check. "Blister, do you honestly think I want to be away from my wife and my children? I love them and miss them terribly. But I might not have a wife and children if the overlords continue unchecked and if Takhisis returns."

"What does your father think about all of this?"

"I didn't ask him."

"Maybe you should."

"Maybe you should mind your own business for a change."

The kender sadly shook her head and stepped aside. "You used to mind other people's business," she said softly.

"I still do," he returned as he walked by.

Blister clucked sadly to herself as Ulin continued down the hallway and disappeared down a flight of steps.

Usha approached her son, holding the skirts of a long green gown to avoid tripping. She started to say something, but he quickly brushed by her, offering her only a hurried goodbye. She'd overheard his conversation with Blister; it was similar to a talk she'd had with him last night. And the ending was the same, though the kender had detained him a little longer. With each passing day, Ulin reminded her more and more of his father and his Great-Uncle Raistlin. Magic was Ulin's passion, as it had been Raistlin's. And working against the evil dragons was foremost in his mind right now. She knew her son's family would have to wait. *If* they could wait, she thought. And if he lived through this experience to return to them.

"Good morning, Blister. Are they still at it?" Usha put on a cheerful front.

The kender nodded, making a mental note to speak to her later about Ulin. It just wasn't right, him leaving. Not when she was stuck here with nothing important to do. It was so unfair. "They're still talking, arguing actually." She waved a hand toward a doorway at the far end of the hall. "I've been trying to talk to Palin, 'bout something important, but he's too busy."

"Let's unbusy him, shall we?"

The kender followed Usha, complimenting her gown as they went, asking if Usha had something smaller in that color that she might wear. Her own brown tunic looked rather drab next to Usha's. All of the kender's clothes had sunk with the *Anvil.* She'd fashioned a few things to wear out of blouses Usha had tired of. And to the kender it seemed Usha tired of the all drab colors. Blister thought it unfortunate that the Majeres only kept a small trunk of clothes and personal possessions high in the tower and that the bulk of their things remained back home.

They stopped in the doorway. The large room beyond was round at the far side, following the exterior curve of the tower, and it was cut in the center by a large window. Walls angled off to the right and left, making the room appear pie-shaped. A triangular table was placed in the center, with Palin, the Master, and the Shadow Sorcerer each taking a side. Maps were spread out across the surface, covering almost every inch of the dark marble.

The sorcerers continued to talk, though they noticed Usha and Blister in the doorway. Not even Palin stopped to offer his wife a greeting.

"There!" The Shadow Sorcerer said. The mysterious mage was stabbing at a place on the map that displayed Neraka, Khur, and Blöde. The sleeves of his gray robe were so voluminous that only the tip of a pale, gloved finger edged out to touch the yellowing parchment. He was pointing at a mountain range.

"I was watching the shadow dragon—the rogue dragon who has been killing smaller dragons. Yesterday morning, I saw him slay a large red, not too terribly far from Brukt where Palin's friends are heading."

"And where is the shadow dragon now?" The Master's gaze rested on the parchment. "Do you think he poses a threat to the Kagonesti and the others?"

"I don't know." The Shadow Sorcerer's hood moved back and forth, the visage hidden from Usha and Blister. "It is difficult to determine. But I believe he is the first dragon that Palin's friends should tend to—after they've recovered the glaive from Dhamon and the crown from the Dimernesti."

"The shadow dragon is not the greatest threat," the Master argued.

"But he is the most unpredictable, and in that respect the most dangerous."

Palin glanced at his two companions. "More dangerous now than when you first took notice of him?"

The Shadow Sorcerer's hood nodded. "He has grown stronger from slaying the large red, the largest dragon I have seen him attack. He has absorbed the red's energy as did the dragons during the Dragon Purge. Perhaps if your friends do not tend to him first, another purge will begin. There are too few good dragons now, and—"

"I will admit the shadow dragon bears watching," Palin interrupted. "But my friends can do nothing about him now, at least not without the artifacts. And you haven't seen him kill a good dragon. Do you know where this shadow dragon is now?"

"Hiding, resting. Somewhere in the mountains."

"Where exactly?" The Master's unnaturally soft voice rose.

"I do not know."

The Master's fingers traced a line from the mountains to Brukt. "Neither do we know exactly where Dhamon Grimwulf is."

"You lost Dhamon?" Blister put her hands on her hips. "You brought me here to help find him. And I did help. You found him. And now you've lost him?"

"I lost track of Dhamon Grimwulf when my attention was distracted by the shadow dragon," the Shadow Sorcerer said.

"Oh, yeah. That happens." The kender brightened. "Well, that reminds me why I've been trying to talk to Palin."

The Shadow Sorcerer, ignoring her, turned back to the map. "Now to important matters," the gray-cloaked mage said.

"Yes, actually this is very important," the kender offered. "And it matters to me."

The sorcerers seemed not to hear her. Blister glanced up at Usha, looking for support, but Usha had become engrossed in the map and the discussion.

"I believe Takhisis will appear here," the Shadow Sorcerer stated. The gloved finger was pointing at a spot in northern Neraka. "At Ariakan's Rest."

"I disagree." The Master stabbed his finger at a location in Khur.

"They're going at it again," Blister muttered.

The Master raised his soft voice; it sounded as if it were painful for him to speak. "The Window to the Stars, here in Khur. It used to be a portal between worlds, dimensions, and planes. My divinations point to this area. I mentioned this to Sunrise and to Ulin. It is not too great a distance from Goodlund, the seat of power of the red overlord. I believe if the Dark Queen were to return, she would choose the domain of the most powerful dragon, and that is where Malys rules. So here will mark the downfall of all Ansalon. Or, perhaps if we are fortunate, here will mark where a god has been rebuffed."

The Shadow Sorcerer batted the Master's hand off the map. "No. Ariakan's Rest! Listen to me. Don't be a fool—there's too much at stake. Takhisis will return here. The Rest is a mountain cave in the Khalkists. Ariakan, one of the greatest warriors in Krynn's history, was led to this cave by the goddess Zeboim, his mother, the trail marked by fragile sea shells placed in the snow. It is part of this great land's history, Krynn's history. Don't tell me you've forgotten all about it?"

"It is also the birthplace of the Knights of Takhisis," Palin said calmly.

"Yes," the Shadow Sorcerer continued. "There is historical precedent here. Takhisis came to the Rest before appearing to Ariakan. Why should not this be the place again?"

"Your words have merit," Palin agreed softly. "And there is a strong concentration of Knights of Takhisis in Neraka."

"Ready worshipers. It is their land," the Shadow Sorcerer added. "And they could support Takhisis here. They could guard—"

"But my divinations," the Master interrupted. His voice had grown hoarse.

"*My* divinations point to Ariakan's Rest!"

"Please stop arguing." Usha glided to Palin's side. "I thought you were supposed to be working *together*."

"We were," the Shadow Sorcerer snapped. "Until you intruded." The gray-cloaked figure looked at Palin, pointedly avoiding Usha's stare. "We will discuss this later, when we are alone." The sorcerer whirled on slippered feet and stalked from the chamber. The kender had to leap out of the way to avoid being knocked down.

"I'm sorry," Usha offered. "I really didn't mean to intrude."

"Ahem," Blister cleared her throat.

"But Blister wanted to talk to you, and—"

"No intrusion." Palin took Usha's hands in his and kissed her cheek. "A welcome break. This discussion was going nowhere. Time will soothe tempers, and we'll attack the problem again in an hour or so."

Usha smiled, her golden eyes twinkling. "Blister?"

Palin turned toward the kender and motioned her farther

into the room. Blister looked about tentatively for a moment, then hurried to join them.

"The Shadow Sorcerer said I'm not needed anymore to find Dhamon."

"You gave the Master and the Shadow Sorcerer enough information earlier. They will use that information again. We'll eventually find him—mostly thanks to you. And it should not take too long."

"Then you really don't need me here anymore."

Palin looked at the kender, smiled, and arched an eyebrow. "You're very helpful Blister. There are plenty of things you can—"

"I'd like to be with Rig and Feril, Jasper, too. And I kinda miss Groller and Fury, even though I can't really talk to either of them. Well, I can. But Groller can't hear me and Fury *can* hear me, but he can't understand—or talk back. Anyway, they're all going to Brukt. At least the Master says they are." She waved her hands in the air. "Gilthanas is gonna help get the glaive for you. He'll probably keep Dhamon from killing Rig, if Rig hasn't already caught up to Dhamon and killed him. I would've gone with Silvara, too, but I didn't know that you didn't really need me anymore. If I would've known that, I would've gone. So I was wondering . . ." She fidgeted with the cord that tied her tunic.

"Yes?"

"I was wondering if you could, you know . . . magically send me to Brukt. Sort of like how you brought Usha and me here from Schallsea. I could go on to the coast with Rig and them and then to Dimernesti. I've never seen a sea elf."

Palin rubbed his chin. Stubble dotted his face; he'd been so busy lately that he hadn't taken time to shave or to eat properly. He was falling into bad habits again. "Are you sure that's what you want?"

Blister nodded. "I've never been to Brukt before, or to any ogre ruin, for that matter. I would've asked Ulin if he and

Sunrise would take me there, but Ulin was kinda grumpy and just said he was going somewhere. And I wasn't sure I wanted to go 'somewhere.' "

"I understand."

"So it's okay?"

"Yes."

"And you can do it? Just send me to them?" Blister smiled wide.

"Well, I'd like to be sure exactly where they are first."

"You can do that?"

"Yes."

The Master cleared his throat, interrupting their conversation. "Tonight I will contact Rig."

Palin mouthed his thanks, then returned his attention to the kender. "And then I'll—"

"You'll send me with Blister." Usha's golden eyes had lost their sparkle, her expression instantly serious.

"What?" Palin's eyes were wide.

"Hmm. I better go pack." Blister hurried from the room, giving the Majeres a chance to be almost alone.

"Perhaps we should continue our discussion of Takhisis and the dragons later." The Master padded up behind Palin, attempting to slip past him and leave.

"No." Usha put her hand out and stopped the mysterious sorcerer. "It is Palin and I who can talk later." She leaned forward, kissed Palin, and left.

Palin watched her go, then rubbed at the stubble on his face again. "I don't think she's serious," he told the Master. "She won't really leave with Blister."

The Master said nothing.

The two returned to their maps. The Master studied his friend's weathered face and began to roll up the parchments. "I still believe the Window to the Stars is the answer."

"Perhaps. But Ariakan's Rest is indeed a possibility and has precedent, as the Shadow Sorcerer says. And . . . perhaps . . .

neither is correct." Palin eased himself into a high-backed chair, steepled his fingers, and stared at his reflection in the dark marble. "I, too, will devote my time to divining the location of Takhisis's arrival," he said finally.

"And together we will discover how to use the artifacts to stop Takhisis' return." The Master tugged the ring free from his hand. "Dalamar's ring," he said softly. "Your ring now." He placed it in Palin's palm. "I've no need of such baubles anyway. So now you have two artifacts."

"The Fist of E'li and Dalamar's ring. Thank you, my friend."

"And soon, if Rig and his companions are fortunate, you'll have the glaive and the crown." The Master walked to a slender bookcase filled with leather-bound volumes. He tugged a thick black book free and brought it to the table. Pale fingers turned the pages. "It took me quite a while to find this. Here. See? I believe this is the weapon Dhamon carries."

Palin leaned over the tome. The words were scratchy, as if they'd been penned in a hurry or by someone with a shaky hand. "Gryendel," he pronounced. "You're right. This could be it." He placed Dalamar's ring in his pocket and traced his finger down the page. "This says it was forged by Reorx centuries upon centuries ago, that it was lost in the All Saints War, before the coming of the last gods and before the Age of Dreams. Indeed it is ancient."

"Reorx's Grin," the Master said. "Crafted to part whatever its wielder desires—wood, armor, stone . . . perhaps even dragonflesh. In any event, it can't be allowed to fall into the clutches of the dragons. Khellendros has Huma's Lance and Goldmoon's medallions already. This cannot be lost too."

"Reorx's Grin," Palin whispered.

* * * * *

In a laboratory upstairs, one with lots of windows, Usha sat at a makeshift easel, putting the last touches on a painting of

Blister. The kender was surrounded by flowers that Usha had painstakingly depicted. All that remained were to add a few highlights to Blister's graying blonde hair and a bit of rose to her lips. Perhaps a half-hour's work at best, she thought.

Usha moved the picture and put another piece of smoothed wood on the easel. She cleaned her brush, drying it on a rag. Then she thrust the tip in dark green paint and began dabbing at the fresh surface. An hour later, she had painted the beginnings of a forest, with trees stretching from the bottom to the top of the canvas. The outline of a dwarf was in the center of the painting.

"Jasper, you're carrying the Fist. I know it," she said to herself. "But you don't know what you carry—and neither, it seems, do I."

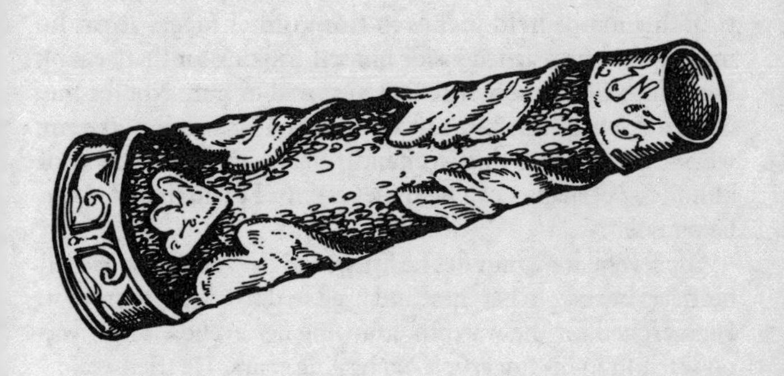

Chapter 9

A Fiery Trail

"They're virtually blind." Rig stood at the edge of the village, in the shade of the crumbling tower of Brukt. Fiona was at his side, watching the villagers who milled about. "All of them—except that man who says Dhamon cut off his arm."

A few of the people were preparing a meal at a central fire pit, their sightless faces turned to fruits and vegetables they were awkwardly peeling. Some of the elves who had been rescued from the lizard creatures were helping the villagers skin a boar they had caught in a trap. Most were gathered at the large building.

A handful of the elves recounted the tale of their capture and rescue and listened to the villagers tell about the dragon.

Nearby, Jasper hovered over a female dwarf who seemed to be the leader of the place. She was sitting with her back against the trunk of a young shaggybark.

Jasper's eyes were closed, his brow furrowed in concentration, his hands held inches in front of her face. *Please*, he mouthed, as he reached inside himself, looking for that healing spark that Goldmoon once had nurtured in him. Not for me, he thought to himself, not to heal my lung and make me whole, but to help this woman. If I can cure one person of blindness, perhaps I can help the rest. And then, maybe, I can help myself.

For several long minutes he listened to her breathing. He felt his heart beating in his chest and tried to draw strength from it. He searched for the warmth, touching her eyelids. There was no warmth in his fingertips. No healing spark. He tried again.

"I'm sorry," he said finally, tears spilling from his eyes. "I can't help you." This should have been easy, he added to himself. He'd done this many times before—before Goldmoon's death.

Groller and Fury were watching him, the wolf leaning against the half-ogre's leg. "Jaz-pear no longer good healer," Groller said glumly. "Jaz-pear has no faith in hiz-zelf."

Feril stood apart from everyone. The Kagonesti had tended to the villagers' injuries, and she had stopped the bleeding and bandaged the stump of the Solamnic spy. Her limited healing skills were enough for that, but she was not skilled enough to attempt to cure the blindness. She glanced to the east, where the swamp melted into the foothills of the mountains of Blöde Then she knelt and studied the ground, merging her senses with it.

"I wonder if the dragon blinded Dhamon too," Rig mused, as he watched the Kagonesti.

"If he's blind, we'll find him easier," said Fiona. "He's only got a day on us, according to these people. That's what the Master said too, when he contacted us last night."

"Nothing's easy, Fiona," Rig chuckled. "At least where Dhamon's concerned. Maybe when—"

"I've found his trail!" Feril exclaimed. Rig and Fiona reached her in several strides.

"I've been over every inch of ground where the villagers claimed Dhamon was," the Kagonesti said. "Most of the tracks belong to the people who live here or the Knights of Takhisis who died. There's even a couple of dragon prints. But I've found a few of Dhamon's. I believe he went out the back of this building and came around to the side, right about here. Then he moved into the foothills. There's a second set of footprints heading away in another direction: a woman's."

"The female commander the villagers mentioned," Fiona said.

Feril nodded. "Probably. They said all the other knights were killed by the dragon." The Kagonesti turned toward the foothills.

Rig shouted. "Jasper, we're leaving!"

Jasper put his hand on the female dwarf's shoulder. They exchanged words the mariner couldn't hear. Then Jasper motioned to Groller and pointed at Rig. The half-ogre shook his head. He tugged on his hair, pointed to his ear, and waggled his fingers skyward.

"Gilthanas," Rig muttered. "And the silver dragon. The Master told me they'd be coming to Brukt, to help us with Dhamon." He turned to Fiona. "Don't let Feril get too far ahead. We'll catch up." The mariner hurried toward Groller.

"Jasper," Rig began, "Gilthanas and Silvara are on their way. They might be here sometime today. Or tomorrow. Who knows when, but it shouldn't be too long. Someone should wait for them, but that someone's not going to be me."

"Nor me," the dwarf returned.

Rig pointed to his ear, pantomimed brushing away long hair, like Gilthanas's, pointed at Groller, then at the ground.

"No," the half-ogre said. "Go wid you and Furl, wid Jaz-pear."

Rig sighed. "Jasper, can you . . ." he gestured at the female dwarf, then whirled to catch up with Feril and Fiona.

Jasper turned back to the female dwarf. "Our companion will come here soon. Can you tell him where we've gone?"

She hesitated a moment, then nodded. "Yes, if you tell me what he sounds like."

Jasper described Gilthanas in great detail: his voice, his height, his laugh. Then he added, "He'll be accompanied by a dragon. She's big. And silver. She won't hurt anybody. Of course, she might not look like a dragon. She might look like an elf . . . Oh, never mind. It's a long story, and we've got to hurry." He smiled warmly at her. "I wish I could help you, but there just doesn't seem to be anything I can do."

"Jaz-pear!"

Groller and Fury were waiting for him. "Good luck to you," the dwarf said, as he squeezed her hand. Then he joined his companions.

* * * * *

The sun was dropping toward the horizon by the time they stopped. They were only halfway up the side of a mountain. Still a good hour of light was left, maybe a little more.

Jasper's chest felt as if it were on fire. The climb was tiring enough for people with two good lungs. Still, the dwarf refused to complain. He was just grateful they had finally decided to rest. "I thought we were going to take the pass through the mountains," he said.

Feril knelt on the ground, her fingers sifting through the dry earth. "He went into the cave over there, but then he came out and continued up."

"How long ago?" Rig glanced up the rocky incline.

"I'm not sure; at least several hours. I don't think he's blind. A blind man's path wouldn't be so confident. I'll scout ahead and be back in a while." Feril ignored Rig's protests. Catlike, she scurried over the rocks, pausing at intervals to examine the ground.

"We should get a little rest." Fiona peered into the cave. "I don't think I can go much farther."

"If you weren't carrying all that armor, you wouldn't be so tired." Rig pointed to her sack.

"Well, I'm not carrying any armor, and I want to rest, too." Jasper climbed into the cave, Fury and Groller following.

Fiona smiled. "Join us?"

"In a minute." Rig scowled, took another look up the mountain. Feril was kneeling next to a rock, her fingers dancing across its surface. "Talking to a rock," he muttered. "All right. A little rest," he said. "But just a little. When she comes back, we'll set out again. Travel by starlight if we have to. Dhamon's too close. He's not going to get away from me this time."

Beyond the narrow mouth of the cave was a large chamber that angled back and down into the side of the mountain. Its floor was covered with soil and leaves. Fiona sat against a wall near the entrance where light spilled in. Her canvas sack was between her legs, and from the bag she removed parts of her armor. She looked up and noticed Rig watching her. "Just checking it," she said.

He sat next to her. The ground was comfortably soft. "They were going to have boar tonight in the village."

"We could have stayed and waited for Gilthanas."

"I'm not hungry anyway." His growling stomach disagreed. He peered into the shadows. "Where's Jasper and Groller?"

She nodded her head toward the back. "There's a passage back there. "They decided to investigate. The wolf, too. Jasper said they'd only be gone a few minutes."

"I thought Jasper was tired."

"Dwarves are comfortable in caves. Guess it was too tempting."

Rig was weary as well, but he was reluctant to allow the conversation to die. "It's dark back there," he said.

Fiona giggled. "Dwarves see very well in the dark. Where have you been all your life, Rig Mer-Krel?"

"On a ship mostly. No dwarves at sea." She edged a little closer, and Rig felt the welcome warmth of her arm against his, then noticed her frown. "What's wrong?" he asked softly.

She held up a small bowl-shaped piece of armor, one that was supposed to fit over her knee. "It's dented. All that jostling around in the sack. I didn't have anything to pad it with."

The mariner reached to take it. His fingers brushed against hers, lingering, then finally moving to the metal, gently plucking it from her. "Shouldn't be too hard to fix." He turned his face toward hers. She was strong, as Shaon had been. But she wasn't Shaon. She wasn't a substitute for her, either. She was a knight: rigid, structured, and everything he wasn't. But she was compelling in her own way. Red hair the color of sunset framed her face. And she was so very close.

Fiona turned her face close to his, raising her lips. He felt her breath against his cheek.

"Rig! Get out here. Hurry!" Feril stood in the cave entrance.

"You found Dhamon?" The mariner pushed himself to his feet, handing Fiona the armor piece.

The Kagonesti shook her head. "No. I lost all trace of him. But I found trouble."

* * * * *

Feril led them up a steep rise, difficult to climb. The Kagonesti moved fast, waiting for them at the top. She didn't give them time to catch their breath, however, as she led them through an uncomfortably narrow gap in the mountains.

From their cramped vantage point they stared out over a gravelly slope and into a small scrub-dotted valley painted orange by the setting sun. More than two dozen creatures the color of flame meandered across the floor, stopping to poke at patches of dirt and craning their necks to spy into crevices.

"Red spawn?" Fiona whispered.

Feril nodded. "I've never seen any like these before, but Palin told me they existed."

"Probably Malystryx's brood," Rig said.

The creatures' legs looked like columns of fire; their scalloped wings were the color of blood, their faces humanoid, with protruding jaws. A spiked ridge ran from the tops of their heads to the tips of their tails. The creatures looked similar to the blue spawn Rig and Feril had battled months past in Khellendros's desert, but their shoulders were broader and their chests more muscular. Even from this distance they looked more intimidating than the blues.

"They breathe fire," Feril said. "I saw one burn a bush just by opening its mouth."

"Too many for the three of us." Fiona kept her voice down. "But with Jasper and Groller, and Fury, maybe we could take them."

"But what about the others?" Rig gestured toward the end of the small valley, where a dozen more red spawn milled about. Then he pointed to a crevice on the slope across from them. It was a cave opening, and other spawn were standing in the shadows. "Mountain's crawlin' with them. Bet they're looking for Dhamon."

Feril's voice grew even softer. "There are a couple more not too far below us. They're coming up. We can't stay here long or they'll see us. Dhamon doesn't stand a chance."

"Maybe they're not after Dhamon." Fiona tapped Rig's shoulder. "You said Dhamon was being controlled by the red dragon. If that's the case, the red dragon wouldn't send her brood out looking for him, would she? She'd know exactly where he was."

"Then what do you think they're after?" Rig asked.

Fiona shrugged.

A dozen spawn in the center of the small valley were conferring, gesturing with long arms, sharp claws glinting. One of them pointed up toward the crevice.

"Maybe we should get out of here," Feril suggested.

A half-dozen spawn took to the air just as Rig, Feril, and Fiona scrambled out of their hiding place. They hurried down the rocky slope, half-running, half-sliding, gravel rolling all around them. Their hands became scratched and blistered as they reached out to keep themselves from falling.

"Think they saw us?" Fiona asked.

"Maybe," Rig grunted.

"Yes," Feril insisted. The Kagonesti pointed up at a pair of red spawn who had materialized above them.

"Damn," the mariner swore. "They're fast." He drew his cutlass. "Get back to the cave!"

There was a hiss of another blade being drawn. "I'll fight alongside you," Fiona declared. She glared up at the creatures.

"Come on, both of you!" Feril spat. "You're too much in the open here."

Fiona and Rig started to run, but by the time the cave mouth came into sight, a third spawn had joined the chase.

"Inside!" Feril darted inside the cave mouth.

Rig and Fiona took up a position just outside the mouth.

"Inside!" the Kagonesti repeated. "Rig, don't argue with me. Hurry!"

The mariner was too busy plucking daggers from his waistband. He held three in his left hand, clutching the cutlass in his right. One of the three spawn was diving at him as he loosed the daggers.

The daggers passed through a ball of flame that erupted from the spawn's mouth. The fire engulfed the spot that Rig and Fiona had vacated moments before.

"Couldn't see if I scratched 'im," Rig huffed as he slid into the cave a second after Fiona.

The Solamnic knight risked a glance. "I can't tell. But all of them are still out there. And there's more of them coming."

"We're sitting targets," the mariner snapped. "Gonna be cooked worse than that boar in the village."

Feril was hugging the shadows, her fingers splayed against the rock. She felt its coolness, its smooth and rough textures. Once before she had merged her senses with the stone floor—in Khellendros's cave several months ago—causing the rock to run like water and flood the blue dragon's guards. Now, once again, the stone felt liquid, pliable as clay. She began to shape it with her mind.

"Move," she whispered to it. "Flow like a river." She poured out her strength. Her senses separated from her body and merged into the cave wall. "Move. Flow," she ordered.

Rig darted outside again, released three more daggers at the lead spawn. This time he knew he hit the mark. The creature bellowed and clutched its chest, flapping its wings furiously to stay aloft. Its claws frantically grasped at the hilts. It screamed once, then exploded in a great ball of orange flame. Though he was several yards away, the mariner's skin blistered.

Two spawn immediately behind closed the distance and landed just outside the cave. Rig slashed at the one on the right, slicing through red scales, and drawing a line of brighter red blood along the spawn's abdomen.

Fiona was suddenly to his left, thrusting forward with her sword. She heard the creature inhale, felt the rush of heated air, then heard the crackle of fire above her. She leapt forward, barreling into the spawn, knocking it back, and narrowly avoiding the ball of fire it had loosed behind her.

The mariner wasn't so lucky. His spawn opened its mouth and breathed, just as the mariner plastered himself against the side of the cave entrance. Rig felt the searing heat against his legs. He screamed and dropped his cutlass, batting at the flames. Then he screamed again as red-hot claws raked his back. The spawn had jumped on top of him and was pressing him to the ground.

"Rig?" Fiona risked a glance over her shoulder as she brought her sword up to defend against her antagonist.

"I'm all right," the mariner said between clenched teeth, as he pushed up, managing to knock his spawn off balance. His fingers fumbled at his waist for more daggers, tugging them free, and he hurled them without further delay. One struck his spawn in the chest. The other two flew wide of their mark.

"Rig, Fiona! Get in the cave!" Feril called. "Now!"

The Solamnic knight slashed with a frenzy belying her fatigue. She drew blood from the spawn, forcing it to keep a respectable distance from her.

The mariner glanced into the opening. It seemed somehow smaller. He reached down to his charred boots and plucked two more daggers free. The pommels were fiery to the touch, so he loosed them at the nearest spawn. Both found their mark this time, one in the creature's throat, the other in its shoulder.

Its scream was inhuman and was answered from somewhere overhead by snarls and hisses—a dozen more of the things were descending. The spawn flailed at the daggers, sizzling red blood flowing over its talons. It opened its mouth wider.

"Fiona!" Rig called. "Get into the cave, now!"

Again the Solamnic jabbed at her target, her sword cutting through red scales and lodging deep in the creature's belly. Not waiting to see if she'd dealt it a mortal blow, she tugged her sword free and retreated. Rig darted into the cave close behind her. The air at the opening was instantly sulphurous, as one of the spawn exploded in a fiery burst.

"Hot!" Fiona gasped, trying to catch her breath. She fumbled at the catches on her breastplate, fingers flying over the shoulder ties until the armor fell free. "Really hot!" Her arms were blistered from the heat, her shoulders raw where the metal of her breastplate had burned her.

"My cutlass is out there," Rig said. He thrust two fingers up the band of his sleeve, pulled out another dagger and crouched at the opening. He let out a low whistle and scooted back. "And it's staying where it is. We've got lots of company. There's an army out there."

Fiona moved forward and stood next to him, watching the cave grow darker as the stone beneath the Kagonesti's fingers shimmered. The rock seemed to melt into gray butter and then billowed to fill the opening. Through the small gap remaining, a spawn's face appeared. The creature inhaled.

"Move. Hurry," Feril implored the stone. "Like water."

The stone flowed together, sealing them inside the cave. It blanketed them with a cocoon of impenetrable darkness, protecting them from the blast of fire the spawn had loosed. The Kagonesti slumped against the wall, out of breath from the effort.

"I can hear them outside," she whispered. "Their feet are clicking against the rocks. There must be dozens now. They're talking. But I can't quite make it all out. There're too many voices." She drew in a deep breath. "Wait. Something about a man the color of mud, about wanting him. One mentioned Malystryx. Malys wants the mud man and his friends. Dead."

"A black man," Rig said finally. "Me. The spawn weren't looking for Dhamon. They were looking for us."

"That's impossible," Fiona replied. No one knows we're here or what we're up to." She was running her fingertips along her arms and shoulders, testing her blisters and burns.

"Except the villagers. They knew we were coming into the mountains," Feril said.

"They wouldn't have betrayed us," Fiona snapped.

"Unless the spawn didn't give them a choice," the Kagonesti countered.

"But the spawn were ahead of us, not following us."

The Solamnic thought a moment. "From Dhamon?"

"He couldn't have known we were following him. At least I don't think he could have. Besides, he would've fought us himself. He wouldn't have needed the spawn. Not with that glaive."

"Then who? How?" Fiona persisted.

"I don't know."

"We've got to slip out of here and get back to Brukt," Fiona said. There was fear in the Solamnic knight's voice. "The village is unprotected, unaware of the spawn. We've got to do something so the monsters don't destroy those people."

Rig groaned softly as he shifted his weight back and forth on his feet. His legs throbbed. "If the spawn are after us, running to Brukt will only endanger those people. We'll lead the spawn right to them."

"The spawn will kill them," Fiona added.

"And us, too, if we lead them there," Rig continued "There were at least forty spawn out there in the valley, Fiona. And those were just the ones we could see. We can take a hobble—a small number—sure; bring 'em on. But not an army." The Solamnic knight leaned against him, and he drew an arm around her shoulders. "We'll leave when Feril's certain they're gone," he said. "We can check on the village, then."

"That could be a few hours," she said.

"Several, at least," Feril interjected. Her voice was soft. "I'm exhausted. We're stuck here, unless you can find another way out of this cave. I can't make a hole in this rock until I get my strength back."

"It's darker than night in here," Rig said. "It feels like a tomb." He and Fiona groped their way toward a wall and slid down it. She put her head on his shoulder, leaning into him. In the still air, they could hear the persistent clicking of spawn's claws beyond the sealed entrance.

"Hey, I wonder where Groller and Jasper are?" Fiona mused. "I can't believe they didn't hear all this. And they should have been back by now."

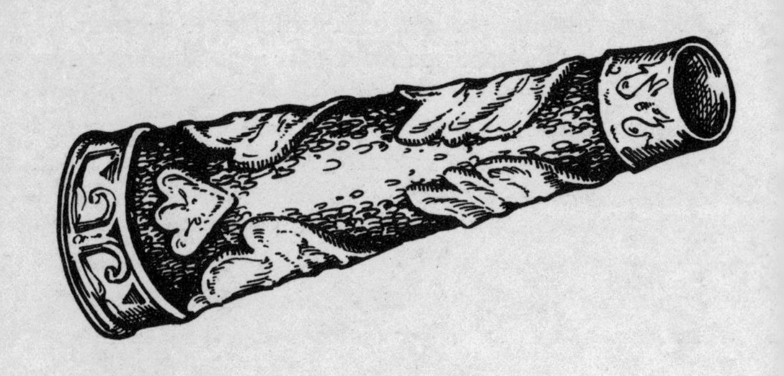

Chapter 10

Shades of Gray

The dragon clung to the shadows deep inside the lime-stone cave, listening to the footfalls of the intruder. His eyes peered through the darkness and glimpsed the black armor of the order of the Knights of Takhisis.

The intruder was a man. This mildly surprised the shadow dragon; he had thought there was only one surviving knight from the village: the woman commander whom he had left alive to inform Malystryx of the slaughter. Perhaps this man had not come from the village or had fled unseen. No matter; the man was a Knight of Takhisis. He would have to die.

The Knights of Takhisis, under the banners of various overlords, had grown too strong as far as the shadow dragon was concerned. Slaying them helped restore the balance of things, as did slaying the red dragon earlier. The shadow dragon's wounds had already healed from that fight, fueled by the energy absorbed from the powerful red.

Like a lengthening shadow, he edged closer to the man.

The warrior slumped against the far wall, illuminated by the merest shard of light. The man was exhausted, oblivious to the living blackness. Sweat-soaked blond hair was plastered against the sides of his head and his face was tinged red with exertion. The man released his weapon, a polearm with a curved blade. Gingerly he flexed his fingers the way a dragon might test an injured claw.

The shadow dragon sensed the magical energy of the weapon. He noticed how the man cupped his hands, as though they were burned from holding it. The dragon concentrated on the weapon, feeling its arcane energy prickle at his senses. The weapon was an instrument of good, ancient and god-made, and it was in the possesion of a Knight of Takhisis, an agent of evil.

Dhamon Grimwulf closed his eyes. His chest ached. His hands throbbed. He had intended to leave the weapon here, then to leave this place. And if then, by some miracle he truly was free, whatever was he to do with himself? What measure of life did he deserve after the acts he had committed? Could he find redemption?

He found some satisfaction in the thought that if he lost himself to the dragon, he would have earned a moral victory by keeping the glaive from her.

The shadow dragon crept closer still. Then he placed a claw upon the man's outstretched legs, pinning him as easily as a child would snare a beetle. Too late Dhamon's eyes flew open and his hand instinctively shot out to grab the glaive. The warmth pulsing up from the haft and into his palm was nothing compared to the feeling in his legs. The dragon's immense weight was crushing them.

Huge gray eyes bore into Dhamon's, and the dragon's cold breath washed over his face, sending shivers down his body. The dragon's mouth opened wide, revealing a cavern filled with jagged quartzlike teeth. A serpentine tongue lolled out, loomed closer, black as night. Dhamon summoned the last of his strength and swept the weapon up from the floor in a clumsy arc that only grazed the dragon. But that was enough. The dragon recoiled in surprise, and Dhamon scurried out from beneath its rising claw, leaping to his feet and shouldering the weapon.

* * * * *

On a volcano-ringed plateau, the red overlord's eyes snapped wide. Malystryx had been brooding over the affront she had suffered at Ferno's death, considering candidates to replace him. She hadn't stopped Dhamon Grimwulf from running from the village. Indeed, from the back of Dhamon's mind she had secretly encouraged him. She had no desire for her pawn to die, as had Ferno and her Knights of Takhisis, and she railed against the thought of the shadow dragon gaining the enchanted glaive.

So Malys had retreated, allowing Dhamon to believe he was free, to run, and then to hide in the mountains. She intended to call him to her once more, but only after she had pondered the matter of Ferno's replacement.

Now, through his eyes, she saw the loathsome shadow dragon move closer. Through Dhamon's senses she felt the growing heat of the haft against his flesh and sensed his heart hammering wildly. There was no place for her pawn to run, she realized, and even with the weapon and her aid, he was no match for the shadow dragon.

The dark wyrm moved to block Dhamon's exit, obstructing the meager light and blanketing the chamber in darkness.

* * * * *

As the blackness filled his vision, Dhamon felt the red dragon overpower him once more.

She forced Dhamon's arms into action, sweeping the glaive in front of him. The blade connected with the reaching claw, digging through the translucent scales and spilling blood. The dragon moaned softly, a pleasing sound to the Red. Where her lieutenant, Ferno, had failed, perhaps she might find consolation after all. She knew her pawn couldn't defeat this dragon. But . . . perhaps . . . through Dhamon she might hurt the shadow dragon—hurt him badly. She directed Dhamon closer, ordering him to press the attack, and she drew from his mind on all the knightly skills he could muster.

He used the haft to parry the dragon's slashes, then twisted the weapon and alternately swept it up and down to keep the shadow dragon from getting too close.

"You cannot have this man, master of shadows," Malys said through Dhamon's mouth. An image of her head superimposed itself over Dhamon's visage.

The shadow dragon's snarl filled the chamber. "I will have what I want," the shadow dragon hissed. "I will have one more of your knights!"

On Malystryx's mountaintop she opened her mouth wide and released a stream of fire into the air. The volcanos rumbled and the peaks trembled.

Dhamon ducked beneath the swipe of the dragon's claw, then darted in close to its belly and swung the blade with all the strength Malystryx provided. He heard the glaive slice through the shadow dragon's thick chest plates and felt the frigid blood spatter his face, seeping into the joints between his armor. As his mind wrestled with Malys's power, Dhamon prayed with all his heart that the shadow dragon might find a way to slay him.

The shadow dragon seemed to fold in upon itself, becoming a smaller target that backed away from the offensive weapon. He inhaled deeply and breathed, a cloud of blackness venting from his mouth and rushing forward to overwhelm Dhamon.

At the same moment, the image of Malystryx's head sparkled and grew, becoming translucent and filling one side of the chamber. The image magically shielded Dhamon from the cloud of blackness. Malyxtryx's mouth opened and drank in the cloud, saving Dhamon from being blinded and weakened.

"You cannot have this man, master of shadows!" the visage repeated.

His legs powered by the Red, Dhamon moved closer to the now-retreating shadow dragon. His arms pumped faster, swinging the glaive in wide arcs that hacked away at the creature. Translucent black scales pelted his face, and black blood cascaded down on him. The shadow dragon drew back.

Dhamon moved toward him over the limestone floor, his legs pounding. *Hurt him again,* Malys ordered. *Hurt him, then run!*

The shadow dragon appeared to cringe, leaning into the cave wall. Dhamon raised the glaive and watched as the shadow dragon's dark eyes glimmered. An inky claw separated itself from the shadows in the cave and struck out at him.

Dhamon fell back from the impact. *Run!* Malystryx screamed in his head. *Leave this cave!* The Red realized the shadow dragon was not as vulnerable as she had thought. Probably he had only been gauging her pawn's strength, while toying with Dhamon. *Run!*

Dhamon's body tried futilely to comply, but his feet slid from under him in the pool of slippery black blood—blood he had drawn with the glaive. He fell forward, the burning glaive slipping from his fingers. His hands flailed about, desperately searching for the weapon. His face was in the blood. His eyes filled with it, as he flopped about like a fish.

Then suddenly his body was stilled, held firmly in place by a shadowy paw. The red dragon within his mind forced his head to the side to keep Dhamon from drowning.

"You will not win this day, Malystryx," the shadow dragon whispered. "Although this man hurt me—hurt me far worse than your red dragon puppet did." His voice was raspy and tinged with venom. "Perhaps you should pick your puppets more wisely—or learn to use them better." The dragon sat back on his haunches, folding its right claw around Dhamon's struggling form. It picked him up and brought him closer to its gray eyes.

Black armor coated with black blood, face and hair black, eyes blinking furiously. The shadow dragon's tongue lolled out, lapping the blood from Dhamon's face. Then the dragon allowed itself to grow larger, a deepening shadow filling the chamber. "One more knight to slay today," the dark dragon observed. "One less knight for you, Malystryx."

The shadow dragon brought its other claw up, snaking a curved talon up to Dhamon's legs and began to pluck away bits of armor.

"I will bring all of your knights down," the shadow dragon continued. "One by one, I will peel away your army. I will eat your knights, Malystryx, and slaughter your dragons. From their strength, I will grow stronger and stronger."

Dhamon heard the muted clang of his borrowed armor as piece by piece it struck the blood-soaked floor. His black leather tunic followed. He felt the crispness of the air all around his now-naked body, and the coldness of the shadow dragon's breath.

The visage of the red dragon disappeared from the chamber, and the black mouth of the shadow dragon filled Dhamon's vision. Quartz teeth loomed closer, clacking open and shut, the harsh sound echoing. From the secret place in his mind, Dhamon felt no fear, only relief that he would no longer be forced to do Malys's bidding and sadness over the deeds she had forced him to commit. Now there would be no chance for redemption.

The shadow dragon's tongue ran up Dhamon's leg, tasting

the blood and salt on his flesh. It touched the red scale on his thigh, then instantly withdrew. "Malystryx," the dragon whispered, "you control this man through magic."

Though she remained silent, the great red overlord seethed in Dhamon's mind. Lava belched from the volcanoes on her plateau. The blessedly intense heat was doing nothing to ease her temper. And it could do nothing to alleviate the loss of the ancient, precious glaive. The other overlords would have to bring her more magic now. And after she became Takhisis, her very first act would be to slay the shadow dragon, to peel off his skin, as he had shed Dhamon's armor. She would kill him slowly and painfully.

"This scale," the shadow dragon murmured. "An interesting spell." The dragon held Dhamon up. "Linked to him, you insinuate your mind into his body. You have become a powerful parasite, Malystryx. Remove the scale, break the link, and he dies. But the parasite lives on elsewhere."

The shadow dragon let out a deep sigh. He leaned forward, pressed Dhamon down against the floor, into the pool of blood. The dragon held him gently now with one claw. A talon on the other drummed softly against the scale. "Weaken the link, and he lives."

Hot white pain shot up Dhamon's leg. Wave after wave washed through him. He slammed his teeth together and writhed.

Malystryx threw back her head and released a gout of fire into the sky. The roar of her defeat was echoed by the rumbling of the volcanoes. The mountains thundered, and her plateau shook violently.

"Damage the scale, and he lives," the shadow dragon observed.

The pain intensified, and Dhamon fought to stay conscious.

Malystryx spread her blood-colored wings, beating them savagely, rose into the sky. She angled her immense head down toward the lava-covered ground, opened her jaws, and released a roaring ball of fire. Flames splashed against the lava to lick at her tail.

Dhamon screamed in agony as the shadow dragon drew an impossibly sharp talon through the scale on his leg, shearing it in two.

The knight thrashed about in the cold blood, squirming and clawing at the stone floor until the pain diminished to a dull throb. He took great gulps of air into his lungs and struggled to sit up.

He wiped at the blood in his eyes and squinted. The chamber was dark, but a soft gray glow shimmered from the shadow dragon, bathing the cave in a surreal light.

"It is time to redeem yourself," the shadow dragon announced.

"It is time to die, dragon!" came a voice from the mouth of the cave.

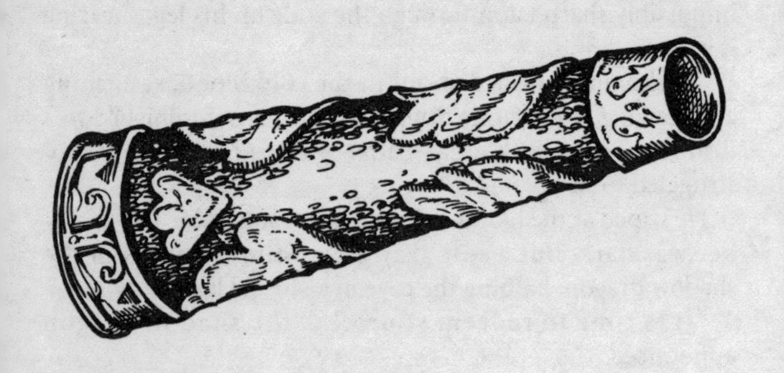

Chapter 11

Dragon Magic

Gilthanas stood just inside the cave entrance, sword in hand, blond hair fluttering about his stern face. Behind him, practically filling the entrance, was a silver dragon.

"Release Dhamon Grimwulf, or you will die!" Gilthanas ordered. The elf, displaying no fear, pointed his sword at the shadow dragon. Gilthanas's keen elven sight allowed him to see in the near-blackness of the cave, to make out Dhamon sitting naked in a pool of blood inches away from the dragon's talons.

Dhamon blinked and turned toward the elf. He opened his mouth but couldn't speak. His throat was impossibly dry. He struggled to his feet, his legs seeming like lead weights. He took a few slow steps nearer the shadow dragon and steadied himself.

"Dhamon," Gilthanas said. "Come toward me."

Dhamon shook his head, swallowed hard, and tried again to draw some moisture into his mouth. Gilthanas, he mouthed, wait.

"I have not harmed this man," the shadow dragon said, his voice haunting and harsh.

The voice of an old man, Gilthanas thought. But not the voice of a feeble dragon, the elf knew. He and Silvara had spoken briefly with the blind villagers when they arrived in Brukt to search for Dhamon. There, they had learned how the shadow dragon slaughtered the Knights of Takhisis and that Rig and the others were on Dhamon's trail.

"Indeed, I have *saved* this man," the shadow dragon continued. "And I will not harm you—unless you force me to do otherwise." Translucent black-gray scales shimmered, and the dragon seemed to shrink, just enough so he could better maneuver in the chamber. He slid by Dhamon and stretched toward Gilthanas. "I would speak with your silver companion now."

"As you wish," came Silvara's musical voice. "Gilthanas . . ."

The elf brandished his sword, but didn't use it. He stood his ground for a moment, then reluctantly stepped aside so the shadow dragon could leave the cave. The limestone chamber brightened a little, and the air seemed to warm a bit.

"You're hurt." Gilthanas heard Silvara say to the shadow dragon.

"I will heal," came the whispered reply.

There were other words exchanged. Gilthanas tried to listen, but the dragon voices dropped to inaudible tones. The elf trusted Silvara to take care of herself, but he hoped she knew what she was doing by talking to the mysterious shadow dragon, a creature as large as she.

Now Gilthanas warily approached Dhamon. The glaive lay

several feet away, all but covered by the blood. Dhamon made no move toward it.

"You killed Goldmoon," Gilthanas began. He glanced over his shoulder toward the cave entrance. The two dragons were snout to snout, as their words, sounding like wind chimes, continued. The elf returned his attention to Dhamon, kept the sword pointed in front of him.

"And Jasper," Dhamon said. His voice was remarkably soft, and it hurt his throat to speak.

"No. You wounded him severely, but the dwarf is alive."

"I deserve death," Dhamon said, looking at Gilthanas's sword, then raising his eyes to meet the elf's.

"Some would argue you deserve worse," the elf returned. "But I'm not your judge, and we're a long way from Schallsea—where you should be tried and punished."

"And killed," Dhamon whispered.

"Maybe," Gilthanas's voice was stern, offering no pity. "That's not for me to decide. Palin would like to believe you weren't responsible for your actions, that the Red was behind everything. Is that true?"

Dhamon didn't answer. He searched for Malystryx in his mind, reaching a hand down to feel the cracked scale still imbedded in his leg. He felt her, briefly, like a whisper on the wind. She still watched like an eavesdropper in the secret part of his mind.

"Is that true?" Gilthanas almost shouted.

"She's still here," Dhamon said, pointing to his forehead. His voice was getting stronger, though his throat still ached, as did the rest of him. "Maybe you should judge me. If I can't be rid of her, I'm not safe. I can't be trusted. Malys wants the glaive. She was forcing me to bring it to her."

The elf let out a deep breath. "I'll take your weapon," he said.

Dhamon gestured toward it.

"And you're coming with me, too. Eventually we'll make

our way back to Schallsea or to the Tower of Wayreth. It depends where Palin wants you. Silvara risked a lot to come here, flying through Sable's realm. We'll take a different route back."

Dhamon shook his head. "You don't want me with you. Believe me."

"Nor do I," came the raspy voice from the cave entrance. "Unlike the silver, I have no desire to be shackled to a man." The shadow dragon slid back inside the cave, bringing with him the cold air and the blackness. In the entrance behind him, the sky glowed dark purple and the stars began to shine through. "But I am not done with you. Dhamon Grimwulf, they call you, a former Knight of Takhisis, a renegade of Goldmoon. Malystryx, I will call you—but for only a few hours more."

"I will help." The voice was Silvara's. She stood in the cave entrance, framed by the twilight sky, looking as she had when Gilthanas first met her—a Kagonesti with sparkling eyes and flowing hair.

The elf noiselessly glided into the cave, following the shadow dragon. She stopped briefly to look at Gilthanas. "Wait for us outside, and be vigilant," she said. "He tells me a legion of red spawn is patrolling the mountains, and there are Rig and the others to watch for."

Gilthanas opened his mouth to protest, but quickly thought better of it. His silver dragon companion had made her mind up about something, and his relationship was too tenuous with her to argue about it right now. "Be careful," was all he said. "Call me if you need me." He watched her follow the shadow dragon into the darkest recesses of the cave. Then he slipped outside.

* * * * *

Gilthanas drew his cloak about him as he paced. The elf knew a lot about dragons and was desperately in love with the silver dragon, but he'd never seen a creature before similar to the one in there with her. The shadow dragon had blinded an entire village. He prayed to the departed gods that Silvara was safe in the creature's presence and that she knew what she was doing.

He'd known Silvara for decades, having met her a lifetime ago, though it had taken him a long time to admit he was in love with her. When she revealed that she was not a Kagonesti, but in reality a silver dragon, he spurned her and went his own way. It took him a long time to realize how lonely was the way, how incomplete was the life he'd chosen.

Palin Majere gave him an opportunity to redeem himself. When Palin and Rig and the others rescued him from the Bastion of Darkness, a Knights of Takhisis stronghold in the Northern Wastes, he threw his lot in with them, vowing to help them fight the overlords. Months ago that promise took him to Southern Ergoth, where he was reunited with Silvara. This time she'd taken on the aspect of a Solamnic knight. He saw a chance to recover the love they once shared. She wanted nothing to do with him at first; she was as cold to him as the frigid landscape that surrounded them. But he was stubborn, and he discovered that she still cared for him.

And so he trod lightly with her now, afraid that to do otherwise would give her cause to leave him. He shoved his stubborn demeanor aside and let his heart rule his actions for a change. He stared at the stars, glimmering like dragon scales.

* * * * *

Silvara gazed at the scale on Dhamon's leg. Behind her the shadow dragon whispered a word, and a pale silver globe of light appeared above her. The shadow dragon shrank away from the light, clinging to the thick shadows and watching the dragon in elven form.

"Malystryx's?" she asked, as she pointed at the cracked scale.

Dhamon nodded and explained how he happened to come by it. A dying Knight of Takhisis had slapped it on his leg and doomed him.

"Diabolical magic," Silvara murmured. She indicated he should sit, and he picked a spot near the shadow dragon, where blood did not soak the floor. Silvara knelt next to him, the globe hovering a few feet away. "You broke the scale?" she asked the dragon.

"Yes," the creature hissed. "I determined that to remove it would kill him—a fate he did not seem to mind."

"I deserve to die," Dhamon whispered. "I killed Goldmoon. Gilthanas said I hurt Jasper. There was a Solamnic spy in Brukt, and I—"

Silvara shushed him and ran her fingers along the scale.

"Malys is still buried deep within him," the shadow dragon said. "The Red refuses to let him go."

"She's watching both of you," Dhamon interrupted. "Through my eyes. I can feel her watching. But I don't think she can control me any more."

"No," the shadow dragon said. "But she must be . . . completely exorcised."

"How?" he asked.

The shadow dragon crept closer. "With a spell."

Silvara looked at the mysterious dragon. "What magic do you know?"

"Some magic is my own. Some magic was taught to me by another," the dragon answered. His voice sounded fragile.

"Who?"

The shadow dragon shook his head. "My demon to bear, and none of your concern. The scale, however, is."

"This spell?"

"Give something of yourself, Silvara, as Malys gave something of herself." The shadow dragon's eyes focused on her elf form's hair. "That will do." He stretched out a talon and cut off a long hank.

Silvara caught the hair, held it, and for several interminable moments met the shadow dragon's gaze. Something unspoken passed between them. She tied the hair about Dhamon's leg, like a tourniquet, just above the scale.

"And something of yourself," Silvara added. She retreated to the pool of blood, cupped a handful, and poured it into the crack between the two halves of the scale.

The shadow dragon closed his eyes, and the cave air grew colder and darker. The silver globe of light faded. The dragon placed a claw over Dhamon's leg, the weight practically crushing it again. Silvara touched the claw, giving her magical strength to the shadow dragon, just as she could give it to Gilthanas, allowing him to increase the power of his spells whenever they were together.

Dhamon felt terribly cold. His teeth chattered, and he shivered uncontrollably. He was pinned to the frigid floor, against the bitter cold wall, anchored beneath the heavy, chilling touch of the dragon. The Red at the back of his mind spat and hissed, fighting to stay inside Dhamon's head. But her magic had been weakened when the scale was fractured.

The cold intensified and Dhamon's eyes drifted shut. He was in a forest, fighting Knights of Takhisis. Feril was there, her tangle of curls fanning away from her unblemished face. Palin and his son, Ulin, were there also, as was Gilthanas. With the glaive, Dhamon could not be bested. He cut down the knights one by one. The last he cradled in his arms, listening to the man's dying words. The knight, an agent of Malys, had tugged a red scale free from his bleeding chest and thrust it upon Dhamon's leg.

He drifted toward unconsciousness, the cold claiming him, the darkness welcoming and swallowing him.

* * * * *

It was dark outside. Gilthanas continued to pace. Silvara had been inside with the shadow dragon for more than an hour. He'd heard nothing—nothing but the wind and chimes that he tried unsuccessfully to decipher. Once he heard Dhamon moan and mention Feril's name, then Palin's, and finally Goldmoon's. The elf flinched at the last name.

"Gilthanas."

The elf turned to look into the cave, then quickly realized the voice came from in front of him. The air shimmered, and a hazy image of a black-cloaked man appeared, seemingly floating like a ghost. The image sharpened and a second one dressed in white joined it.

"The Master. Palin," the elf stated.

The image of Palin nodded, and Gilthanas noted that his sorcerer-friend looked especially tired. "The Master and I were searching for Feril and the others," Palin began. His voice sounded hollow and distant.

"As were we," Gilthanas added.

"We discovered they passed through Brukt and went into the mountains. But we have not found them," the Master interjected. "Not yet."

"We have found Dhamon," the elf said.

"Is he . . ." Palin's question hung unfinished in the air.

"I don't know how he is. Silvara's with him, inside, along with some mysterious black dragon. I think it's a shadow dragon. But I intend to find out what's going on."

Behind Gilthanas, a large black shadow slipped from the cave and dropped over the ledge, spreading its wings and disappearing into the deepening night.

* * * * *

Dhamon's eyes fluttered open. Silvara was in front of him. The shadow dragon was nowhere to be seen.

"The dragon said we could stay until morning. How are you feeling?"

"Cold."

She helped him to his feet. "There's some water over here.

Let's get you cleaned and wash that blood out of your clothes. Then let's get you dressed."

* * * * *

"Silvara?"

"You can come in."

Gilthanas stepped inside. The cave was lit softly by the glowing silver orb that continued to hover in the air.

Dhamon was at the back of the cave, dressed in tattered black leggings and the black leather tunic he'd worn under the Knights of Takhisis armor. He was holding the glaive. It felt warm in his grip, though no longer uncomfortable. He leaned it against the cave wall and put on his black cloak. The garments were still damp from the washing.

"Dhamon? It is Dhamon! Usha, look!" Blister rushed in, nearly knocking over a surprised Gilthanas. Usha Majere followed, stopping just ahead of the elf. The kender hurried toward the back of the cave, pausing only a moment to ogle the light globe and to edge around the pool of blood. "What happened to your hair? Your hair's black." She put her hands on her hips. "It used to be blond."

Dhamon glanced at the pool of the shadow dragon's blood that spread on the floor. His eyes were flecked with silver.

"What happened?" the kender persisted.

"The dragon's blood," Dhamon said finally. "The blood wouldn't wash out."

Silvara smiled a hello to Usha, joining Gilthanas at the cave entrance. She read the myriad questions on his face, and her eyes told him the answers would come later. "Did Palin send them?" she asked softly.

He nodded. "Do you think you can carry all of us?

"Of course." She grinned, her elven fingers folding over his. He squeezed her hand, drew her close. "Where are we going?" she asked.

"I don't know yet," he replied. "Palin will contact us in the morning. I suspect he'll first want us to head toward the coast of Khur, maybe search for Feril and Rig."

She tipped her head. "And then find the land of the Dimernesti?"

He nodded.

"There's a sea dragon there, you know," Silvara said. "A very big one."

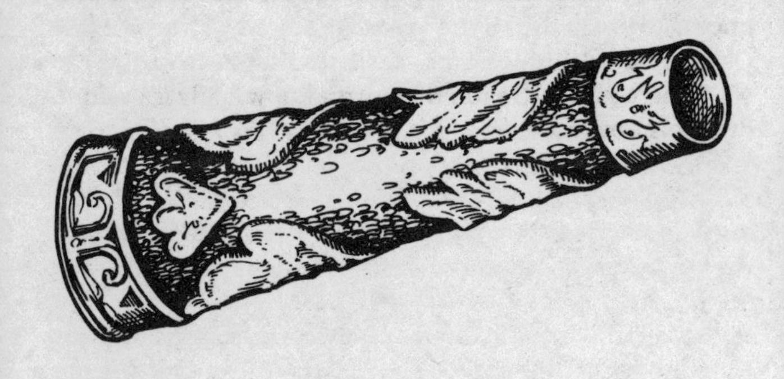

Chapter 12

Blue Intrigues

The blue dragon could not smell the giant scorpions, and this bothered him. Gale could hear them with little effort. Their mandibles were clacking together for no apparent reason, their feet skittering over the stone floor of Khellendros's lair. He could sense the magic in them, hear their heartbeats whenever he concentrated—the identical rhythms never varied.

The sentries obeyed Gale to the letter, giving him no cause to doubt them. But the blind dragon did not like them, and he especially did not like the fact that they were created by Fissure, the huldre.

When Khellendros became sole consort to the reborn

Malystryx—the new Takhisis as she dared call herself—when this lair and this realm became Gale's, the giant scorpions would die. Gale relished this thought, just as he eagerly anticipated banishing the dark faerie. If Khellendros managed to open the portal, the huldre would be left on Krynn—of this Gale had no doubt. But the faerie would not be left in the Northern Wastes. The lesser blue dragon would not tolerate the presence of a creature he could not bring himself to trust. Spawn would guard Gale's lair, loyal only to him.

The blue dragon stretched out on Khellendros's desert sand, the scorpions behind him at the lair's entrance, still clacking and skittering. Four barbarian women stood in front of him. Gale smelled the sweetness of the persistent evening rain, fouled by the scent of the wet animal skins the humans wore. Above all, the dragon smelled their fear. One human had actually soiled herself. Gale smiled grimly. He imagined what they looked like: muscular humans, skin baked from the sun, their hair a mass of tangles. In his mind's eye, he saw their eyes, wide and staring, afraid to blink or to look away from him. Their legs must be aching, Gale thought smugly. He had not permitted them to sit for hours.

He detested them.

The humans reminded him of Dhamon Grimwulf—the man who had stolen his sight, who in years past tricked the dragon into thinking the pair could be allies. Dhamon had deceived him into believing a human could befriend a dragon.

He hated them with all his soul.

Gale had been busy, raiding the smallest of the barbarian villages that dotted the Northern Wastes. He relied on his hearing to select those individuals with the strongest heartbeats, the youngest, healthiest, and most suitable to become spawn. These humans would make superior spawn to the ones Khellendros had captured. The Storm Over Krynn had decided a female body was necessary for Kitiara. The overlord could transform these women into spawn and select one of them for the ultimate transformation.

Gale intended to pay very close attention. When the Northern Wastes was his, and he was an overlord, he would create his own spawn army.

The blue wished Dhamon Grimwulf were here. What would Dhamon's fear smell like as he was turned into a spawn, as his human shell melted away to be replaced by scales? But first Gale wished he could blind Dhamon, stealing the most precious of his former partner's senses.

The rain fell harder as Gale studied the barbarian women. It was coming in driving sheets now. The wind had picked up, too, howling to announce the approach of the blue dragon overlord. Gale imagined the lightning flicker, smelled the trace of heat in the air. He knew almost precisely when the thunder would boom, coaxed by the violent change in the temperature of the air.

The thunder came quicker and louder, and now he could barely hear the flap of the overlord's wings.

"Khellendros," Gale said, nodding his head as the blue overlord landed.

The Storm Over Krynn studied the four humans. Their fear had grown measurably since the larger dragon arrived.

"You have done well," the overlord announced after several moments. "These are fine shells."

"Fine enough for your Kitiara?"

Khellendros narrowed his eyes, as his gaze drifted from one specimen to the next. Four women, all muscular, young and strong. "The females," the Storm said. "Prepare them."

Gale herded the four into the lair, the giant scorpions skittering out of his way. The barbarians' fear had reached a fever pitch, and the lesser blue dragon found the scent intoxicating.

Khellendros remained just beyond the entrance, concentrating on the storm, demanding the wind keen louder.

These women were the best human subjects he had seen. Kitiara would approve, he decided.

He stared into the driving rain, picturing her again. Blue-scaled armor, cloak falling about her ankles, black curls whipping in the wind, eyes wide and staring into his. He recalled what he felt when he first lost her: immeasurably empty, though in truth no emptier than he felt now. He'd been bitter, and had felt ineffectual, as he had not been able to prevent her death. With her passing, he had lacked the motivation to do anything important—except to keep his pledge to her.

He remembered what he felt like when he searched for her spirit beyond Krynn's portals. For centuries he had pursued her, though only a few decades passed on Krynn. Toward the end, he gave up hope, resigning himself to living as though incomplete. But as he turned toward Ansalon, passing through the Gray—the realm between realms where faeries lived and men's spirits drifted—he sensed her anew. Her spirit welcomed his, embracing it. The dragon made it clear he would return for her when he had a proper form. Her spirit seemed pleased.

"Soon," Khellendros hissed. "The time shall be soon." He closed his great eyes and felt the rain strike his scales. Energy from the lighting flowed into him.

Malystryx would not understand his ties to this human, he knew. She would be furious to discover that he harbored artifacts he intended to use to regain Kitiara. He had no plans to give the precious items to the Red for her transformation into godhood. Let the other overlords relinquish their treasures.

Malystryx would not understand that he could love a human more than he could possibly love her. The Storm had to admit that Malys's offer was tempting. To rule Krynn at her side as consort to a dragon goddess would mean untold power. But that power would not fill his emptiness.

"Ah, Kitiara," Khellendros breathed. An idea tickled the back of his mind. He nurtured it, as his jowls edged upward into a sly grin. "You would have made a better mate than Malys." He drew a claw through the sand, watched the rain quickly fill the depression. "Perhaps the gods dealt you a cruel hand, Kitiara uth Matar, in making you a human. But perhaps The Storm Over Krynn can deal you a more merciful one."

He cast his head toward the heavens and opened his maw, feeling the energy inside him build and then erupt into lightning. The sky thundered in response.

"I shall place your spirit in Malys's form, dear Kit. You shall ascend to godhood and be Krynn's sole goddess. And I shall rule at your side. Now it is all a matter of timing."

He turned and slipped into the darkness of his lair.

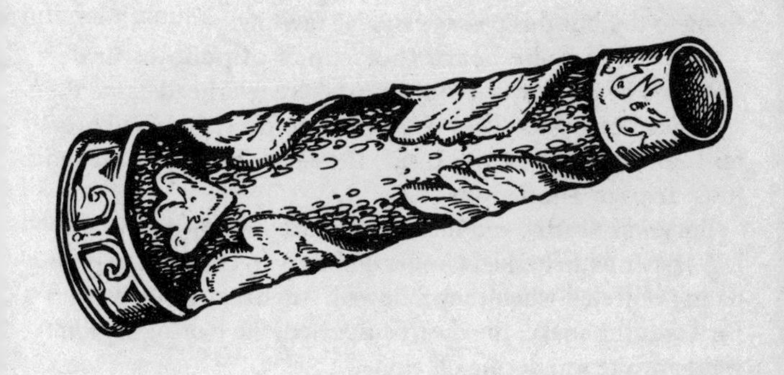

Chapter 13

Pitfalls and Revelations

Jasper was tired. His feet were sore, his stomach growling, and he was in desperate need of a bath. But he didn't complain—at least not so anyone could hear him. The boar in the village would have been delicious, he knew, and staying to help eat it wouldn't have slowed them down all that much. It would have let him spend a few more hours with Garta Stonejaw—that was the name of the village leader. It had been more than a year since he'd spent any time with another dwarf.

The dwarf ran his stubby fingers over the limestone walls. He liked the feel of the rock; he always had. As a youth he had learned to appreciate stone when he visited Thorbardin. He liked the smell of it.

He moved through the passage slowly, in part because he was enjoying his surroundings, but mostly because he was fatigued. He knew he probably should have rested with the others near the cave entrance; it would have been the sensible thing to do. But this passage was . . . inviting.

Behind him, he heard the crunch of pebbles under Groller's heavy boots. From somewhere overhead came the squeals of cave bats. They were music to his ears. It had been far too long since he was inside the earth. He sorely missed those trips to Thorbardin.

Fury was nearby, and the dwarf heard the wolf softly panting. Jasper hadn't asked Groller and Fury to come, though he hadn't objected when they followed. After that incident with Feril and the snake, the dwarf suspected, the half-ogre didn't want anyone wandering off alone.

The passage narrowed and twisted downward. They were now so far from the entrance that no light reached them. The dwarf's eyes picked through the blackness. He glanced over his shoulder. Groller was feeling his way, his long fingers running along the right-hand wall. His left hand dangled down to brush Fury's head.

Water ran in thin rivulets down the wall, hinting there was a mountain stream somewhere above them. Jasper brought the water to his lips and smiled. It tasted sweet. "We'll not go too much farther," the dwarf said to himself. "Just around this corner." His hands stretched out to touch the rock, which was much smoother here. Judging by the way the passage twisted and dipped, he guessed it had been formed long ago by an underground river.

"Lifetimes ago," he whispered. "Maybe before the dragons. I wonder how far down this tunnel goes? We should go back. Yes, we should go back. Wait. What's this?"

The passage forked, one side heading steeply upward and drastically narrowing, the other continuing to spiral down. The passage walls were shot through with minerals. Jasper noted the marks of picks along the wall. So this passage was mined, he thought. Maybe mined by dwarves. I wonder when.

A layer of slate cut through the rock. The dwarf chipped a piece away with his thumb and stuck the rock in his mouth to suck on.

"Just a little farther," Jasper said to Groller, tugging on the half-ogre's ragged tunic to let him know which direction he intended to take.

"You're going too fur," Groller said.

The dwarf felt for Groller's hands. He cupped them and brought them together in front of the half-ogre, then slowly drew them apart. It was the gesture Groller had taught him for *more.* Then he drew Groller's hands close together, the sign for small.

"Just a little more," Jasper said to himself.

Groller got the idea. "Not much mer, Jaz-pear. Furl be worried."

The dwarf moved ahead, prodding here and there with his fingers, trying to determine how long ago this passage was worked. "Hmm. The floor is slate here. Smooth. Gotta watch my step. A little slippery." He hoped Groller could tell that he was being more cautious. He reached to his belt, where the leather sack containing the Fist of E'li dangled. He didn't want the sack to come loose.

"No, no. We won't go too much farther. Just a little bit, a few more feet. Rig'll probably be worried, too. Just down this corridor, around this corner, and . . ." He heard the crack of the stone beneath his feet, then felt himself falling.

He let out a shout of surprise, lost on Groller. The wolf howled as Jasper fell. The dwarf's arms and legs churned, his fingers struck rock, and his knees were badly scraped. He shifted himself and dropped his right hand to his waist, holding the sack tight.

Then he slammed into a small shelf and lay still. He tried to stand, but sharp pains shot upward from his right leg. "Broken," he muttered. He ran his fingers along the wall, then started crawling. How far did I fall? he wondered. His head had begun to throb, too. Gotta find a way back, he thought. Then, once again, he felt the ground give way.

He fell, bouncing against the walls, and then striking the hard floor many feet below. Mercifully he lost consciousness.

Above, Groller had seen Jasper disappear. The wolf brushed by the half-ogre and peered over the ledge.

"Jaz-pear!" Groller called. "Jaz-pear!" He reached down to Fury, feeling for the wolf's head. "Jaz-pear!" Maybe Jasper couldn't talk, Groller thought. Maybe Jasper had hurt himself. "Fuhree. Find Jaz-pear."

Groller nudged the wolf forward and reached a hand up to either side of the tunnel, groping his way along. The half-ogre dropped to his knees and felt with his hands. He cursed himself for not arguing with the dwarf. Jasper was weak from the blow Dhamon had dealt him, tired from climbing the mountain. He should have rested, Groller thought. He's probably passed out from exhaustion.

Instead of the dwarf, however, Groller found a jagged hole in the floor. "Jaz-pear!" he called. The wolf pawed nervously at the edge of the hole.

"Jaz-pear fell," Groller said. He glanced over his shoulder, back the way they had come, debating whether he should retrace his steps and get the others to help.

But Jasper and he had been walking for quite some time and had covered a good bit of distance. If the dwarf was hurt—if he wasn't already dead—going back might lose precious minutes. Groller couldn't risk it.

"Fuhree! Go ged Rig!" Groller called. The wolf retreated down the tunnel, while Groller tested the edges of the hole. He found a secure hold where the slate was firm and lowered himself over the side. He swung his feet around. Nothing to stand on immediately below. He swung his legs in widening circles until they connected with something solid several feet away: another rock wall. Keeping one hand firmly on the ledge above, he began to feel about in the chamber below for another hold.

His fingers wedged themselves into a crack. Then he released his hand on the ledge above and repeated the process, finding cracks and working himself downward as a spider might. At last, his feet brushed against something to stand on, a narrow horizontal ledge that seemed sturdy enough to support his considerable weight.

Jasper must have fallen straight down, Groller guessed. And that's where the half-ogre was going, too, hand over hand, cautiously but at a steady pace. He suspected he must have descended at least ten feet by the time his groping hands found a wide crack in the wall. He braced himself against the sides and moved farther down.

It was eerie, seeing nothing, unable to hear anything, unable to tell for certain what distance he had descended. All he could smell was musty air and something foul—bat droppings he guessed, when his fingers encountered a sticky mass on an outcropping.

Groller found another ledge and paused a moment to catch his breath. His aching fingers were scratched and bleeding from the rocks. He glanced around, seeing nothing except darkness. Nothing but an eternal sheet of gray. Nothing but . . . his eyes peered down and saw a bit of lighter gray. "Jaz-pear?" The light gray area didn't move.

The ledge widened, angling down after a while, and he took this course. It seemed to drop steeply now, going right toward where he wanted to go. He hurried, moving quickly, almost falling a few times. His feet scrabbled across loose rock, and he fought to keep his balance.

He was getting closer now. Just another moment and then . . . The ledge beneath the half-ogre gave out and he fell. He bumped repeatedly against the cavern wall. The rock scratched his face and knees and arms, as he flailed madly to find a hold. From out of nowhere a spike of rock struck his chest.

Groller groaned and felt a greater impact: the floor of the cavern. His head struck hard, and the dark gray all around him turned to black.

* * * * *

The half-ogre stood in a farming village in Kern, not far from the shores of the Blood Sea. His wife was by his side, a plain-looking human woman to whom he was passionately devoted. He held her small hands in his large, calloused ones and looked over her shoulder toward their home, made of stone and thatch. They'd recently built it themselves, built it in the shade of a pair of large oaks. There was a vegetable garden behind the home, and by craning his neck, Groller could see the crops coming up—beans, carrots, and a row of turnips. Their daughter was playing at the side of the home, chattering to a cloth doll and straightening its flower-dotted dress. Groller intended to build an addition to the home, now that his wife was pregnant with their second child. The baby would be a boy, he hoped; someone to carry on the name of Dagmar.

Groller was accepted in this village—more than accepted, he was considered a vital part of the community. He was strong and able to help with the toughest of tasks. Amiable and caring, he was liked by everyone. The village suited him, and he was happy.

He was working in the garden late one morning when the green dragon came. The beast skimmed twice over the village, watching as the people shouted and ran for cover, like scurrying ants. Then the beast banked away, and Groller prayed it was gone, that it had found nothing to interest it in this small place. He grabbed his hoe and headed toward the house, where his wife and daughter were.

But the dragon hadn't left. It was merely biding its time, selecting the best vantage for its attack. It returned just as Groller reached the front door, flying low, jaws open, breathing a cloud of noxious sticky liquid that coated everything.

Those people still outside who were caught in the cloud began screaming. They grabbed their faces and pitched forward, twisting on the ground. Groller yelled to his wife and daughter to stay inside, and he darted out into the center of the village, hoe held high.

The dragon landed, its tail lashing out at the smallest homes, the ones made only of wood. Its wings whipped up the air and blew the thatch off buildings. Several people were snatched up in the creature's claws or smothered by its noxious, lethal breath.

The screams filled Groller's senses. They wouldn't stop; they rose to a fever pitch as the dragon continued its terrible assault. The half-ogre watched his friends die. He swung his hoe at the dragon, but it bounced off the thick green scales. The dragon glanced amusedly at him; or perhaps it was looking beyond him, not seeing him at all. Then it pushed off from the ground. The air from its wings knocked Groller over as well as the handful of others who'd dared to make a stand.

The dragon flew from one home to the next, crushing each building and pulling out the people. It ate most, swallowing them whole. Others it simply killed and tossed aside.

"Maethrel!" Groller shouted. His wife was in the doorway. Then suddenly there was no doorway, no home. The dragon had landed atop it, turning it to rubble, then vaulted away to demolish another building.

Groller's legs pumped over the ground, which was still sticky from the green dragon's caustic breath. His hands tore at the thatch and stones until his fingers were bloody from the effort, until they located Maethrel. She was dead, crushed. Groller's daughter too was slain.

Tears streamed down the half-ogre's face, and he screamed

in sadness and rage. His screams mixed with the cries of those few still alive. Only half-aware of his actions, he grabbed his hoe and ran toward the dragon, crying with anger, trying to get the dragon's attention. "Fight me!" he yelled. But the dragon seemed uninterested. It was tearing at the building that used to be the village hall.

The air was saturated with the cries of the dying, the screams of the few survivors. The cries rose louder than the dragon's snarls, than the whoosh of its horrible breath. They were all Groller heard.

"Make the noise stop," Groller prayed as he raced toward the dragon. "Please make the screams stop."

He was only a few yards away from the dragon when it lifted from the ground again and banked toward the east. It flew out over the Blood Sea, finished with the village. All around Groller, the moans continued.

He fell to his knees, dropping the hoe and cupping his bloody hands over his ears. "Please make it stop."

Out of the corner of his eye he saw a tiny man, gnome-sized and golden, with golden eyes. The man was watching him. Then the creature nodded to him, and suddenly the screaming stopped.

Groller looked around. The little gold man was gone, as were all the noises. He stumbled back toward his ruined home, glancing at the survivors, wondering why a handful had been spared. They were talking to him, yelling at him perhaps. He saw their mouths move, tears streaming from their eyes, but he could no longer hear them.

He couldn't hear anything.

"Maethrel," he cried. He couldn't even hear his own words. He sat beside her, placing his bloody hand over her heart, and wept.

He buried his wife and daughter that night and slept by their graves.

He awoke to the sensation of something rough and wet

running across his cheek. He lay on his back, blinking. He thought he saw the small gold-skinned man again. The one with the golden eyes. He blinked again, and reached his fingers up, entwining them in Fury's long red hair. No little man. Only the wolf. Somehow the wolf was with him. Somehow the beast had found a way down into the cavern. Fury continued to lap at Groller's face.

"Rig?" Groller asked, hoping the wolf had somehow brought the mariner down too. "Furl? Fee-oh-na?"

Groller tried to push himself up, but his legs wouldn't move and his waist wouldn't bend. Panic rose in his chest. He couldn't *feel* his legs. He struggled to move his arms, his long fingers prodding the back of his head. Blood, and a growing bump. He gingerly felt the rest of his body. His chest felt on fire and his arms and head ached. He touched his thighs. His sensitive fingertips registered the feel of the fabric, the warm wetness of the blood, the give of the flesh. But his legs felt nothing.

"Fuhree?"

Groller turned his head this way and that, trying to see through the darkness. Where were Rig and Feril? He glanced about again, his eyes coming to rest on the lumpy form of the dwarf. "Jaz-pear!" Groller called. "Jaz-pear!" Shouting hurt his chest.

Groller couldn't tell if the dwarf was alive. The grayness was unmoving. His own chest hurt, and breathing was painful. "Maethrel," Groller breathed. Perhaps he would see his wife again when he died. That would not be so bad. But he didn't want to die yet. Rig and Palin needed his help against the dragons. "Jaz-pear!"

* * * * *

Jasper heard his name. It was a whisper, hard to make out, indistinct. Goldmoon? he thought. It sounded as if she were calling to him from a distance. It was as if he was on the Walk on Schallsea Island and she was in the Citadel of Light, calling him to come to another lesson. Her body was in the Citadel of Light, he knew, in a crystal coffin that magically preserved her so the mystic missionaries could travel to the island and bid their final farewells.

"Jasper," he thought he heard Goldmoon call again. If it *is* her, he thought, I'm dead.

"Jasper." Definitely Goldmoon's voice, he decided. The dwarf searched for her face, but all he could see was the darkness. "Jasper. Have faith."

He imagined her, full of life, gold hair tumbling to her shoulders and spilling down her back. Her eyes were pensive and expressive. When he'd given serious thought to going to Thorbardin before the dwarves sealed the kingdom, those eyes had talked him out of it. Goldmoon wanted him to stay with her, to learn more of the healing arts and of mysticism. He hadn't been able to say no to those eyes.

The shifting bands of gray became paler, and tendrils of hair framed a smooth face. "Goldmoon," Jasper whispered. "It is you."

"Jaz-pear!"

The dwarf's eyes fluttered open. He blinked, focused on a lighter patch close to the floor of the cave. No Goldmoon. Only his imagination.

"Jaz-pear!"

"Groller?"

The half-ogre saw Jasper move. "Jaz-pear! Wuz fraid you dead."

"I thought I was too, my friend. In fact . . ." Jasper let his words trail off. "I might as well be talking to myself. You can't hear me. Ouch!" The dwarf tried to pull himself closer to Groller, but his broken leg hurt too much. He saw the half-ogre lying next to him, a trickle of blood on his forehead. Groller must have fallen, too. "We'll wait for Rig," the dwarf decided. "Rig'll miss us, eventually find us. He'll get us out of here."

"Jaz-pear. Hurd bad."

Yes, I am, the dwarf answered to himself. My leg's broken. I'm one big bruise. I'm surprised I'm alive.

"Jaz-pear. I cand feel by legs. Cand move."

The dwarf cursed himself for not thinking first of Groller. Goldmoon would have never thought of herself first.

He gritted his teeth and inched forward, relying on his good leg. The floor was slick with guano. He gasped. The air was foul, stale and heavy. The dwarf gagged on the scent, felt what little he'd eaten today rise into his throat.

"Almost there," he said. "A few more yards." Might as well be miles, he thought. And once I get to Groller—if I can get to Groller—I won't be able to do anything for him. "Rig! Feril! Fiona!" the dwarf bellowed. He heard his voice echo off the walls, paused and listened for a response. After several heartbeats the echos died. The dwarf sighed and fought to blot out the pain in his leg and chest.

He wasn't sure how long it took him to reach Groller, maybe several minutes, though it felt like hours. His chest burned from his fall and from the exertion.

"Jaz-pear," the half-ogre said when he felt the dwarf's stubby fingers. "Jaz-pear all ride?"

Jasper's fingers found Groller's hand. "No," the dwarf coughed. "I'm not all right." The dwarf grimaced. He coughed again and tasted blood in his mouth, a bad sign. Perhaps his good lung had been punctured as well.

Groller peered through the darkness, making out the dwarf's face. "Jaz-pear, fix by legs."

The dwarf shook his head. My faith isn't so strong anymore, my friend, he said to himself. He knew the words were lost on Groller. I couldn't heal Goldmoon. I couldn't even heal myself after Dhamon struck me. The mystics at the Citadel couldn't heal me either—my lack of faith prevented them. *I can't heal.* We'll have to wait for Rig.

"Jaz-pear, fix," Groller repeated. "Fix by legs."

The dwarf sighed and began to carefully prod Groller.

"Feel dat," the half-ogre said. "Hurts bad. Real bad. Dat. Feel dat."

Groller's words stopped when the dwarf put pressure on his hips. Back's broken, Jasper sadly noted. And several ribs. The half-ogre wouldn't be leaving the cave. Even if Rig finds us, the dwarf thought, he's not going to be able to get Groller out of here alive.

The dwarf coughed again, feeling blood trickle over his bottom lip. "Rig might not get here in time anyway," he whispered. "I think I'm dying. But I have the Fist. Rig and Palin need the Fist."

"Fix by legs," Groller encouraged.

Jasper closed his eyes. The dwarf had only a little energy left, and it was quickly dissipating. The fall had left him all but incapacitated. The blood felt thick in his mouth.

"Code," Groller whispered. "So code down here." The half-ogre was shivering.

"Concentrate," Jasper admonished himself. "Not for me. For Groller. Reorx, Mishakal, please." He tried to focus, as Goldmoon had taught him, reaching inside himself for the inner strength she claimed everyone possessed. She had taught him how to apply that strength, to call it up and channel it into healing magic and other mystical spells. He looked for it now. But he couldn't find it. The energy was gone.

"Jasper." It was Goldmoon's voice, the dwarf was certain of it.

"Goldmoon?"

"You must have faith."

The dwarf smiled weakly. Her voice was real—he hadn't imagined hearing her. Just as she, no doubt had really been speaking to Riverwind for all those years when she stood by the window in the Citadel of Light and carried on what the dwarf had thought was a one-sided conversation. Goldmoon hadn't realized anyone was listening to her. Probably anyone else would have considered her mad. But Jasper had listened and wondered.

Maybe I'm the one who is mad now, he mused, to hear voices, to think I might be able to heal. But I have to try.

"Have faith."

"Goldmoon." He found it then, that tiny spark of inner strength buried deep inside him. It felt warm, and the more he concentrated on it, the brighter the spark glowed. "Faith," he whispered. "Goldmoon, I must have faith again."

A wave of warmth radiated down his arms to his fingers. He placed his hands on the half-ogre's waist, working around until he touched the small of his back. The warmth felt invigorating. His fingers traveled up to Groller's chest, to his neck and down his arms.

Jasper felt the half-ogre moving and used his hands to still him. "I'm not finished yet," the dwarf said. His fingers found the gashes and bump on Groller's head. He touched cuts and scrapes, raised spots where bruises were forming. Then his hands ranged down the half-ogre's legs, which were twisted at odd angles.

"Shouldn't have followed me in the cave," Jasper grunted. The heat from his hands radiated out, mending the broken bones.

"Jaz-pear, you're good healer," Groller stated. "Feel by legs now. Can move now."

Jasper's hands tried to hold the half-ogre down, but Groller was too strong, and he pushed himself up into a sitting position.

"Jaz-pear, you're hurd," he observed.

"Have faith," Goldmoon's spirit whispered.

"Jaz-pear, fix y'zelf."

"I'm trying, my friend." The dwarf continued to concentrate on the warmth, coaxing it to flow. "Trying."

"Faith," Goldmoon repeated.

The warmth lingered in his chest and in his leg, spreading

to his own back and dancing along his ribs. He felt as if he was floating, growing stronger. And yet at the same time he knew he was becoming weaker, as the magic sapped the last bit of his physical strength. His leg and chest tingled. The sensation reminded him of his studies with Goldmoon, and previous occasions in which he had healed himself from minor tumbles.

"Your faith is strong."

From nearby he heard Groller's nasal words. "Jaz-pear, be bedder." High above, he heard the soft squeals of bats, as he heard his heart beating stronger and heard Goldmoon's voice drift to nothingness.

"Tired," he murmured, as the warmth receded, the spell ended, and the last of his energy was sapped.

"Jaz-pear, you're good healer," Groller repeated.

The dwarf felt himself being lifted. "I'm fine," he insisted. "I can walk." The dwarf's fingers fluttered to the sack at his belt, as Groller shufled along, carrying him.

Somehow the half-ogre found his way to a wall. Groller had looked around for the wolf, and found no trace. He wanted to know how Fury had gotten down here—no doubt it was an easier path than he had taken. Where had the wolf gone?

Groller tucked Jasper under one arm, felt along the wall, and began to use the other arm to climb.

Where were Rig and Feril, Fiona? Groller wondered. He'd sent the wolf to get them. Can't wait for them, he decided. Can't stay down here. Don't want to stay down here. It stinks.

Groller twisted his fingers and feet into cracks, steadied himself, and then reached up with his hand. The going was slow, but Groller was persistent. He slid a few times but made progress and eventually reached a support ledge.

This one was narrower than the one he'd found when he was trying to climb down to Jasper. Groller inched his way along, wedging the fingers of his free hand into cracks here and there. Jasper tugged on the half-ogre's tunic. They were near the opening through which the dwarf had fallen. Groller squinted in the darkness. Jasper patted his shoulder to let him know they had made it.

Now came the hard part. The half-ogre was going to need both of his hands. He balanced himself carefully on the ledge. "Jaz-pear, hode tight," he said. The dwarf snaked his arms around Groller's neck. The half-ogre found another handhold.

He climbed like a spider again, hanging from a rocky wall that tilted at a slant toward the opening. Groller's fingers ached from the rocks, and from supporting the weight of the dwarf. He scrabbled for holds and swung his legs about desperately.

The frantic movements upset the bats nearby. Their squeals filled the air. Groller couldn't hear the bats, but he felt them. The air was stirred by their wings, and a few of them struck him with their movements.

Finally Groller's legs found a deep crack, and he was able to continue his climb. A few moments more, and the two were lying in the tunnel.

Jasper was the first to move, but then Groller took the lead again, using his sore fingers to guide them along the passage. He spotted Fury ahead of him in the tunnel. The beast pawed at the ground and then whirled away. The wolf was apparently alone and had not brought Rig or Feril with him. Perhaps something had happened to them, Groller thought. The half-ogre hurried along, twisting his head to make sure Jasper was following.

The passage coiled like a snake, just as he remembered, and he saw the wolf pawing at the ground again. Groller started to run. Fury turned the corner and disappeared from sight.

Groller sped around an outcropping and into the mouth of the cave. It was dark. For a moment the half-ogre suspected he'd made a wrong turn and found a different chamber. But then his eyes saw gray patches.

Jasper practically barreled into him, as the dwarf rounded the corner.

"Several hours, at least." Jasper recognized Feril's voice. "I'm exhausted," she said. "We're stuck here until I can get my strength back—unless you can find another way out of this cave."

"It's darker than night in here." That was Rig's voice. "Like a tomb."

Jasper heard other sounds, an odd clicking-clacking that came from beyond the chamber.

"I wonder where Groller and Jasper are? They should have been back by now."

"We are back, Fiona," Jasper said.

"And just where have you two been?" Rig demanded. "We've been fighting spawn. They're still out there. Feril sealed the cave off to keep 'em from killing us."

"Whew! What's that smell?" Fiona asked.

"Uh, bat droppings," Jasper answered.

The dwarf tugged on Groller's tunic, and the half-ogre followed him into the large chamber. Groller headed toward Feril and the wolf. Fury's golden eyes greeted the half-ogre. Groller stared at them.

"Bat droppings. You find bat droppings, and we find spawn," Rig said. "Where were you?"

"Exploring," the dwarf said. Exploring this cave and myself, he silently added. Finding my faith. He took a deep breath and walked toward Rig. His lungs felt healed—both of them—and his faith was restored. A smile spread wide across his face. "Groller and I just did a little exploring."

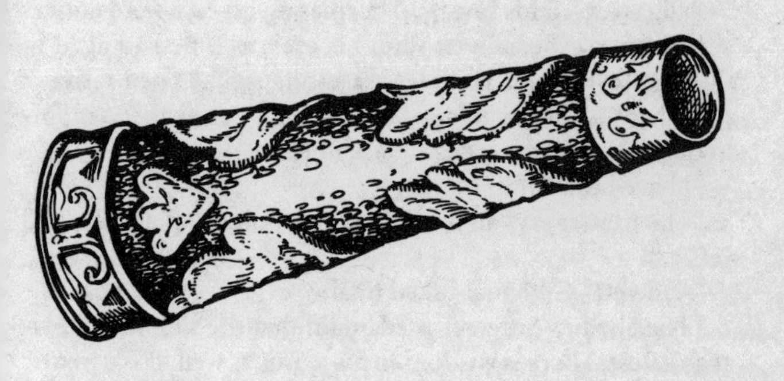

Chapter 14

Sunken Ships

"I've been exploring the possibilities surrounding Takhisis's return," Palin said. "Something . . . bothers me." The anxiety in his voice was evident as he stared into the water-filled crystal bowl. Gilthanas's face stared back at him through the widening ripples.

"Bothers you more than the dragon goddess coming back?"

"No," Palin said with a laugh. "There is little worse that could befall Krynn. It is where she will return that is bothering me. If we guess wrong—"

"No one will be there to stop her," Gilthanas finished. "If we guess right, we might not have the power to stop her anyway."

"But we must guess right if we are to have the slightest chance."

"Agreed. What are the options?" The elf's voice sounded soft and hollow.

Palin steepled his fingers. The lines on his face were noticeably deeper, especially around his eyes, as if he had aged in the past few weeks. He released a long sigh. "The Master is confident Takhisis will appear somewhere near the Window to the Stars. It is an ancient place in Khur."

"I have heard of it."

"The Master says all his divinations point to that area, and yet . . ."

"And yet?" Gilthanas asked finally.

"The Shadow Sorcerer is adamant that the site will be Ariakan's Rest. There is wisdom in his words as well. It is a mystic place for the Knights of Takhisis."

"Takhisis appeared there before," Gilthanas said.

Palin nodded. "My associates refuse to come to an agreement. Neither will consider the other's position. They have almost come to blows over the matter."

"Our forces are too small to split up," the elf said.

"And the two places are far apart."

"Are you alone?"

Palin nodded.

"Then tell me, whose counsel do you trust more? Perhaps that should make the decision."

Palin shook his head, shrugging his stooped shoulders. "I don't know." The Master was the personification of the Tower of Wayreth, he thought, and the embodiment of high sorcery in the form of a man. He could wear the face of any sorcerer he chose. The Shadow Sorcerer was wrapped in mystery, as well. Perhaps he was a man, perhaps a woman. Palin had come to rely on both mages heavily during the past several years. But he did not trust one above the other.

"How can I help?" asked Gilthanas.

"You've got magic on your side," Palin began, "and a dragon. If Silvara is willing, the two of you could explore the area around the Window after you've taken Usha and Blister to the coast, to Ak-Khurman. Check for signs and see if you notice anything unusual."

"Khur's a big country. It will take time."

"It will take the others time to obtain the crown. With the Shadow Sorcerer's help, the Master was finally able to contact Feril and Rig. It took some doing. They had sealed themselves in a cave, several miles away, to avoid dozens of spawn. The Master told them you found Dhamon, and they decided to head to Ak-Khurman."

Palin sighed. "And I cannot risk destroying any more of the arcane items here to power a spell to send them to Ak-Khurman."

"In Ak-Khurman—" Gilthanas began.

"Feril and the others will meet Blister and Usha there. Then they'll all head to Dimernesti. Usha has plenty of steel with her to rent a ship."

"And Dhamon. . . ?"

"What of him?" asked Palin.

Gilthanas let the question hang in the air. Quickly he explained how the mysterious shadow dragon and Silvara had broken Dhamon's link with Malys, and how the former Knight of Takhisis no longer appeared to be a threat.

"Do you trust Dhamon?" the sorcerer asked in a cracked voice.

"I trust Silvara."

Palin cocked his head. "If there is no threat, he could be helpful. Still . . ."

"Your wife and Blister are capable and, I believe, safe in his company. But I'll take the glaive away from Dhamon to be sure. He's *different,* Palin, changed. But I suppose anyone would be after what he went through. Silvara claims he is completely out from under the red dragon's control.

And, as I said, I do trust Silvara."

"Then he can accompany Usha and Blister." Palin seemed to relax a little. "We will deal with the matter of Goldmoon's death later. Be careful on your journey, my friend. The wilds of Khur are dangerous."

"I have learned to be careful. And you?"

"I will go to Ariakan's Rest."

"What signs should we look for?"

Palin pursed his lips. "Dragons gathering," he answered finally. "Wherever Takhisis intends to arrive, there will be other dragons and their minions. And there will be Knights of Takhisis."

* * * * *

"Look, there's some more knights!" Blister waggled her gnarled fingers toward the marketplace, indicating a trio of Legion of Steel knights who were questioning a merchant.

"Keep your voice down," Dhamon urged. He drew Usha and Blister under an awning. "We don't want to raise their suspicions. We've done nothing wrong, nothing to cause them to bother us," he whispered. "In fact, they might be able to help us. But just in case . . ."

The knights moved on to another merchant and his shoppers, one stall closer.

"Let's get to the harbor by another route, shall we? Just in case," Usha suggested. "The Legion of Steel is honorable. It has protected the people in this town. But—"

"Just in case," Blister finished.

The trio ducked around a corner and followed the dusty streets that wound between homes and scattered businesses. The buildings were large, some three stories tall, and made of stone with tiled roofs. Wood seemed to be scarce; even building signs and shutters were made of slate. A new home was being built on a narrow lot between two older structures. Since they'd arrived at Ak-Khurman, they'd noticed several new constructions.

"Doesn't seem to be that many people," Blister said. "Certainly not for all these buildings."

"Anticipation," Usha said. "This is one of the largest cities in Khur, and it's the only one with a safe port."

"So they figure more people will move here?" the kender asked.

Usha nodded. "Khur barbarians loyal to Neraka are driving people from the plains. The people have nowhere else to go. Nowhere safe."

"And I thought the dragons were the only ones who did nasty things like that. Hey, Dhamon, when you were . . . you know . . . working for Malystryx, did she make you do nasty things?"

A tense look crossed Dhamon's face. He had adroitly avoided talking about the time he spent under the dragon's control, except to satisfy Gilthanas's curiosity and win some measure of trust from the elf and Silvara. He lengthened his stride, and Usha and Blister had to hurry to keep up.

"Touchy," the kender whispered to Usha. "He didn't used to be so touchy, not when he had blond hair."

The trio rounded another corner. The top of a lighthouse poked above the buildings that sprawled in front of them. Made of stone, it stretched high into the early morning sky. Khurman Tor, the lighthouse was called. The city had grown up around it. The local people had walled the city so barbarians and rampaging Neraka tribesmen would leave them alone, and they had stationed lookouts in the lighthouse to guard against threats coming from sea or land. The wall that swept around the city and down to the sea was twenty feet high and solid, with iron-bound gates manned by the Legion of Steel. Knights also walked these streets, chatting with merchants and passersby, questioning people they didn't know.

Usha knew to expect the knights. Palin had researched the city before suggesting they meet Rig there and hire a ship. It wasn't the site closest to the underwater realm of the sea elves, but it was the closest port not in dragon territory, and it offered a deep harbor.

They headed toward the harbor, selecting a street that cut through a small merchant district filled with butchers, bakers, and fishmongers. It was all Usha and Dhamon could do to keep Blister from darting into each shop to investigate inviting odors.

"Cinnamon," the kender said, sniffing at a window. "Raisins, too. Apples."

"We'll have time for something to eat later," Usha said. "I want to make sure we have enough steel to rent a good ship first."

The kender cheerfully acquiesced. "And maybe we'll even have enough left over to get Dhamon something else to wear. Something black to go with his hair. Or something a little brighter. Hey, Dhamon, did the red dragon ever—"

Dhamon scowled and walked faster still. Usha and Blister had to run to keep up with him.

The sounds of gulls crying and water gently lapping against the docks greeted them as they hurried down an especially dusty street that opened into Ak-Khurman's bustling wharf district. The hot breeze that blew in from the ocean washed over them and loosed graying hair from Blister's braid.

A small fortress stood on the northeastern side of the waterfront. Several Legion of Steel knights milled around outside it. There were more knights on the docks. Despite the number of people roaming the waterfront, there appeared to be no sailors or ship captains. Indeed, there were no ships moored to the docks.

But there was evidence of vessels. Usha noticed them first. Jutting barely above the waterline were several broken masts. Bits of mastheads and rigging floated in the shallow water, caught in the roots of the willows that edged the bank. Blister counted at least twelve sunken ships.

Farther out in the harbor were anchored a half-dozen

ships, among them two impressive galleys. Each flew a black flag with the death lily emblem.

"Dark Knights," Usha whispered. "Palin said the Legion of Steel ran this town."

"They do," Dhamon said solemnly. "But the Knights of Takhisis have blockaded it. That's probably why the Legion of Steel knights were questioning so many people. They are looking for Dark Knight spies or sympathizers."

"Palin couldn't have known," Usha continued. "He would've sent us somewhere else."

"Skulls and crossbones would make me feel a whole lot better than death lilies." Blister wrinkled her nose. "Rig was a pirate once, and I bet we could deal with pirates better than with those black knights. Wonder if the knights sunk the ships?"

"I'd bet on it," Dhamon said grimly.

The kender put her hands on her hips and pouted. "Now how're we gonna get to Dimernesti? Swim?"

* * * * *

There wasn't a table large enough for all of them in The Flowing Flagon, so Rig and Fiona sat alone at a small table against the back wall. She had donned the rest of her armor, and presented a sharp contrast to the mariner, whose clothes hung on him in tatters.

Jasper, Groller, and Feril hugged one side of the long table near the window, all of them looking like ragged beggars. Blister, Usha, and Dhamon, dressed in new clothes, occupied the other side, picking at the food on their plates—their second meal of the day—while their companions made short work of what was in front of them.

When the companions were reunited on the waterfront just after sunset, Rig had slammed his fist into the side of Dhamon's face. It took Jasper and Usha to keep him from drawing a dagger. The mariner refused to listen to Dhamon's explanations about being under Malystryx's control. However, he paid a little more attention to Blister and Usha as they relayed what Silvara told them about Dhamon and the shadow dragon. As he ate his mutton, Rig glared at Dhamon and mouthed "later."

The others guardedly welcomed Dhamon. Jasper was the friendliest. He looked up from his meal and offered Dhamon a smile.

"I don't like the way people are lookin' at us, Fiona," Rig said. "See 'em? Just staring—at us and at them." He pointed to Dhamon's end of the table.

"Maybe it's the clothes some of us are wearing," Fiona suggested. "This place doesn't cater to the most well-to-do Ak-Khurmans, but on the other hand, the rest of the customers are far better dressed than you and—"

"My clothes?" Rig snorted.

"Or maybe it's mine." Her armor gleamed in the light of the oil lamp on the wall.

"Maybe they think I'm your prisoner."

"So I've captured you, eh?" She smiled slyly. "Maybe, Rig Mer-Krel, they're looking at us just because they're nosy. We're outsiders here. Obvious strangers. These days you can't trust strangers."

Rig's eyes narrowed, and he made sure Dhamon caught his look. "Sometimes you can't trust people you thought were your friends."

Fiona ran her fingers up his arm, drawing his attention to her, for a few moments, at least. Then Rig glanced around the room again.

"Strangers. Yeah, that's part of the attraction, I suppose. But look at the way that fellow is staring at Dhamon." Rig pointed to a dark-clad man who hadn't touched his mug of ale.

"You're imagining things. Besides, you're staring at Dhamon, too. He's a striking man." Fiona finished the last of her honey bread. "At least Dhamon has been cured of the Red's influence."

"Cured," Rig chuckled, as he took Fiona's hands. His eyes still rested on Dhamon. "Being a dragon's pawn isn't a disease. How are you cured of it?"

"You must give him a chance," she returned. The young Solamnic reached her fingers to his face, turned it to meet her gaze. "Dhamon didn't have to involve himself in this, you know. He didn't have to come here with Usha and Blister. He could have gone his own way."

"If Gilthanas would've let him—which I doubt. Who knows? That wouldn't have been so bad, would it?" Rig snapped. "We don't need him." His expression softened as he stared into Fiona's eyes. "And what about you? After we get the crown will you be going your own way, back to your order?"

"There will still be the dragons to deal with. There will be Takhisis."

"And then?"

She smiled. "You could come back with me. You'd be welcomed in the Solamnic knights, Rig Mer-Krel. You're an honorable man."

He cringed at the word "honorable." "I always considered myself a rogue."

"An honorable rogue then." She leaned over the table and kissed him. "Would you consider it?"

"Me, a knight?" Rig released her hands, brought his fingers up to touch her smooth cheek. "I don't think so, Fiona. All that armor—it's just not me."

"Think about it," she insisted.

* * * * *

Dhamon was watching Feril, outwardly oblivious to Blister's continuing questions about where he'd been since Schallsea, what the dragon had made him do, and what it was like to have a dragon in control of your body, forcing you to do things you didn't want to do. The Kagonesti glanced Dhamon's way, then quickly returned to studying a whorl in the tabletop. Groller offered Dhamon a sympathetic smile.

"Feril needs time," Blister said. "I'm sure everything will be back to normal in a little while. She's just gotta get used to you again, you know. Maybe if your hair was blond and you were wearing something that wasn't black and gray. Besides—"

"Blister!" Jasper's stern gaze stopped the kender's prattle.

For a moment. "Feril just needs time," Blister repeated.

"And we need a ship," Dhamon said. He took a long swallow from his mug of cider and leaned back in his chair.

"I don't think the Knights of Takhisis are going to let us rent one of theirs," Jasper said. "No matter how much steel we offer." The dwarf stuffed the last of his roast beef into his mouth, then waved for dessert. "We'd better find another city with a port."

"It's Ak-Khurman or nothing," Usha said. "Palin believes Takhisis's arrival will happen within the next two months. It would take us too long to travel somewhere else."

"So we go wait for Takhisis without the crown," Jasper said.

"No. We've come to far to give up on that," said Fiona. The Solamnic knight had walked over and was leaning over Dhamon's shoulder.

"So let's steal a ship," Rig said, joining them.

Blister beamed. "A great idea. The Knights of Takhisis have so many out there anyway, they're not going to miss one little boat."

"A big boat," Rig corrected. "We need a ship where we're going."

"When do we steal it?" Blister's tone grew more excited. "I've never stolen a boat before. Sounds like it'll be exciting. And then we can use Usha's steel to buy you and Feril and Jasper and Fury some clothes. Fiona, too, in case she wants to wear something instead of armor. Maybe another new dress for me. We'll save money by stealing a boat . . . er, ship. With what we save, we can buy new clothes and . . ." She wrinkled her nose at what was left of Rig's attire, and waggled her fingers toward Jasper, Groller, and Feril. "Clothes for everybody. Baths, too. So, anyway, when are we gonna do all this?"

"Tonight. Just before dawn." Rig lowered his voice. "When it's real dark." The mariner caught the dwarf and half-ogre looking at him and made a few gestures with his hands and fingers in the silent language Groller had taught him.

"Anyone figure out why they're blockading the harbor?" the kender asked.

Fiona shook her head. "The barkeep says the knights haven't given anyone a clue. They won't even talk to the city officials. They just came in force almost a month ago and destroyed the ships along the docks. They even wrecked the fishing boats and killed a couple of the captains who protested and the Legion of Steel knights who tried to fight them. Ever since, they've been preventing anyone from entering or leaving the harbor."

"Except us," Blister said. "We'll get out. After we get a boat."

"A ship," Rig corrected again. "Feril, come with me. And you"—he gestured at Dhamon—"Time to take a stroll and see what's available."

"What about me?" Blister pushed out her bottom lip. "What about Fiona and Usha?"

"I need you to come with me," Jasper said to the kender, as he stuffed a piece of apple pie into his mouth and nodded at the mariner. He had understood Rig's earlier gestures and knew what was needed. "Groller, too, and Fury. Hmm . . . Fiona and Usha better stay here and wait for us. We've got to get some . . . uh supplies. Then we'll all meet by the docks in an hour or so. By that huge willow tree."

The kender was quick out of her seat, beating Groller to the door. "Where we gonna buy supplies? Everything but the taverns is closed." The dwarf nudged the kender outside, but the others could hear her shrill voice through the open doorway. "What kind of supplies? Huh?"

Feril glanced warily back and forth between Rig and Dhamon.

"Feril, I need your elven eyes," the mariner told her. "Your vision is better than ours. I don't want to get too close to the docks, not just yet. But I need you to get a good look at the harbor. Tell us how many knights you see on those ships and what kind of defenses the ships have." To Dhamon, Rig said coldly, "And I want you along, traitor, because I don't trust you out of my sight. Fiona, Jasper's right. You should stay here." He pointed to her armor. "You stick out a little too much."

Fiona and Usha were left alone at the table. Usha toyed with her half-eaten piece of pie.

The Solamnic knight finally broke the silence. "Why did you come here, Usha? Blister I can understand. This is all a grand adventure to the kender. But why you? Why didn't you stay with Palin?"

Usha speared a slice of apple on her fork, seeming to study it, then put it in her mouth. After several moments she answered. "It's the Fist of E'li."

"The scepter Jasper's carrying?"

"I'm trying to remember something the elves told me about it."

"And you think you can remember better here than with Palin in the tower?"

"I certainly can't remember any worse."

The knight's expression was puzzled. Then it turned alert as she rose from her seat.

"Don't like my company?" Usha asked.

"No, it's that man who just left. He didn't touch his drink. I just saw him follow Feril past the window." Fiona stepped away from the table. "Something's prickling at my neck now. I've a bad feeling about that man." She turned away from Usha and hurried out into the night.

Usha dropped several silver pieces on the table and followed her.

* * * * *

Outside, Dhamon blended in with the night, his dark clothes and black hair allowing him to melt into the shadows. Feril walked at his side, not as well concealed, with Rig several paces ahead of them.

"I don't know what I'm feeling," she said softly. "About you. I thought I loved you. Maybe I still do. I don't know. I . . ."

"I understand. I killed Goldmoon. And that changed everything."

"It was the dragon. I know that. But it's hard . . ."

"*I* killed Goldmoon," he repeated. "And I almost killed Jasper, Rig, and you."

"Dhamon, why did you join with us again?"

He was silent for a moment. "I want revenge," he whispered. "And I can't get it alone. Every night, all I see is the shock on Goldmoon's face, the blood on my hands. I want the red dragon to pay. And I'll do whatever I can to ensure that happens. Maybe it's the only way I can redeem myself. Maybe it's the only way I can have peace—if I deserve peace." He took her hand, and peered through the darkness to study her face. She dropped her gaze to the street without reply. He released her hand.

"*Peace.*" Rig softly spat the word from in front of them. "You deserve a lot less than peace." The journey to the harbor continued in uncomfortable silence.

Out in the bay the lights on the prows of all the knights' ships reflected on the water like giant fireflies. A light fog was stealing in to wrap around the harbor. The trio stood silent for several minutes, watching and waiting.

"There's a dozen ships out there," Rig muttered finally. "We ought to be able to figure out how to steal one."

"Seven," Feril softly corrected. "There are seven ships."

"Seven, a dozen, a hundred, a thousand. What difference does it make? There're none close enough to the docks where we could reach them without a long swim."

"Then we'll just have to go for a long swim." It was Fiona's voice.

She and Usha ducked under some willow leaves. Between them they held a dark-clad man, a wad of cloth stuffed in his mouth.

"He was following you," Fiona said, as she pinned the man against the tree trunk. "He was watching us in the tavern. I think he was listening to our conversation, too. At first I thought he was just curious, that he didn't have anything better to do than ogle a tableful of strangers. But then I got this twitchy feeling."

Rig stepped closer, tugged a dagger from his belt and held it up to the man's throat. With his other hand, the mariner loosened the gag.

"You scream, you die." It was dark under the willow, but just enough light spilled down from the moon and out of a nearby inn, so that the mariner could tell the man wasn't frightened. There wasn't a single drop of sweat on his brow, no telltale quiver of his lip. Rig pressed the dagger deep, drawing a thin line of blood. "Why were you following us?"

The man didn't answer. Rig moved his face in closer, inches from the stranger's. The man's face was smooth, his hair short, his clothes well-made. He smelled like musk. Not a laborer. A fancy man, the mariner decided, but one who still didn't flinch.

"Nothing's going to make him talk," Usha said. "We've already tried."

"Well, maybe a little pain will set his tongue to wagging," the mariner growled.

"There's another way." The willow leaves parted again and Jasper joined them. Blister was at his side, tugging a leather sack. Groller stood behind the pair, a sack in each hand and the wolf at his feet.

"Then demonstrate." The mariner shoved the stranger to the ground.

The dwarf moved closer, bringing his stubby fingers near the man's chest and closing his eyes. "I learned this from Goldmoon," he whispered. "I just didn't have any cause to use it before." The dwarf had no trouble finding his inner strength this time. He'd had no trouble since his fall in the cave and his vision of Goldmoon. He nurtured the spark inside of him, feeling it quickly grow and bend to his urging.

A tingling sensation rushed from his chest and down his arms, centering on his fingers, which touched the man's expensive dark shirt. The dwarf opened his eyes. They were wide and shining now, locking onto the man's. The man's stern expression relaxed noticeably and his eyes fixed on the dwarf's.

"What's Jasper doing?" Rig asked.

"Magic," Feril whispered. "Of a sort I didn't know he could cast. He's more than a healer. He's a mystic, like Goldmoon was."

"Friend," Jasper said warmly.

"Friend," the stranger replied.

"You were following us."

The man nodded, his eyes never leaving the dwarf's. "Yes, following you."

"Why?"

"Had to be certain you were the ones. Orders."

"What orders? Who's orders?"

"The knight-commander's orders."

"From the Legion of Steel?"

The man shook his head.

"You're a Knight of Takhisis?"

"No." The man shook his head again, keeping his eyes focused on the dwarf's. "Not a military man. Doesn't pay well enough. I spy for the Dark Knights. For that, they pay me well, friend. There's plenty of steel in my pocket."

"He's worse than a Knight of Takhisis," Rig mumbled.

"The knight-commander ordered you to watch *us*?" Surprise was in Jasper's voice. "Us?"

"I was to watch *for* you. I and a few others—and the knights in the harbor. We've been waiting for a while. Knew you were coming to Ak-Khurman. It was just a matter of time. Had to be careful. The Legion of Steel knew there were Dark Knight spies in town. They were questioning townsfolk, trying to find us."

"You were watching for *us*?" the dwarf repeated.

"A Kagonesti with an oakleaf on her face, a black man with a cutlass," the stranger continued. "You, a short-bearded dwarf. A female Solamnic knight. A big half-ogre with a red wolf. And Dhamon Grimwulf. Spotted him a week ago, but didn't recognize him then, too far away. Not with black hair."

The man paused, then added, "Malys. The red overlord wants you stopped and killed. She wants Dhamon Grimwulf captured and tortured."

"Wonderful," the dwarf said. "A very pleasant way to earn some steel."

"But I wasn't paid to kill you, just to report when and where I'd seen you, where the Dark Knights could find you. I wouldn't want to hurt you, friend. Not by my own hand, anyway."

"So the knights blockaded the city because of *us*?" Jasper asked.

The man nodded. "More ships down the coast left an hour or so ago, in case you accidentally wandered into an ogre village to the south."

"All these Ak-Khurman ships sunk," Feril murmured. "Because of us."

"The red spawn in the mountains were probably sent for us, too," Fiona said. "And because that didn't work . . ."

"Why?" Jasper pressed, a hint of anger creeping into his voice. "Why are the Knights of Takhisis so keen on stopping us?"

"The Red knows you mean to prevent Takhisis from returning. Wants you dead."

"Now how could she know that? And how could she know we were coming here?" The question was Usha's.

Behind the dwarf, Rig shot a glare at Dhamon. Yes, how could she know that? the mariner mouthed.

The stranger shrugged. "I don't know how dragons know these things. I was just paid good steel to watch for you. I was on my way to tell the knight-commander I spotted you in the tavern."

"And just how were you going to tell him?" Rig asked. He knelt next to the dwarf.

"A boat," the man answered. He gestured in the direction of a massive lilac bush growing along the shore. "A boat hidden under that bush. I was going to take the boat to the knight-commander's ship."

"So I guess we're not going to have to swim after all," Fiona said.

"Good thing," Jasper said. "I can't swim. I'd sink like a stone."

Rig bent next to the spy, twisting the dagger in his hand so he was carefully holding the blade in his fingers. Then he rapped the pommel against the stranger's head. The man crumpled, unconscious, at the base of the willow.

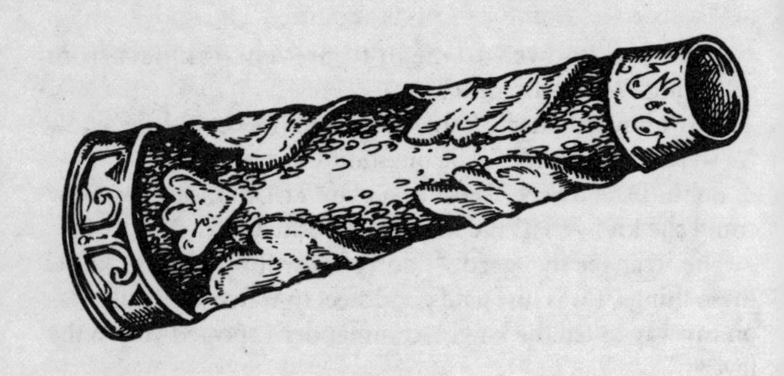

Chapter 15

Fire on the Water

"Are we gonna sail this all the way to Dimernesti?" Blister eyed the fishing boat. "I don't think all of us can even fit in it."

"All of us can't," Rig said, as he eased the boat into the water and motioned for Blister to get in. "Hurry," he whispered.

"But I thought we weren't gonna do this until just about dawn," the kender complained.

"Change in plans. I want to get out of here now before any more spies see us." Rig looked over his shoulder, eyeing Dhamon. "Blister, will you please hurry!"

The kender and the dwarf sat together, a sack full of jugs

and rags wedged under them—the supplies the dwarf wanted. Blister had tried to explain to Rig how they obtained them from a closed store, but Jasper cut her off.

"I'm not proud of what we did," he whispered.

"But you left some steel on the counter," she said.

"Still, it wasn't right. It was justified," he said, eyeing the ships in the harbor. "But it wasn't right. Still, maybe the shop owner will be happy if what I think Rig has in mind works out."

"What's Rig . . ."

"Shhh!" the mariner cautioned. "They can't see us. Too dark. But that doesn't mean the Knights of Takhisis can't hear us."

Dhamon and Rig took the middle seat, under which was tucked a few lengths of rope, and Groller sat between Usha and Fiona. The small boat wasn't meant to hold so many and sat heavily in the water. The lip of it bobbed only a few inches above the choppy surface. Rig passed Dhamon a paddle and stuck his own in the oar mount.

While they'd questioned the spy, the fog had grown thicker. It hugged the water and wrapped around all the ships, making their lights look soft and indistinct.

"Looks spooky," Blister whispered.

"The fog'll help hide us," the mariner said. "If they see us, they can sink us. Now, nobody breathe too deep. We can't handle an ounce more weight." The mariner dipped a paddle in, slow and easy so the water wouldn't splash. Dhamon's oar moved together with Rig's.

Feril and the wolf swam ahead of them, heading toward the closest ship, a good-sized galley. The water was warm and soothing to the Kagonesti, and the cool air felt good on her face, as she swam forward with strong kicks. The only sound she heard was the wolf paddling near her and the almost imperceptible creak of the twisting oar mounts from the fishing boat coming a few yards behind her.

The Kagonesti focused on the fog, thin all around her and spreading toward the horizon as far as she could see. Too thin, she knew. If she could easily see the Knights of Takhisis's ships through it, then Rig's boat could be seen by anyone on deck who chanced to look this way. She slowed her strokes, concentrating on the air where it met the water. Her senses were teased by the tendrils of fog.

"Hide me," she whispered to the fog. She was pouring all her energy into the thought, leaving herself just enough strength to stay afloat. "Hide me," she repeated. She focused only on the fog, letting it intoxicate her.

Fury swept by her, paddling to keep his head above the water. He nuzzled her cheek, then pulled ahead, his churning legs brushing her arm.

"Hide us," Feril said. The Kagonesti felt her magical strength growing. By the time the fishing boat caught up to her, the fog had thickened, like a dark, gray blanket that had been thrown across the Ak-Khurman harbor. She heard Blister chattering behind her. Rig hushed the kender, seeing the lights on the knights' ships now as opaque as a gathering of will-o-wisps. "Perfect," she whispered.

"I can't see anything," the kender was saying.

"Quiet!" Jasper softly scolded her.

"How can you tell where you're going?" she persisted. "If I can't see anything, you can't see anything either. Neither can Groller, I bet. Or Fiona. Or Dhamon. What if you're paddling the wrong way?"

"We're not going the wrong way." It was Dhamon's voice. "We're going against the current."

"Oh."

Feril stopped Dhamon's paddle with her hands, and trod water next to the boat. "Go slower," she said. "Follow me. I can see through the fog."

"The ships," Rig whispered. "Did you get a good look at them? Describe them."

She did.

"Two galleys. Can't steal either of them. It would take too many men to handle 'em. Four carracks and a small cog. I want one of the carracks, the biggest one," he whispered. "But we have to take out the galleys first, or they'll chase us down."

Feril nodded. "We're nearing the closest galley."

Rig *heard* the galley before he saw it, heard the gentle groaning of the ship's timbers, the water lapping against the sides, the musical creak of the great masts. It was a shame what he was planning, he thought to himself, a crime against the sea. "Can't be helped," he mused aloud. "Pass her by," he said softly to Feril. "Take us to one of the smaller carracks, the closest one."

The Kagonesti led the boat beyond the galley. Gazing up through the fog, she made out *Pride of the Dark Queen*, painted in white letters on its side. Several minutes later, they neared one of the smallest carracks. If it had a name, Feril couldn't read it. Only one lantern burned from the bow of this ship.

The boat scraped against the carrack's hull, and Rig ran his fingers along the wood just above the water line. The carrack was an older ship; he could tell by the condition of the timbers and the thickness of the paint, but it was well-maintained and had been recently scraped for barnacles. He held a hand out to Dhamon. The knight fumbled under the seat and produced a rope, passing it to the mariner.

Rig carefully stood, balancing himself, and quickly worked a knot into the rope. He whirled the rope above his head, then released it, grinning when his lasso landed around a railing post on his first try. Blister passed him two jugs and a couple of rags, all of which he held under an arm. He looked down at Dhamon. "Grab two more and follow me, if you can. Fiona, take the boat out a little bit. I don't want the rest of you too close when the trouble starts."

"I don't have a weapon," Dhamon whispered to the mariner.

"Then you'd better not get in a fight," Rig returned. Catlike, the mariner started up the rope one-handed, using his feet against the side and scaling it as if he were a mountain climber heading toward a peak.

"Here." Fiona extended her long sword.

Dhamon shook his head, tucking two jugs under an arm, and followed Rig up and over the side. The mariner was crouched low behind the capstan and was stuffing the rags in the jugs. Dhamon joined him and did likewise. "Tinder?"

The mariner shook his head. "Not yet." He plucked a dagger from his belt, stuck it between his teeth, crept a few feet away to the anchor chain, and began winching it up.

The anchor thudded against the hull. Someone was approaching. Two someones, from the sounds of boot heels. Dhamon couldn't see the men through the fog until they were practically on top of Rig. He set his jugs next to the mariner's and waited.

At the same time, Rig saw the men. He plucked the dagger from between his teeth, hurling it at the man on the right, and drew a worn cutlass, one he had acquired in town. The dagger found the mark, sinking to the hilt into a Knight of Takhisis's unarmored chest. The man thumped heavily on the deck. Dhamon was on the second, pinning him stomach first to the deck and clamping a hand over his mouth. The man continued to struggle, hammering his feet against the deck.

"No noise," the mariner advised. He rapped the pommel of his cutlass against the back of the knight's head. "See?" he said to Dhamon. "I told you that you didn't need a weapon. Not when I'm around."

Rig scuttled back to the capstan. "Current'll take her right into that galley now, but I'm gonna hurry her along." He looked toward the rear mast, cloaked in fog. "I'll cut one of the sails to speed her up a bit. You stop anybody that wanders by."

"With what?" Dhamon quietly shot back.

"Your charm." A heartbeat later the mariner had climbed up the mast into the fog.

Dhamon crept back to the two bodies and tugged a long sword free from one. From the body of the other, he retrieved Rig's dagger, wiping the blood off on the dead man's tabard. He spotted a shadow in the fog; someone else was approaching, he could hear voices.

"I can't see in this pea soup," one man said.

"It'll lift by morning," a second shadow said.

"The fog's not your concern." A third voice. "Just find out why we're drifting, and stop her. I don't want to hit one of the other ships."

"Aye, sir!" replied the first man.

They'd find the bodies, Dhamon thought. He clutched the dagger in his left hand, the long sword in his right. Hurry, Rig, he said to himself. He glanced at the mast. There was still no sign of the mariner, but he heard the canvas drop and heard the breeze catch it.

"Hey!" one of the men barked. "We're not drifting! We're under sail. Better get the sub-commander."

Dhamon rushed toward the shadows, leading with the sword, wanting them to see him. There'll be no more ambushes, he thought. It'll be an honorable fight this time. A few steps more and the shadows came into focus: two Knights of Takhisis in black tabards and leather shirts. One had a sword in his hand, while the other started to draw his weapon as soon as he spied Dhamon.

"Sub-commander!" the one with sword already out called. "We've got company!"

Dhamon tossed the dagger at the man drawing his sword, and muttered a soft curse when it sank into the fellow's thigh instead of his chest. Still, the wound was enough to stop him. The man dropped to one knee, hands clawing at the dagger.

At the same moment, his companion lunged. Dhamon

ducked below the sweeping blade and thrust his long sword forward, impaling the knight on it. The man's sword clattered to the deck and he pitched forward, just as footsteps thundered from below. Dhamon turned to face the wounded knight, who was now on his feet.

"Trouble, sub-commander!" someone hidden by the fog called.

"Trouble, all right," growled the wounded knight. The dagger free from his leg, he tugged his sword from its sheath, quickly parrying Dhamon's blow. "I don't know who you are," he snarled, but it doesn't matter." He effortlessly parried another thrust. "You'll be dead soon enough."

Dhamon increased the force of his swings, marveling at the man's defense. The knight was well-trained in the classic strikes and parries taught by the knighthood. Dhamon leapt in close, using a maneuver he'd borrowed from Rig, catching the man off guard. Dhamon brought the long sword out to his side and swung it in hard, slicing through the leather shirt and deep into the man's midsection.

"Fire!" came another voice. "She's on fire!"

Rig was responsible, Dhamon knew. The mariner had been busy. Dhamon cut at the man again, killing him quickly. Then he rushed back to the capstan. The mariner was there, holding two jugs, the rags in them burning merrily. The other two had been smashed on the deck and were responsible for the fire the knights were rushing to put out.

"You were supposed to wait for me here," Rig snapped, as he lobbed the two remaining jugs toward the rear mast. "Let's move."

The mariner darted toward the rear of the ship, glancing over his shoulder once to make sure Dhamon was following. Then he dropped over the side. Dhamon paused long enough to stick the long sword in his belt, then he too vaulted over the rail.

"Feril'll find us," Rig said as he trod water near Dhamon.

"The boat can't be far."

Dhamon didn't say anything. He was watching the burning carrack. The ship was moving quickly, its anchor up and sail billowing. Some of the men on deck were concentrating on the fire. But other men and the slaves who had manned the ship were jumping overboard.

The flames grew smaller as the ship drifted. Then Dhamon and Rig heard a heavy thud, as the carrack struck something.

"I remembered where the galley was," Rig said matter-of-factly. "I knew the way the wind was blowing, so I figured out just where to aim her."

The air was filled with the cries of "Fire!" Smoke roiled off the carrack's deck, and flames spilled onto the galley. The scent of burning wood hung heavy in the fog. More men and slaves were jumping over the side.

"Well, you don't have to congratulate me or anything," Rig continued. "But I just took out two ships. We take out another carrack or two, and it's clear sailing."

Dhamon watched the fire, made hazy now by the still-thick fog.

"They'll burn right down to the waterline if they can't put them out," the mariner continued. "You know, you surprised me up there. You didn't have any qualms about killing those knights on deck: your comrades-in-arms. I would've thought . . ."

Dhamon thrust the mariner's words to the back of his mind, listening to the burning timbers. Then he picked out the sound of oars and of Feril's voice. He quickly climbed aboard the fishing boat.

Gaps were appearing in the fog by the time Feril and Fury guided the boat toward the three remaining carracks, bobbing side by side only a dozen or so yards apart. Feril had dropped her concentration on the fog, and was too tired from treading water to spend her energy on deepening the mist again. Men were gathered on the bows of all three carracks, spyglasses pressed to their faces. The carracks had not made a move to raise their sails and come in closer. No doubt the captains didn't want to risk the fire spreading.

"Risky," Rig said. "They're awfully close together. Where's the other galley?"

"Farther out," Feril said. "At the mouth of the harbor. Near the little cog."

"That's our target," the mariner said. "The other galley. We'll do the same thing, lead the galley into one of the carracks, the one on the right. I want the bigger one, to the far left—the three-master."

"How are we going to man it?" Feril whispered. It was a question Blister had asked earlier and that the mariner had ignored.

"Legion of Steel maybe," he replied. "I don't know. I'll think of something."

The fog had thinned considerably by the time the fishing boat reached the far side of the galley. Dhamon and Rig no longer needed Feril to guide them. They could see well enough through the wispy fog. Fortunately the men on deck were all watching the fire and had not seen them approach.

Rig found his balance, threw the rope up, and cursed when it missed its mark and splashed in the water behind him. He rolled it up and tried again.

"There's nothing to hook it on," Blister said. "You'll have to try the other side."

Rig shook his head and coiled the rope over his arm. He pulled two daggers from his belt and worked them into the ship's hull, a few feet above the waterline and between the oar ports.

"Hey, that's pretty clever!" the kender squealed. "He's making a ladder. Maybe I could . . ."

A cross look from Dhamon and Jasper silenced her.

Rig took two more daggers and wedged them in higher in the hull. Then he stood on the first two daggers and climbed to the higher pair. Precariously balanced, he wedged in another couple, and continued climbing, using his makeshift footholds. Several minutes later he was out of daggers, but he was at the top. He disappeared over the side.

Blister fidgeted. "I don't think he should be up there all by himself," she whispered. "I'd like to have a little of the fun."

The rope dropped over the side, as did a rope ladder the knights probably used for boarding. Rig hung over the railing, motioning to Groller. The half-ogre pointed to the sack under Blister and Jasper. Dhamon brought it out and carefully tied it to the rope.

Dhamon climbed up the ladder, retrieving two of Rig's daggers in the process and sticking them in his belt next to his long sword. He guided the sack up the side, careful to avoid scraping the hull and shattering the jugs inside. He helped Rig lift it over the rail and joined the mariner on deck.

"Same as before," Rig whispered.

They looked toward the ship's starboard side, where nearly two dozen Knights of Takhisis stood against the railing, watching the fire.

"I don't think so," Dhamon said quietly. He pointed at midships, then gestured at the mainmast, where a knight stood perched in the crow's nest. The knight had noticed them.

"Pirates!" the knight bellowed, instantly drawing everyone's attention away from the fire. The knight waved his arm toward Rig and Dhamon.

"We could use some help up here!" Rig called over the side. He felt for his daggers. "Damn! Used 'em all."

"Here!" Dhamon passed him the two daggers he had retrieved, then darted forward, meeting the charge of the first three knights. This is suicide, he thought. He ducked below a wide swing and stabbed up with his long sword. The blade dug into one knight, and Dhamon leapt back just as the man pitched forward.

He did not leap far enough, and the knight's falling body knocked him over. Dhamon scrambled out from under the corpse and leapt to his feet as one of the other advancing knights stabbed his thigh. Dhamon swung toward a knight wearing black chain mail. The sword bounced off the armor. Dhamon jumped back a few steps. Both of the knights rushing toward him were wearing chain mail; four more in leather were behind him somewhere.

"Suicide," he repeated half under his breath.

Several yards behind him, Rig was engaging a pair of unarmored knights. A third lay on the ground with two daggers protruding from his chest. The mariner had snatched a sword from the body and was deftly parrying the knights' swings and hurling insults at them at the same time.

The thunder of more footsteps from below made Dhamon swallow hard. He was good with a blade but overwhelming odds were another matter. And a ship this size would have dozens of men on board—not to mention dozens of slaves chained in the hold and at the oar ports. Suicide definitely.

"Oh no you don't!" taunted Blister. "You leave Dhamon alone!" The kender had climbed onto the deck and was expertly pelting the knights attacking Dhamon. Sea shells she'd gathered from somewhere struck the backs of their heads.

The knights lifted their hands to protect them from the fusillade, giving Dhamon an opening. He kicked out at one knight, forcing the man back and impaling him on the out thrust sword of one of four advancing knights. At the same moment, he slashed hard to his left, cutting through links of chain to find the skin beneath. The knight howled, and Dhamon followed through with a strong thrust that pushed the long sword deep into the man's belly.

Dhamon tugged his blade free just as Feril darted past him. The Kagonesti was heading toward the mast, down which the knight who'd been in the crow's nest was climbing. Agile as a monkey, Feril scrambled up the rigging and kicked out at the man. He held tight to the mast and drew his sword, but she kicked again, ferociously and repeatedly, until man and blade fell to the deck.

"Cut the sail while you're up there!" Rig called to her.

She paused.

"Unfurl it!" Rig bellowed. "Let it down to catch the wind!"

A quartet of knights drew Dhamon's attention back to the battle. He guessed that counting the ones who'd just come up from below, there must be at least three dozen on deck to contend with. He backed toward the rail, parrying blows, although one got through his defenses, wounding his arm.

"Swim for it!" one of the knights shouted.

Dhamon had no intention of jumping over the side, he just wanted to feel the rail at his back. Several feet away, he noticed Fiona, her armor gleaming in the light of the lanterns spaced around the deck. She had her back to Rig, and the two of them were keeping another quartet of knights busy. Other knights crowded around, looking for an opening.

"The carracks!" Feril called from the rigging. "They're raising their sails. All three of them!"

Rig muttered a string of curses. "We're gonna have more company than we can handle!" he yelled. Under his breath, he added, "I didn't think they'd all come over here."

"Let's finish this fight quickly!" Fiona called.

"Finish it?" The voice belonged to Jasper. The dwarf awkwardly climbed over the rail and fumbled with the sack at his waist. Groller climbed over behind him and headed toward midships. "Finish it? They're going to finish us." Jasper pulled the Fist of E'li from the sack and smacked it into the leg of an approaching knight. The man doubled over and Jasper swung the Fist into his head, grimacing as he heard the man's skull crack. The dwarf stepped over the body and waded into the fray.

"The half-ogre!" a knight bellowed. "And an Ergothian!

These are the ones we came here for! And they came right to us! Kill them all! Malys will reward us!"

Groller met the charge of two knights, pitching one over the side. He barreled into the other, pinning him to the deck. His big hands found their way to the man's throat and squeezed. The knight struggled for several moments, then lay still.

Groller pushed himself off the knight and caught a blow to his arm. The cut was deep, and the half-ogre howled as he brought his uninjured arm up to punch the knight. The man was momentarily stunned, and Groller pressed his attack, kicking the knight in the chest, then tugging a belaying pin from his belt and cracking it against the side of the man's head. Four more knights were heading his way.

"We can win this!" Rig shouted above the clash of swords.

"Losing's not an alternative I want to think about!" the kender called back. She'd climbed onto the capstan and was hurling sea shells, rocks, buttons, and an assortment of other oddities with her sling. She caught a couple of the knights off-guard, buying Rig a little time with his cutlass. Then she looked about for Dhamon.

The mariner had downed two men and whirled to take on one of Fiona's targets.

"I don't need help!" Fiona yelled.

"Just being honorable," he returned.

"Be honorable to those over there!" She gestured toward a pair of knights who had stepped up to take their fallen comrades' places. Rig leapt back from one of the two Knights of Takhisis, who thrust upward with his blade. Had the mariner not moved, the sword would have pierced his heart. Rig ducked below another swing, then twisted to the side and drove his blade into the knight. A moment later, he heard Fiona's target fall to the deck.

More than a dozen knights had been killed, but there were three times that many still on their feet. Rig suspected there were still more below deck putting on armor and grabbing weapons.

"See why we couldn't steal a galley?" Rig called as he stood back-to-back with Fiona again, careful not to trip over the bodies. "It takes too many sailors to man her!"

"Too many to man a carrack, too," Blister muttered.

The canvas dropped from the mainmast and billowed, and the Kagonesti dropped in a crouch.

"That's great, Feril!" Rig yelled. "But we aren't going anywhere with the anchor still down."

"I'll get it!" the Kagonesti called to him, then sprinted toward the rear of the ship, leaping over a fallen knight and sidestepping another.

"It's got two anchors!" he yelled. But the Kagonesti was too far away, and the sounds of the battle drowned any hope of being heard. "One at the front," he added to himself.

"Get the kender!" a knight cried.

"No!" Dhamon had dispatched the four knights in leather, suffering more than a few cuts in the process. Now he was fighting a towering man, whom he could tell was a commander, perhaps the man to whom the spy was supposed to report.

"Dhamon Grimwulf," the towering commander hissed between clenched teeth. "Don't quite match your description. Thought you had blond hair. Malys wants you alive." The commander shifted the grip of his sword, intending to strike Dhamon with the flat of the blade. "I can take you alive."

"Not if I can help it." Dhamon parried the man's wide swing, forcing him toward the capstan. As the knight drew back for another blow, Dhamon stepped closer, thrusting the blade up and through a gap in his armor. The wounded knight stepped back, clutching his stomach and brought his long sword down. The impact knocked the weapon out of Dhamon's hand. The sword clattered to the deck.

Blood flowed from the knight-commander. "Malys wants

you alive," he repeated through clenched teeth. He coughed deeply and backed Dhamon toward the rail. "But I'm not going to see tomorrow. And now neither are you. Don't know why Malys is so keen on you. Word is you were a knight." He coughed again, rosy saliva spilling over his lip. "That would make you a traitor."

The knight-commander drew back his blade, careful not to give Dhamon room to escape. "Rogue knights carry a death sentence."

His sword arced toward Dhamon but stopped short, falling from his grip even as the knight-commander dropped to his knees. Dhamon's sword stuck through the man, and Blister's hands were on the hilt.

Dhamon bent and retrieved the commander's sword, just as Blister huffed and tugged Dhamon's sword free. Her hands were trembling.

"I think you better use this sword," she said. "Too heavy for me. I like my sling better. I have to admit, though, he just wasn't gonna be stopped by my buttons."

"You saved my life," Dhamon panted, as he plucked the sword from her grasp and dashed forward just in time to stop a knight from reaching Blister. He glanced over his shoulder and spotted the kender heading toward the rail, where Usha was climbing over.

"You saved my life," he repeated as he parried the thrust of a new opponent. "But Palin will take my life sure enough if something happens to his wife."

Feril had managed to pull up the rear anchor. A burly knight was headed her way, sword out and cursing.

"You're the wild elf," the knight said. He slowed and stood a few feet away. "Tattoo on the cheek. We're 'sposed to kill you. Pity. You're a pretty thing."

He moved forward, and Feril spun to the side. Then she darted past him, her bare feet sounding on the deck. She ran hard, leaving him behind, but she still heard the pounding of his footsteps. She rushed to Dhamon's side. He had just dropped another knight and was standing in front of Usha and Blister, trying to keep them safe.

The Kagonesti glanced around. Bodies littered the deck. Dhamon was bleeding from cuts on his arms and legs, and there was a gash across his stomach. Several yards beyond him, Jasper kept two knights at bay. Despite their longer reaches, they gave the dwarf a wide berth, keeping their eyes on the scepter.

Feril got Dhamon's attention, pointing to the dwarf, and then to Rig and Fiona on the other side of the ship. Five knights jockeyed for position around the Solamnic and the mariner.

Dhamon pushed his sword into Feril's hands, and bent to scoop up a blade from a fallen knight. "The Knights of Takhisis use slaves to man their oars," he shouted above the din of battle. "They'd be down in the hold." Then he spun on his heels and headed toward Rig and Fiona. "Free them if you can!" he called over his shoulder.

"We have to try," Usha said, her voice difficult for the Kagonesti to hear over the clang of swords.

"Then let's go." The Kagonesti darted toward the open hatch, Usha at her heels. Blister followed, but paused to pelt a knight with a slingful of buttons.

Feril stepped over the body of a knight lying at the edge of the hatch. She bent and pried a long sword out of his cold fingers. She held it out to Usha. "Take it!" The elf pressed the pommel into Usha's hands. "There might be more knights below."

The Kagonesti and Usha disappeared below deck. Blister stood at the hatch, sling ready, watching for any knights. None seemed to be interested in the kender any longer. They were directing most of their efforts against Dhamon, Rig, and Fiona and Groller.

"I'm not afraid of you," Blister taunted softly. "I can take you. I can . . . hmmm. Maybe weapons aren't the answer."

The kender glanced toward the rear of the ship, at the sack Rig and Dhamon had hauled over the side. It sat undisturbed. "Or maybe a different kind of weapon would work," she said to herself. Blister took a look into the hatch and strained to hear Feril and Usha. "Nothing. Must mean they're okay so far and not in trouble." She stuffed her sling in her pocket and headed toward the sack.

At midships, Dhamon was fighting at the side of Rig and Fiona, quickly slashing through two of the five men who surrounded them. That left one foe for each, and Dhamon faced the one in armor.

Several yards beyond them, Groller struggled against three knights, with another three heading toward him. Dhamon tried to keep the half-ogre in sight as he continued to assault his foe.

"There can't be more than two dozen left now!" Rig cried cheerfully. The mariner was hurt badly, bleeding from a gash in his side and from several deep cuts on his leg. Fiona was exhausted, but uninjured. Her Solamnic armor had protected her well. "We can take 'em!" Rig continued. "We can . . ." Out of the corner of his eye he saw Groller slump to the deck, six knights around him now. "Groller!"

Dhamon saw what was happening to Groller too, but he could not get past the armored knight in front of him.

The mariner summoned all that was left of his strength and swung his sword. But each thrust was parried, preventing Rig from reaching the half-ogre. "No!" he screamed, as he watched one of the knights shove a sword in Groller's back. The knight stepped on the half-ogre, tugged the blade free, then pointed toward Rig. The six men turned as one and advanced.

Dhamon tried not to think about Groller as he fought on. He managed to stab his opponent. The knight howled in pain, and when Dhamon struck him again, he dropped his sword and fell to his knees. With one swift stroke, Dhamon whipped his blade across the man's neck. So much for honor, he said to himself as he stepped forward to fight the half-dozen knights who'd finished off Groller.

Dhamon met the lead knight head-on, plunging his long sword into the man's unarmored chest. The sword lodged deep and stuck, as the man fell.

Behind him , he heard a throaty groan and a loud thump, but he couldn't afford to take his eyes off the five men in front of him. Two of those he faced carried shields, black as night with lilies gleaming around the edges. One wielded a wicked-looking morning star.

"Bastards!" Rig, clutching his bleeding side, raced past Dhamon to grapple with the two knights with shields.

"Rig, don't be a fool!" Dhamon called to him. "You're badly hurt!" He scanned the deck, spotted a discarded sword, and dove for it, his fingers closing on the pommel, just as three of the knights reached him. He jumped to his feet, and out of the corner of his eye saw Rig reeling from blows.

"Dhamon!" Fiona screamed. "Rig's down! Help him!" She had her hands full, dueling with two knights. She cast worried glances at the mariner, while swinging her sword erratically.

Rig slumped to his knees, in a growing pool of blood. Somehow he raised his sword just in time to block one of the knight's blows. Another cut at his sword arm. Rig screamed, and his sword spun away.

"Fight me!" Dhamon challenged the three men in front of him.

"All right, let's be done with this," the one with the morning star returned. He took up a position in front of Dhamon, while the knights with swords lined up alongside him.

One of the other two swung again at Rig, and the mariner pitched forward. The knight placed a conquering foot on the body.

"You used to be honorable!" Dhamon snarled. "Honorable!"

The knight with the morning star grinned. "Only you and the lady knight left," he said as he whirled the weapon in a circle above his head. "And the women who went below decks. We'll take our time with them. Save 'em for last. I'm not too worried about the kender."

Or the dwarf, Dhamon thought, wondering where Jasper was. He growled, feeling the morning star pass over his head as he ducked. Slashing to the right, he caught a knight in the abdomen, and quickly repeated the stroke, downing the man. At the same time, steel bit into his left side. The other knight had scored a cut. Dhamon felt his side grow wet and warm. He spun and stood, slashing at the knight on his left side, while dodging another blow from the morning star.

The knight stopped, his blade suspended, his mouth gaping in surprise. Dhamon had pierced the man's stomach with his long sword.

Dhamon pulled back his sword and brought it up in an attempt to parry another blow by the morning star. The chain of the weapon caught around the blade, and his opponent jerked the sword from Dhamon's hand.

Without pausing, Dhamon lowered his shoulder and rammed it into the knight, pushing him backward. He swept his leg behind the knight's feet and sent the knight tumbling to the deck, the morning star spinning away with his sword.

"Honor be damned then!" Dhamon drove the heel of his boot into the knight's stomach. The knight rolled, and Dhamon staggered. As he struggled to keep his balance, the knight's fingers closed about the morning star. The warrior started to rise, but Dhamon moved fast. He kicked the man's stomach again, then drove the blade into his throat, tugged it free, and whirled toward the fallen Rig.

"There's no honor in fighting an unarmed man!" Dhamon cried.

Two knights still stood over Rig, one ready to stab a sword

into the mariner's back. Dhamon rushed forward, sliding in the blood, clutching his side.

The taller of the two knights sneered at him and lunged, but the other pointed toward the rear of the ship. "Fire! She's burning!"

Dhamon registered the smell of burning timbers as he engaged the tall knight. He stepped beneath the man's swing and drove his sword to the left, meeting the man's shield. Then he jammed his elbow into the man's abdomen, pushing the knight back several paces.

Dhamon spun about and met the challenge of the other knight. Their swords clashed above their heads, but Dhamon couldn't find a decent opening. He concentrated on staying alive.

"Rig!" Fiona was at the mariner's side, having vanquished her foe. Her armor was splattered with blood; the hair that spilled from under her helmet was matted with it.

Rig groaned and waved her off, trying futilely to push himself off the deck. "Help Dhamon," he breathed. "Get to Groller. I'll be all right. Find Jasper."

She paused only a moment, then joined Dhamon, taking on the taller of the two knights. The man leveled swing after swing at her. She parried several strokes, but one found its way through her defenses, and the sword came down hard on her breastplate. He followed up the attack, slamming his shield into her chest. The impact knocked her to the deck.

Dhamon gritted his teeth and drove forward, putting everything into one final thrust. The blade glanced off the knight's weapon. At the same time, Dhamon knocked the knight's shield aside with his free hand. He swung again, the blade finding its way between the knight's ribs.

Dhamon stepped over the dying man, and met the swing of the tall knight who had been striking down at the fallen Fiona. "Fiona! Drag Rig to the rail! Get everyone to the rail," Dhamon called to her. "The ship's burning fast! And those carracks are coming! They'll be on top of us in a moment!"

"She's on fire!" came a shout from off the starboard bow, from the deck of one of the carracks. The three carracks were closing; they would be upon the galley within seconds.

"Drop anchor!" someone shouted. "Don't get too close! Send longboats over!"

Dhamon heard Rig groan and heard Fiona's boots tromping through the blood. "Rig, stay here," she said. "I've got to help Jasper. I can see him—barely—behind the mainmast."

Dhamon returned his attention to the tall knight. The man had dropped his shield and snatched up a smaller sword, was wielding it in his other hand. He wove the two blades before him in a gleaming tapestry of steel.

"You're not leaving this ship alive," the knight hissed. His voice was deep. He'd been one of the last ones to come up on deck, and from the bloodied insignia on his tabard he was a sub-commander.

"Sorry, have to leave," Dhamon replied.

"Oh, you'll leave, all right. You'll leave straight to the Abyss." The man laughed, a deep, throaty chuckle that rose above the crackling of the fire. "Too bad you won't be alive to see Takhisis return!" Smoke wafted past the knight and Dhamon, and they felt the heat of the fire that was swiftly consuming the ship. The knight lunged with his long sword, drawing back with the other blade. Dhamon jumped and turned, reversing their positions so the knight's back was to the fire now.

Dhamon glanced past him. The entire rear of the ship was on fire. The sail Feril had lowered was engulfed, lighting up the night sky and cutting through what little fog remained in the harbor.

Blister was at the edge of the blaze, firing jugs from a small ballista at the approaching carracks. Lit rags were in the bottles' mouths, and Dhamon realized, with a curious detachment, that the kender was responsible for starting the fire on the galley.

More men were racing up on deck, though they were not in the livery of the Knights of Takhisis. They were thin, dressed in torn and dirty clothes. Feril and Usha led them around the flames. The Kagonesti coughed, talking to Usha, then pointing toward the rail.

"Blister!" Feril yelled. "We're leaving!"

Behind them, Blister catapulted two more jugs and headed toward the rail.

Beyond the galley were two carracks. One had caught fire and was burning merrily. Dhamon could see its glowing sails. The third carrack had held to a safer distance and was lowering longboats that would rescue the knights and slaves.

If Dhamon could finish this man, he and the others could escape to the relative safety of the small fishing boat. This man, and . . . out of the corner of his eye he spotted Jasper.

The dwarf was between the main and forward masts. He held the scepter extended in one hand and was slowly waving it back and forth between two armored knights. The knights eyed the dwarf, but were making no attempt to rush him. Then Dhamon spotted Fiona coming to the dwarf's aid. She had caught one of the men's attention, and he charged her.

"We've got to hurry, Jasper," she grunted, parrying the knight's thrust. "This ship isn't going to be floating too much longer. Blister saw to that." As if to give credence to her words, a flaming piece of sail broke free and fluttered to the deck right behind the knights. Fire leapt from it, adding to the flames already lapping at the ship. It broke the stalemate between the dwarf and the knight closest to him. The warrior growled and stepped toward Jasper.

Fiona held the advantage over her foe. He moved sluggishly as the smoke grew thicker.

"I'll spare you your life!" she offered, as she dodged a poorly aimed blow. The man shook his head, as if he was trying to clear his senses. "I'll give you your life, if you drop the sword!" she repeated.

He shook his head again and swung his blade low. The blow glanced off her sword, and she aimed her weapon at an opening where his armored breastplate met a short chain skirt. He pitched forward, she freed her sword and moved on to help the dwarf.

Because the dwarf was so much smaller, the knight had difficulty penetrating his defenses. Each time the man thrust at the dwarf's chest, Jasper raised the First, and each time the blade harmlessly bounced off the enchanted wood.

"We don't have time for this!" Fiona shouted. She was coughing now, and waving the smoke out of her eyes. "Get to the side, the fishing boat! Help Rig over the side! He's hurt real bad, Jasper. And I think Groller's dead."

Jasper didn't argue, knowing she could handle the knight better than he could. As the dwarf moved toward the railing, sliding in the blood, stepping over the bodies, he heard the clang of Fiona's sword against the man's sword and armor. There was a rhythm to it. Then the rhythm stopped, and through the crackling of the flames he heard a dull thud. Fiona coughed, her boots slapping across the deck, and he breathed a sigh of relief. The Knight of Takhisis had fallen.

Rig was on his knees, holding onto the rail, his breathing ragged and uneven. The dwarf looked about frantically for the rope ladder he'd climbed up. It was too far away, toward the rear of the ship, which now looked like one big ball of fire. "We'll have to swim. At least you'll have to," the dwarf said. "I can't. But maybe I can keep from sinking like a stone."

The dwarf raised the Fist of E'li and battered it against the rail, breaking a section of it free and knocking it into the water. "It floats. And maybe with its help, I can float too."

The mariner raised his head, his eyes stung by smoke. "I can swim. I'll help you."

Not in your condition, Jasper thought. The dwarf helped Rig over the side, so that the mariner hung like a sack of flour, dangling in the air. The dwarf looked for the fishing boat. The dark gray smoke from the galley mingled with the wispy fog, and at first he could see nothing.

But through gaps in the smoke he finally spied people in the water: the slaves Feril and Usha had rescued. They were treading water and backing away from the galley. And then he saw the floating rail.

"My sword," Rig gasped. "Got to get my sword. Can't lose another one."

"Fury!" the dwarf shouted, ignoring the mariner. "Blister!"

A moment later he was rewarded with the wolf's frantic barks. "Jasper! We're down here!" It was Blister's voice. "We're in the boat!" So the boat was somewhere below. It couldn't be too far away if he could hear her this easily. Jasper thrust the Fist into the sack at his waist, making sure it was secure, then pushed Rig over the side. The dwarf took a quick look around the deck. Feril was toward the bow, cranking furiously on the anchor chain and coaxing over the last of the freed slaves. Usha gathered her skirts and jumped over the side.

Dhamon was nearby, struggling with a tall knight.

I should help him, Jasper thought. But then Rig might drown. The dwarf leaped over the side after the mariner, angling his body and praying to the departed gods that he wouldn't sink.

Fiona had doubled over coughing. She couldn't see more than a few feet in front of her now, but she knew where to go. She heard metal striking metal. Dhamon was still fighting the tall knight. That was the only battle still going on. She peeled off pieces of her armor and staggered toward the noise.

Both men were covered with blood. The tall knight was using two weapons, parrying Dhamon's sword with his longer blade and slashing at Dhamon's chest with the shorter weapon.

Dhamon's tunic was blood-soaked. She realized most of the blood was his, the tall knight's tabard was practically pristine. She pulled off her breastplate, letting it fall to the deck, and then rushed forward, stopping just short of Dhamon.

"Unfair odds," the tall knight hissed. "Two against one. There's no honor in that."

"You didn't think the odds were unfair when you were fighting my friend!" Fiona spat.

"The black man?" the knight laughed. "Malys wants the Ergothian dead. But you," he tipped his head toward Dhamon. "You—I want an honorable fight with you!"

"Not this time," Dhamon retorted. He let Fiona parry the knight's long sword, while his blade clanged against the shorter weapon. Dhamon awkwardly spun about and jabbed at the man's side. His blade sunk in only a few inches. But the pain was enough to make the tall knight glance at his wound. Fiona stepped closer and slashed at his chest, then crouched and sliced at his legs, her blade striking black plates, clanging hollowly. The knight stepped back and wildly waved his weapons at the pair to keep them at a safe distance.

"I'll give you your life!" Fiona called. "Drop your blades!"

The knight let out a guttural cry and dashed forward. Fiona stepped up to meet him, while Dhamon slid to one side. Dhamon raised his long sword high over his head and brought it down with all the strength left in his arms. The sword bit into the man's shoulder. Dhamon pulled it loose and struck again. The knight gasped and dropped the shorter blade, fighting only with the longer weapon now.

The Dark Knight gave Fiona a tight smile and jockeyed to the side so he could see both her and Dhamon. The smoke around him was thick, and he was gasping for air. Fiona was having trouble breathing as well, and Dhamon gestured toward the side of the ship. Go! he mouthed.

She shook her head. "Not without you!"

Dhamon, choking on smoke, moved forward clumsily now, swinging his sword in a broad, uneven arc. The knight stepped back, staying just beyond the weapon. The black-haired warrior steadied himself, and brought his blade up. As the knight waited for an opening, Dhamon gave him the illusion of one.

The knight stepped forward, bringing his blade down. At the last possible moment, Dhamon stepped close to the man and into his swing. The long sword hit Dhamon's shoulder, but his own sword cut at the man's already-injured side. Dhamon pulled the sword back and slammed the blade in again, and the knight collapsed on him, pinning him to the deck.

Fiona was there, coughing, gasping for air, pulling the dead knight off Dhamon and tugging him toward the rail. "We've got to get off this ship! It's listing. Can't you feel it?"

She was right. The deck slanted toward the sea, as if the ship were taking on water. And the ship was moving toward the shore. Somehow the forward anchor must have come loose.

Dhamon leaned on Fiona for a moment, and both grabbed the rail as the galley stopped, a crunching sound that competed with the roar of the fire.

"She's hit one of the other ships!" Fiona gasped. The galley lurched again, and the Solamnic started to fall. Dhamon caught her, leaned her over the rail where she could gulp in a bit of fresh air.

"You first," he said, waving his arm. "I'll follow."

She tugged at the last few metal plates on her arms, her fingers fumbling with the fastenings, then tossed her helmet off. I should've left it all in the swamp, she thought. When the last piece clanged against the deck, she sheathed her sword and dove over the side.

"I'll follow after I find Groller," Dhamon called. He closed his eyes and imagined the deck. Then he dropped down to all fours and crawled forward, picturing the mainmast, the forward mast, and the place where he'd seen the half-ogre go down between the two. Dead or not, Dhamon intended to bring Groller with him.

Dhamon's hands connected with body after body, none of them large enough, all in the garb of the Dark Queen's knights. He crawled steadily over them, slipping in the blood and cutting his fingers on dropped swords. It felt as if he'd crawled for hours. His chest was on fire, water ran from his closed eyes, and he ached from a dozen wounds.

He was feeling faint, dizzy from lack of air and loss of blood, by the time he reached a large body.

It was face down and bloody. With considerable effort, Dhamon turned it over, ran his fingers over the long hair, felt about around the broad shoulders, and touched the man's face. His hands felt Groller's wide nose and thick brow. Dropping lower, they felt for the worn leather tunic, now cut and slick with blood.

"Be alive," Dhamon prayed. He pressed his cheek to the half-ogre's nose, at first feeling nothing. Then, barely detectable, he sensed a trace of shallow breath. The sensation did not cheer him. Dhamon had tended enough wounded on various battlefields to know that the half-ogre was dying.

Dhamon struggled to his feet, carrying Groller under the armpits. He staggered toward the railing, dragging the half-ogre with him. Going back was easier; the deck was tilting more in that direction.

"Dhamon!" Someone was calling for him, a woman. The voice was faint, and he couldn't make out who it was. Feril? Usha? It wasn't the kender—Blister's voice was more child-like. Perhaps it was Fiona.

He wrestled with Groller's body, pulling it up and propping it against the rail. He threw one of his legs over the rail, the one with the blackened scale. The scale shone through the numerous cuts in his leggings. It was one of the few spots not spattered with blood. The half-ogre was heavy, and Dhamon was growing increasingly weak. He hauled him up, and the rail snapped under their combined weight. Dhamon clutched Groller to him, and together they struck the water.

He felt himself sinking, the weight of the half-ogre pulling him down. Dhamon held tight to Groller and kicked hard. The saltwater stung his wounds and helped to revive him. It seemed to give him a burst of renewed strength. He heard sounds through the water, things he couldn't describe but guessed were pieces of the galley falling into the harbor. Then suddenly his burden was lighter. Something or someone was helping him with Groller.

Dhamon's head broke the surface, and he gulped in air. Feril swam at his side, helping to keep Groller's head above the surface.

"He's dying," Dhamon managed to get out.

She waved an arm and whistled, and Dhamon heard the splash of oars. Finally he saw the small fishing boat cutting through the fog and smoke. Jasper leaned over the side, stretching his fingers out toward Groller.

The dwarf was singed and soaked, as well as exhausted. His face looked oddly pale in the firelight. "Bring . . . him . . . closer," the dwarf gasped. Fury stuck his head over the side of the ship and howled. The wolf tried to jump in, but Fiona's arms were locked around him.

"Is Groller all right?" Blister asked.

Feril and Dhamon struggled to pull Groller up over the edge of the small boat. Jasper touched the half-ogre's face, closed his eyes, and worked to find the healing spark again. He'd spent the past several minutes tending to Rig, while struggling to hold onto the floating railing until the fishing boat came to their rescue.

The mariner had been seriously wounded, and it took most of the dwarf's energy to heal Rig's worst injuries and keep him alive. Jasper, too, was injured, as was Fiona, but neither were in danger of dying.

Groller was another matter. The dwarf coaxed his spark to grow stronger, searching for the half-ogre's familiar life essence. It was weak and hard to find, like an ember growing cold. Groller was slipping from Krynn, as Goldmoon had slipped from the world. Jasper knew the half-ogre was injured worse than he had been in the cavern. Behind him Fury howled again, struggling against Fiona, and now Blister, too, as she helped to hold back the wolf.

"You'll get in Jasper's way," Blister scolded Fury. "Stay here."

Groller's cheek felt unnaturally cold beneath the dwarf's fingers. "No," Jasper whispered. "I'll not lose you, too. I can't." The dwarf barely clung to the side of the boat now, putting all his effort into his healing spell. "Don't die on me. I saved you once. I can do it again." He heard his own heart beating, thumping over the distant sounds of fire and men shouting. It beat in time with the choppy waves lapping against the side of the boat. The dwarf focused on the rhythm, using it to build the spark.

He felt a warmth radiating from his chest and slipping down his arm to his fingers and Groller's face. He felt the fishing boat lurch.

"Jasper!" he heard Fiona shout. "Grab the boat!"

He made no move to do so, not wanting to interrupt his spell. He felt his free hand touch the water, then sink below it. He spilled over the edge of the boat and started to sink, but he made no effort to keep himself afloat. Everything was directed toward the spark and saving Groller.

Then Jasper heard the half-ogre gasp and felt Feril grab his stubby arms. Her legs churned. His eyes snapped open, and he saw Dhamon helping Fiona and Usha bring Groller into the boat. Fiona slipped over the side to make room for the half-ogre. Then her hands joined Feril's in lifting Jasper out of the water. He was deposited next to Groller and Rig in the center of the boat.

"Jaz-pear good healer," he heard Groller whisper, as he drifted off to sleep.

Feril, Dhamon, and Fiona trod water next to the fishing boat. The freed slaves were nearby in the water, some holding the edge of the fishing boat, others holding onto bits of broken, floating rails.

"What now?" Usha asked. "The shore's too far for the slaves to swim.

"The carracks are all burning," Blister said. "It's my fault. I raised the anchor and let the ship drift into them. Then I fired flaming jugs at them. Kind of neat, huh?"

"You saved us," Dhamon said. "Those knights would have joined the fight on the galley and killed us. There were just too many of them. This was not one of Rig's better ideas."

"There's still one ship left." Fiona pointed toward the east. "That little cog Feril saw."

The Kagonesti grinned. "Yes! It stayed back when we set the galley on fire."

"Then let's make for it," Dhamon said. "It's closer than the shore. Let's hope there aren't very many knights on board. There can't be. It's pretty small."

"And we've got people to man it!" Blister beamed, gesturing at the freed slaves.

"Only if they're willing," Feril returned. "Otherwise, we'll put them ashore."

"Let's discuss this after we've taken over the cog," Dhamon said. His voice was weak. He started swimming towards the cog. "*If* we can take it," he added.

It seemed like hours before the fishing boat scraped and bumped against the seaward side of the cog. The smoke was still thick on the water; it cloaked them from the knights on board, most of whom were busy watching the fires from the far railing.

Dhamon squinted through the darkness, fighting to stay awake. The light from the fire didn't reach this side of the ship. He pointed toward the bow. "I see an anchor rope. There's our ladder up."

"You're not going," Fiona whispered harshly. "You're bleeding."

"I'm not hurt that badly," the knight lied. "And I'm not staying in the water. It's only a matter of time before the sharks show up." He paused. "Unfortunately, I don't have a weapon. I left the ones I borrowed on the galley."

Feril guided the fishing boat to the anchor rope. Usha took a rope from under the middle seat and looped it around the cog's anchor rope. "We won't drift this time," she said. Then she reached toward the center of the boat, fumbling with something. A moment later, she handed two daggers over the side to Dhamon. "Rig's sword is on that burning galley, too. But I saw these sticking out of his boots. I don't think he'll mind."

Dhamon grinned. Though it was dark, he could make out the pearl inlaid lilies on the black pommels. Rig must have expropriated them from a high-ranking knight. He stuck them in his belt and started up the rope, hand over hand. It took a lot of effort. As he neared the railing, he felt someone climbing up after him.

He let out a soft moan as he lifted himself over the side, and pressed a hand to his side. A wave of dizziness washed over him. He ached from his injuries.

Fiona was next. As she hit the deck, she drew her sword and looked toward the line of men against the far rail, all of their eyes trained on the burning ships. Feril silently slipped over the railing, and glanced at Dhamon. Blood trickled through his fingers. More ran down his arm from another deep slash. She gave him a concerned look.

He gripped the railing and pulled himself to his feet, plucking the daggers from his waistband.

Stay here, she mouthed to him.

He shook his head and stepped toward the center of the small ship. It had a single mast, and its sails were lowered. He moved stealithly around the rigging, Fiona and Feril behind him. He balanced a dagger in each hand. Eleven men against three. Not the best of odds, he decided, but they were oblivious to the threat behind them.

He searched for a clue as to which was the sub-commander, but with their backs to him, he couldn't see any braid or insignia. His eyes locked onto the largest man, one with a broad back, taller than the others. First target. The knight thought of shouting a challenge, but his caution got the better of him. Better to be alive with diminished honor, he thought wryly. Dhamon raised the dagger over his shoulder.

"Surrender!" Fiona's shout caught Dhamon by surprise. "So much for stealth," he muttered, as the men whirled. Seven of them wearing the black chain mail of the Dark Knights drew long swords and cutlasses. The other four were sailors, and they fumbled for belaying pins and daggers.

"We're responsible for the fires!" the young Solamnic continued. "And we'll not hesitate to burn this ship, too. But we offer you your lives. Don't be as foolish as your brothers. Drop your weapons! Surrender to us!"

The sailors hesitated, one of them glancing over his shoulder toward the burning ships. The large knight Dhamon had singled out rushed forward. Dhamon inhaled deeply and hurled a dagger. The blade pierced the man's body just above his waist. The knight took a few more steps, then dropped his sword and fell to the deck.

Dhamon readied the other dagger.

"There's ten of us!" one of the knights shouted. "Three of them. Let's take 'em." This knight darted toward the Solamnic, then pitched forward, clutching his throat. He gave a gargled scream before he died. Dhamon's second dagger had hit the mark.

"We'll make this offer only once more!" Fiona barked. "You can surrender and flee on the longboat, help your fellow knights on their burning ships—or you can die."

"This ship can burn, too!" This came from the kender, who had climbed onto the deck. She was holding a jug in one hand, and the rag stuffed into the top of it was on fire.

The men glanced toward the fires on the other ships, and a second later their steel hit the deck. Only two knights remained defiant, sheathing their swords rather than dropping them. Fiona did not press the matter, and Feril darted forward, kicking the swords out of the men's reach.

"Are there any others below deck?" the young Solamnic continued.

The men shook their heads. "The Red wants you," one of the older knights sneered. He pointed at the Kagonesti. "The elf with the tattoos. Bad luck for you. The dragon'll get what she wants. She always does."

"Not always." Dhamon moved forward and snatched up one of the fallen knight's swords. He felt weak and dizzy, but he forced a thin smile to his lips. "Count yourselves lucky that you're all still alive."

"We left no survivors on the galley!" Feril added.

A knight toward the middle of the line took a step forward. His sword remained in his scabbard, but his fingers were edging toward it.

"Don't try anything!" shouted Blister. The kender had moved up behind Fiona, and was holding the flaming jug toward the rigging. "And there's more of us coming," she added. The sounds of feet thudding against the hull backed her up. In a moment, three of the freed slaves stood behind her ominously. "If I were you," the kender continued, "I'd listen to Fiona. She's awfully good with that sword. And I'm getting pretty good at playing with fire."

"Those of you with armor, lose it!" the Solamnic ordered. "You're going over the side in the longboat. Unless you want that boat to sink to the bottom of the harbor from all the extra weight, you'd better get rid of it."

Glaring back at them, the five knights slowly removed their black chain mail.

"Now over the side and into the boat!" Fiona's face was grim. She waved her sword for emphasis. "Be quick!"

The four men who were sailors, not Knights of Takhisis, were the first to comply. That left the five knights. The oldest among them glowered at Fiona.

"She'll get you, the dragon will," he spat. "She'll make you pay!"

Dhamon stepped toward the man, pointing his sword. "I'd worry about myself if I were you. I doubt the dragon rewards failure." He clamped down on his bottom lip as he felt faint. The pain helped keep him alert, but he knew he wouldn't be on his feet much longer. "Into the longboat! Now!"

The man opened his mouth to say something else, but the knights on either side of him grabbed him and hustled him over the rail. The remaining knights followed. Fiona and Feril lowered the boat, and Blister tossed the flaming jug over the other side of the ship into the sea.

When the men were safely in the boat, Dhamon stumbled to the mast, sagged against it, and slid down to the deck. He held his side, closing his eyes. "Fiona, when Jasper wakes up, could you have him . . ." The rest of his words were lost.

* * * * *

It was morning before Dhamon, Rig, and Groller opened their eyes. The three were in a well-appointed cabin paneled in sweet-smelling cedar. Dhamon and Rig were on beds, and Groller, too large for one of the narrow mattresses, was wrapped in blankets on the floor.

They were all bandaged and washed beneath fresh sheets. And an assortment of clothes were piled on a chair for them to try on—what had been left behind by the sailors and Knights of Takhisis.

"Didn't lose a single patient," the dwarf said proudly. Jasper was immensely pleased with himself, grinning broadly as he paced. "Though I'll admit it wasn't for the lack of your trying. Picking fights with that many of the Dark Queen's knights. That was a dose of foolishness if you ask me." He clucked concernedly at them. "Amazing how many sheets and shirts we ripped up just to make bandages. I think you lost more blood than you've got left in you."

Dhamon was the first to stand, though somewhat shakily. Rig's and Groller's gazes locked on the black scale on his leg. Dhamon padded toward the chair and started picking through the clothes, selecting the drabbest of the lot.

"Leave me that red shirt," the mariner said, as he struggled out of the bed. "Mind telling us what happened to that scale?"

"Yes," Dhamon answered tersely. "I do mind."

Groller sluggishly joined the two.

"Now, none of you move around too fast, understand? You were all less than an inch from death, and I don't want any of my meticulous work undone. Or the ladies' handiwork. They put on most of the bandages."

Dhamon slowly drew on a pair of gray leggings, baggy enough to fit over the bandages on his legs. The cuffs hung just above his ankles. Next he put on a dark gray linen shirt, belted it with a black sash. The clean material felt good against his bruised skin.

Rig had the red shirt. Made of silk, its voluminous sleeves suited him. He picked out a pair of black leather trousers, started putting them on, and grinned when he noticed the half-ogre's dilemma. Nothing was large enough for Groller.

The mariner snapped up a long green and black striped nightshirt, held it up to the half-ogre's back and grimaced. Blood showed through the bandage wrapped around

Groller's chest. Rig ripped out the sleeves and handed Groller the altered garment.

The half-ogre struggled into it, testing the limits of the seams. The garment fell just above his knees, and wouldn't button from midchest up. Groller scowled and shook his head when he caught sight of himself in the mirror.

Jasper tugged on the shirt to get Groller's attention. The dwarf drummed his stubby fingers against his temple, shook his head and frowned.

"Jaz-pear zayz I shud not worry," Groller translated. The half-ogre let out a chuckle and glanced down at his bare legs, each of which had a thick bandage on it. "But Jaz-pear haz clothez that fid. Jaz-pear haz zhoes."

"Your boots are drying," the dwarf replied, though he knew Groller couldn't hear him. "They're blood-soaked. Usha washed them. Usha can sew, too. She'll fix something for you. I'm sure we've got days to go before we reach Dimernesti, wherever it is. She'll make you something that fits."

"I know where Dimernesti is—at least if the Master gave me the right directions." Rig was admiring himself in the mirror that hung on a maple frame between the two beds. He glanced at his surroundings. The wood trim was lacquered, polished to a soft shine, and the furniture that was nailed to the floor was expensive and inlaid with brass. They were in the second mate's or bosun's quarters, he guessed.

Jasper pointed toward a table in the far corner. A beveled glass-door cabinet over it was filled with rolled parchments. "Nautical maps," the dwarf said. "Fiona found one with the Khur coast, has it laid out and ready."

"She okay?" Rig gave the dwarf a worried look.

"A few cuts, but I healed them. Lots of bruises, but they'll have to heal on their own. Feril and Usha are in good shape, too—now. I tended to them this morning. They had to wait. The three of you took all my energy last night. Blister didn't even suffer a scratch."

"Now why would they put all the maps in the bosun's quarters? Why not the captain's?"

This is the captain's, Jasper observed.

Rig strode over to the table, glanced at the map. "How long've I been out? How long've we been sailing? Did you pick up some Legion of Steel knights in town to help man her?"

"One question at a time," the dwarf answered. "We've been sailing since late last night. The women got us underway right after they brought you down here. The former slaves from the galley—all three dozen—are taking turns manning the ship and sleeping in the hold. They demanded to come along as payment for their freedom."

"Three dozen. Not nearly enough for a carrack. We'll need at least twice that many."

"Actually," Jasper said softly, "that's about twice as many as we need."

The mariner hadn't heard him. "I better get up top quick. The ship needs a real captain."

"As a matter of fact," Jasper said a little louder, "Blister was at the wheel when I looked a few minutes ago."

Rig groaned and went to the door, catching himself as the ship rose and rocked. He stepped out into the hall. Teakwood panels gleamed in the light of a lantern that burned scented oil. It was a narrow hallway, with only four other doors. There must be another way into the rest of the ship, the mariner decided as he walked toward the ladder that led up top. Groller and Dhamon followed him.

At the base of the steps, the mariner turned to Dhamon. "I don't remember much after the Dark Queen's men took care of me last night," he said in a voice a little above a whisper. "But I recall Fiona saying that you kept them from finishing me off. You saved Groller, too." It was as close to a thank you as Rig was going to offer Dhamon.

The dwarf closed the door. "Well, don't everyone thank me

all at once for tending to them," Jasper chuckled. "At least the ladies were much more polite." The dwarf yawned and scratched at his own bandages. He eyed the beds, picked out the softer-looking one that Rig had vacated, and settled himself into it. He closed his eyes, feeling the ship rise and fall with the waves, and quickly fell asleep.

On deck, Rig took a deep breath, pulling the welcome sea air into his lungs. He spotted Fiona first. She was near the wheel, wearing baggy black leggings and a crisp white shirt that was a couple of sizes too big. It snapped and billowed about her like a sail. Her red hair fluttered in the breeze. Blister was in front of her, standing on a crate and steering. The kender, dressed in a bright yellow cutoff shirt that was belted at the waist and hung to her ankles, was doing a pretty good job of keeping the ship on course. He decided to let her continue a while longer.

Dhamon brushed by Rig, walking toward Feril at the bow. The Kagonesti was leaning into the wind, her hair fanning out around her head. She was humming something, and Dhamon stood quietly for several moments and listened. She was clad in a pale green shirt the color of sea foam. She had torn out the sleeves. She also wore darker green leggings she'd cut off just above her knees. A bandage was wrapped around her arm, and another was around her ankle, which looked badly swollen. She turned to face him.

"Feeling better?" she asked.

Dhamon nodded. "I'll survive."

"I'm grateful—and surprised," Feril said. "But then, I'm surprised we all lived through *that.*" She stepped aside, making room for him. They looked over a bowsprit that reminded Dhamon of a lance. "She's called the *Narwhal.* I don't think she belonged to the Knights of Takhisis. Fiona thinks she's a coastal ship, a small merchant trader. She's beautiful. The knights probably took her because she's obviously got some value to her. Someone put a lot of steel into this ship."

"She's a little small for the ocean," Dhamon observed. He stood next to her, the wind whipping his black tresses.

"She's cozy," Feril argued. "I've been thinking, Dhamon, and talking to Jasper. About forgiveness. About a lot of things." She leaned into him, and he raised his arm as if to drape it around her shoulder, then dropped it to his side.

I killed Goldmoon, he thought to himself. I don't deserve happiness.

* * * * *

After Rig said his good mornings to Fiona, he took a good look around the deck. Usha was sitting against the mainmast—the only mast—mending a spare sail. She looked up, waved, and smiled.

One mast, Rig said to himself. "This isn't one of the carracks," he said aloud, the size of the ship sinking in.

"No. All of them caught fire." Fiona came up behind him, wrapped her arms around his waist and leaned her head into his neck. "But you probably weren't awake to see them burn. They lit up the sky for miles and miles."

"One mast. Twenty-five feet long at the most," he said. "The cog."

"Twenty-two. Blister paced it off."

"Wonderful."

"At least we got a ship," Fiona consoled him. "The one ship that didn't catch fire. And she is awfully pretty."

"No," Rig softly grumbled. He shook his head then closed his eyes. "We don't have a ship, Fiona. We have a boat."

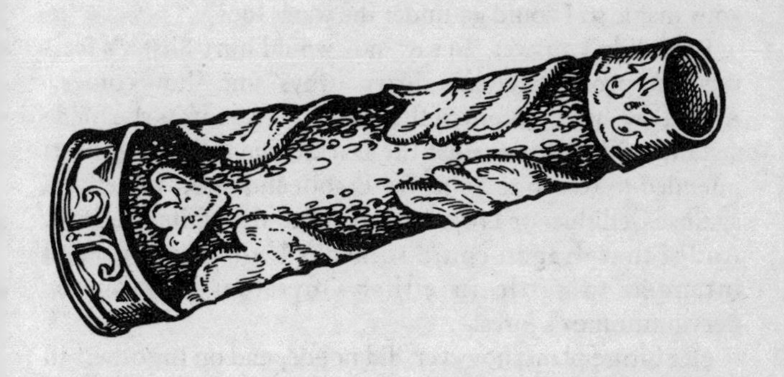

Chapter 16

Dimernesti

Feril stood poised on the railing, near the port side of the *Narwhal*'s bowsprit. She gazed at the rolling water as it captured glimmering shards of the late morning sun. The light sparkled like stars glittering in a night sky. In the distance she spotted a darker patch of blue that indicated the presence of a reef. And at the very edge of her vision was a rocky ridge she knew was dotted with sea caves, where ships had moored and traded with the Dimernesti before the great sea dragon came to rule the area.

The sunken land of the sea elves was said to rest somewhere between the reef and ridge.

"Wish I could go with you." Blister stood a few feet behind

her. "I've never been under the water before. Well, other than swimming a little bit, and that doesn't count. I mean, I've never seen a whole underwater country and elves and everything. Do you think someday you could teach me how to do your magic so I could go under the water too?"

Feril didn't answer. To say "no" would hurt Blister's feelings and probably elicit a dozen "whys" and "how comes." And to say "yes" was out of the question. As soon as she made a stand with Palin against the Dark Queen, the Kagonesti intended to return to Southern Ergoth and direct her efforts against Gellidus, or Frost as men called the white overlord. And if that dragon could someday be driven off, Feril intended to settle in either Onysablet's swamp or Beryllinthranox's forest.

Her future plans, however, did not depend on the others in the party. She felt close to Blister and the others, to Dhamon especially. But that closeness couldn't substitute for her need to be alone and in the wilderness.

The kender spoke a little louder, thinking perhaps that the waves washing against the ship had drowned out her voice. "Feril, do you think some day maybe you could teach me . . ."

The Kagonesti pulled a deep breath of salt-tinged air into her lungs and dove over the side.

" . . . how to cast magic?" Blister's lower lip stuck out and she shuffled to the rail, catching a glimpse of Feril's feet. Then the Kagonesti was gone.

The sea closed like a cocoon, and Feril concentrated on the feel of the water against her skin, focusing on a spell that would transform her into a creature she had studied years earlier. She'd spent most of the previous day sleeping and gathering her strength. The rest was necessary, as magic was taxing.

She felt her skin tingle as her lungs started calling for air. As the Kagonesti angled herself deeper, she saw the skin of her outstretched arms darken and become the color of mud. The water felt different now; her skin, too, was different: thicker, rubbery. Her tunic slipped from her and floated toward the sea floor.

Her hands disappeared, her feet vanished, and her limbs became snakelike. They writhed in the water, propelling her on. Her lungs ached, and she took a tentative gulp of water. Not yet! The spell had not yet progressed far enough. She concentrated harder as her head pounded.

Feril's snakelike limbs thickened, and more sprouted from her body—two arms on each side, growing from ribs that were snapping and popping and changing.

She dove deeper, as the light diminished, looking hazy now. The plants around her were plentiful, pointing their stalks and leaves toward the surface, trying to drink in the dim light. Her leggings slipped away.

The hair that fluttered around her face receded, her torso shortened, became bulbous, melding with her enlarging head. Her fingers and toes reformed and multiplied, becoming hundreds of suction-cup appendages. So sensitive were the cups that as they brushed against sea fronds, a myriad of sensations flooded into the Kagonesti's brain. Feril gasped, this time taking a great gulp of water into her lungs. The feeling was strange, as if she were drowning, the water inside of her and part of her. But she wasn't drowning; she was finally breathing the water. Her heart hammered wildly, and she focused on calming herself, accepting the new experience.

The octopus dropped toward the white sandy floor. Feril's new body felt liquid and malleable, the tentacles undulating to carry her across the bottom, the suction cups registering the smoothness of stones, the roughness of sand, and the suppleness of the few plants. It was impossible to catalog all the impressions. Feril concentrated on taking in the landscape.

Her new eyes, no longer needing sun-filtered light, easily peered through the now-dark water. The colors were intense. She had a wide range of vision and quickly learned to focus.

She noted the cuttlefish and squid that swam just above the sea floor to the right and a little behind her, and she saw a large reef shark that swam ahead in the distance. The shark was hunting, practically inhaling a scurrying school of black-saddled pufferfish. The shark would leave her alone, Feril thought. She was too large, and probably not on its list of preferred morsels.

Feril continued toward the reef, as she visually explored her surroundings. Then the sea floor abruptly sloped upward, and she gathered her limbs behind her, jetting forward. The water rushed around her, as she finally spread her limbs to slow her pace.

The coral reef was breathtaking, and Feril found herself staring at it in amazement. Turtle grass grew in profusion along its base and was scattered in clumps here and there. Elkhorn coral, green and yellow growths, predominated in the section of reef closest to her. She saw patches of fire coral—yellow, white, and pale orange animals that looked like tendrils of fire. In some spots the coral was only a few yards across before it was cut by the sea bed. In others, it stretched for a few hundred yards.

The fish were as colorful as the reef. A school of blue tang swam above the elkhorn. Box crabs clawed their way up toward the surface, snapping at tiny fish as they went. There were porcupine fish, star-eyed hermit crabs, delicate-looking leaf scorpionfish, and brittle stars. She wished her companions could see the marvels spread out before her. She watched a white ball sea urchin collecting bits of shells to cover itself. Nearby, a flamingo's tongue, a small mollusc, was feeding on the polyps of soft coral, leaving a swath of death behind it.

Her tentacles propelled her up the reef where the colors became brighter, a rainbow of life, as more sunlight spilled down. Then she was traveling over the top of the reef and down the other side, steeply down toward a great ravine that looked like a dark scar against the sea floor's white sand.

Feril gathered her tentacles and jetted across, glancing down into the darkness and seeing nothing but shadows which seemed to move in rhythm with the current and the seaweed.

* * * * *

"Do you think there's a city under the water?" Blister stood next to Usha, who was sitting on a coil of rope, her back against the mast.

Usha nodded. "Several."

"And do you think there're elves there?"

"They're called the Dimernesti."

"Ever see one?"

Usha shook her head.

"Do you think Feril will find the place?"

"I hope so."

"You know, we might not be in the right spot. The ocean's awfully big." The kender threw her hands out to the side, then shrugged.

"I'm sure Rig followed the Master's directions correctly," said Usha soothingly. "We must be close."

"But Feril's been gone for hours." The kender had an uncharacteristically worried look on her face. "She missed lunch. What if she's not back in time for dinner?"

Usha smiled. "Give her time, Blister. Not only does she have to find Dimernesti, she has to find the crown."

The kender stared into Usha's golden eyes. "I hope she doesn't find the dragon. I remember Silvara telling us about Brine."

"Feril can take care of herself." Rig had moved up behind Blister. "I'm more concerned about the dragon finding us. We're the only ship on this part of the ocean. That makes us a sitting target. The dragon's been known to sink ships that travel these waters." He had a spyglass in his hand. It was elaborate, made of onyx and silver and inlaid with mother-of-pearl, one of the nautical treasures he'd found in the cabin. "I haven't seen another ship since we left Khur about two weeks ago. All the smart captains keep their ships to the coasts."

"You don't have to worry about the dragon," Blister said. "The *Narwhal*'s much too small. The dragon's not going to notice a boat."

Rig closed his eyes and let out a deep breath, balancing himself as the *Narwhal* pitched violently. The kender latched her arms around the mariner's leg to keep from falling.

When the sea finally calmed, she let go, steadied herself, and looked up into his dark eyes. "Have you ever seen a Dimernesti? A sea elf, not the land kind. They're called the same thing even though they're not the same thing. I know you haven't seen the land. But you might have seen one of the elves. Usha told me that the sea elves can breathe air. You've sailed all over Ansalon, and I thought maybe . . ."

"No. I haven't seen one." Rig handed Blister the spyglass. "Mind taking a turn at watch?"

Blister grinned broadly and puffed out her chest, snatched the spyglass, and hurried toward the rear of the ship, where Groller was teaching Dhamon some of his sign language.

"Thanks," Usha said.

"Don't mention it," replied the mariner, grinning. "I'm going to get some sleep and then take the evening watch. You should think about a little rest, too."

"Rest?" The new voice was craggy and accompanied by the tromp of boots. "There'll be plenty of time to rest when we've stopped the Dark Queen from coming back." Jasper had his canvas sack clutched in his hands. Fury was following him.

Jasper reached in the sack, handing the scepter to Usha. She ran her thin fingers over its wooden surface, tracing the gems with her thumbs. "You really want to try again? You've been doing this every day," he said.

"I know."

"Ever think that maybe you can't remember because there is nothing to remember?"

"You're sounding like Blister," she teased him. "No. The elves made me forget because they were worried the scepter might fall into the wrong hands, and they didn't want it used for evil. It wasn't that they didn't trust Palin and I. And they didn't think we'd voluntarily tell someone of its powers. They just didn't want to take any chances."

Jasper sat next to her, looked between a gap in the railing at the waves, and held his stomach. Usha would never remember, he decided. Just as he would never get over being seasick.

* * * * *

The sea floor dropped off and the current became much stronger. Feril continued in the same direction, following the Master's instructions. The water was even darker now, both because she was deeper and because it was evening. She knew several hours had passed, but felt no fatigue.

She wouldn't have had to swim so far if they had taken the *Narwhal* closer. But neither she nor Rig wanted that. They didn't want to risk losing everyone on the ship to a dragon that, according to Silvara, liked to sink anything that came too close to Dimernesti.

Her eyes picked through the murky shades, separating rocks from shadows from plants from . . .

She stopped, her tentacles waving gently over the sand to keep her in place. A few dozen yards ahead, strange shapes rose from the sea floor. Black and angular, they weren't rocks.

Dimernesti? she wondered. Feril crept closer, squeezing herself through a pair of coral spires, and jetted toward a bulky shadow. A shipwreck, she realized a moment later. A large three-masted carrack lay on the sea floor, its masts stretching futilely toward the surface. Bits of sail and long sections of rope flapped in the current, making the whole thing look like the underside of a giant jellyfish.

Her tentacles touched the hull, feeling the smoothness of the wood and the rough barnacles that dotted its surface. She moved to a gaping hole in the side and slipped inside. It was dark as midnight in the cargo hold. She made out crates, coils of rope, and barrels labeled in a tongue she couldn't read. A body, completely covered with tiny red crabs, thumped against the hull's interior. She spotted other sailors, or rather what was left of them, mostly picked clean by the local denizens.

Shuddering, she scooted out of the wreck and continued on. Several dozen broken ships littered the sea floor: massive whalers, four- and five-masted galleons, caravels, cogs, merchant vessels and traders. All had become home to thousands of fish, lobsters, and crabs. As she threaded her way through the wreckaged, she noted that some of the ships had been down here for decades, the largest of them claimed by sharks and squid. The algae was thick on the older wrecks, like blue-green carpets covering every inch.

Buntlines wagged in the water like tethered sea snakes. Crow's nests were canted at crazy angles, some still affixed to masts, others caught up in seaweed-draped rigging. The place was eerily peaceful. Small sharks skimmed over the decks, and a school of a yellow tang darted inside a three-masted caravel. Feril spied another octopus, not so large as herself. Its tentacles curled and uncurled through a gash in a small galley's hull.

There were more recent wrecks, too, and Feril could make out names along their hulls: *Seawind, Balifor's Darling, Blood Sea Bounty, Sanguine Lady*, and *Cuda's Gem*. Feril paid closer attention. Her tentacles carried her across their decks and into their holds, while her senses shut out the bodies trapped there.

All of the ships had one thing in common—holes gaped in their hulls, as if they'd run aground on dangerous shoals. But there were no shoals in this deep water, no coral spikes hiding just below the surface. The dragon must have done this, she realized.

Feril moved more quickly now. She had visions of the *Narwhal* joining this graveyard. She passed beyond the wrecks and followed the still sloping sea floor. Life here was sparse in comparison to what thrived elsewhere.

Finally, she spotted the glimmering lights of what she was certain was an underwater kingdom. A school of palm-size triggerfish—bluechins, half-moons, clowns, and pinktails swam into view. Fish darted toward and away from a city that surpassed the coral reef in beauty. Feril's eyes focused on spires and domes that looked as if they had been sculpted by an artist. The colors were dazzling oranges and greens, shimmering whites, pale blues and yellows. Along the buildings' surfaces were windows. Light spilled from them, illuminating the city and making it look like a jeweled brooch.

The city was at the edge of an underwater continent, nestled amid hills. It reminded Feril of Palanthas, held in cupped lands ringed by finger hills and mountains. White sand stretched beyond it.

As she moved closer, she concentrated on the triggerfish. Within a few heartbeats, she felt her body shrinking, folding in upon itself. Her brown rubbery skin was replaced by scales, pale yellow along her sides, green atop her back, and white along her belly. Her limbs dissolved, becoming gills. A tail appeared, and her eyes moved atop her head, giving her a disconcertingly wide range of vision. Her new body was angular, a diamond shape with a tail, and it weighed no more than a few pounds. Her lips were bulbous and bright yellow, like the yellow band that shot just below her eyes.

She joined the school of triggerfish and swam toward the city. The fish fed on the small coral growths that sprouted here and there along the mountains and near the base of the buildings. Feril saw shapes passing by the windows, manlike, some pausing to look out before moving away.

Part of the triggerfish school darted toward a dome, and she followed. The buildings toward the center of the city were smaller. Some buildings were curved, sweeping like a horn from the ground. Others looked like overturned vases, and a few resembled lobster tails and conch shells. There were no people outside the buildings. She continued to swim with the fish, giving herself a tour of the city, and wondering if all the elven cities in Dimernesti looked like this.

Toward the south was what looked like a park. There were coral spires artfully arranged, as a gardener might purposefully plant trees and bushes. There were statues, too, though only one was intact: a tall sea elf with a trident clutched to his chest.

Beyond the park stretched other evidence of destruction, a row of once-tall buildings that were now nothing more than rubble. The triggerfish swam toward this, spotting coral and algae growing on a collapsed wall. They feasted on the algae and on tiny animals that looked like lace floating just above it.

Feril considered staying with the fish, hoping they would lead her around the city until she found a likely place where the crown might be. But the triggerfish showed no interest in leaving their algae snack, and Feril was in a hurry. She swam past the rubble to a smaller dome with a single light toward the roof. She darted in a window and found herself in a bedroom illuminated by a glowing shell on the wall. A net hammock fluttered between two poles. Cabinets lined one wall. An oval doorway led from this room, and Feril swam through it. Beyond was a room filled with benches and chairs, lit by more of the shells. Sculptures of sea creatures were arranged on low tables. The furniture was white, edged in pearls.

Her heart leaped in surprise as something touched her. Fingers. She pumped her fins and turned about, stared face to face with a young pale blue elf. Long silvery-white hair streamed behind her, silver like the tunic she wore. At first, Feril thought the elf had no eyebrows, but then she saw they were so pale as to seem invisible.

The sea elf's hands were webbed, her ears gracefully pointed, eyes wide and expressive, hinting at warmth and kindness. Her lips, a darker shade of blue, were moving. She was saying something. Veil? Veil-long? Feril felt the vibrations in the water before she heard the words. But the Kagonesti couldn't understand the words. As the sea elf spoke, fragments of words sounded familiar to Feril; they reminded her of her native tongue. Again, the sea elf ran her fingers along Feril's sides.

Feril shut out the sensation and selected another spell. As it took effect, she watched the sea elf step back, filled with surprise. The Dimernesti grabbed a piece of sculpture, holding it in front of her, and Feril prayed the sea elf wouldn't hit her with it. The Kagonesti desperately needed her first encounter with a Dimernesti to be a friendly one.

The sea elf replaced the sculpture, and Feril breathed a sigh of relief. The Kagonesti continued to change. Her tail elongated and split, forming legs covered with pale yellow scales. Her fins thrust out to her sides, fleshed out and became scale-covered arms. Within several moments, Feril floated before the sea elf, her hair fluttering like a lion's mane in the water, the tattoos on her face and arm visible. She had taken on her Kagonesti form, but her body retained the triggerfish's scales and coloration, and her neck preserved the fish's gills.

Veil. The word the sea elf repeated again sounded like "veil." The Dimernesti cautiously approached Feril. More words spilled from her mouth. "Elf" was the only one Feril could make out.

The Kagonesti tried to respond but found she couldn't speak intelligibly in this form. Her own elven words were foreign to the sea elf. She settled on a different tact, thinking of Groller so far distant. Pointing toward the ceiling, she cupped her hands in front of her, as if she were holding something. Then she moved her hands forward, as if they were a boat. Finally she placed her hands flat against each other and tilted them down, pantomiming diving.

The sea elf looked at her quizzically, but friendly, extended a hand, and led her from the room. As they went, the sea elf continued to talk; her words sounded musical. Only a few had any similarity to the elven tongue Feril knew. The only ones she recognized were elf, magic, and dragon.

Their path took them across the park. Nowhere did Feril see any other beings, only the triggerfish and a few crabs that scuttled along the sandy streets. The sea elf swam quickly, furtively glancing above and down each waterway between rows of buildings. She slipped between a pair of rose-colored dwellings, coaxing Feril along.

Then the Dimernesti turned down a street lined with massive, polished conch shells. They passed several more ruined buildings along the way. Feril wanted to ask her guide about them, but she filed the questions away for later, for a time when communication might become possible. Perhaps the elf was taking her to someone who could help her.

They approached a building that Feril guessed stretched upward five or six stories. It was a pale gray, shot through in places by streaks of silver. Soft orange light spilled from windows that spiraled up its sides.

The sea elf started talking again, faster, words that didn't register with the Kagonesti. She pulled Feril toward a round door, rapping her pale blue hand against it. After several moments, the door opened, and a male sea elf stood in the frame.

His skin was a shade of bright blue, and his hair was dark green and short. He looked at the pair with a puzzled expression, as the female sea elf guide rattled off what Feril assumed was an explanation of how a fish swam into her home and turned into a scaly elf.

The man stepped aside, gesturing, and Feril allowed herself to be conducted into a circular chamber, the walls of which were covered in shell mosaics depicting fish, blue-skinned elves, and fantastical creatures. There was a hole in the ceiling, providing access to another floor. A similar hole at the edge of the room led to somewhere below.

Three more sea elves swam through an oval doorway directly across from Feril. They were young and muscular, wearing only shimmering cloths about their thighs. And they carried nets. Feril moved back toward the door, panic rising in her throat.

Her guide shook her head at the men, waving her webbed hands and speaking rapidly. But the men seemed to ignore her and headed straight toward Feril.

The Kagonesti felt the rush of water behind her as the door was closed, blocking her way out. She whirled and bumped into the bright blue elf. He grabbed her shoulders, and spoke words she couldn't decipher. She struggled, but his hands were surprisingly strong and locked about her arms. He pushed her against the wall, continued to talk.

"I mean no harm!" Feril shouted in her native tongue, then again in the common tongue. Both times her words were distorted and lost on the sea elves. "I can't let this happen!"

She summoned her strength, placing her feet against the wall, and pushed back as hard as she could, managing to break the grip of the blue sea elf.

Then she kicked out with as much force as she could manage. She bought herself a few yards, though the men with the nets were coming closer as her guide still argued with them.

She swam toward the oval doorway, narrowly avoiding the outstretched nets. Then she quickly altered her course. More elves might be in the chambers beyond. At the last moment, she kicked her legs hard and angled herself toward the hole in the ceiling. She was about to kick harder when a hand clamped around her ankle.

Her foot struck a face, and she bucked wildly to tear loose. But a hand grabbed her other ankle, and though she continued to struggle, the hands pulled her down. A net was thrown over her. Feril ripped through several of the strands. A second net was added, the weave uncomfortably tight. And then a third.

Bundled up, the Kagonesti was carried through the hole in the ceiling. The sea elf who had guided Feril to this building was left behind as she was taken to the third story of the tower. She was kept here under the guard of a pair of elves who tried to talk to her. It was hopeless—she still couldn't fathom a word. The nets in which she was trapped were secured to a decorative post.

There was furniture in this room, and her three guards sat on slabs extending from the walls. The largest of the sea elves commanded a net chair that hung from a corner. Having given up on communicating with her, they conversed among themselves. Feril listened as she struggled to free herself. "Elf" was the word repeated most often. "Magic, fish, and dragon" always followed. Other elves came and went, chattering to her guards and ogling the prisoner.

She could use her magic to alter her form, become small enough, perhaps, to slip through gaps in the net. Other spells could split and rend the net and let her flee in this form. But should she cast such spells? Or should she wait, bide her time? The sea elves had not hurt her. And if they operated like other elven societies, no doubt leaders were being summoned to decide what to do with her. Perhaps she would be able to explain to them about the crown.

But how long should she wait?

A while, at least, she finally decided; long enough to rest and rebuild her strength. Feril was tired. She drifted in and out of an uneasy sleep, regaining some of her strength. She suspected the better part of the day had passed by the time her guards changed. The two new watchers chatted with her former captors in the doorway.

She concentrated, remembering the triggerfish, deciding a small one might wriggle its way free and lose itself in this city. One triggerfish among dozens. She felt her skin tighten, her form start to shrink. Then she stopped the spell. One of the new guards was approaching.

"Do you understand the common tongue?" he asked, the words muffled through the water, but distinct enough for her to make them out. "Veylona thought she heard you speak it. Are you from the surface?"

Her heart soared with excitement. She nodded vigorously. She tried to talk and failed miserably, though a few words came across. "Feril" sounded like Groller's "Furl", and "crown" sounded more like "round." Another form would be best, she considered, something that might . . .

The sea elf yanked the nets free. "This was a precaution, nothing more," he said. "We did not intend to harm you. Veylona—she was certain you meant no harm to us, though we had to be convinced."

Veylona, Feril thought. Veil? The word the sea elf woman had repeated.

"These are difficult times for us," the Dimernesti continued. "And you must understand that visitors here are most rare. Our mystics divined that you were alone, not a spy for the dragon."

"Veylona?" Feril said the word loud and slow.

"Veylona, she brought you here. Her command of the common tongue is not as good as mine. Veylona, she asked me to guide you. She thinks you are a sorceress."

Feril swam free of the nets and flexed her arms and legs.

"*Are* you a sorceress?"

The Kagonesti shook her head. How to explain? Perhaps it was better not to. At last, she nodded slowly.

"A sorceress from the surface. Then you require air? Prefer air?"

Feril nodded again, more vigorously. If she had air to

breathe, she could better talk to him, and explain why she was here and what she needed.

He motioned for her, and she followed, the other guard swimming behind her. His fingers were wrapped around the haft of a trident.

"I am Beldargh," he said. "One of the city guardians. I am taking you to a room with air, where in decades past we brought visitors from the surface. It has not been used in a most long time."

This room was at the top of the tower, the water in it shallow, held at bay, Feril suspected, by an enchantment cast long ago. Her face broke the surface as she concentrated on her body again, this time returning it fully to her Kagonesti form. The guard poked his head above the water next to her.

"Feril," she gasped, as she took in a lungful of the stale air. "My name is Feril."

"Sorceress Feril of the Surface," Beldargh said slowly, his words sounding breathy in the air. "Were you on a ship that Brine sank? Did you survive by magic?"

"No. The dragon hasn't sunk our ship. I hope it's beyond his reach. But I'm here because of the dragon—all the dragons. I need your help. I need the crown."

"The Crown of Tides?"

Feril nodded.

"Feril, I do not think that will be possible." Beldargh's expression darkened, and he shook his head.

"Please listen to me," she begged. While Beldargh listened, the Kagonesti began the long tale of what brought her to the underwater realm.

"Dimernost," Beldargh said when she was finally finished. "It will take us a day to reach there. In Dimernost you will ask our . . ." He groped for a word in her tongue. "Our leader. Our most wise leader will decide. We leave now."

He motioned for her to follow, then added. "Expect disappointment, Sorceress Feril of the Surface."

* * * * *

Dimernost, the capital of the underwater realm, looked much like the city Feril had first visited, though much larger. Beldargh served as her guide, and she was accompanied by a handful of other sea elves, including Veylona, the first sea elf that the Kagonesti had met.

She was led through a series of domes partially filled with air. The party stopped at an ornate room containing dozens of sea elves. Most wore few clothes and had pale blue skin, Feril noted, though others had gray skin, and a few were dark blue. Their hair color varied, as well, from white to almost blond, to green, and in many cases various shades of blue.

In the center of the assemblage stood a robed woman to whom the other elves seemed to defer. She had a matronly air, and her unblinking eyes carefully regarded Feril.

"I am Nuqala, Speaker of the Sea," the woman began in the common tongue. Her accent was one Feril had heard spoken in Khur. "And you are a Kagonesti. Only once do I recall one of your kind visiting with us. That was a long while ago, and he was with a merchant trader seeking to barter goods. Like the trader, you appear to wish something from us."

Feril nodded and opened her mouth to explain, but Nuqala continued.

"Word moves quickly through the water. What you wish is very valuable, precious to us and life-sustaining." She paused a moment, and then continued. "You seem to have a considerable command of magic. That magic allowed you to avoid Bryndelsemir."

Again Feril nodded.

"Explain yourself," the woman stated.

Words tumbled from Feril's lips. It was the same story she earlier had told Beldargh, but now it was much more complete: how she came across the Southern Courrain Ocean with her companions in search of Dimernesti, and how she elected to make this part of the journey alone because of her command of nature magic. She explained that she had seen no signs of the dragon, but had seen the ship graveyard.

"Ships sail here no longer," Nuqala said. Her voice was tinged with melancholy. "We have no more trade with the surface. We are prisoners here. But we are fighters. We do not give up. Our people hunt, though some in turn are hunted by Bryndelsemir. We tend crops, and the dragon devours some of our farmers. But we will never surrender to the dragon. I believe Bryndelsemir does not want to kill us all, as he would have nothing to toy with. We use the Crown of Tides to keep him at bay, preventing him from destroying all of our cities. And you want the crown that is our defense?" Nuqala's laughed sadly and shook her head. "You, surface elf, want us to surrender. You would doom us, and for what purpose?"

"I don't wish to doom you but to save you and to save all of Krynn," Feril replied. There was urgency in the Kagonesti's voice. "The crown is old, an artifact from the Age of Dreams. Palin Majere believes . . . "

"Majere? Palin, nephew of Raistlin?" The sea elf tilted her head. "That is a name I have not heard for decades. Palin Majere lives?"

"Yes. He sent us here, to recover the crown. He believes that with the crown, and with other artifacts, we can stop Takhisis from returning and can make a stand against the overlords."

"You want to help your people against the dragons on the surface. You want me to hand over something sacred to save the surface dwellers."

"I won't deny that," Feril returned. "But I also want to help you. Please believe me. We haven't much time. Takhisis is returning. And if the Dark Queen comes back to Krynn, your people will have worse things to worry about than a sea dragon."

The other elves in the domed chamber spoke among

themselves, some arguing. A few chattered heatedly to Nuqala in the tongue Feril could only catch pieces of. Nuqala seemed to absorb all their conversations.

"The crown is one of our most hallowed treasures," she said at last, turning back to Feril. "It belongs to the Dimernesti. It is part of our heritage, linked to our lives."

"There will be no Dimernesti if the dragons have their way and Takhisis returns," said the Kagonesti.

"I will consider your words, as I will consider the words of my people. You will stay as our guest for the day, surface elf. In the morning, you shall have my answer."

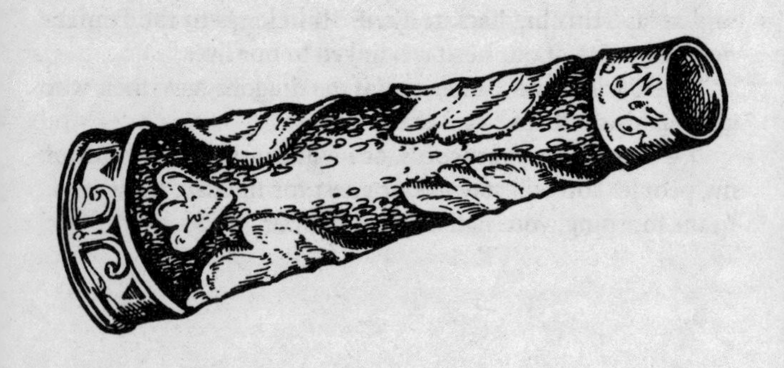

Chapter 17

Rough Waters

"I don't like this one bit." Rig pressed the spyglass to his eye, looking out across the choppy water tinted pink by the dawn sun. "She should've been back by now. It's been three days."

Dhamon leaned against the railing nearby, his gazed fixed on a swell in the distance. "We have to wait for her."

"I don't intend to pull up the anchor . . . just yet," the mariner returned. "So you don't have to be all worried that I'll leave her stranded—if she's still alive. She's a friend of mine, and I'm not one to abandon my friends. But waiting isn't my style either. If Palin contacts Usha again tonight, I'll see how much longer we can afford to stay here." He thrust the glass at Dhamon. "I'm gonna wake up Fiona, and the two of us'll fix some breakfast. Something edible. Something better than what Blister came up with last night."

The mariner glided across the deck, silent as a cat. Dhamon held the glass to his eye and looked out over the water.

"Still lookin' at that scepter?" Blister addressed Usha, who was sitting on a thick coil of rope. "I'll admit it is pretty. And awfully valuable what with all those gems on it. But I'd get tired of looking at the same thing all the time. Of course, there isn't much else to look at, I suppose. There's water. Lots of water. You could count the panels of wood in the captain's cabin. I already did that, though. So maybe we could—"

"Good morning, Blister!"

"Good morning to you, Jasper." The kender turned her attention to the dwarf. "Usha's lookin' at the scepter again."

"I can see that."

"She's still trying to remember something."

"I think I've figured out a way to help her do just that."

The kender's eyes grew wide. "Really? What? How?"

The dwarf sniffed the air. "Mmmm. Breakfast. Rig and Fiona are in the galley, working on something tasty."

The kender scurried toward the stairs. "I told Rig I'd cook breakfast! I wanted to use that jar of blue flour I found last night!"

"What did you have in mind?" Usha asked the dwarf.

"Something I should have thought of a long time ago, if I'd been thinking right. Remember when we were in Ak-Khurman, and I, uh, . . . made the spy a little more cooperative? The spell might work on you, too."

Usha's eyes sparkled as she set the scepter at her feet. "Please, Jasper. Anything to help me remember."

The dwarf reached inside himself, felt for the spark, and coaxed it to grow. The sooner he accomplished this, he told himself, the sooner he could go back below deck where he didn't have to watch the water pitch and roll and where his stomach didn't seem to rise quite so high into his throat. He held a stubby hand out toward Usha, rested it on her leg and stared into her golden eyes.

"Friend," the dwarf began.

"Friend," Usha heard herself reply. She closed her eyes, and the blue of the Southern Courrain Ocean disappeared. Her world was filled, instead, with green.

Usha watched Palin leave, the forest of the Qualinesti swallowing him along with Feril and Jasper. The green filled her vision and made her feel suddenly empty and isolated, somehow frightening her a little. For several moments all she heard was her own uneasy breathing. She felt in her ears the beating of her heart, and faintly she heard the rustling of the leaves in the slight breeze.

Then the birds in the tall willows around her resumed singing, signaling to her that Palin was moving farther away, no longer worrying them. The chittering of chipmunks, chucks, and ground squirrels reached her, and she sagged against the thick trunk of a shaggybark, taking the myriad sounds of the tropical forest. She tried to relax. Had the circumstances been different, or had her husband been accompanying her, she might have enjoyed her surroundings or at the very least appreciated them. However, as it was, she couldn't help but feel uncomfortable, a wary intruder in the elven woods.

Once again, as it had happened before, the elf stepped into view. Once more she heard her name as if it were a curse. The details were as vivid as if she were back in the Qualinesti Forest.

"It is called the Fist of E'li," the Qualinesti woman was saying, "an ancient thing once wielded by Silvanos himself. Ornate, it is said, bejeweled and pulsing with power. Perhaps if we had the Fist, we could do something against the dragon's minions."

"If Palin gains it, you can't take it away!" Usha surprised herself by the vehemence of her tone. "We need—"

"I'll not take it, if he finds it—though I doubt that will happen. I'll be glad enough to keep it away from the occupants of the tower. But I'll accept a promise from you, provided your husband returns here with it." The elf's eyes glowed. "If the scepter is not consumed by whatever your husband has planned for its use, then you will do everything in your power, Usha Majere, to keep it safe and to return it to us. You will risk your very life for this scepter—the Fist of E'li—if need be. Do you understand?"

"Risk my life," Usha murmured. "Keep it safe. I promise. But you must tell me what the Fist does. You owe that to me after stealing my memories."

"I will tell you, Usha, but only because I do not believe Palin Majere will ever return from the tower. Legends claim Silvanos used the Fist of E'li, the Fist of Paladine, to rally the elves, to incite them, to inspire them, to urge them to champion his causes. Some say the Fist of E'li is a mind-controlling device. I prefer to believe those elven scholars, however, who insist the Fist only reinforces what people already believe or support. It simply lends them the courage to stand up for their convictions. The Fist, these scholars say, gives people the resolve to embrace with deeds what is harbored by their thoughts. I believe this, too. The Fist is not capable of corrupting people."

"I understand," Usha said softly. "The Fist can't change people's minds or control their thoughts. But it can give them confidence."

"Yes. And it cannot force them to do something out of character," the elf continued. "E'li would not have had that. He would not have wanted unwilling armies, followers who were no more than marionettes to be controlled by his thoughts."

The elven woman reached up and twirled a strand of

Usha's hair about a slender finger. "Some scholars say the Fist has other properties, too, Usha Majere: that it makes its wielder more confident, and that it can enhance the appearance of the wielder, making him more pleasing to the eye or more accepted by his audience perhaps. Or, perhaps it is merely the beauty of all the gems, making the wielder seem more attractive or stately."

"Stately," Usha repeated. Her brow furrowed. "But if the Fist of E'li doesn't change people's minds or accomplish anything drastic, what makes it so powerful and valuable to my husband?"

The elf's eyes twinkled. "I suspect Palin Majere knows nothing of what the scepter can actually do. He simply thinks it is an ancient artifact that will help fulfill his quest. It does possess arcane power, Usha. For the Fist is also a weapon, and it can slay at command, provided the wielder concentrates on his foe and knows how to call upon its killing force. With one strike it can reduce enemies to cinders."

"Could it slay a dragon?"

The elf stepped away, regarding Usha. "A dragon? Perhaps, perhaps not. I doubt it would do more than wound a great overlord such as Beryl. E'li would not have had such a foe in mind when the scepter was fashioned. Besides, an overlord such as the Green Peril would sense the magic in the scepter and would unleash her horrible breath, destroying the wielder and the Fist before the artifact could be used against her."

"We must tell Palin about the scepter's powers. It is possible that he might find a way to—"

"No. The powers of the Fist are like your isle of the Irda: a precious secret the two of us have shared. The secret belongs to me and my chosen followers, and with elven scholars. Palin might indeed wield the Fist capably as it was intended. But if he fails and it is stolen from him, the knowledge of its abilities will also be stolen, and the Fist could be turned into a force for evil. That will be his test. Secrecy is best, I think."

"Secrecy," Usha repeated. "I understand secrets."

"You know nothing about the secrets of the Fist of E'li," the elf said, her voice monotonic, spellbinding. "You will remember nothing of our conversation. You will remember none of these things, Usha Majere. You will only remember our forest and your vow about the Fist."

After a pause, the elf said softly, "You were telling me about your voyage to this forest."

Usha's fingers fluttered across her temples, rubbing away a minor headache. "Yes," she said haltingly. "A ship brought us here."

"What did you call it, this ship?"

"*Flint's Anvil.* Jasper named it, bought it with a gem his uncle Flint gave him."

"That uncle would be . . ."

"Flint Fireforge. He was one of the Heroes of the Lance."

"The legendary dwarf." The elf cocked her head. "Is something wrong, Usha?"

"I remember."

Usha blinked and grasped Jasper's hand.

* * * * *

"I have reached a decision, surface elf." Nuqala floated in front of Feril in a small room devoid of furnishings. The building, Feril had learned, was called the Tower of the Sea. "The crown is a treasure," Nuqala said. "It is part of our heritage, crucial to our defenses. It has been useful in deterring Brine."

Feril's hopes sank.

"I also realize that perhaps it could be more useful in helping to bring down all of the dragon overlords, not just the one that plagues us. The Crown of Tides is yours in return for a pledge. If you keep Takhisis from returning to Krynn, and then launch a plot against the dragon overlords, you must promise first to attempt to slay Bryndelsemir."

I can't make such a promise, Feril thought. How can I guarantee that my friends will agree? Still, she said to herself, she could guarantee her own actions. Feril nodded to the woman. "I promise."

"I sent for the crown last night," Nuqala continued. "We keep it elsewhere in this tower." She reached into the folds of her robe, which fluttered like sea fronds about her slight frame, and retrieved a tall blue coral crown studded with pearls. It was breathtakingly beautiful, and the Kagonesti could sense the vibrations of power.

Nuqala held it out to Feril. The Kagonesti's fingers tentatively stretched forward, touched the crown.

"The Crown of Tides," the sea elf whispered. "The waters are yours to command with it." Nuqala stepped aside, gestured toward the open oval doorway behind her. "Surface elf, inform Palin Majere of your promise to me. And make sure that you keep it."

* * * * *

The mountains of Dimernesti grew small behind her as Feril hurried toward the ship graveyard, the first landmark that would bring her back to the *Narwhal*. She kept her scaly-elf form, and the Crown of Tides rested securely on her head.

She kept close to the sand, swimming between the dark hulks, not wanting to attract the attention of the small sharks or any of the larger reef sharks that might be in the vicinity. It was early in the morning, she could tell, and pale light was filtering down, painting the ships a murky green. *Sanguine Lady*, she mused, as she passed that ship. She would have to tell Rig of the fate of the vessel. She remembered he had once told her that he had sailed on it years ago.

The graveyard behind her, she swam faster toward the ravine and the reef beyond. Rather than focus on the riot of marine life all around her, she forced herself to concentrate on the crown. She felt the magic in the blue coral; it invigorated and emboldened her.

It controls water, she mused. The crown fairly hummed, and her eyes snapped wide. The crown was responding to her! Feril shot over the ravine, her legs kicking hard, the water jetting away from her. She focused on her fingers now, holding them before her face, and watching as water streamed away from her hands.

The Crown of Tides, she thought. Yes, I could control the very tides with this! But what will it do above water? How can it help Palin?

She kicked toward the reef, oblivious to the shadow that broke away from the ravine wall, following her.

The creature propelled itself after the Kagonesti, which it had mistaken in the murky water for an insolent sea elf. The great dragon didn't like the Dimernesti elves straying outside in their underwater realm, and he ate those who tempted his anger.

As she crested the reef, Feril felt the sea growing hot. Puzzling at this new sensation, she thought perhaps it was a side effect of using the crown. Perhaps. . .

She gasped, as the hot water flowed in through her gills. No! Not the crown. Something else. She spun about, looking behind her, almost too late as her mouth fell open and the heat grew impossibly intense.

Brine, she thought.

The great dragon looked like a sea monster from children's folk tales. Feril guessed he must be more than two hundred feet from pointed snout to barbed tail. His long, black body was legless and was closing the distance. Dark green scales covered his neck and head, while lighter green scales lined his lower jaw and belly.

As Brine opened his jaws, Feril felt a great surge in the current, the water churning all around her. She gasped, unable to breathe the overheated water, and doubled over from the excruciating pain. Her fingers reached for the crown and touched it as she felt herself slipping toward unconsciousness.

No! she screamed wordlessly. I can't give in. I can't be boiled alive before Palin has a chance to use the crown!

She thought of the water, boiling all around her, willing it to be cooler. And within the span of a few heartbeats it was so. The Crown of Tides had worked its wonders.

But the dragon was so close now, she could see his iridescent blue eyes. As the creature bore down on her, she imagined her reflection in the orbs. She kicked, concentrating on the crown, as the dragon loomed closer still. His undulating body pushed through the water, mouth wide, and snapped rapaciously. Jagged-looking mother-of-pearl teeth glistened in the light that spilled down from the surface.

She kicked harder, at the same time gesturing with her arms, sending a more intense jet of water Brine's way. Feril risked a glance over her shoulder, saw to her surprise that the dragon had been pushed back a little by the increased force. She focused again on the jets of water she was creating, pushing the dragon back a little into a rocky outcropping near the reef.

A howl carried through the water, and Feril saw that the dragon's tail was skewered on a spire of coral. Brine howled again, the water boiling all around, destroying the small creatures, the coral, and the living rock in the area and shooting a wave of unbearable heat Feril's way.

The Kagonesti swam faster, drawing on the Crown of Tides to augment her strength, trying to put distance between herself and the dragon.

A moment later she felt a surge of renewed heat in the water around her and realized that Brine had extricated himself. Dark boiling blood colored the water. The dragon opened his mouth and roared, then shot forward, his tail whipping furiously.

Feril pumped her legs, concentrating on the crown to maintain the water jets. At the same time her mind reached out to the nearby plant life. She merged her senses with them, asking for their help. She'd used the enchantment numerous times on land and knew instinctively it would work here, too.

The turtle grass, fronds, kelp, and soft coral responded, stretching to wrap about the dragon's tail. A dense patch of seaweed rose to entwine about the dragon's sinewy neck.

The dragon howled in anger, thrashing wildly. He opened his mouth and released another boiling blast that Feril was barely able to cool. Then the Kagonesti stopped, floating and staring at the dragon, as she ran her fingers along the coral band and focused on the plants.

Grow, she willed.

Powered by the artifact, her spell came alive, and the effects were startling. The seaweed doubled in size, then doubled again. The soft coral multiplied and surrounded Brine. The kelp became thick, all but obscuring the dragon.

Grow, she continued. Tighter.

She heard the dragon's scream clearly. It was painfully loud, even in the water. She sensed the grasses tightening around Brine's neck, keeping him from taking in life-sustaining water.

Tighter. Grow.

The grass stretched, blotting out all traces of Brine now. Then in the span of a heartbeat it withered and died. Feril stared as her heart hammered. The dragon had found the strength for one more ferocious breath and wiped out all the plants around him.

The great dragon's eyes narrowed, and again he shot toward her. Feril turned and cut toward what she believed was east, away from where she knew the *Narwhal* was. She couldn't risk running to the ship for safety, not when the dragon would easily destroy the small ship.

She used the crown to force jets of water away from her legs and arms, working to buy time. Then she felt herself propelled forward, not by her own means, but by Brine. She was hurled, somersaulting through the water, toward a coral outcropping. Feril fought to slow herself, then struck the reef. Her eyes closed.

The dragon eyed the unconscious elf. Not blue, like the Dimernesti, but an elf, and a powerful one. One from the surface? From a ship?

* * * * *

Dhamon spotted another swell and trained the spyglass on it. Something about it was different. It was dark green, perhaps black. Maybe a whale. The swell flattened and he lost track of it. A whale, especially a large one, could pose problems if it got too close. It might even capsize the *Narwhal.*

"Where are you?" Dhamon whispered. "Where?"

The ship's bow rose suddenly, riding up high until the ship was practically perched on its rear rudder. Dhamon grabbed onto the rail. His feet flew out behind him as a spray of incredibly hot water hit him in the face.

A handful of the freed slaves who were on the deck slid toward the rear of the ship, their hands scrabbling for anything to grab onto.

"No!" Jasper tumbled head over feet when the ship lurched. Usha, at midships, reached out to grab him and the scepter. At the last moment her fingers locked around the polished handle, while her other hand managed to catch the dwarf's pant leg. But the material ripped, and Jasper fell headlong. Then Usha felt herself sliding, as well. She heard the ship's timbers groan, heard startled cries from below deck. She careened after Jasper, and they both struck the capstan.

"I've got you!" the dwarf yelled. He wrapped one stubby arm around Usha's waist, clamping the other one onto the capstan. "Don't drop that scepter!"

She opened her mouth to reply, but instead gave a scream of surprise. The front end of the ship crashed down, slamming against the water and jarring her and Jasper loose, eliciting pitiable cries from the former slaves. The dwarf was on his feet first, helping Usha up.

"What was *that*?" Usha asked.

"Don't know." He shrugged and clutched his stomach as a wave of nausea began to overwhelm him. "But I intend to find out." The dwarf steadied himself against the capstan while looking about. "Dhamon!" Jasper glanced toward the bow, where a drenched Dhamon, his face red and blistered, was struggling to his feet.

Dhamon thrust the spyglass in his pocket and drew a long sword that was strapped to his waist—one of a dozen weapons he and Rig had unearthed below. He was edging backward, keeping wary eyes on the water. "Rig!" Dhamon hollered. "Rig get up here!"

"Untangle the rigging," Jasper instructed the freed slaves, as he and Usha hurried toward Dhamon. "And brace yourselves. I think we've really found trouble this time."

The dwarf took the scepter from her. "What is it?"

"I thought it was a whale," Dhamon said. He brushed his free hand at his face, scowling when his fingers touched the blisters. "But I don't think so. I think . . ."

"Dragon!" Usha shouted. She was pointing off the port side. "It's a dragon!"

"What?" It was Rig's voice. "A dragon?" Fiona was behind him, Groller towering next to her.

"What happened?" Blister scooted around them. The kender's hair was blue. Her face was smudged with blue flour, and some gooey yellow mixture was evident on her tunic. "Did we hit something?"

"Dragon!" Usha repeated.

They all saw Brine then, as his head broke the waves. His jaws were longer than the *Narwhal*, his teeth as big around as the ship's mainmast. His blue eyes locked onto the ship. The dragon rose higher.

His serpentine neck, shimmering green and black in the morning sun, looked oddly beautiful. He craned his head about, opened his mouth, and blasted the *Narwhal* with a gout of steam.

Fury howled. The wolf had just come on deck and was rushing to the rail when it caught the first of the steamy breath. It was knocked off its feet, howling, and tore free large clumps of hair.

"Brine!" Blister yelled as she pawed at her pockets, searching for her sling. "I said I wanted to see a Dimernesti, not a dragon," she muttered to herself. "I didn't want to see a dragon at all. No, no. Not at all."

"If that thing gets close to this ship, we're all done for!" Rig yelled. He plucked daggers from his waist, holding three in each hand. He steadied himself by the port rail, waiting until the dragon came within range.

Dhamon was at the mariner's side, a leg thrown over the rail. "It's going to try to take the ship down."

"What do you think you're doing?" Rig stared as Dhamon slipped his other leg over the rail.

"Taking the initiative and giving you a chance to get the ship under sail. I fought a dragon before, remember? Get the *Narwhal* out of here." Then without another word, Dhamon dropped into the water and began to swim awkwardly toward the dragon, holding his sword in his hand. Rig was too astonished to say anything.

Dhamon *had* fought Gale, the great blue dragon which descended on the *Anvil* when it was moored in the Palanthas harbor. That was the battle that cost the life of Shaon, the marnier's love. Rig had blamed Dhamon for Shaon's death and had said that if Dhamon had stayed with the Knights of Takhisis and remained partnered with Gale, Shaon would still be alive. But Dhamon had indeed fought Gale. Rig had watched him battle the dragon over the Palanthas hills, had watched Dhamon and Gale plunge into a deep lake.

"These won't do anything," Rig muttered as he threw the daggers at the dragon. Only one of the six managed to lodge in the dragon's neck, the rest falling into the water. The mariner suspected the small blade was no more than a pin-prick to the beast. "Jasper! Up anchor! Fiona, drop the sails!" He called to the former slaves to watch the rudder, keep the rigging tight, and to warn the men in the hold.

The mariner dashed toward the bow, seeking the *Narwhal*'s lone ballista. He opened a chest affixed to the deck, and began pulling bolts from it. "Daggers didn't hurt you, but these might," he yelled.

At midships, Fiona unfurled the sails with Usha's and the ex-slaves' help. The ship budged, then caught, held by its anchor. The women glanced toward the stern, where Jasper and Groller were busy pulling at the anchor rope. "Hurry, Jasper," Usha urged.

"Yes!" Fiona cheered, as she watched the anchor rise from the water. Then she shook her head. "No!" she called to the half-ogre, knowing he couldn't hear her and that even if he could her words wouldn't dissuade him. Sure enough, finished with the task, Groller did the unthinkable. He plunged into the water, his long arms taking him toward Dhamon and the dragon.

"What does he think he's doing?" Usha gasped.

"Helping Dhamon," Fiona solemnly replied, as her hand drifted to her sword. "He knows there's only one ballista, and Rig's using it."

"But he's committing suicide."

The Solamnic knight nodded. "And I'll be joining him in the great hereafter unless we can find something else to shoot at the dragon from a distance."

"In the hold," Usha urged. "There are spears."

"Then let's hurry."

"Blister!" they heard Rig bellow as they made their way below. "Forget your sling. Useless! Get on the wheel! Get us some distance!"

The mariner was aiming the large crossbow, shooting bolts at the great sea dragon. He was unaccustomed to the weapon, but after a few shots he had already begun to aim it better.

Now, several dozen yards out from the retreating *Narwhal*, Dhamon trod water and held the sword above his head as the dragon rose above the surface, then slammed down. A spray of hot water coated Dhamon. He gritted his teeth to keep from crying out. The beast's head rose again, his eyes fixed on the man in the water. His jaws opened and released another searing blast of steam.

Dhamon dove just in time to avoid the brunt of the blast. The water was achingly hot, and he fought to stay conscious and to keep hold of the weapon.

Determined, the knight held his breath and kicked forward. Closer! Dhamon screamed to himself. Closer! There! He jammed the sword into the dragon's neck with all of his strength. The blade found its way between green-black scales and drew blood.

Stung by a man! Brine howled in astonishment. The sword hadn't truly hurt; it was more of an annoyance. Yet the dragon howled in fury that something so puny would challenge him. Another man was swimming this way. This man was larger and would be eaten first.

Brine sank lower, even as the first man pulled the sword from his throat and stabbed again. The dragon angled his head, then his neck shot forward, jaws opened wide.

On the deck of the *Narwhal*, Blister worked the wheel, turning the bow of the ship away from the dragon, even as Rig swiveled the ballista in the mount for a better shot.

Jasper was behind her on the deck, grasping the Fist and staring at the dragon. "Can't swim," he said. "I'll sink like a stone. Groller!"

The dwarf spotted the half-ogre. He was holding onto a spine on Brine's back, sword in hand, stabbing at the beast. Rig saw Groller too and spun the ballista about.

"Blister!" Rig shouted. "Steer toward the dragon!"

"I thought you wanted us to get away!"

"Change in plans!" Rig shot back. "Get us closer." Groller forced the change in plans, the mariner thought. Rig wouldn't risk his life for Dhamon Grimwulf; he wouldn't put the ship in jeopardy for that man. But Groller was another matter. "Closer!"

Usha and Fiona ran up from below deck, arms laden with spears from the armory. A dozen men followed, similarly burdened.

"The dragon," Usha murmured in disbelief. "We're heading toward it, not away."

"Easier to hit if it's closer," the Solamnic said. She stood by the rail, her feet planted, hefting a spear in each hand. "One at a time," she said to Usha. Then the spears flew from her hands toward the great sea dragon. Usha passed her two more spears, while readying another pair.

The others joined her, futilely trying to wound the beast.

"Uh-oh," Jasper said.

The dragon was rising up again in the water, preparing for another dive. Its massive form disappeared below the waves in a great rush that sent a shower of boiling water across the *Narwhal*'s deck.

Beneath the surface, the sea dragon's body writhed, flinging the man away. The dragon roared, furious, turning his head and breathing a gout of steam in the half-ogre's direction, just as Groller surfaced near the ship. Brine heard the small cry of the man, caught on the edge of the blast. He allowed himself a moment of anger that the man was not close enough to be killed by the heat, then felt another stab at his neck. The man with the black hair had returned. The dragon dove deeper.

Dhamon's sword was lodged in Brine's neck, his hands tight about the pommel.

The man would die now, Brine knew. He did not have the pointed ears of the Dimernesti and could not breathe water.

The dragon headed for the sea floor. Dhamon desperately hung onto the sword that was still buried in the creature's neck.

On the surface, Rig, at the railing of the *Narwhal*, extended a pole to the battered half-ogre. Groller reached a hand up and grabbed it, allowed himself to be pulled back on board.

The mariner eyed his friend.

"I'm all ride," the half-ogre told him. He was scalded and bruised and had come close to death, but he was alive. "Dried do help Day-mon." He brushed the saltwater out of his eyes, then saw Fury and Jasper approaching. "Jaz-pear good healer. Jaz-pear, fix me again."

"Where's Dhamon?" Rig muttered. "Where's the damn dragon?"

Below the waves, Dhamon struggled to stay conscious. His lungs ached and his head throbbed, but he forced his hands to pull the sword free one more time, to stab the sea dragon again. Brine was larger than Gale, his skin much thicker, but Dhamon had been hammering at the same spot over and over. He had pierced the scales and finally drawn a significant amount of blood. Black like the shadow dragon's blood, it pooled about him, clouding his vision.

He drove the blade in deeper, and the dragon recoiled. He raised his neck, then slammed it down against a coral ledge, pressing Dhamon between its body and the coral. The last bit of air rushed from the knight's lungs, and his hands lost their grip.

Brine raised his neck and felt pain where the sword was lodged. The man lay unmoving, ready to be devoured. First the dragon would sink the ship. Then he would return to deal with this man—and the vexing woman with the crown.

He'd destroy the ship first, before it could sail away. The dragon would kill all of those on the ship, devour them one by one, savor the taste of their insolent flesh. Brine pushed off and shot toward the surface, clearing the waves several yards from the *Narwhal.*

"There's the dragon!" Rig bellowed. "Hard to port, Blister. Now! Hard to port!"

The kender complied.

"Good healer," the half-ogre said. He was propped against the base of the ballista.

The dwarf had used his healing magic to ease the pain of the blisters on Groller's skin. The wolf hovered over the half-ogre, pawing at the deck and glancing from Groller to the dragon.

"No," the half-ogre told the wolf. "Won't go zwimming again."

"We might all be going swimming!" Rig shouted. "Unless Blister can get us farther away! Port!"

"Trying!" the kender called in as loud a voice as she could muster. "But the dragon's pretty darn fast!"

Brine reached the side of the *Narwhal* and raised his head above the deck to eye the men crawling about. Fiona and the others continued hurling spears at the beast, but nearly all of them bounced off the creature's thick hide.

"The dragon's much too fast! And much too big!" Blister squealed when she got a closer look at the wyrm.

The dragon's tail curled up over the railing, gripping it and tipping the *Narwhal.* The move threatened to spill Fiona, Usha, and the crew into the water.

"The mast!" the Solamnic knight called to Usha and the others. "Climb to it! Hang onto it." Before Usha and the others could reply, Fiona reached for her sword and began slashing at the section of the dragon's tail that was within her reach.

"Come on!" one of the former slaves urged Usha. He helped her climb up the steeply tilting deck, where she accepted a hand from Jasper. The dwarf and Groller were holding to the rigging and helping the others find things to grab onto.

Fury did his best to keep on his feet, but he was sliding toward the rail. Usha grabbed at the wolf and lost her own footing, just as Groller pulled her and Fury to safety. The wolf rubbed against her side, and all of them watched the dragon.

"I didn't think it would end like this," Usha whispered, "so far from Palin."

"It's not finished yet," Jasper said. "Time for me to join the fight." The dwarf swallowed hard and released the rope he'd been holding. He slid toward the rail, the Fist of E'li gripped firmly in one hand.

The dwarf reached Fiona's side just as Brine's head once again reared above the mast, his jaws open. A gout of steam erupted, and the fringe of the blast struck the dwarf and Solamnic knight and Rig.

The dwarf was wracked with pain. It felt as if he was on fire. He felt his skin blister, his eyes burn, and he knew if the dragon released another breath, they'd all be finished. The scepter in his hand grew incredibly hot, the inlaid bands of precious metal branding his skin. But he refused to drop the Fist, refused to give into the pain.

Black water hit the deck. Blood, the dwarf realized when he noticed the long sword protruding from the dragon's neck.

"So you can bleed," Jasper muttered. "That means you can die."

To his right, Fiona swung at Brine's tail. Her skin was blistered, too, though she didn't appear to be slowed by the pain.

"You can die," Jasper repeated, as he glared at the dragon. The dwarf concentrated on the Fist, remembered Usha's words about its powers. Find the slaying power, he told himself. Then he closed his eyes so he wouldn't be distracted by looking at the beast that was looming closer. The rancid smell was bad enough. Find that power! Find that . . .

Suddenly the dwarf's fingers felt chilled and the icy cold traveled up his arms. His teeth chattered. He was shivering uncontrollably now, as his fingers loosened their grip ever so slightly on the scepter. And the icy feeling started to fade.

"The power!" Jasper cried out as he raised the Fist of E'li. He was terribly cold, but he managed to slam the scepter down against the dragon's jaw just as Brine bore down on him to swallow him.

The dragon reared back, trembled and roared, an almost human scream that drowned out the shouts of everyone on board. Brine's eyes narrowed at the dwarf. He opened his jaws again and lashed his tail against the deck, striking Fiona over the side. Then he dove toward Jasper.

"Again!" Jasper swung the scepter once more. The dwarf felt overwhelmed by cold now. He feared he would pass out from the sensation. His limbs felt thick, and the cold dazed him; yet at the same time he felt strong. Silvanos the elven king wielded this weapon, he thought. If an elf could endure this cold, certainly a dwarf can.

"You can die!" He raised the scepter again, swinging it once more and this time landing a solid blow against the beast's throat.

Then the dragon rose above the ship again, rose, teetered—and fell backward, away from the *Narwhal.*

"Die!" Jasper screamed again.

"Blister, hard to starboard!" Jasper heard Rig's voice. "Ram the dragon, Blister! Ram it before it goes under!"

"First port then starboard, then port, then starboard," the kender muttered as she pulled hard on the wheel. "Make up your mind or come steer the ship yourself."

The *Narwal*'s timbers groaned.

"Hold onto something!" Rig instructed everyone on deck. "We're going to . . ."

The rest of the mariner's words were drowned out as the bowsprit struck the dragon, penetrating his underbelly like a lance.

Groller, scrambling toward the bow, was the first to be showered by the spray of dragon blood. He pawed at his eyes, wiping it away.

The great sea dragon threw back his head, then flung it forward like a whip, striking the ship. His jaws snapped at the mast, shearing it in two and sending Usha and Fury and several of the others scrambling toward the rear of the ship.

The dragon reared again, but his body jerked spasmodically, his tail twitching. Blood poured from the wound caused by the *Narwhal.* It spouted from the gash on the dragon's neck where the sword was still lodged. Chills raced up and down Brine's body, thanks to the scepter.

Brine's neck hit the water, the impact threatening to take the *Narwhal* under.

Then the sea dragon felt himself sinking, and his first conscious thought was relief to be under the water again and free of the ship. Brine grew colder. His tail grew still. The sea dragon's eyes fluttered closed as his spiny back touched the sand. His chest rose and fell once more, then stopped.

* * * * *

"Fuhree!" Groller motioned the wolf near. His long arms wrapped around the wolf. Fury's side was bloody from where the mainmast spar had struck him. "Jaz-pear fix," Groller told his animal companion. "Jaz-pear fix."

Jasper was at midships, where Usha was heading. The dwarf threw a rope to Fiona, who had narrowly avoided being hit by the dragon's falling body.

"Dhamon!" the dwarf exclaimed, as he and Usha tugged the Solamnic on board. "Did you see Dhamon in the water?"

Fiona shook her head.

"I think we got the dragon!" Rig shouted. He was at the ballista, with a bolt notched, ready to fire. "I think we killed it!"

"And it got us," Fiona observed, as she glanced around the deck. "It crippled us."

"And ate Dhamon," Blister added glumly. She climbed off the crate behind the wheel. She wasn't needed there at the moment, especially not with the ship's mast ruined.

The bowsprit had gone under with Brine. Most of the railing that wrapped around the front of the ship was gone, too. Lines lay across midships, tangled in the sail that shrouded the broken mast.

Usha was wrapping a blanket around Fiona, despite the knight's protests that she was all right.

"I never would've picked a one-masted ship," Rig muttered. He backed away from the ballista and looked at Fiona, his expression instantly softening. "No mast. No oars. We're stuck."

"At least we don't have to worry about the sea dragon anymore," Blister said.

The mariner gave her a slight smile. "Maybe Palin can wiggle his fingers and whisk us away," he said. "Maybe he'll even . . ."

"Rig!" Jasper, leaning over the port side of the ship, was calling to him.

"Now what?" The mariner tromped over.

"Who are you? What are you?" Rig stared over the railing into a pale blue face that was peering back at him. It was framed by glistening silver white hair that fanned out in the water. "And how did you find Dhamon Grimwulf?" The mariner watched as the sea elf hoisted an unconscious Dhamon into Jasper's hands.

"Veylona," she said. "Found Day-mon Grimwulf on coral shelf." The pale blue elf spoke haltingly. "Near death. Might die. Watched Brine . . . squeeze . . . Day-mon against coral."

Quickly, in her broken speech, she recounted the tale of Dhamon caught beneath Brine. Occasionally, in frustration with the unfamiliar language, she slipped into her sea elven dialect.

Rig asked her more questions, which she brushed aside.

"Please to wait," she said. Then she disappeared below the surface of the water.

"Wait. Ha! We're not able to go anywhere," the mariner muttered as he looked over Dhamon. "Lots of broken ribs. Lots of blood. He feels cold. Looks pale. You don't need to be a healer to tell he's dying."

Fiona, Groller, and Fury joined them at the rail. The Solamnic took the blanket from around her shoulders and draped it over Dhamon.

"Can you help him?" Usha asked as she glided up behind Jasper.

"I have faith," the dwarf said, as he bent and searched for his inner spark. The dwarf paused to pick up the scepter. "But this'll help. I don't have much of my own energy left," he added.

"Jaz-pear fix?" Groller asked, oblivious to the conversation around him.

The dwarf nodded. "Yes, I can fix him again. Hobby of mine. Fixing." He grinned as the spark grew.

"Feril," Dhamon mumbled. "Feril . . ."

"Feril?" It was Rig's voice this time. The mariner was still looking over the side at where the sea elf had disappeared. She resurfaced in almost the same spot, this time with the Kagonesti at her side.

"I was afraid you were dead," the mariner said, as he extended a hand and helped Feril on board. His eyes opened wide as he noticed she wore no clothes, only a crown on her head.

"I thought I was dead, too," she said, as she rubbed at a spot on the back of her head. "Veylona saved me."

"Dragon more interest for ship," the sea elf said, as she scrambled over the side.

"A Dimernesti!" Blister squealed. The kender skittered to the sea elf's side and stretched up a gnarled hand in a greeting. "A real, living sea elf!" The kender raised an eyebrow at Feril's lack of attire, then gave her attention to Veylona.

Rig shoved the kender's questions to Veylona to the back of his mind and stared at Feril another moment, then felt the flush of embarrassment rise to his face. He quickly removed his shirt and handed it to her.

"Veylona," Feril said by way of introduction, interrupting Blister's prattle. The others joined the gathering. "She's a Dimernesti healer," Feril explained. "I owe her my life, and she saved Dhamon."

"Tried," the sea elf said. "Day-mon." Her smooth face showed concern as she peered over the dwarf's shoulders as he cared for Dhamon. "Student of Nuqala."

"Nuqala will be happy to know that Brine is dead," Feril added.

"Most glad," Veylona replied. Her eyes studied the dwarf, watching his fingers and the way his brow furrowed as he worked his healing magic.

Dhamon gasped, his eyes fluttered open, and his hand reached up to grab at the dwarf's. He coughed, water rushing from his mouth. Jasper helped him up, pounding his back. Dhamon coughed deeply several more times.

"You'll be sore for a while," the dwarf said, "and you'll have a few bruises. You'd better rest."

"Thank you," Dhamon said to the dwarf. "Again."

Jasper smiled, but his eyes were riveted on the comely sea elf. "Always happy to help people who appreciate me." He shook his head, as if clearing his senses, sighed, then turned his attention back toward Dhamon. He helped him to his feet and frowned when Dhamon clutched his side.

"I guess a little rest wouldn't hurt," Dhamon told him. "Veylona, thank you, too." He met Feril's gaze; his expression showed relief that the Kagonesti was all right. She nodded to him and watched Jasper lead him toward the ladder, Blister's questions following them down the stairs.

Then the air buzzed with voices around Feril and Veylona. "Stay here time," Veylona announced. "Nuqala say stay. Help."

"You're welcome to stay as long as you like," Rig offered. "Since we aren't going anywhere." He gestured at the broken mast. "Unless Palin can magic us someplace."

Veylona and Feril exchanged glances. The elves smiled as Feril's fingers brushed the coral crown on her head.

"What?" Rig asked, wondering what had passed between the two women.

"Give me a few minutes," Feril answered. "Let me find something else to wear. I'll let Veylona explain."

"Explain what?" the mariner continued. Fiona had moved up beside him, her fingers enfolding his.

"Maybe you should find something for Veylona to wear, too," Fiona called to Feril as the Kagonesti slipped below deck.

"Zea elf." Groller finally spoke. He was staring at Veylona, at her shimmering hair that hung to her waist and at the slight silver tunic that clung to her body. His mouth was agape. He didn't hear Rig chuckle when the half-ogre proffered a big hand to shake hers. "Bootiful blue zea elf."

Veylona's cheeks darkened slightly. She smiled and listened to Rig explain Groller's deafness. "But he's definitely not blind," the mariner whispered into Fiona's ear.

"And neither are you," she answered. "I think I'll help Feril find Veylona something a little *warmer* for her to wear."

* * * * *

It was shortly after noon that the *Narwhal* got underway, heading back toward the Khur coast, but avoiding the Ak-Khurman harbor. Rig decided not to chance running into any more Knights of Takhisis ships that might have found their way there.

Groller was at the wheel, with the wolf curled comfortably

about his feet. Rig and Fiona sat with Veylona near the capstan. The sea elf was now garbed in a voluminous dark green tunic, belted at the waist and hanging halfway down her thighs. Though her command of their language was limited, she did her best to regale the pair with stories about life in Dimernost and the horrors the people there suffered because of the dragon.

Jasper was below deck, fretting over Dhamon and trying to heal the blisters on his skin.

The kender was below deck, too, rummaging around in the small galley to find foodstuffs that hadn't been spilled during the ordeal with the dragon. She had promised something "tasty and interesting" for dinner to celebrate the death of the sea dragon overlord. And she had found a bottle of something purple that might pass for wine.

Feril sat by the ship's rudder, watching the water as it jetted toward the *Narwhal.* She had helped create the narrow, powerful wave, which was guiding the ship. The *Narwhal* was moving as fast as if it was under full sail. Veylona had volunteered to relieve the Kagonesti from time to time.

A week and a half, Rig guessed the journey would take them, three fewer days than it had taken to get them to the kingdom of the Dimernesti. Then where to? he wondered. And if Palin knew where to go, would there be time to stop Takhisis?

Had Palin found out where the Dark Queen was to appear?

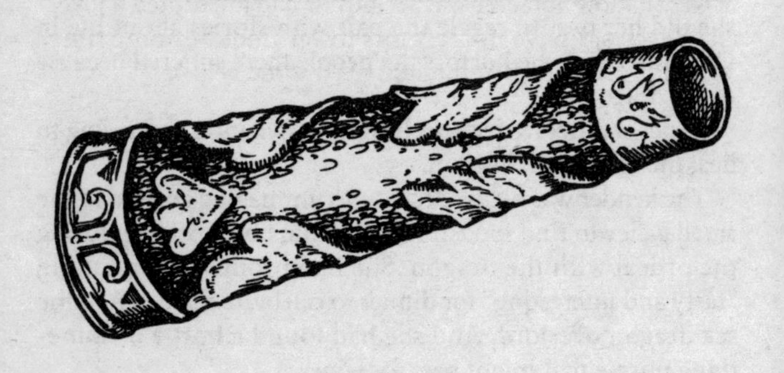

Chapter 18

Ariakan's Rest

Palin concentrated on the enchantment that would spirit him to Ariakan's Rest, more than a thousand miles from where he stood in the Tower of Wayreth.

"Wait!" The soft, indistinct voice made him start, and the incantation slipped away from him, unfinished. The Shadow Sorcerer glided into the room. "I am so certain Takhisis will appear in the cave, I will risk traveling with you."

Palin looked at the dark figure narrowly. "If you're correct, there should be dragons nearby. Certainly there will be Knights of Takhisis. It could be dangerous."

The hooded figure nodded. "I have studied dragons

longer than you, Majere. To see one up close might be the appropriate culmination of my studies."

"Culmination," Palin softly chuckled, then stopped, unsure if the Shadow Sorcerer was serious or had attempted a joke.

"Besides, I have not left this tower in quite some time," added the sorcerer. "You might need some help."

"I'll not argue with that."

Palin glanced at his left hand. Dalamar's ring sat next to his marriage band.

The Shadow Sorcerer watched his face closely. "You have not cast magic with such an ancient and powerful artifact before?" he inquired.

"Many times," Palin replied. "I carried the Staff of Magius for years. But it has been a while."

"Then shall we be on our way?"

"I welcome your company." Palin briefly thought of Usha, vowing to contact her as soon as he investigated Ariakan's Rest. He had not spoken to her in several days, for he'd been wrapped up in his studies. He wanted the Shadow Sorcerer to be right, and he hoped to find some evidence that the goddess was returning to Krynn *inside* a cave. Then Palin would transport his companions there, along with the artifacts they'd been gathering. He had been mulling over the possibilities of using the artifacts to bring the mountain down on top of the Dark Queen and any dragons gathered there—even if such an act might end their own lives. It would be a trivial sacrifice, he thought, if it kept Takhisis away from Krynn. "Ready?"

The Shadow Sorcerer nodded almost imperceptibly.

Palin concentrated on the spell again and on Dalamar's ring. He drew the energy from the ring, and the magic came quickly, whisking them away from the room high in the Tower of Wayreth. The stone floor of the tower disappeared beneath their feet, and within a few passing moments, the two sorcerers stood on uneven rocky ground on the side of a mountain in the heart of Neraka.

"This is not the cave," the Shadow Sorcerer observed.

Palin shook his head. "No, but we are close. I did not want to appear in the midst of some evil gathering. Better that we investigate a little."

"As you wish," the Shadow Sorcerer said. "Lead the way, Majere."

Palin picked his way along the mountainside. It was late afternoon, and an orange glow painted the rocks and warmed his skin. He inhaled deeply. The air seemed sweeter outside the tower, away from the powders and smokes of magical studies and incantations. He had caged himself in the Tower of Wayreth for too long.

He heard the Shadow Sorcerer softly muttering behind him, felt his skin tingle and realized his companion was cloaking their presence with an invisibility spell. It was a precaution Palin would not have bothered with, as he was certain dragons did not need to *see* trespassers to know they were near. Their other senses were highly acute. Still, Palin admitted to himself that being invisible was wise. At least any Knights of Takhisis stationed in the mountains would be unable to see them.

"What do you know of Ariakan?" the Shadow Sorcerer whispered.

"That he was an evil man, but one who demonstrated some honor. He had traits to be admired, and he endured much."

The Shadow Sorcerer nodded. "Including captivity for many years at the hands of his foes, the Knights of Solamnia."

"He learned from them."

"Yes. And undoubtedly some of that knowledge led him to establish the Knights of Takhisis."

Palin nodded. "I suppose," he said. "It was fitting that following the Chaos War, the remnants of the Dark Queen's knights withdrew to this land, which is named for the city that once belonged to Takhisis."

"She built the city of Neraka, did she not?"

"In a manner of speaking. It would be more accurate to say she caused it to be built. Legend says she planted the cornerstone of the Kingpriest's Temple of Istar, which grew into a terrible edifice from which she mustered and rallied her forces. The city grew up around that great, dark place."

"And all in the city served her," the Shadow Sorcerer said. "Ariakan's Rest is where she will return. The Master was wrong to think otherwise. Our trip here will make him realize his bad judgment."

The pair lapsed into silence as they continued along a thin trail. Most of the countryside was like this place: barren, inhospitable, rugged, and steep. Between the mountain ranges that crisscrossed the land were nestled dry, narrow valleys. Volcanoes dotted the country. It was a perfect climate for red and blue dragons, and Palin knew there were a few in the area.

Shortly before sunset, the two men reached the entrance to the cave. It looked like a wide, deep scar, large enough for even dragons to fit through. As the two sorcerers made their way on the last bit of trail, they noticed smoke curling upward from three encampments. The Shadow Sorcerer, with the aid of his magic, confirmed their suspicions that garrisons of Knights of Takhisis were camped nearby.

"We should go inside Ariakan's Rest to be certain," he observed to Palin. "After all, we have come this far."

"No debate." Palin took a deep breath and realized his hands were trembling from anticipation, and from fear of what might await them in the bowels of the mountain. He slipped inside the cave, hugging the wall. His skin tingled, and he knew the invisibility spell had lapsed. He hoped he wouldn't need it here. He stood silent for a moment, listening. The only sound he could hear was the teasing wind. The air was still and dry. He crept forward, working to calm his nerves and his shaking fingers.

The cave was deep, and the farther in he went, the darker it became. Palin thought to himself that Feril's vision would come in handy. He could not see the Shadow Sorcerer behind him, but he sensed the mage was there.

Palin used his left hand to guide him. He walked purposefully, but not too fast. He could no longer see anything but blackness and did not want to risk tripping. The cave floor sloped downward, steeply in places, and wound in a slow spiral. He imagined for a moment that he was following the same course Ariakan had pursued those many decades ago when he followed the seashells that led him to safety. But there were no seashells to lead Palin. And he doubted the cave was safe.

He stopped abruptly and heard the Shadow Sorcerer behind him.

"Majere?"

"I see it."

There was a soft light ahead, pale gray and flickering. Palin steadied himself and pressed forward. Within moments found himself in a massive chamber—massive enough to contain several dragons.

A dozen torches faintly lit the chamber. They burned magically, leaving no trace of smoke.

"Empty," Palin whispered. He padded toward the center of the chamber, scrutinizing the floor. On it was a thick layer of dirt in which the tracks of a small dragon were evident. He knelt near a clawprint, glancing toward the opposite wall. "Dragon spoor. Indeed you could be right."

"Indeed, Majere," the Shadow Sorcerer said.

A ball of hot light materialized where Palin knelt. The searing flash burned away the sorcerer's clothes and hair.

Palin writhed in agony, screaming, while the cold, logical part of his mind realized he would be dead in a moment or two if he didn't act. The sorcerer concentrated on Dalamar's ring and tried his best to blot out the pain—which was impossible. He rolled in the dirt, trying to cool himself. Naked and scarred, he staggered to his feet, gasping for air. He found that breathing was painful. His lungs ached. He looked about for the Shadow Sorcerer but could not penetrate the darkness. The fireball had half-blinded him. An unusual form of dragon breath? Palin wondered as he backed toward a cavern wall. A spell? He glanced at the torches. They still glowed. There was no trace of the Shadow Sorcerer. Every inch of Palin's body cried out to be cooled, and he suspected Dalamar's ring had been the only thing that kept him from being turned into a pile of ash.

"Majere." The Shadow Sorcerer's voice.

Palin peered into the dark crevices. Nothing. Something made him look up. Hovering in the center of the chamber was the Shadow Sorcerer, unmarred gray robes billowing about him, hood thrown back. A silver mask gleamed on the sorcerer's face, hiding any expression there. Voluminous sleeves were pulled back to reveal gloved hands.

Beams of light leapt from the Shadow Sorcerer's fingers, streaking like ribbons of red and yellow fireflies toward Palin.

Palin dropped to his stomach and rolled out of the way, feeling the ferocious heat from the light above. "What are you doing?" Palin cried as he sprang to his feet. He concentrated on Dalamar's ring, focusing an enchantment that might protect him.

"Ending this foolishness," came the icy reply. "Ending your attempt to stop the Dark Queen's coming! Die, Majere!" Again shards of light shot from the gray-cloaked wizard's fingers.

Palin did not completely elude the blast this time. The shards struck him and sent a fresh jolt of agony into his body. He screamed, losing the incantation he'd been attempting.

"Stop this!" Palin gasped.

"Oh, I have hardly begun, Majere," the Shadow Sorcerer taunted. His voice was no longer a whisper. It rose and echoed through the chamber, shrill and brimming with hatred. To Palin, it seemed almost as if another man were speaking through the sorcerer's mouth. "By believing me, by believing that Takhisis might return here, you have lost. You allowed yourself to be spirited away from your precious tower. You walked away from all your friends and from all your defenses. You left the Master—whom you should have trusted. He is right, you know. The Dark Queen will be reborn at the Window to the Stars. She will be reborn there a little earlier than you anticipated. Three weeks, Majere. Three weeks from this very night. It is a pity you will not be there to witness it. But die, Majere, knowing that you have helped the dragons to win. The dragon goddess cannot be challenged now!"

"Traitor," Palin spat, as he circled around the chamber. "Traitor!"

"I am no traitor to the Dark Queen. I am loyal, Majere, loyal enough to spend these past many years with you and the Master. I worked with you, ate with you, listened to your simpering stories of your wife, children, and grandchildren. Listened to your laments over poor, dead Goldmoon. Listened to your foolish hopes of beating the dragons. I won your confidence, Majere, admit it. I even helped you against lesser dragons to gain your trust. And you were such a trusting fool.

"I joined the Last Conclave and helped you discover new magic years ago because Malystryx the Red feared Beryl's growing threat. By allowing you to challenge Malystryx's enemies, Beryl could better be held in check."

"Why?" Palin shouted as he barely dodged another bolt of light. "Why such an elaborate game?"

"Spying is a necessary game in war, Majere," the Shadow Sorcerer returned. "By being one of you, I was apprised of your every move. I could report where your pitiable friends were traveling—your wild elf Ferilleeagh, the insolent mariner and his deaf lackey—all of them. Even your dear, sweet wife, and that tormented puppet Dhamon Grimwulf. All of them. All of them dead. Dead by now because you always let me know where they were. Dead because you helped me!" The sorcerer's words ended in a wild shriek of laughter that died away in something very like a sob.

"No!" Palin's hands shook, and he made no move to calm himself. Instead, he focused on another spell, concentrating on the ring on his finger.

"Dead. Yes," the Shadow Sorcerer continued, recovering himself. "My reports allowed the great Red to send her spawn into the Blöde hills looking for them."

"The spawn failed!"

"They were expected to fail, you idiot! They were merely meant to worry your friends and drive them quicker—like cattle, Majere. But the Knights of Takhisis did not fail. The knights blockaded the harbor in Khur. They were waiting for your wife and the others. The knights will kill them all."

Palin shook his head in disbelief. "They got by the blockade. I contacted them! They ran your damn blockade!"

"The first blockade, Majere. The Red wanted them to. Don't you see? The Red wants the Crown of Tides, just as you want it. She wants the ancient magic. She wanted your friends to fetch it. Brine had been unable to obtain it for her. But your friends. Ah, they were successful. Malystryx will be most pleased. You see, there are Dark Knights stationed all along the coast now, waiting for their return. More Knights of Takhisis than there were in the Ak-Khurman harbor. If they return at all. The Red intended to alert the sea dragon of tasty morsels headed away from Dimernesti. She can magically communicate with all the overlords, you know. Dead, your friends. All of them. And the Crown of Tides and the Fist of E'li in the Red's clutches." The Shadow Sorcerer's hands glowed red as hot coals and his voice rose to a scream. "And now you will die, too, Majere."

Light raced from the mage's fingertips, streaks of red and

white so bright and intense they shattered the rock above Palin's head. Bits of rock rained down on Palin's aching flesh, just as he finished his own incantation. A bright red shield formed in his hand. Made of flame and birthed by Dalamar's ring, it reflected like a mirror.

Palin raised the shield and felt the impact as the beams of light and the shattered rock struck it. The sound of crackling flames filled his senses. He roared as loud as he imagined a dragon might roar. The heat generated by both spells made the air difficult to breathe. "Return," Palin whispered, focusing on his fiery shield, on the ring, on the Shadow Sorcerer. "Return."

A scream echoed shrilly in the chamber. A woman's voice. The Shadow Sorcerer was a woman! Palin craned his aching neck around his shield, saw the gray-cloaked mage engulfed in the streaks of light that had been reflected by his shield spell.

The Shadow Sorcerer squirmed and twisted, her garments shredding, the silver mask falling away. Her face was struck by shattered bits of stone and intense light. Then she fell below the beams of light, striking dully against the cavern floor. A cloud of dirt flew up through the blazing air.

Palin released the shield, stumbling away from the wall and dropping to his knees a few feet from his former ally. The woman's chest rose and fell slightly. Her face blistered and scarred.

"Why?" Palin whispered as he crawled toward her.

"To side with the dragons is to live," the Shadow Sorcerer gasped. "I must serve the great Red. She will be . . . she will be . . ." Blood trickled over the woman's cracked lips.

"No," Palin said. He got to his feet and stumbled to the cavern wall, grabbed a rock and returned to the Shadow Sorcerer. Her eyes glowed red, and her twitching fingers clasping a medallion that hung about her neck. He raised the rock above her head and brought it down. . .

. . . on nothing.

The Shadow Sorcerer had been in the midst of a spell, had spirited herself away. Palin fell to his knees and doubled over—from the pain that still wracked his body, and from the betrayal at the hands of someone he had for years considered a trusted friend. His sobs echoed softly in the chamber, and he prayed for Usha.

One by one the torches went out. Palin closed his eyes. The vision of Dalamar's ring swam before him, gleaming dimly. Then, beneath his back he felt cool stone paving. He had returned to the Tower of Wayreth.

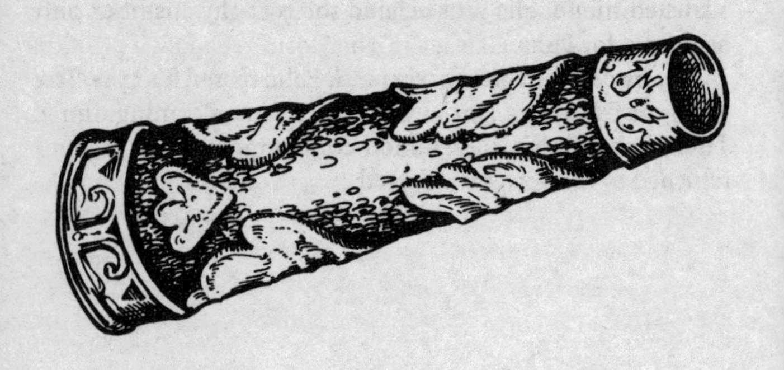

Chapter 19

An Evil Congregation

The final rays of the day's sun touched the Window to the Stars, a great plateau in Khur, making the ground appear as if it were molten bronze, warm and rich. It reflected the visages of the seven great dragons who ringed it, framed by great weathered stones, bleached white as giants' teeth, that stretched toward the sky behind them.

The dragons' massive bodies looked like colorful mountains, each contrasting sharply with the one beside it.

Malystryx sat at the north compass point, before the most angular of the Window's stones. Behind her rose a megalith: the Window to the Stars. The air between the twin upright monoliths churned with enchanted smoke. Occasionally a spot of light, like a distant star, was visible, but then the roiling smoke covered it.

A new lieutenant, a large female called Hollintress, lay to Malys's right. To Malys's left sat Khellendros, her consort, his scales shining violet and regal in the twilight, his head only slightly below hers. Gale lay in The Storm's shadow, a position that branded him as subservient and respectful to the blue overlord. Malystryx had made it clear that a great honor had been bestowed upon Gale in allowing him to participate in the ceremony—and an even greater honor lay in store when he would inherit, this night, the Northern Wastes and Palanthas.

The other lieutenants, as well as a few reds she chose to honor, waited at the base of the plateau with troops of barbarians, hobgoblins, goblins, ogres, draconians, and talons of the Knights of Takhisis.

Gellidus the White suffered the heat wordlessly, directly across from Malystryx. His icy blue eyes were fixed on hers, watching her every move and studying her expressions.

Onysablet regarded the Red carefully, though the great black's eyes also took in the other overlords and gauged their moods.

Beryllinthranox avoided Malystryx's gaze.

In front of each dragon was a mound of treasure, glittering pieces of jewelry that once lined the coffers of Ansalon's richest families, magical items that pulsed with energy, and artifacts that had been won at the price of valued pawns.

Gellidus's prize sat atop his pile: a half-moon-shaped shield of platinum said to have been crafted by Lunitari for a favored priest. Its edge glimmered like twinkling stars, was said to be hammered bits of the goddess's moon captured and held in the metal.

Beryl's gift was a true sacrifice. It included a platter-sized mortar and pestle carved of amethyst and enchanted, it was said, by Chislev. The tale said the goddess many ages past gave the worked gem to a selfless Irda. When properly used it could create a cure for any malady, including age. The mortar and pestle sat atop a gleaming shield; the Shield of Dwarven Kings, it was called.

Onysablet had been able to gain only one piece of ancient magic, a finely crafted long sword called the Sword of Elven Glory. To this, the great Black had added a considerable number of lesser magical items. In fact, she had offered everything magical she possessed, along with enchanted items taken from smaller dragons in her dark realm. She knew that under a new dragon goddess's banner, she could collect more magic.

Khellendros's offering, however, was the most auspicious, one he said was meant to honor the Queen of his Heart. Two Medallions of Faith topped the pile, once worn by the famed healer, Goldmoon. Crystal keys, able to negotiate any lock, glimmered orange in the sunset. The greatest prize, Huma's lance, sat closest to the great blue dragon. It had pained the Storm Over Krynn to carry it here, further wounding a claw that was still red and scarred.

"When the sky is dark and the moon is full and high, haloed by storm clouds, I will ascend to godhood," Malystryx began. "The night will herald a new goddess born to Krynn, the only goddess the land will know. I will lead you to a greatness you only dreamed of. And no one will stop us from claiming all of Krynn."

"Malystryx," Gellidus said, staring at Malys. The White bowed.

"The Dark Queen," the others repeated.

"The stars will witness my rebirth," she continued. "The stars will witness a new age. The Age of Dragons! The death of men!"

* * * * *

In the foothills beyond the plateau, Gilthanas held out the glaive. "I believe you can wield this weapon, Dhamon, much better than I."

Rig's brow furrowed. The mariner opened his mouth to say something, but stopped when he saw Dhamon shake his head.

"I'd rather have no part of that particular weapon," Dhamon replied. He patted a long sword that hung from his hip. "I'll settle for this one."

"I much prefer a sword myself, too," Gilthanas added. "Rig?"

The mariner was quick to accept the glaive. A cutlass already hung from his left side, and at least a dozen daggers were visible sticking out of the leather sheaths that crisscrossed his chest. A few more pommels poked above his black boots. "I'd rather be using Sturm's dragonlance," he said, looking at Dhamon. "Unfortunately, it's resting with the *Anvil*." Under his breath, he added, "And I intend to retrieve that lance, if we manage to live through this experience."

"Slings don't work against dragons," Blister observed, as she took a couple of Rig's daggers. "But I don't think these will do much either."

Fiona, Groller, Veylona, and Usha carried swords and shields. All of the weapons had been provided by Palin, who had borrowed them from the magical treasure trove of the Tower of Wayreth. There was residual magic in all the blades, though not as much as that radiating from the glaive. Nonetheless, they might pierce a dragon's tough hide.

The sorcerer was scarred from head to toe, hairless, and looking considerably older than his fifty-odd years. But determination sparkled in his eyes, and Dalamar's ring gleamed on his finger. He had intended to send Usha back to the tower, knowing this was no place for someone not trained as a fighter and unable to cast spells. But after looking into her golden eyes and seeing her firmly set jaw—and after explaining what had happened at Ariakan's Rest—he knew better than to order her away. They would live or die together this day. She had faced Chaos in the Abyss. How could she not be a part of this battle that would play as pivotal a role in determining Krynn's fate?

Palin only wished Ulin had joined them. He'd had no contact with his son since the day Ulin left the tower with the gold dragon. However, he knew a force of good dragons was headed this way and would soon fill the sky, Knights of Solamnia on silvers for certain. Perhaps Ulin would be among them.

Feril wore the Crown of Tides, telling Palin she needed no other weapon. She had used it to sink several Knights of Takhisis ships that tried to prevent them from landing near Port Balifor, and she would continue to use it to augment her spells.

Jasper carried the Fist of E'li. No one argued with the dwarf's right to wield it.

Silvara and Gilthanas had provided information about the gathered dragons, and about the armies that were camped around the base of the plateau. Silvara assured them that there were indeed many good dragons on their way, ones she personally knew who would offer their lives to prevent Takhisis from returning to Krynn.

"This is suicide," Gilthanas whispered to Palin, as he pulled the sorcerer aside. "The armies here alone are too much for us to handle, let alone five dragon overlords and two lieutenents—and Takhisis is coming too. Suicide, my friend."

Palin nodded, gesturing toward the others. He held his wife's gaze. "They know it too," he said. "But not to try . . . "

". . . is to willingly hand all of Krynn over to the dragons. I know. And that would be suicide, too," the elf said. "Silvara and I will wait until the sun is down, then take to the sky. We'll watch for you to reach the plateau."

"And if we don't . . . "

Gilthanas ran his fingers along his sword's pommel. "Then Silvara and I will begin the fight." Much softer, he added, "And join Goldmoon's spirit far earlier than we had planned." Sorcerer and elf clasped hands. Several moments later, Silvara and Gilthanas were gone.

The small group worked its way along a trail that led between the foothills and toward the mountaintop plateau. Blister fretted as they neared the place. "The Knights of Takhisis," she muttered. "A sea of black. It makes my fingers itch. I don't see any goblins yet, or hobgoblins or ogres or draconians like Silvara and Gilthanas noticed when they were scouting around. And who knows what else is really there? How are we gonna get by all that? Walk?"

"Of course," Palin returned. His thumb played against Dalamar's ring.

Within moments, they all resembled Knights of Takhisis, all tall and human. Even Fury, although he could not help but paw at the ground and constantly sniff the air, was clad in black armor. The only clue to the others' identities was the color of hair that spilled out from beneath their helmets.

"This gives me the creeps," Rig said to Fiona, as he looked down at the skull emblem on his black breastplate. His fingers traced the design, and he cocked his head toward Palin. He hadn't felt metal. Instead he felt the smooth skin of his chest and the daggers strapped there.

"It's a mask," the sorcerer said by way of explanation. "An elaborate one, which we should pray those armies can't see through."

"Wow!" Blister squealed. She was admiring her gleaming armor and gauntlets. "I look wonderful!" Then she instantly frowned. The spell certainly made her look impressive, but her voice sounded just the same.

"The mask is for appearances only," Palin said. "Be careful not to speak. That could give us away."

Blister nodded. The red-haired knight growled softly and stopped pawing.

Dhamon led the way through the first encampment. Several dozen knights were stationed on the outer rim, but none paid the masked group any attention. They were more interested in the feast being prepared. Several large pigs were roasting on spits, and barbarians from some of the local Khur villages were passing around bread and cheese.

It was but the first of several camps they passed through, each roughly the same size and each characterized by the same celebratory atmosphere. Yet there was no ale or mead, Dhamon noted, nothing that would dull the knights' senses.

The goblin armies were another matter. Drums pounded out an odd rhythm, and the youngest goblin warriors danced around tables heavy with food. Barrels of something pungent and fermented were conspicuous. Dhamon found the least-crowded paths through these camps and hurried toward the plateau, the others following. He didn't want to risk a drunken goblin bumping into Blister or Jasper and seeing through Palin's mask. He also avoided the camps of the ogres and draconians they spotted.

The hobgoblins and barbarians seemed to be the most disciplined of the lot, and there were no intoxicants in these camps. However, the air was filled with scattered war cries and victory speeches, as blustery sergeants and captains boasted how their lot in life would improve when the dragon goddess returned to Ansalon.

At the base of the mountain plateau, an elite force of the Dark Queen's knights were camped in the shadows of four red dragons, a small black, and a small green.

Dhamon recognized Jalan Telith-Moor, and quickly steered his entourage the long way around the camp to avoid her. The commander might be blind, but Dhamon doubted it. He knew she had access to a group of Skull Knights who probably had the ability to cure her malady. Out of the corner of his eye he spotted several black-robed men and women: Knights of the Thorn. He didn't want to risk the spellcasters seeing through his disguise either.

"This way," he said, as he picked his way past a pair of knight-officers and started up a winding path.

"There're so many of them," Usha whispered to Palin.

"More perhaps than there were in the Abyss."

"It's easier to come here than it was to the Abyss," Palin replied.

"Stop, you!" A knight-commander faced Dhamon, where the path veered around a rocky outcropping and climbed an even steeper slope. Only Dhamon, Rig, and Fiona had turned the corner. The rest were unable to see the man who had stopped them. He spoke again. "Malystryx the Red is allowing no one to come closer! Return to your posts immediately."

Dhamon squared his shoulders. "Malystryx's orders were to come to the top. I was to bring these men to her."

The knight-commander's eyes narrowed. "I doubt that the dragon would have—"

"You doubt the dragon, sir? I have Palin Majere with me, a prisoner she wants. Perhaps she means to offer him to Takhisis." Dhamon's eyes didn't blink.

"Let me see this Palin Majere."

Palin couldn't see the man, but heard his and Dhamon's clipped conversation, felt Usha's fingers nervously brush with his. "It will be all right," he whispered. "Dhamon knows what he's doing." Palin squeezed around the corner, through Rig and Fiona, dropping the masking enchantment that covered him.

The knight-commander stared at the sorcerer, his eyes studying the burns and scars on his face, head, and hands.

"Injuring him was unavoidable. Malystryx's orders, sir?" Dhamon said, gesturing at Palin and tapping his foot impatiently. "If you will not permit me to escort Palin Majere and these knights to the top of the plateau, then you must explain your reasoning to her. I hope the red dragon is understanding."

The knight-commander's eyes narrowed, but his lips trembled ever so slightly. "Go!" he barked, waving Dhamon along. "Take the sorcerer to her. No doubt he'll make a tasty morsel for the Dark Queen."

Dhamon nodded and started past the man.

"It worked!" came a childlike female voice. "See, Jasper, I told you that lying lesson I gave Dhamon months and months ago would pay off."

Dhamon was at the knight-commander's shoulder when he heard the hiss of steel being drawn and the sharp intake of the knight's breath. Dhamon reached for his own blade, wheeled, and watched as the knight-commander was cut down. The man hit the ground, the blood pooling around him.

Rig stared at the glaive he clutched and whistled softly.

"Someone might find him!" Dhamon warned the mariner.

Palin closed his eyes, ran his thumb along the metal of Dalamar's ring. Fiona propped the man up against the side of the mountain. She and Rig worked to balance the body so it wouldn't fall over.

"If he was alive, we wouldn't be breathing for long," Rig mumbled.

"I think they'll notice all the blood, and that his armor's been sawed in half," the kender observed. "It's kinda hard not to notice it."

Rig scowled, and then his face brightened. "Thanks Palin," he said. In the span of a few seconds, the man looked alive and untouched, his eyes closed as if he'd fallen asleep at his post. Palin again looked like a Knight of Takhisis.

"Let's hope no one comes this way and slips in the blood," the sorcerer whispered. He glanced at Dhamon, who had resumed the climb. "Better hurry."

They were nearing the top when the last sliver of sun slipped below the horizon. The land was bathed in a bright, early twilight. The wind picked up quickly and without warning, blowing strongly and whipping their hair about their faces. Palin grimaced.

Clouds gathered, plunging the area into an eerie darkness. Dhamon's legs pounded up the last of the narrowing path, and as thunder rocked the mountain, he gripped his sword tightly. "Hurry!" he called to the others.

Lightning cut through the sky, revealing the forms of dragons—blues and reds, greens, circling in the air above the Window to the Stars. They stood out starkly against the storm clouds. High in the sky, flecks of metal also glimmered—the silver and gold dragons were arriving. Palin knew Knights of Solamnia would be astride many of them.

A voice boomed above the thunder and the wind, sibilant, inhuman and commanding. "Prepare yourselves!" the voice cried. "The ceremony to herald a new age begins!"

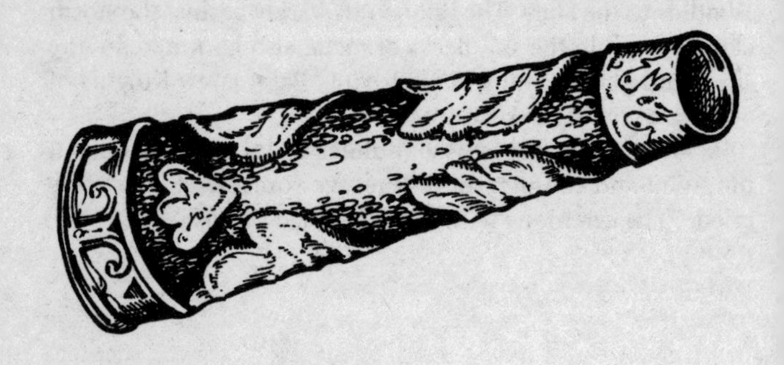

Chapter 20

Rebirth

Deylona's knees shook and her teeth chattered, and she cupped both hands over her mouth so no sound would escape. The Dimernesti was peering around a rock at the lip of the plateau, staring at the nine massive dragons, five of them overlords. She was sweating more than she had after trudging for days through the desert of the Northern Wastes. The dragons terrified her.

Jasper knelt beside her, his hand on her shoulder giving her no comfort. Groller and Fury were right behind them, and a trembling glance over the kender's shoulder told Blister that the big half-ogre was every bit as overcome with fear as she.

"Dragonfear," Palin whispered to Veylona. "It's an aura the dragons exude."

"Can you do something?" asked Usha. Her gold eyes were wide. She'd been around dragons before, when dozens of them battled Chaos in the Abyss, but she had never seen dragons so huge.

"I can," Jasper softly offered. The fingers of his right hand were wrapped tightly around the Fist. "This can influence others, bolstering their courage," he whispered as he began to concentrate. "If it doesn't bolster our courage quickly, I think a few of us will be running back down this mountain any moment."

Jasper closed his eyes. "Goldmoon, I have faith," he said in a hushed tone. "Have I the strength to . . . ?" His mind wrapped around the energy that played along the scepter's haft. "Praise the departed gods."

Across the plateau, the wind started blowing. Hot as a furnace, it was tinged with the scent of sulphur. Lightning flashed repeatedly, illuminating the dragons circling in the sky.

Jasper opened his eyes, studying Dhamon, Rig, and Fiona as they came closer. The expressions on their faces told him they were no longer as afraid. Veylona quietly moved behind him.

"So dry," she said, her voice faint. "Skin hurts. My eyes burn. So far from ocean home." The Dimernesti looked up at the sky, her eyes blinking at each lightning stroke. Her pale blue nose quivered, and her lips turned down in a slight frown. A storm was brewing, but she could tell there would be no cleansing rain, only this dry, uncomfortable heat. "Stand a chance, I thought," she continued. "When Brine died, thought more dragons could die." Her pupils were wide, her hand clenched around the pommel of the sword Palin had given her, knuckles so pale they looked deathly white.

"There's always a chance," Usha said. "There's—"

Suddenly the wind keened loudly, and the ground was rocked by thunder. Palin and the others swayed, struggling to keep from being pitched over the side of the mountain.

Malystryx was moving slow and stately. All dragon eyes were on her, all dragon heads lowered in respect.

"What's happening?" Jasper whispered as he tried to peek around the rocks in front of him.

"Something," Blister replied. "I think the red is going to summon Takhisis."

Palin pursed his lips and eyed the dragons, trying to pick out the weakest. He wanted to launch a strike but realized they might have to fight all the dragons at once if they revealed themselves now. Gilthanas is right, he thought to himself, this is suicide. We haven't the strength to defeat even *one* of them. Aloud, he whispered, "I don't know what Malys is doing. But I think our time to act may be nearing. We should—"

Khellendros unleashed a bolt of lightning that struck the smooth surface of the plateau and blasted away chunks that harmlessly pelted the overlords' thick hides. When the sulphurous smell and dust dissipated, the humans saw that the bolt had been directed near a rocky altar that stood alone in the midst of that vast space.

"The magical treasure," Malys said, her thick, inhuman voice louder than the drumlike thunder, easily carrying above the howling wind. "Place it here."

One by one, the dragons complied. Their great paws gently scooped up the arcane baubles and carefully placed them on the altar and around its base, oblivious to the people who watched.

"When?" Blister's voice sounded fragile. "When do we . . . you know . . ." Her fingers touched the dagger pommels. "When—"

"Everything!" Malys cried. Her voice rocked the mountain, and the stone formations trembled. She threw back her head and opened her mouth, breathing a stream of fire high into the sky. Then her eyes widened, as she spied the silver and gold dragons descending, so high in the sky they looked like stars toppling toward the earth. The black, green, and blue dragons that had been circling rose to meet them. "Everything! Now!"

Save Khellendros, the dragon overlords worked faster. His paw slowly moved to his treasure pile, nudged the crystal keys, the Medallion of Faith.

A single medallion?

"Fissure!" the blue dragon spat the word so softly that Malys couldn't hear it. He glanced behind him and saw a small gray shadow. He'd kept the huldre's presence secret and brought him here, intending to use him to help open the portal when the propitious moment came. "The other medallion, faerie!"

The little gray man shrugged.

"Give it back," the dragon hissed.

"I don't have it." The huldre returned Khellendros's stare, his smooth face impassive.

Khellendros growled, casting his gaze around the arena. He nudged the keys closer to the altar, and also the lone medallion, keeping the lance at the edge of the treasure circle, near his wounded claw. All this time, he watched Malys.

"Too long has this world been without a dragon goddess!" Malystryx cried. The great red dragon reared back on her haunches, her neck stretched toward the heavens. "Too long has there been no undisputed power, no mighty voice setting the course of Ansalon. Now one has arisen. It is I, and I am all!"

"Malystryx!" Gellidus roared. The air shimmered white around him, as ice crystals spilled from between his jagged teeth and instantly melted in the hot air.

"The new Dark Queen!" Beryl and Onysablet cried practically in unison. Acid spilled from the Black's jowls, hissing and popping and melting coins and bits of jewelry on the altar.

"The Dark Queen!" began a chant from the rest of the dragons. It was picked up almost as a whisper by the dragons waiting at the base of the plateau. Faint, almost imperceptible, the voices of men joined them.

Steam spiraled from the Red's cavernous nostrils, and flames licked around her teeth. The tendrils of fire seemed to take on a life of their own. They looked like miniature red dragons sprouting from her vast, horrible mouth.

Palin Majere's face paled. Somewhere, amid the leaping fires, his aching eyes seemed for a moment to see again the silver visage of the Shadow Sorcerer, who had betrayed them.

"What's happening?" called Blister, her tiny voice almost lost amid the tumult of sky and mountain.

"It's a spell," replied Palin. His voice trembled. "She's not summoning Takhisis. She thinks she *is* Takhisis!"

"But I always thought Takhisis was supposed to be beautiful," persisted the kender. "Sounds to me as if Malys has gone funny in the head. Sounds to me . . ."

Palin hushed her with a gesture. "Now!" he urged his friends. "We must act now! We cannot wait for Gilthanas and Silvara! The silver and gold dragons are too far away and have the evil dragons above to contend with!" The sorcerer stood and pointed at Gellidus, drawing on the power of Dalamar's ring, summoning his own fire. Bright red flames leapt from Palin's scarred hands toward the white overlord.

The masking spell abandoned, their Knights of Takhisis guises ran off them like water. They stood revealed in their true forms.

"Now!" Palin shouted.

Gellidus's chanting erupted in a howl as frosty scales melted beneath Palin's artifact-powered blast of fire.

Rig and Fiona rushed forward, keeping under Palin's fiery blast and charging at Gellidus. The young Knight of Solamnia had insisted on attacking this particular dragon, the one who held Southern Ergoth in his frigid grip and terrorized the people her knighthood had sworn to protect. And Rig had volunteered to help her.

Blister and Jasper wheeled toward Onysablet, the great Black, Veylona at their heels.

Groller charged Beryl, the green. For my wife, he thought, and for my daughter too. For the people of my village. Beryl had not been responsible, it was a smaller dragon, he knew. But this was a green one all the same, and the half-ogre was aided by Fury racing alongside him.

Usha began to move forward, but Palin clamped his right hand down on her shoulder. "Don't try to protect me," she said. Her long sword gleamed.

"I'm not," he said, his voice faint. "I need you to protect me."

She instantly understood. He was the greatest threat to the dragons and would become their most likely target. "With my life," she answered, raising the shield, hefting the sword, and waiting.

Dhamon was darting toward the center of the plateau, straight at the great red overlord. Feril was torn. She stared at Gellidus, the dragon who had ruined her homeland. She wanted to fight him with every fiber of her being. But her heart . . . Dhamon closed on Malys, alone. An instant later, however, Feril was behind Dhamon, focusing on the Crown of Tides and calling forth what little moisture was held in the air.

"Malystryx!" Dhamon roared. "You made me a murderer! You made me kill Goldmoon! You stole my life, damn you!"

The great red overlord glanced down and noted the presence of the detested human, the lowly man who had defied her and broken free of her control and kept the glaive. Moments ago she would have stopped anything to slay him. But moments ago she was merely a dragon. Now she was a goddess, a being beneath the pettiness of such revenge.

Malys continued her spell, only vaguely registering the sound of human feet that scrabbled up the treasure pile, only mildly feeling the tickle of a sword striking against the thick plates of her belly. Dhamon Grimwulf could not harm her. Perhaps she would slay him when she finished, as a warning to men who dared defy dragonkind.

The Kagonesti watched as Dhamon struck again and again at Malys. His sword clanged ineffectually against her bright red hide, as if each of his blows were parried by a thick metal shield. Tears spilled from her cheeks as she watched him, realizing now how fully the dragon had been responsible for his heinous acts. "How could I have blamed you for Goldmoon?" she murmured.

The Crown of Tides tingled, swept up her tears and began to multiply them into a river of tears.

In the sky overhead, the black, green, and blue dragons closed the distance to a swarm of glittering silvers carrying Knights of Solamnia. Gold dragons were in the lead and the most numerous. But copper, brass, and bronze dragons were among them, as well.

Gilthanas was astride Silvara, hands clasping a long sword. He spotted a fork of lightning as it stretched down toward the mountains, and his mind snared it, twisting it in midair and hurling it back against the lead black dragon. The black howled and flapped madly to stay aloft, its scales and blood raining down on the plateau.

The dozen silvers behind Silvara were streaking forward. She had called more, but these were the first to reach the Window of the Stars portal, perhaps the only ones who would make it here in time. They would not be enough, Silvara knew, but they could be trusted to sacrifice themselves to keep these foul dragons from joining the overlords below and interfering with Palin's bid to stop Takhisis. She and Gilthanas would gladly sacrifice themselves, too, if necessary.

Fast behind her were Terror and Splendor, bronze and brass dragons who wanted no part of living beneath the Dark Queen again. They, too, would sacrifice themselves for this just cause.

* * * * *

"A man?" On the plateau, Beryl, the green overlord, paused in her chant and spotted the half-ogre rushing toward her. She inhaled sharply and dropped her head, opened her mouth and breathed a cloud of caustic gas. It drifted toward the half-ogre and the red-haired wolf. Both flattened themselves against the ground as the cloud passed over their heads.

Groller groaned. The liquid burned his eyes and lungs, stung his skin and overwhelmed his senses. Fury nudged his side. The wolf's coat was drenched with the stuff, but it did not seem to affect him. With the wolf's prodding, Groller kept going toward the dragon.

Beryl smelled them as Groller and the wolf came closer. She felt the man's sword strike her and felt the wolf nip at her dew claws. They could not hurt her; they were not worthy of her attention.

Instead, Beryl stared at Malys. She saw the Red shimmer. Something was happening! The ceremony was working! Beryl's chant came louder and quicker.

"Malystryx, my queen!" Gellidus the White howled. Palin's flames had melted away a patch of Gellidus's scales. And now a woman with flame-colored hair and a dark man, Fiona and Rig, struck at the white dragon. Fiona's sword drew blood, as she targeted her swings for places where the flames had melted away the scales. The mariner labored at the white dragon's side, the glaive light in his hands. He swung the weapon and watched with amazement as it sheared through the dragon's scales and yielded a line of red.

"Malystryx!" Gellidus called again. The man was hurting

him. A human was causing him pain! The White turned his head, his icy blue eyes narrowing on Rig.

The white dragon inhaled sharply, drawing the hot hateful air into his lungs. Then he exhaled, releasing a blast of cold, a winter storm.

Fiona was familiar with Frost's tactics. She barreled into Rig, knocking the mariner away from the force of the sharp ice crystals.

Rig slammed his teeth together and felt his legs shake from the intense cold. He sank to the ground, now wet with the melted ice particles. His arms and chest bled from dozens of wounds where the rapierlike crystals had struck him. He knew he would have been killed, had Fiona not knocked him away.

His hands stayed tight around the glaive haft, and he somehow found the strength to stand and swing the blade again.

"Rig!" Fiona called. Struggling to her feet, she saw he was badly hurt. She was shivering, too. "Move in close, where his breath can't reach you! Hurry!"

The mariner complied, pressing against Gellidus's underbelly. He swung the glaive at the thick plates that protected the dragon.

Fiona stabbed at the dragon's open wound, her arm pumping faster as she heard the dragon's intake of breath. She pressed herself against Gellidus's side, feeling an intense rush of cold against her back. She was barely out of the reach of the icy shards.

Malys watched Gellidus breathe ice again, staring at the glaive the man was wielding against the white overlord. It was the one she had coveted and had wanted to help fuel her ceremony. The man was gravely hurt. He was stubborn, determinedly clinging to life and to the weapon, as he struck again.

Malystryx felt power flowing from the magical treasure

pile and into her—into her claws, up her legs and toward her furnacelike heart. The ceremony was working! The world before her stood stock-still for a single, delicious, unbearable instant, and in that moment she *knew* she was a goddess.

She would kill Dhamon Grimwulf, then the man swinging the glaive. She would take the glaive and secret it away from all men. She was Takhisis, the All. She tossed back her head and breathed a gout of flame into the heavens. Fire fell back on her, and she relished the sensation.

Dhamon felt the fire strike his shoulders, biting into him. Not so painful as the glaive had felt after he killed Goldmoon, he told himself, nor so painful as being under the red overlord's total domination.

"Malys!" Dhamon bellowed.

Feril stared up at the red dragon's massive chin, felt the air cool about her from the gathering water, felt the crown pulse on her head. She concentrated on the ancient bauble, on the dragon, and felt a rush of energy. A beam of water erupted from the crown, a spray as tight and straight as a spear. The water reached up to Malys, knocking the red overlord off balance, sending her back from her magical treasure pile. A white cloud of steam rose into the air, engulfing the dragon.

"You dare!" came a rumbling cry from inside the cloud.

Dhamon spun away from the dragon, his feet slamming against the treasure and carrying him toward Feril. He leapt at her, knocking her to the ground in the same instant that a ball of fire shot out of the steam. It crackled above their bodies and, by happenstance, struck Gellidus squarely in his chest.

"My queen!" Gellidus bellowed.

Fiona fell at the white dragon's side, catching only the misdirected heat of Malys's fiery blast. But it was enough to blister her skin and send a wave of pain through her body. Despite her training, the young Knight of Solamnia screamed. Her sword branded her palm, the blade clattering to the ground, and Fiona doubled over.

Rig, too, narrowly avoided the fire blast, protected by Gellidus's belly. He saw Fiona fall, felt tears well up in his eyes. "Shaon," he whispered, fearing that Fiona would succumb to a dragon as Shaon had. He didn't rush to her, though. Instead, he raised the glaive again and struck a blow at the White, cleaving through dragonflesh and striking bone beneath.

Gellidus screamed, beating his wings, and headed into the sky, away from the cloud of black, green, blue and silver dragons overhead. He wanted no part of any more fighting. Krynn's new dragon goddess could damn him, he realized, but Gellidus, who detested pain and heat, turned his great head toward the west and with painful strokes of his wings started back toward the blessed cold of Southern Ergoth.

"Palin!" Usha yelled. "One of them's leaving: the white one. I think Rig drove it off!" She watched the mariner hurry to Fiona's side. Usha breathed a sigh of relief when Rig tugged Fiona to her feet and they moved together toward Onysablet. "Palin, perhaps we truly can win."

The sorcerer shook his head. "We can't beat them," Palin said. "We can't kill them, not even one of them. We haven't the power. But we can disrupt what Malys has planned. That would be some measure of victory."

"Don't talk like that Palin. Maybe we . . ."

The words died in her throat. Coming from around the pile of magical treasure were the blue and red lieutenants, Gale and Hollintress. Khellendros had sent his most trusted lieutenant to deal with Palin Majere, the hated sorcerer he thought he'd killed months ago on Schallsea Island.

"Finish him," The Storm hissed. "Finish Palin Majere for Kitiara."

"Palin . . ."

"I see them, Usha." The sorcerer lifted Dalamar's ring.

Khellendros cast a last glance at Palin and moved toward the treasure and the altar. The blue overlord had little interest in what the men who trespassed here were attempting. He was thinking now only of Kitiara, the queen of his heart.

"Rig!" Blister had her daggers out and hammered with them against Onysablet's rear claw.

The mariner grimaced. The kender was doing her best, but the daggers were doing nothing to the black dragon. At the kender's side, Veylona was faring little better. It was clear the sea elf's blade was enchanted, for it chipped away at some of the black scales and had drawn a thin line of black blood. But it was doubtful the beast was very much hampered.

Fiona and Rig hurried to join the kender and sea elf. Rig glanced toward the front of the dragon, where Jasper was barely holding his own.

The dwarf had struck the black dragon's front claw with the Fist of E'li. Chilling energy tingled up from the polished wooden haft, rushing into the dwarf's chest, and sped outward from the scepter into Onysablet.

The Black snarled so loudly the ground shook beneath Jasper's feet. Acid dripped from her jaws, spattering over the ground and the dwarf. The liquid ate through the dwarf's clothes, burning his skin, dissolving parts of his short beard and making him gasp.

"Die!" Jasper swung the scepter again, then screamed as acid rained down on him. This time he caught the full brunt of her horrible acidic onslaught.

"I should be dead," he coughed. "Should be . . . why?" The Fist, the dwarf suspected. Somehow, god-made, it was keeping him alive. The Fist and . . . Goldmoon? He sensed her presence near him, as he had felt her when he almost died in the cave. She had helped him regain his faith. Was her spirit helping him now?

Jasper heard his skin sizzle, saw it bubble up, and felt intense pain.

"Jasper!" Rig was coming closer. "Jasper, get out of there. Get—"

A wail divided Rig's attention. At the same time Onysablet breathed on Jasper, she had kicked backward with her rear leg. Blister and Veylona somersaulted through the air, heading toward the edge of the plateau. Fiona reached out to them, though she was in danger of tumbling over the side herself.

The mariner lunged after her, his arm outstretching, fingers finding the sea elf's tunic and pulling even as Fiona's hand locked onto Blister's wrist. Fiona struggled to keep herself from falling over the side and quickly pulled the kender up.

Rig tugged Veylona over, frowning when he noticed she was unconscious. A trickle of dark blue blood ran over her lips. More blood stained the front of her tunic where the dragon's rear claw had dug into her flesh. The stain was growing. He laid her down and turned back toward the black dragon. Tending to the sea elf would have to wait—if there was time. If they survived.

"Beast!" Jasper screamed at Onysablet. The dwarf's eyes were slits, the lids hurt so badly from the acid he couldn't open them farther. The Black lowered her head, still keeping her eyes on Malystryx and Khellendros. The latter was not bothered by the little men and inched forward, nearer to the magical treasure.

The massive black grinned, more acid spilling from her midnight lips. From the corner of her eye, she caught sight of the man with the glaive approaching her, and she sensed the magic in the weapon he held, knowing it had wounded Gellidus. Onysablet lashed out with a wing, catching the dark man unawares, sending him away from her and nearly into the path of a lightning bolt breathed by the blind blue dragon.

Rig felt himself flying from the impact. For an instant he feared he would be catapulted into Palin and Usha. A lightning bolt cut through the air near him, ending his musings and sending a searing jolt through him. He saw miniature bolts of lighting dance across the blade of the glaive, but he refused to drop the weapon. A wave of dizziness washed over him.

Can't lose consciousness! he thought. I must stay awake! He slammed into the ground, the air rushing from his lungs, and the blackness overwhelmed him.

"Beast!" Jasper repeated. The dwarf had realized within moments of coming upon Onysablet that she was more formidable than Brine, the sea dragon he had helped slay. "Foul dragon!" Somehow a little of the acid had found its way inside his mouth. It was burning his tongue and making it difficult for him to speak. He swallowed, and his throat felt on fire.

The Black snaked a claw up, then brought it down, intending to slash at the tiny dwarf, to rip him in two so she could devote her full attention to the red overlord's ceremony. Instead, the dwarf darted out of the way, and she caught only a piece of him.

Jasper howled and felt his left arm go limp. The pain was ghastly, as the acid ate away at his skin. "I have faith," he said through clenched teeth. "I have faith!"

He felt about for the presence of Goldmoon's spirit. It was there, stronger than before, reassuring and comforting. "Faith!" The dwarf stepped closer, trying to find the strength to stay on his feet and to raise the scepter with his still-serviceable right arm. "Die, dragon!" he spat. "Die!" But his arm burned from the acid.

"Your faith is strong," Goldmoon whispered. "Rely on your faith, my friend."

The air shimmered next to the dwarf, and suddenly there was the ghostlike image of the healer. Her Medallion of Faith glistened around her neck, sparkling brighter as her form took on substance.

"Goldmoon?" Jasper could barely manage the word.

She nodded, brushing against him, her flesh warm and solid. No ghost. Not any longer. She was dressed in leather leggings and a tunic. Her hair was sprinkled with beads and feathers. She was as his Uncle Flint had described her: young and full of fire. She looked as she had during the War of the Lance.

"I'm here, Jasper," she said softly, a hint of sadness to her voice. "And I am truly alive. It wasn't my time to die. Riverwind convinced me to return."

How? He wanted to ask her. How is it possible you're here? The gods? Did they have a hand in this? Are they not truly gone? I watched Dhamon Grimwulf kill you, he thought. I tried to save you, but I didn't have the faith to sustain you and keep you alive. I failed you. Forgive me.

She smiled, as if she had heard his thoughts. "There is nothing to forgive, my friend," she said. "Trust your faith, Jasper. Use your faith."

He did trust his faith. He saw the spark inside of him and somehow found the strength to lift the scepter. He held it high above and behind him even as Goldmoon leapt forward with a thick quarterstaff.

"Goldmoon's alive!" Jasper shouted as he slammed the scepter against the black dragon's leg. "Goldmoon's alive!" He was practically beaming as the dragon roared. Black scales fell on Jasper, black blood spattered his head. He shut out the pain and thought only of the joy. Goldmoon lived!

The dwarf pulled back on the Fist of E'li, thinking now only of the dragon's death, and swung it even harder. "My faith will protect me!"

The dragon roared again, lashing out with her other claw. This time she aimed not for the dwarf, but for the silver- and gold-haired woman who had also struck her. The woman's goodness sickened Onysablet; it was a purity that threatened the black dragon's perfect foulness and corruption.

The claw barely connected with Goldmoon; only a talon ripped at her tunic. Onysablet howled again, anticipating victory. The black dragon gave all her attention to the healer.

The dwarf would come second. One more thrust and the woman of goodness would be gone.

Behind her, the ceremony in the center of the plateau continued. Onysablet could feel the energy pulsing from the magic items, could sense the electricity in the air. Her black heart pounded in rhythm with the thunder Khellendros was summoning in the skies overhead. It would take her but a moment to kill this woman, then the dwarf would follow. Then she would watch Malystryx as a dragon goddess was reborn.

Khellendros edged closer to the treasure, his claw clutched around the burning lance once wielded by Huma.

Malystryx had weathered a second blast of water from the Kagonesti's crown, which had pushed her farther away from the magical treasure. The red dragon had not been hurt, merely thrown off balance. Malystryx launched another fiery breath at Feril. This time the elf dodged it on her own and continued to fight at the side of Dhamon Grimwulf, the human who had been Malystryx's most promising pawn. The only pawn to defy her.

The red overlord snarled, flames wreathing her head. "Dhamon Grimwulf," she hissed in her deep, inhuman voice, as she slouched toward him. "I intended to slay you after I became a goddess, to punish you then for your foolish insolence. But I will do so now, taking from you the glory of watching me ascend. I shall destroy you and the accursed elf."

Malys moved closer, snaking her head forward, her malevolent eyes narrowed to gleaming slits.

Behind her, Khellendros's claws touched the mound of treasure. He now stood where Malystryx had been standing. The blue overlord looked to the sky, where small forms—black, green, blue and silver, gold, and more—dove and swooped. His keen eyes separated the shapes, saw blasts of quicksilver pelt the greens, and watched clouds of acid strike the gold dragon in the lead. The gold dragon had a rider, as did many of the silvers. And that human element made both of those dragons more curious, more threatening.

Three of the blacks were attacking the silver with the elf upon her back. Khellendros watched as the blacks breathed streams of acid. The silver slipped away at the last possible moment, saving herself and her rider.

As Khellendros wished he could have saved Kitiara's life those long years ago.

"Ah, Kitiara," he breathed. "My queen. Malystryx's form is not good enough for you. It is tainted. I shall choose another."

Fissure was pressed against The Storm's leg, hiding in his shadow, adding to the magical essence, and thinking of The Gray.

"Khellendros!" Malystryx keened. She had cast a glance over her shoulder, spotted Khellendros in her place. "Move aside! The ceremony is mine! Move away from my treasure!"

The Storm Over Krynn watched Malystryx turn more toward him now, fury etched across her massive red face, flames licking out to burn him. But the fire burned only faintly now. It hurt less than the lance he grasped. The magical energy pulsing into him from the treasure beneath his claws, and the strength the lightning gave him as it raced down from the clouds and pulsed through his scales, was keeping him safe, making him stronger.

Khellendros watched Gale and Hollintress glide toward Palin Majere and a silver-haired woman with golden eyes.

He saw Beryl, the green overlord, claw at a big half-ogre, saw a red-haired wolf dash in front of the Green's talons and save the big man—as he wished he had saved Kitiara. As Beryl's claw connected, the wolf seemed to explode in a golden flash of energy, leaving nothing but a stunned half-ogre and an angry green dragon with a sore claw. Khellendros sensed that the wolf, or whatever it truly was, was still nearby, reforming itself.

Then Khellendros watched as Goldmoon, a woman he recognized as the mistress of the Citadel of Light, narrowly dodged Onysablet's jaws. Acid rained down on her deerskin tunic, sizzling and popping as the dwarf's skin had done minutes ago.

"Goldmoon!" the dwarf was yelling. "Get out of the way!"

"My faith will protect me!" she called back. There was a deep sadness in her voice and in her eyes. Her fingers trembled as she brought the staff up to strike Onysablet's descending claw. "My faith." She sobbed openly, her tears spilling over her cheeks and down her neck to wash over the Medallion of Faith that hung there.

The Medallion! The Storm finally realized Goldmoon, not Fissure, had taken the second medallion from his pile of treasure. Back from the dead to claim her cherished possession. Back from the dead, as Kitiara should be.

"My faith!" she exulted.

Onysablet's claw bounced harmlessly away from the healer, knocked back by her simple wooden staff. But a second claw was moving in, talons razor sharp and gleaming. Talons aimed at Goldmoon's heart.

The Storm Over Krynn heard the dwarf calling out, watched the dwarf wield the magical scepter, throwing off Onsyablet's aim.

The Storm watched as the dwarf gathered his strength and leaped to interpose himself between Goldmoon and the claw, while at the same time bringing his own weapon down hard against it.

The talon pierced the dwarf's heart instead of the healer's.

But light blossomed forth from the Fist of E'li, scorching Onysablet and hurling the black dragon back into the path of a series of well-aimed blows from the man with the glaive and a red-haired woman. Before them was a small kender, who was also raining jabs against the dragon. They could not kill Onysablet, Khellendros knew. But they could distract the Black for some time.

Goldmoon knelt over the fallen dwarf, tears falling from her face onto his body. "My faith," she whispered. "*You* were supposed to die, Jasper, on Schallsea Island. Not me. You were to die that day, my dear, precious friend. I have students to teach. And while I, alone, can do nothing against the dragons, all of my students—and others who will come to me in the future—can do something. That is why I had to come back."

Nearby, Khellendros watched Dhamon Grimwulf step forward, the black-haired man intent on Malystryx, the elf equally intent at his side. She was using the magic of the coral crown again. Water shot from the band a third time, striking Malystryx as she opened her mouth, creating steam instead of fire. It did not hurt the great red overlord. Dhamon and the elf did not have the power, The Storm knew that. Nor did the attack deter her; instead, it succeeded only in angering her. Dhamon and the elf were less than gnats to Malystryx. Unless . . .

"Khellendros!" Malystryx cried. "Move away from the treasure! The ceremony is mine! Mine!"

The Storm Over Krynn gave one last look at the tumultuous scene before him. And then the blue dragon saw, seated upon a distant peak, sitting calmly, patiently, the dark form of another wyrm. It was not black; rather, it seemed cloaked in shadow. As he spied it, Khellendros felt, for the briefest of moments, a chill of doubt, as though he beheld a power vast and terrible, hidden behind a cold, inscrutable mask.

"Kitiara," The Storm repeated to himself. The moment of weakness as gone, and his course lay plain before him. Squarely behind the altar now, Khellendros felt the earth tremble beneath the pile of magical treasure, felt energy flow into his claws and up his legs, down into his belly, across his back. He threw back his head and shot a thick bolt of lightning into the sky, felt a myriad of tiny bolts race down to caress him, to fuel him, to increase his power. The ceremony was working its magical wonders on him.

"No!" Malystryx roared. "*I* am to ascend! *I* am to be the one!"

The beautiful vision that had possessed the red overlord's mind split apart, like a shattered crystal. The world around her dissolved into fire, ice, and steam. Malys felt her mind bleed away, flitting across the plateau in an infinite series of shadows. Yet some part remained within the dragon and glared balefully at the humans who had attacked her.

Khellendros's legs pulsated with arcane energy. Energy crackled from his horns.

"By all I count holy," Palin said. He and Usha stared wide-eyed. Khellendros's scales glowed as bright as the sun, and his eyes glistened like gems.

Light cascading off The Storm Over Krynn illuminated the Window to the Stars and cast a harsh glare over the dragons. The massive blue overlord reared back on his hind legs, standing as a man might stand, wings swept out to his sides, with Huma's lance still clutched in his claw. The weapon no longer burned him. Lightning flickered around his teeth and eyes, cavorted around his claws, and made the lance glow dazzlingly bright.

The dark huldrefolk at Khellendros's side squinted, gazing up in disbelief.

"Storm?" Fissure whispered.

Beryl paused in her attack on the half-ogre, lowering her head in deference to The Storm.

Onysablet directed all her attention to Khellendros now, not caring that Goldmoon was pulling away the dwarf's body, tugging it toward the unconscious blue-skinned woman. "Khellendros!" Onysablet screamed in surprise.

Hollintress and Gale turned to face the blue dragon. Hollintress registered the power that now emanated from Khellendros, while Gale only understood that magical energy covered the overlord and made the plateau tremble wildly.

"No!" Malystryx wailed. "It was to be me! Me!" Her eyes

rolled back in her head, and she clawed deep fissues in the ground before her. She glared at Dhamon Grimwulf. "Human!" she spat. "You caused this! You distracted me! You will pay!"

"Dhamon Grimwulf." The words sounded long and drawn out, coming from The Storm Over Krynn. "Do you want Malystryx, Dhamon Grimwulf?"

Dhamon looked up, squinting through the bright light and the lightning. He saw something glowing fall toward him.

"Do you want the Red?" the thunderous voice repeated. The words were so loud, they hurt his ears.

Dhamon stretched out his hands and caught Huma's lance. He whirled as Malystryx bore down on him, and darted forward, scrabbling clumsily over the last bits of treasure, closing the gap.

The lance parted Malystryx's flesh, running deep into her chest and drawing from her a bone-jarring scream that shook the sky. Dhamon tried to pull the lance free, but it was lodged too deeply. Its haft scalded against his palms as the red dragon's fiery blood spilled across the weapon. Dhamon released the lance and stepped back, watched Malys writhe. Khellendros's claw streaked toward her, striking her, batting the huge red dragon away and off through the sky.

Malystryx sailed from the plateau, Huma's lance buried in her, fire erupting from her mouth.

"Khellendros!" Onysablet called. "Khellendros!" The Black lowered her head in respect.

Beryl, the green overlord, snarled, but did the same. "Khellendros!' she cried.

The cry was picked up by Hollintress and Gale, echoed by the dragons at the base of the mountain.

"Hear me!" Khellendros roared, the words causing the mountain to shudder violently. "I am Khellendros, The

Storm Over Krynn! Khellendros, The Portal Master! Khellendros, once called Skie by Kitiara!"

The great blue dragon gestured toward the rocky formations that ringed that plateau. The glow that radiated from him stretched out to bathe the stones. The rocks absorbed the light and began to resonate, their loud hum filling the sky.

Overhead, where black, green, blue, and silver, gold, brass, copper, and bronze dragons clashed, the hum could be heard, too. The dragons paused in their aerial battle. The Knights of Solamnia atop their silvers peered down, eyes straining to see what was happening.

Khellendros drew the last of the magical energy from the treasure at his feet and from Fissure. Weakened so he could no longer stand, Fissure fell.

Then Khellendros's mind reached out to the stones, calling for access to The Gray. The megalith glowed, the smoky air between the twin pillars of rock sparkled, and then it parted. Stars shone through. Stars and wisps of gray.

"Home," The huldrefolk whispered. He tried crawling toward the megalith, but Gale's claw held him in place. "The Gray."

The stones hummed louder, as Palin and the others covered their ears.

"Palin Majere!" Khellendros called. "I give you your life and the lives of your friends this day. The dragons here will not harm you, on my word. Neither will the armies below. You are free to go. But this day only!" His voice trailed off. "Leave now!" the dragon continued. "When next we meet, Palin Majere, I will not be so generous."

His legs bunched and he leapt, rocking the mountain and tossing Palin and the others to their knees.

Khellendros flew toward the megalith. One vast claw reached out for a blue female dragon—Kellendros's chosen vessel for Kitiana's spirit. The blue female instinctively shrank back, and for a moment Khellendros wavered in his flight. As he did so, the surface of The Gray seemed to ripple and pulse. Tendrils of mist reached out and encircled the blue dragon. They stroked and embraced his great body, seeming to lift it toward the darkened canopy of the sky.

"Kitiara," cried Khellendros, "at last I come to you!"

The portal's surface shivered and Palin, staring at it, thought he beheld, for a single, eternal instant, a dark face of enormous, heart-wrenching beauty. Then the body of the blue seemed to elongate impossibly, stretching out between the stones. A thunderclap shattered the mountain-tops, and in the distance, unnoticed now by anyone, the shadow dragon lifted his wings and sailed silently into a cloud.

Khellendros was gone.

"Kitiara!" the wind whispered.

Beryllinthranox stepped away from the half-ogre, gesturing toward the side of the mountain. Onysablet did the same, then nudged Rig and his fellows with her snakelike tail. "Leave," the dragon overlords hissed.

Rig picked up Veylona, as Goldmoon cradled Jasper's body in her arms, the scepter resting atop his blistered, bloody chest.

Fiona took the kender's hand and led her toward Palin and Usha, who had started down the mountain.

Feril stood with Dhamon, looking up at the sky. She leaned into him, her hand closing into his, drawing him toward the edge of the plateau. He mutely followed her, eyes incredulously staring at Goldmoon's back.

The group walked unmolested past the lesser dragons at the base of the mountain. In silence, the rows of Knights of Takhisis parted, allowing them safe passage, as did the goblins, hobgoblins, ogres, draconians, and barbarians.

They didn't stop until they were well beyond the armies

and until the sun was rising in a cloudless sky. Ulin, Sunrise, Gilthanas, and Silvara were there waiting for them. They all showed surprise at seeing Goldmoon, and sadness at the sight of Jasper. Their glances spoke volumes, though not one word was uttered. There would be time for words and tears later.

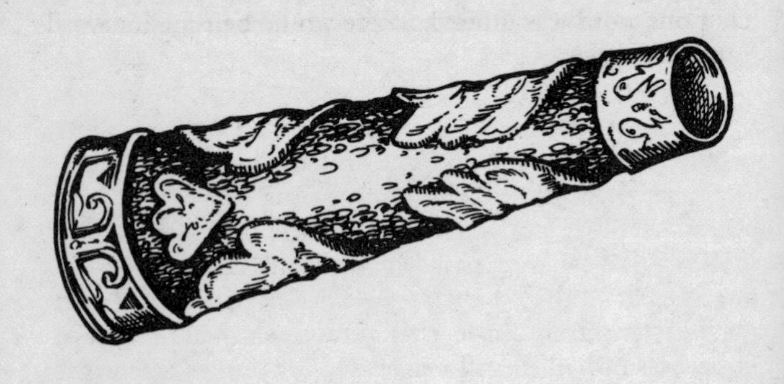

Chapter 21

Deaths and Beginnings

The half-ogre caught a ferry from Schallsea Island shortly after Jasper was buried. He intended to go home, to visit the graves of his wife and daughter, and to search for a red-haired wolf whom he was certain was not dead—and that he and the others now knew was not a wolf at all.

There were still dragons to fight, and Groller made it clear to Palin he would return within a few months. He needed some time for himself first. He gestured goodbye to the mariner, crossing his arms in front of his chest and nodded farewell toward Rig. The mariner repeated the gesture, tears welling in his dark eyes.

* * * * *

Palin and Usha returned to the Tower of Wayreth after spending several hours in conference with Goldmoon. They had loose ends to tie up, including determining the extent of the damage caused by the traitorous Shadow Sorcerer. They had plans to make and needed to decide how to continue the fight against the dragons.

* * * * *

Blister elected to stay with the healer as her newest pupil. The kender had talked Veylona into staying also, at least for a little while. Blister intended to follow in Jasper's footsteps, and she was already wearing a Medallion of Faith around her neck, one similar to that worn by Goldmoon. Blister seemed uncharacteristically serious and quiet, as she had been since Jasper was buried. "I will make you very proud," she whispered, as she threw a handful of dirt on the dwarf's grave. "And I will always remember you."

* * * * *

Ulin and Sunrise never returned to Schallsea. They left from Khur, not revealing where they were going or hinting at when they intended to return. The younger Majere had made no mention of his wife and children to Usha, only of the magic he would command in the future.

However, it was indeed home to his family that Ulin was headed with his gold companion. They could study there together. Privately he smiled to think of how his children and wife would react to Sunrise.

* * * * *

Gilthanas stood next to Silvara's elven form. Their arms were locked around each other, their eyes joined. "So much to do," Silvara said. "There are still overlords, though Khellendros is gone. Those who survive now understand that men will not lie down and be dominated. We will fight back."

Gilthanas shivered, remembering the cold of Southern Ergoth, knowing he would feel that cold again, since that was where they had decided to head next. They were going to rally the people there, organizing all the Solamnic knights and directing their efforts toward pushing the White out of the former homeland of the Kagonesti.

And they were going to start a life together there: elf and dragon. Gilthanas swore he was not going to let Silvara slip away from him again.

* * * * *

Rig and Fiona held each other closely, too. Unlike Silvara, Fiona was not returning to Southern Ergoth. She had been unable to convince Rig to join the knighthood; neither had he succeeded in convincing her to abandon the order. So she had compromised, agreeing to take a temporary leave from the knighthood.

He brushed an errant red curl away from her face and kissed her. She was not Shaon. He didn't want her to serve as a replacement for his first love. But he had to admit to himself that he loved Fiona as fiercely.

"Marry me," Rig asked her, simply.

Her green eyes sparkled mischievously. "I'll think about it," she said.

"Don't think too long," he teased. "There are dragons to fight."

"And we'd fight them better if we were married?"

He grinned. "I know that *I* would."

"Then I accept, Rig Mer-Krel."

He held her close, gently, as if she might break apart and ruin this moment of happiness.

* * * * *

Dhamon stood on the shore of Schallsea Island, watching Groller's ferry depart, waving farewell. Feril stepped quietly behind him.

"I love you," she said. He turned to face her, and she slipped into his arms, buried her face in his neck.

He closed his eyes and held her for several minutes, inhaling her sweet scent.

"But I can't stay here," she added, pulling back just a little. "I'm going home. I'll travel with Silvara and Gilthanas."

"I could go with you," he said. "Goldmoon has forgiven me, and I . . ."

She shook her head. "I need some time alone. I need to find myself again."

He swallowed hard, looked into her eyes and felt his chest grow tight. "Feril, I . . ."

She put a finger to his lips. "Don't say anything, Dhamon. Please. It would be so easy for you to convince me to stay with you. And that's not what I need right now."

He nodded. "I will miss you, Ferilleeagh."

"I will be with you again," she promised. "When I'm ready. There are still dragons to fight, and I don't intend to let you carry on alone. Look after Rig and Fiona. Palin has promised to keep an eye on the three of you, to send me to wherever you are when a crisis calls. . ."

" . . . whenever you're ready," he finished.

They stood together and looked out over the glimmering water of the New Sea.

* * * * *

Thousands of miles to the north and east stretched the glimmering waters of a different sea, the Blood Sea of Istar that lapped at the shores of Malystryx's realm.

A ripple formed on the water's glasslike surface, then another and another. Bubbles appeared, small and few at first. Then they increased in number and size, as if the sea were a boiling pot.

A dragon's head cleared the surface, red and angry, eyes gleaming darkly. Then a claw appeared, one holding a lance.

The weapon was red with blood. She had plucked it from her chest.

"This is war," Malystryx hissed. Her claw sizzled, and steam spiraled up from where the lance burned her. "And this is just the beginning."

The Dhamon Saga

Jean Rabe

The sensational conclusion to the trilogy!

Redemption

Volume Three

Dhamon's dragon-scale curse forces him deep into evil territory, where he must follow the orders of an unknown entity. Time is running out for him and his motley companions—a mad Solamnic Knight, a wingless draconian, and a treacherous ogre mage. Is it too late for Dhamon to redeem his nefarious past?

July 2002

Now available in paperback

Betrayal

Volume Two

Haunted by the past, Dhamon Grimwulf suffers daily torture from the dragon scale attached to his leg. As he searches for a cure, he must venture into a treacherous black dragon's swamp. The swamp is filled with terrors bent on destroying him, but the true danger to Dhamon is much closer than he thinks.

April 2002

DRAGONLANCE is a registered trademark owned by Wizards of the Coast, Inc., a subsidiary of Hasbro, Inc. ©2002 Wizards of the Coast, Inc.

All-new editions from Margaret Weis & Tracy Hickman

The Second Generation

Meet them again for the first time – the children of the Heroes of the Lance, those who inherited the sword, the staff, and the legacy of the heroes who came before them. This all-new paperback edition features stunning cover art from DRAGONLANCE® artist Matt Stawicki.

February 2002

Dragons of Summer Flame

When the father of the gods returns to Krynn, the world is shaken to its core. The battle that rages in this hottest of summers will change the people and deities of Ansalon forever. Striking cover art from Matt Stawicki graces this all-new paperback edition!

February 2002

Legends Trilogy Gift Set

A handsome hardcover case surrounds this trilogy of classic titles from the foundation of the DRAGONLANCE saga. Each title in this collectible boxed set features paintings by Matt Stawicki and is a must-have for any DRAGONLANCE fan.

September 2002

DRAGONLANCE is a registered trademark owned by Wizards of the Coast, Inc., a subsidiary of Hasbro, Inc. ©2002 Wizards of the Coast, Inc.